Praise for

THE DEPTHS OF TIME

"[A] well-rendered hero and a maddeningly
provocative ending." —*Publishers Weekly*

"Allen meets his usual high standard in
the far-future combination of speculative hard
science, social SF, and pure adventure."
—*Booklist*

Novels by
ROGER MACBRIDE ALLEN

The Torch of Honor
Rogue Powers
Orphan of Creation
The Modular Man*
The War Machine (with David Drake)
Supernova (with Eric Kotani)
Farside Cannon
The Ring of Charon
The Shattered Sphere
Caliban
Inferno
Utopia
Ambush at Corellia*
Assault at Selonia*
Showdown at Centerpoint*
The Game of Worlds
The Depths of Time*
The Ocean of Years*

Nonfiction

A Quick Guide to
Book-on-Demand Printing

Published by Bantam Books

THE
SHORES
OF
TOMORROW

**Third book of
THE CHRONICLES
OF SOLACE**

ROGER MacBRIDE ALLEN

BANTAM BOOKS

THE SHORES OF TOMORROW
A Bantam Spectra Book / December 2003

Published by
Bantam Dell
A Division of Random House, Inc.
New York, New York

ISBN 0-553-58365-4

Manufactured in the United States of America
Published simultaneously in Canada

OPM   10 9 8 7 6 5 4 3 2

To the Memory of Dr. Charles Sheffield:
A good father, a good husband, a good friend,
a good scientist, a good writer—
A good man.

TABLE OF CONTENTS

He hath set eternity in their heart, yet so that man cannot find out the work that God hath done from the beginning even to the end. —*Ecclesiastes 3:12*

That which is hath been long ago; and that which is to be hath long ago been: and God seeketh again that which is passed away. —*Ecclesiastes 3:15*

Wherefore I saw that there is nothing better, than that a man should rejoice in his works; for that is his portion: for who shall bring him back to see what shall be after him? —*Ecclesiastes 3:22*

DRAMATIS PERSONAE

Note: A Glossary of Terms and Gazetteer of Places and Ship Names appears after the main text of the book.

Wandella Ashdin: A historian and expert on Oskar De-Silvo.

Ulan Baskaw: Scientist who lived approximately five centuries before the main action of the story. Little is known about her—it is not even certain whether Baskaw was a woman or in fact a man. Baskaw invented many terraforming techniques that were later appropriated by DeSilvo. Baskaw also discovered certain mathematical principles underlying the science of terraforming.

Villjae Benzen: Acting Director, Groundside Power Reception, NovaSpot Ignition Project.

Haress Bevard: Chief Engineer, NovaSpot Ignition Project.

Jerand Bolt: Member of the crew of the *Dom Pedro IV*, recruited after departure from Solace.

Lieutenant Commander Burl Chalmers: Commanding officer, operations section, Chronologic Patrol Intelligence Command Headquarters.

Norla Chandray: Second Officer aboard the *Dom Pedro IV*.

Sindra Chon: Starship crew member aboard the *Dom Pedro IV*.

Oskar DeSilvo: Architect and terraformist and director of the project to colonize Solace. He managed the centuries-long project by using cryosleep and temporal confinement, arranging to have himself revived from time to time in order to oversee critical points in the process.

Zak Destan: A rabble-rouser who touched off the Long Boulevard riots and vanished the next day. Apparently commenced criminal/political operation upon return to Solace.

Berana Drayax: Director of the NovaSpot Ignition Project.

Neshobe Kalzant: Planetary Executive, Solace.

Admiral Anton Koffield: Formerly commander of the Chronologic Patrol Ship *Upholder,* then a passenger aboard the *Dom Pedro IV* when she was sabotaged. Indeed, the ship was sabotaged because he was aboard. Later, he received authority from the Planetary Executive of Solace to hunt down Oskar DeSilvo.

Beseda Mahrlin: Engineer, Groundside Power Reception, NovaSpot Ignition Project.

Elber Malloon: A former "gluefoot," or refugee, on SCO Station, who has become a file clerk in a shipping office on the station.

Jassa Malloon: Wife to Elber Malloon. Their dead son Belrad lies buried in the grounds of a drowned farm on Solace.

Zari Malloon: Infant daughter to Elber and Jassa.

Captain Felipe Henrique Marquez: Captain of the *Dom Pedro IV*.

Bosley Ortem: Junior Engineer, Groundside Power Reception, NovaSpot Ignition Project.

Dixon Phelby: Cargo officer of the *Dom Pedro IV.*

Karlin Raenau: Station commander of SCO Station, orbiting Solace.

Hues Renblant: Disaffected officer aboard the *Dom Pedro IV* who resigned from the ship's company.

Buran Rufdrop: Chief Designer and Director of Groundside Power Reception, NovaSpot Ignition Project. Killed in a crash three months before Ignition Day.

Boland Xavier Shelte VI: System Maintenance Director, Canyon City, Last Chance Canyon, Glister. Sixth of that name since the founding of the city.

Captain Olar Sotales: Director of the Station Security Force aboard SCO Station.

Curthaus Spar: Junior Engineer, Groundside Power Reception, NovaSpot Ignition Project.

Yuri Sparten: Formerly an assistant to Karlin Raenau on SCO Station. His parents, as children, were refugees from the fall of Glister. Later, assigned to accompany—and monitor—Anton Koffield as Koffield searched for DeSilvo.

Lieutenant Kalani Temblar: Chronologic Patrol Intelligence Investigator.

Ballsto Vaihop: Junior Engineer, Groundside Power Reception, NovaSpot Ignition Project.

James "Jay" Ruthan Verlant V: Alternate Member of the City Council for Technical Issues, Canyon City, Last Chance Canyon, Glister. Fifth of that name since the founding of the city.

Clemsen Wahl: Starship crew member stranded on Asgard Five by equipment malfunctions aboard his ship. Later, recruited to serve aboard the *Dom Pedro IV.* He ran off from a landing party during a visit to Rio de Janeiro.

THE TIMESHAFT WORMHOLE
TRANSPORTATION SYSTEM

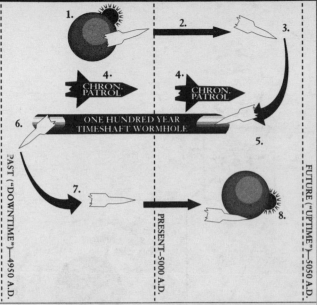

1. Spacecraft departs home star system, bound for target system, ten light-years away. Crew enters cryosleep hibernation and/or temporal confinement for duration of voyage.
2. Spacecraft travels for fifty years at one-tenth light-speed, thus traveling fifty years uptime and a distance of five light-years.
3. Spacecraft reaches timeshaft wormhole, midway between home and target systems. Captain is revived briefly to pilot ship through timeshaft.
4. Both uptime and downtime ends of wormhole are guarded by Chronologic Patrol ships.
5. Spacecraft drops through timeshaft and is propelled one hundred years downtime, into the past.
6. Spacecraft emerges from wormhole, fifty years before its departure from its home system and one hundred years before it enters the wormhole. Captain returns to temporal confinement.
7. Spacecraft onces again travels fifty years at one-tenth light-speed, again traveling fifty years uptime and five more light-years.
8. After traveling for one hundred years shipboard time, spacecraft arrives at target system a few days or weeks after departure in objective time. Crew is revived from one-hundred-year hibernation to find less than a month has passed.

THE NOVASPOT IGNITION PROJECT

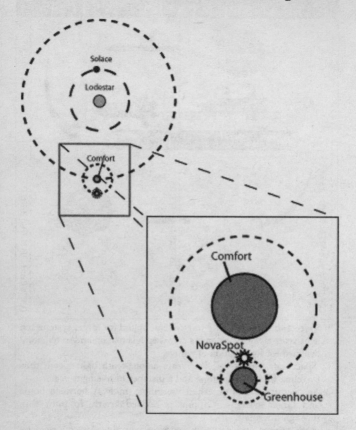

The NovaSpot, a massive artificial fusion reactor, orbits Greenhouse, which is a moon of the planet Comfort, a planet with an orbit exterior to that of Solace.

The plans for NovaSpot's Ignition call for Ignition itself to take place when the planet Solace is shielded from the blast by virtue of the fact that both the local primary, Lodestar, and the gas giant planet, Comfort, stand directly between it and the NovaSpot. Greenhouse will shield the worlds and habitats of the outer system for which Greenhouse eclipses NovaSpot.

Planetary alignments that will afford complete shielding from an event as violent as NovaSpot Ignition are extremely rare.

Part One

THE PRESENT PAST

Chapter One

THE RUINED WORLD

MARINER CITY
MARS

June 15, 5343 (Earth Reckoning, Common Era)

The lift door opened, and Kalani Temblar stepped out
into the wreckage of the ruined city. She had been working hard, but that wasn't what had her perspiring. It was
fear of what came next, not the effort of what she had
just done, that had drenched her brow and neck with
sweat.

She did not attempt to wipe the sweat away. That
would have been impossible, even had she been wearing
an ordinary pressure suit, and the suit she wore was far
from ordinary.

She stepped away from what was officially called the
Emergency Evaluation Vertical Covert Entrance, Technology Storage Facility. According to the files, the last
Chrono Patrol agents to use it, hundreds of years before,
had simply called it the Dark Museum Drop Shaft.
Whatever it was called, Kalani sincerely hoped she never
had to go down it again. There was too much down
there in the underground museum, too much in too
many ways.

Still beats being out on the surface, she told herself.
Best to be off-planet as soon as possible. She patted the

bulge of the data recorder in her suit pocket. What she had recorded already in there would turn everything—*everything*—upside down. The evidence she had uncovered in the Dark Museum was going to give the Chronologic Patrol's Central Command fits. If she stayed alive long enough to get it to them.

She stumbled through the thrice-cursed cityscape. Mariner City had been abandoned to plague a thousand years before, then entombed by the murderous symbiote-mold—then wrecked by an explosion in the Dark Museum hidden underneath it. She made her way around the smashed buildings, giving as wide a berth as possible to the thicker clumps of symbiote-mold that covered everything. The old files said that, way back when, the stuff had been even thicker and more virulent outside the city. Unfortunately, she was about to have the chance to find out if that was still true.

Lurching and stumbling through the crumbling, mold-covered wreckage, she arrived back at her lander— and was disheartened to see that it had already acquired a thin dusting of mold. She could almost imagine that she could see it growing. She glanced at the arm of her suit and didn't need to imagine anything. The thin tufts she had first noticed a few hours ago were now plainly visible.

The lander was purpose-built for landing on, and traveling across, Mars: a short fat cone with three legs and thrusters in the base. Nothing fancy. The cabin wasn't even pressurized. No sense sending something sophisticated down to this place. The Interdict Law made it clear that any ship that landed on Mars had to be incinerated, for fear of contaminating whatever else it might touch.

Her pressure suit was actually two suits, one inside the other. Once she was off-planet and safely back in space, alongside the one-person Chrono Patrol transport that had gotten her to Mars orbit, the first thing she would do would be to beam all the data she had captured over to a datastore that wasn't hopelessly saturated with Martian contaminates. Then she would abandon the lander, sending it into a burn-up trajectory with the Martian atmosphere. Then she'd seal herself in a fabric bubble, pump in a pure oxygen environment, and ignite the outer suit. It would disintegrate completely, leaving her in the supposedly fireproof inner suit. She sure as hell hoped it was fireproof.

Watching from the inside as her pressure suit burned was going to be a new experience for Kalani, but the people she was tracking had done it, or something very like it. She was going to have to do a lot of the things they had done. She could see that now.

She climbed up into the lander and sealed the hatch. The hatch, and the hull itself, for that matter, weren't designed to hold pressure in but merely to provide a reasonably smooth aerodynamic surface during transit through the atmosphere. Even so, it felt good to have *something* between herself and that horrific landscape.

But she wouldn't just get to lift off and leave the damned planet. Oh, no. She would have to land one more time, in order to finish her investigations here and seal off a massive breach in security that had been there for at least a century before she was born. What was the near-ancient phrase—"closing the barn doors after the horses have already gone"—something like that. Still, orders were orders. The tunnel would have to be shut.

She strapped herself in and fired the lander's main thruster, not even bothering to calculate a flight plan. Her destination was so close that it wasn't worth the effort. She had the coordinates she needed from her suit's inertial-tracking system. All she had to do was fly up, fly due east five kilometers, and land again.

The lander jumped into the sullen sky and nosed over as it reached the apex of its flight. Kalani squirted the coordinates from her suit's tracker into the lander's flight systems, and told the lander to paint a bright red x on her heads-up display.

There, that six-sided building out in the middle of the mold fields. That must be it. She did a lock-in on the lander's flight systems, and told it to do a slow-speed approach and autoland fifty meters shy of the structure.

The lander took over the flying, and Kalani was able to concentrate on the landscape below. Time had passed, and the symbiote-mold grew quickly. Still, she could read traces of her quarry's visit. At a guess, she was about to land almost precisely where they had. It was also quite clear they had run into trouble. The surface was still broken and disturbed, and showed some signs of fire. The wreckage of several one-shot cargo landers, and the remains of the burned-off camouflage covers that had hidden them, were nearby. She made sure her recorders were running, getting a visual record of it all, just in case there was ever an occasion that the evidence might prove useful.

But it was the rough-hewn six-sided structure that drew her attention. It looked for all the world like a long-abandoned temple to some long-forgotten god.

Never mind the poetic imagery, she told herself severely. *What matters is that it has to be the place I'm looking for.* Just a few hours before, she had been in the tunnel that ran under that structure, and even walked up a flight of stone stairs that led to what had to be the inner chamber of that building, but the steel door between the inner and outer chamber had been locked against her. She had been forced to backtrack all the way through the tunnel, back through the wreckage of the Dark Museum, back out onto the surface, then fly her lander here, in order to get to the other side of that door.

She studied the area closely as the lander brought itself in but learned little more than she had seen at first glance. The desolation, the gloom, the symbiote-mold growing over everything; there was little she had not seen in the city. All of Mars was that way, in each place as in all places. The temple and the tunnel beneath it were the only novelties in the landscape—and it was her job to destroy them both.

The lander eased itself down onto the ground with one gentle bump as the craft set down. A perfect landing—but with a disconcerting sequel. The whole craft shuddered once, twice, then dropped another meter or so before coming to a final stop.

It took Kalani a moment to understand. The lander had set down on the "surface"—but the surface was merely the outer crust of the symbiote-mold. The weak and crumbly stuff was like crusted-over snow. Break through the outer layer, and the decayed mold underneath could provide no solid support. The ship only came to a complete rest when it reached the underlying solidity of rock and soil.

Kalani refused to indulge in the obvious by framing a metaphor for the Chronologic Patrol, or the state of things in general. She had work to do. She pulled the charges and detonators out of their locker, stuffed them into a pocket on her suit, and got moving.

She climbed out of the stubby little lander and stepped gingerly down onto the mold-crusted surface. The stuff looked even nastier from ground level, and, sure enough, it was even more unpleasant than in the city. The mold was a crumpled, wrinkled, dirty grey-green blanket that covered the world. Here and there the crust had broken open, and a cleansing wind had blown long enough to expose the actual surface of stone and soil. But it was plain to see such flaws soon healed themselves, the mold quickly swallowing up the land again wherever it showed itself

Strange things grew up out of the mold—great obscene brown mushrooms, reddish fanlike stalks, orange spikes, clusters of long knobbly fingerlike stalks, the hands of blue-grey corpses reaching up from under the mold to grab her and pull her down.

Kalani tried to get her imagination under control, even as she promised herself not to get too close to those finger-things. She started walking, moving carefully toward the temple. With every step, she could feel the mold crust giving under her feet just a little, creaking and groaning as she passed.

Almost against her will, she paused and looked around now and again as she made the short walk toward the temple. She dutifully recorded the views from each position, getting detailed shots of the wrecked landers and the temple from various angles, and of patches of surface that plainly had been torn up and had mold grow back over it.

They must have kept damned busy while they were down here, Kalani thought. It looked as if they had been dragging gear from the abandoned one-shot landers to their own ship. She could see bits of discarded equipment here and there, and a major collection of junk strewn right about where she figured their lander had set down. It looked very much as if they had been dumping hardware overboard in order to shed weight, and doing it in a hurry. There was obvious fire damage to the dumped equipment, and to the mold surface, and to the old one-shots. But there wasn't enough oxygen in the current Martian atmosphere to support much in the way of combustion. *You'd have to dump oxygen into the atmosphere in order for anything to burn. What the hell had gone on here? How had they even stayed alive on this planet long enough to do so much?* From all the evidence, it seemed clear that they had been in burn-off suits like hers, albeit less sophisticated ones, with more limited duration.

Which reminded her to check her own suit's status. She had to scrape a film of mold spores off the wrist display before she could read it clearly. She'd been in the suit for nearly three days, and slept in it twice. Even for a military-specification pressure suit, that was getting close to the duration limit. The displays said she had about eight hours left. She had no desire to spend anywhere near that much more time in such a hideous place.

She moved forward, hurrying a bit, toward the steps of the six-sided temple. She stepped on a thinner patch of mold crust, and her boot broke through. She fell, facefirst, into the miserable stuff. She pushed herself back up with both hands and came floundering out of the broken, crumbling, grey-green nightmare. She knelt there for a moment, calming herself, making sure that she wasn't going to panic. The spores that were now all over her helmet and suit would kill her quickly, but most unpleasantly, if they reached her skin or lungs. They'd start digesting her before she was actually dead. But they *hadn't* reached her skin or her lungs. They were safely on the other side of her suit. *A whole four or five centimeters away,* she told herself. *Isn't that comforting?*

She gave herself a few more seconds to settle down, then stood back up, brushed herself off as best she could, and moved on toward the temple. The best thing she could do for herself was get out of here as soon as possible—which meant getting the job done as soon as possible.

The steps leading up to the temple itself were all but completely buried in mold, to the point that it was difficult to see where they were. She moved carefully onto the upper platform on which the temple itself stood, and walked around it, searching for a way in. She spotted it on the western side of the structure. One wall panel had a handhold on one side and hinges on the other. She pulled hard on the handle and got exactly nowhere. She tried again, and started wondering what sort of tools she had on the lander. But on the third try the door finally shifted, grinding against the sand and the mold and opening about a quarter of the way before jamming up hard, completely immobile.

Never mind. It was open far enough for her to get in, even if she had to edge in sideways to manage it. She powered up her suit lights and went inside.

She stopped dead just inside the entrance, and started up full-image recording. They'd need to see this back at HQ, or else they'd figure she had imagined it. There had been faint marks on the floors down in the tunnel, but nothing this clear or distinct.

Footprints. Living footprints. Three sets of them, if she was reading it right, leading directly from where she stood straight to the solid wall on the far side of the room. Their boots must have picked up spores outside and planted them inside. The mold must have grown since where the boots had left the spores. She was undoubtedly about to plant her own set of spores with her own boots.

So, three of them got this far, at least, she thought.

And then back out again. Now that she knew what to look for, she could just see fainter traces of three sets of prints pointed toward the exit.

If she had needed any evidence that there was something behind that wall, she had it now. One set of prints ended exactly *at* the wall, with a bootmark that was cut off just ahead of the heel, and the front of the foot missing, as if the owner had simply walked straight on through.

She recorded it all, then walked to that wall, looking for the way in. She spotted it quickly enough—a handle set into the middle panel, the hinges set so it would swing to the left. She pulled it open and found a massive reinforced vault door behind it.

She checked the display on her inertial tracker and nodded. About eighteen hours before, she had stood on the far side of this door—about a meter east of her current location. It had required a hell of a backtrack to move that one meter, but she had done it. Now she had to make sure no one else ever did.

She examined the vault door. It had three sets of spin dials on it. The single word OR was stamped into the metal between the top and middle row of dials, and again, between the middle and bottom rows. Kalani nodded again. That was plain enough: The door had three possible combinations, any of which would open it.

Nor would she have to look far for clues to the combinations. They were right there, on the inside of the outer door. She carefully recorded images of the vault door, and of the inside of the outer door.

There were four thick pieces of transparent material sealed to the door panel. The top one held a sign reading THE RIGHT TIME AND PLACE. The second was an image of one side of a room more or less the size she was in, though of much finer material than the roughly hewn rock in this temple. There was some sort of inscription on one wall in the image, but that portion of the image had been deliberately blurred out. The third panel showed an image similar to the first, though apparently of the opposite side of the same room. Once again, the writing on the wall was deliberately blurred out and made illegible.

None of it made any sense to her. She could add it to the stack of puzzles she had found already. Let the big brains back at HQ take a crack at them.

The fourth panel was what she was interested in. It was another notice, printed in thick red block letters.

Warning. Locks and Security System Contain Embedded Piezo-Thermal-Optical Detectors Linked to Self-Destruct System. Any Attempt to Break Through Locks will Initiate Self-Destruct.

She was not in the least surprised or alarmed—now. She had been, down in the tunnel, when she had finally recognized the white tubing in the vault of the tunnel as a rope charge. But no one set charges like that unless they had a way to detonate them, and booby-trapping the entrance was a fairly obvious guess as to how it might be done.

Should you locate an unauthorized entrance into the Technology Storage Facility, you are to destroy it.

So her orders read, and she was not going to argue with them. Not given what she had been through in order to get approval for a Mars visit in the first place—and not after what she had seen down there.

That was in fact the trouble: It was too obviously the next move. The tunnel's builder had obviously known that the previous three visitors, or someone like them, would come here. Plainly, all had been prepared for them. She could not help but wonder if the tunnel's builder had foreseen *her* visit as well. Had the builder anticipated that an officer of the Chronologic Patrol would, sooner or later, stand where she was standing, intent on destroying the place? Suppose he *wished* to have it wrecked, now that it had served its purpose? If so, was she then playing his game, doing his bidding?

But Kalani Temblar had already spent long enough in intelligence to shy away from such hall-of-mirrors worries. It was too easy to become immobilized, to start believing that *everything* could be a trap, that any move you made could have been part of the Enemy's master plan. She forced the worries from her mind. After all, her orders were explicit and provided no room for judgment on her part in this matter. She pulled out the charges and the detonators. She had brought four medium-sized bricks of flex-and-stick explosive with her. She peeled each one out of its container, then pressed one up against each set of spin dials. The fourth she set around the vault door handle. It was the work of a moment to set detonators into each charge, then string the detonators together to work off the same timer.

It was, however, with a vast reluctance that she reached for the timer itself. Long before she had headed to Mars, the Chronologic Patrol had known that someone might well have gotten into the Dark Museum. As the official entrance was well hidden, there were obviously good odds that someone had built his or her *own* entrance. The planning group for this job had given Kalani the explosives in order to wreck the entrance if she found it. No one had expected the illegal entrance to be anything more elaborate than a drilled vertical shaft like the Chrono Patrol's own drop shaft, or perhaps some sort of chance pathway through the rubble left by the collapse of the upper levels.

No one had expected to find a massive, kilometers-long engineering project, let alone one with its own self-destruct mechanism. Now Kalani was planning to touch off that self-destruct system, destroying a fair-sized building and the tunnel under it. The folks back at HQ wanted a full visual record of her mission—and that would most certainly have to include images of the tunnel's and temple's destruction. That in turn meant she would have to stay close enough to record them.

A nice, simple, radio-controlled remote detonator would have suited the situation admirably. Head back to the lander, do a detailed preboost checkout, do a high-hover to, say, fifteen hundred meters, push the button, watch the bang, and boost for orbit. Unfortunately, she didn't have a remote detonator.

A timer-controlled detonator made things far too exciting, forced her into too many guesses about how long it would take to get her ship to that high-hover, and too much faith that nothing would go wrong. Suppose she set the timer for too long and stood at high-hover for so much time she didn't have enough propellant left to reach orbit? Suppose she set it short, and the whole damn place went up while her ship was still on the ground? Suppose she tripped and broke her wrist and couldn't climb into the lander with just one hand before the damned thing went off? Or suppose it didn't matter when she set the thing for, because the symbiote-mold had already eaten through the lander's propellant plumbing? Or suppose she was so tired she'd just wired things up with a short across the leads, so the detonators would go off the moment she attached the timer? There was no way to be sure which, if any, answer would be right.

Just make the best guess you can, she told herself. Sensible advice, but what would the best guess be? She thought it through as carefully as she could, balancing the dangers of too fast against those of too slow. *Call it twenty minutes,* she told herself at last. She made the setting at once, before she was tempted to work it all through again, and then again, just to be sure. She could invent enough doubt to paralyze herself that way, too.

But she should at least check her wiring before she started the timer. She traced back her leads and confirmed they were all where they should be. Then she looked, not at the leads, but at the explosive charges. She could *see* the mold growing on it, a thin fuzz already coating the entire exposed surface of each charge, with thicker patches blooming here and there, growing moment by moment as she stood there and watched. *Twenty minutes.* Would there even be any explosive left to detonate by then? She looked to the timer again and thought hard. Suddenly, she was sweating again, sweating as if her suit cooling had cut out altogether. *Heat.* That mold was digesting the explosive fast enough that it had to be generating some significant heat and some extremely weird chemical by-products. And for all she knew, the mold had already infiltrated the detonators and was digesting the safeties on their mechanisms. The mold could set off all or part of the charges at any moment—or else keep them from going off at all.

The sooner, the better, she told herself. She was tempted to crank the timer down to ten minutes, but it would be all but impossible for her to take off that fast. She compromised on fifteen minutes, reset the timer, noted the exact time, started the countdown, and watched the numbers change from 15:00 to 14:59. She put the timer down carefully on the stone floor, making sure not to jostle any wires—then got the hell out of the temple as fast as she could go.

Not that she could go all that fast. Not in the big, clumsy burn-off suit. Not through the broken-up, dirty, treacherous surface crust that seemed to find new ways to kick up dust and spores with every step. Not with her eyes half-blinded by droplets of sweat, and more sweat spattering on the inside of her visor and drying there. Not moving as close as she was to the absolute ragged edge of exhaustion. And not stopping every five steps to see how much time she had left.

She forced herself to stop halfway, to kneel forward, hands on her knees, and catch her breath. *Steady down, Lieutenant,* she told herself. *Panic is what will kill you fastest. Slow. Steady. Don't wear yourself out floundering through the mold crust. It isn't far to go.*

Kalani soon discovered that last was a good thing, because she sure as hell wasn't about to cover much distance. With the mold crust weakened and broken by her walking on it already, the going was at least twice as bad as it had been moving in the other direction. She fell twice, then gave up and deliberately walked ten meters south, ninety degrees away from where she was trying to go, in hopes of finding a steadier walking surface. Her boots still broke through with every step, but only by a couple of centimeters, rather than up to her ankles or knees. That helped, if only a little.

After what seemed a most unreasonably long time, she made it back to the base of the lander—and more hopelessly chewed-up surface. Whatever scraps of calm she had managed to gather to herself evaporated when she checked the countdown status again. Somehow, five minutes and thirty seconds had already gone poof. *And you'll go poof too, if you don't start up that ladder fast,* she warned herself.

She had another series of bad moments when she tried to reach up for the lowest rung of the ladder, which was set into the side of the lander, exactly between two of the lander legs. Just as she had her left arm fully extended to grab the rung, she broke completely through the mold crust and fell. The broken mold collapsed in around her, and she was buried nearly to her thighs. She looked up, and for one terrible moment thought the whole lander was toppling over on top of her. But no, it was just the weird low angle that made it look that way— plus her own agitated state of mind. Nor did it help that, with the surface fallen away, the lowest rung of the ladder was not only above her head, it was nearly out of sight, given the limited visibility her helmet's visor permitted. She literally had to bend over backward even to see it.

Somehow, she dragged herself up and managed to find a solid enough bit of mold crust so that she could jump just high enough to grab that lowest rung. She pulled herself up, thankful for the low gravity, and grabbed the next rung, and the next, and the next. She opened the hatch, climbed in, and closed and sealed it behind her. She checked the countdown: seven minutes left. *Not even exciting,* she thought as she turned around. *Plenty of time to do a quick prelaunch check and get out of here.*

But just as she was about to indulge in a sigh of relief, she made the mistake of looking at the lander's tiny control panel—and at the pilot chair. Vigorous new growths of mold spores had sprouted in both places. Kalani automatically reached out to brush the greyish fuzz off her seat—and realized there was twice as thick a growth on the arm of her suit. She looked down at herself, as best she could in the bulky suit, and discovered that virtually every part of her suit was covered in the stuff, as if her outer suit were growing a thin, patchy coat of grey-green fur. Something had stimulated the spores to very active growth. The idea of having the outer suit burned off was starting to seem downright appealing.

The suit and the chair didn't matter so much. They'd still function if covered with grey fuzz. *But if that crud is growing into the controls the way it's growing into the explosive . . .*

She sat down, strapped herself in, and, working carefully so as to not activate any of the controls by accident, brushed and peeled away as much of the stuff from the panel as she could. With all that crud hiding the display and gumming up the controls, she wasn't going to be able to perform a preflight safety check—

And what the hell is the point of a preflight safety check? she asked herself. *What safety issue am I going to find that's going to make taking off more dangerous than staying here seven—make it six—more minutes?* Besides, if there were anything wrong, how the hell was she going to be able to fix it?

She finished clearing the mold off the control panel as best she could and wished she could do something to clear her mind as well. Mars was getting to her, no doubt about it. Go straight to preflight prep and just hope the mold hadn't gotten into anything important just yet. Pressurize main propellant tank. Power to stabilizers. Nozzle temperature low but inside tolerance. Check trim-tank levels. Engine gimbal check, solid-state gyro check. Pressure to the main tank wasn't coming up very fast. Was there a leak somewhere, or a valve stuck? She cycled the switches on and off a couple of times, and was rewarded with a much-improved rate of pressurization. *Some crud in the line,* she told herself. *Don't ask yourself where it's from or what it is. Just be glad it's gone and don't wonder if more is on the way.* Time check—three minutes thirty seconds to go. Basic preflight sequence complete. *Okay. Let the main tank get to pressure, and let's just go.*

She watched the tank-pressure gauge, cheering it on, urging the numbers to rise. And they did so, quite briskly, for a little while, nearly edging over into low-acceptable range before slowing even more abruptly than before.

Something was plainly not right in the tank-pressure system. But there was no time to troubleshoot, no time to figure it out—and besides, there was also a very good chance that whatever was wrong would only get worse as the mold infiltrated farther into whatever it was jamming.

Two minutes left, then the landscape would open up with a bang. She cycled the tank-pressure switches again, and once again, the jolt was enough to knock the obstruction loose—for the moment. The tank pressure teetered on the low end of the acceptable range—and then jumped over, suddenly sailing right up into the middle of the preferred range.

Kalani wasted no time questioning the gift she had been given. Whatever had nudged the system back to normal performance could nudge it back out at any time.

She powered up the main thruster and cranked it up to full throttle. She was slammed down into her couch as the lander shot up into the sky. The moment the lander was in motion, Kalani knew it was going too far, too fast. She throttled down to 1 percent, not daring to shut the thruster off completely for fear of not being able to restart it in midair. The lander streaked upward, riding its momentum, reaching the apex of its initial boost about three thousand meters up. Kalani, vastly relieved that the ship had boosted at all, was tempted to stay right there, but she knew that really was a little too high for a good view of the show that was about to begin. Best to settle in a little lower. She pushed forward on the main throttle, again powering the thruster up—or at least intending to do so.

For a long, sickening moment, the thruster did not

respond to her commands. Instead of throttling up, it held at 1 percent, barely ticking over. The lander started to fall, faster and farther than Kalani had intended. She jammed the throttle hard against the stop, full power, and felt it kick in hard. She eased down again, slowly, to about one-third power. For whatever reason, the thruster chose that moment to respond properly to the controls. Kalani put on the brakes, slowly but surely, and came to a high-hover. The flight instructors called it a "landing on air"—a complete halt in midair. Pilots called it the most inefficient of all possible maneuvers. The lander was burning irreplaceable propellant in order to remain motionless.

And motionless in the wrong place. Somehow she had skewed about a half kilometer west, and was a good thousand meters lower than she wanted to be. She checked the countdown. Thirty seconds to go. She barely had time to lock the lander's cameras in on the temple and the surrounding area. Twenty seconds. *Some more altitude would be a good idea right now.* She throttled up, and felt that same sickening delay from the thruster before it finally responded to commands. What the hell was wrong? The lander oozed slowly upward. Kalani resisted the urge to slam the throttle forward again. The controls were in bad enough shape without her roughing them up needlessly.

Fifteen seconds. Ten seconds. She throttled back down again, as gently as she could, compensating reasonably well for the delay in response. The lander was at seven hundred meters, still much lower than Kalani had intended—but two hundred meters better than five hundred.

Five seconds. Four. Three. Two. One. Zero.

Nothing. The lander hung over a landscape quiet enough for a tomb, let alone a temple. The clocks kept counting forward from zero, as Kalani wondered frantically what to do. What had happened? Had she set the timer wrong? *One.* Had the mold eaten that much of the explosive? *Two.* Should she go down and check? *Three.* Her orders gave her no option, but the information she had already was vital. *Four.* It would be suicidal to go back. Those charges could still blow any second. *Fi—*

Four bright bursts of light, like concentrated bolts of lightning. The temple flashed with brilliance, then blossomed outward in all directions, a cloud of fire and shrapnel. The shock wave and the sound struck at the lander in the same moment, with the debris close behind.

The little ship shuddered and lurched from side to side, just barely holding upright. The racket was terrifying as the hull was peppered with dust and small gravel. Only dumb luck kept the larger chunks of flying rock clear of the lander.

Down below, there was a smoking, dust-choked crater where the temple had been. Suddenly, a ruler-straight fissure in the ground erupted, drawing a line in the sand, an arrow pointing straight back toward Mariner City. The ground surged up, throwing fresh gouts of angry orange fire, more fountains of dust and rock and mold chunks into the sky. The tunnel charges had gone off, exactly as the placard had threatened—or promised.

The lander's viewports were blinded by the upwelling dust and smoke. More debris struck the hull, and the dull shriek of three or four alarms started sounding. Kalani had to fight hard to hold the ship under control. Finally, she brought it back down to a steady high-hover. But with the surface below completely obscured, there was nothing left to record, and certainly no further reason to stay where she was. *Past time to get out,* she told herself. She had everything she had come for, and much more besides.

She throttled up the main thruster one more time, and again felt that slow, sickening delay between command and response. She nosed the ship over to point due east and started the run for orbit.

If she was reading the clues properly, then the Chronologic Patrol was likely about to face the biggest threat in its very long history. The hunt she had started would continue.

But she had learned about more than threats down there.

The Dark Museum had taught her a great deal about the Chronologic Patrol as well—and Kalani Temblar was far from sure she was happy with what she knew. The Chronologic Patrol was supposed to keep the past safe from the future—but what she had seen in the Dark Museum told her it was spending a great deal of effort to suppress all change, in effect to keep the future from happening.

Behind and below her, secondary explosions boomed and rumbled across the ruined land. Ahead of her, the transport awaited, then headquarters on the Moon. From there, her quest would continue—but the way forward seemed no clearer than the chaos she left in her wake.

The little ship streaked upward toward orbit.

Chapter Two

PRESSURIZED
ENVIRONMENTS

BASE GLISTER
OSKAR DESILVO'S OPERATIONS CENTER
THE PLANET GLISTER
GLISTER SYSTEM

Admiral Anton Koffield, late of the Chronologic Patrol, long-ago and faraway master of the Chronologic Patrol Ship *Upholder*, a ship long since sent to the breaker's yard—Anton Koffield, marooned twice in time, and now, perhaps, a captive as well—Anton Koffield glared out the viewport of the buried habitat and moodily watched the earthmoving equipment outside. The robotic machines were busily erasing all the external evidence that this place even existed.

Koffield had his doubts that they could possibly succeed in hiding it, but their host—or was he their jailer?—had not asked for Koffield's opinion. *Best to think of him as host*, Koffield decided. *If I think of him as jailer, it will just get my anger that much closer to the surface.*

"What was it your people named this place?" his host inquired. Oskar DeSilvo stood next to him, watching the same view, and no doubt seeing something completely different. Koffield saw the trap being taken down, hidden away, now that it had served its purpose in catching him. Probably DeSilvo was simply enjoying the site of robotic tractors and bulldozers moving dirt and rock and ice around the frozen hell outside, an overgrown small boy watching his toys moving around in his very own giant sandbox.

"DeSilvo City," Koffield replied, knowing full well that DeSilvo knew the answer. The man just liked hearing the name. "It looked something like a city from orbit when we came in. At any rate it looked big enough." It had, in fact, resembled nothing so much as a giant bull's-eye, made up of concentric circular walls of loose rock and ice, surrounding a central dome, with a complete midsize spaceport landing field in the dome. The moment DeSilvo had detected their ship, he'd lit the place up like a near-ancient Christmas tree. Now the lights were gone, the dome was already half-buried, and the dozers were hard at work flattening the loose-rock walls as well.

"That was the idea," DeSilvo said, plainly pleased with himself. "But now that DeSilvo City, as you call this station, has done the job of attracting your team, it is time to hide." He gestured out the window. "The robots should have completely erased all outward sign of this place in another week or so. They will return the surface to its prestation appearance, as recorded before I started construction."

"They won't get it perfect," Koffield observed. "Anyone walking the surface will be able to tell there's been recent activity."

"Quite likely," DeSilvo conceded cheerfully. "Perhaps even a low-level flyover would be enough to detect us, though I think not. But the robots will be thorough—and there is frequent violent weather that will serve to blow sufficient dust and dirt around so that the activity won't look recent for long. The winds scour this whole landscape, as well. It will be difficult, from any range at all, to distinguish what we have done from the effects of weathering. The odds are very much against your pursuers electing to do a surface search in this place.

"Nor are your potential pursuers likely to have

brought along long-duration search aircraft capable of flying in the sort of frozen low-pressure environment we have outside—and I might add Glister's surface is a most difficult environment to work in. Furthermore, the planet Glister is a large place, nearly all of it frozen, abandoned, wild, and littered with abandoned equipment and habitats. That is our chief protection. We are a needle, and my robots are busy at work piling up the haystack around us."

He reached out and pressed a stud set into the frame of the viewport. The camouflaged blast shields swung back into place, concealing the outside view from Koffield, and any outward sign of the viewport from the exterior.

"But being hidden from view changes very little for us," DeSilvo went on. "Most of the station is underground anyway, and the aboveground portions we will simply bury. We shall continue doing business as usual during and after the concealment operation. Come, my dear Admiral," he said, and led Koffield down the corridor.

Business as usual, Koffield thought as he followed along. *He makes it sound as if we've all been working along down here for months, or years.* In point of fact, Koffield's party had arrived only a few days before—and the first day had not gone well. DeSilvo had managed, quite accidentally, to goad Yuri Sparten into an attack that had left DeSilvo and Sparten both injured and both sedated.

DeSilvo was wearing workers' coveralls again today, with the sleeves rolled up and the collar open. The bandages at his throat and his right forearm were plainly visible, yet DeSilvo himself strode purposefully past the point in the corridor where Sparten had attacked him, past the bullet hole in the corridor and the spatters of blood on the walls and floor that the robot cleaners had not quite managed to clear away.

Apparently a near-miss gunshot and a knife at his throat were not sufficient to remind the man of his own mortality. Probably nothing but his own demise would be enough, given how long the man had lived and the number of times and ways he had cheated death already.

But some hint of age, of well-hidden weariness, shone out from underneath that youthful aura. His eyes and teeth and hair were too perfect, too unmarked by time. A very slight yellowish cast to his skin hinted that his last regeneration treatment was wearing out—and that the next was not likely to work well.

Oskar DeSilvo was of medium height, with a lean, wiry frame. His face was square-jawed and high-cheekboned, with piercing blue eyes and thick black eyebrows. He looked fit. Back in the old days, he had been clean-shaven, and had worn his jet-black hair in a very dramatic shoulder-length cut. Now it was trimmed back to a crew cut, and he sported a small neat black goatee with a streak or two of grey running through it. For the moment at least, he had turned in his scholar's robe for much more utilitarian garb. Whether the change in clothes and appearance was meant to be significant, Koffield had not the slightest idea.

DeSilvo arrived at the doors of the lift, which opened at his approach. The doors slid shut, and the lift car descended rapidly, a hundred meters down at least. The doors opened, and DeSilvo led Koffield out into a corridor that was a near duplicate of the one they had just left. The temperature was a bit higher, and the walls and floors were a bit more scuffed and worn. *And there aren't any bloodstains or bullet holes,* Koffield thought. *Maybe that's why we're on this level today.* Koffield could think of no other reason for meeting below ground, rather than above. Unless it was to hide, just that much more completely, from the outside world.

DeSilvo led him through the shabby warrens of his buried kingdom. Koffield had explored at least part of that kingdom already—and had been astonished by its extent. The tunnels and chambers went on and on, corridor after corridor, level after level. The eerie caverns were just starting to come out of the centuries of frozen sleep. *Half-frozen and buried alive,* Koffield thought. Knowing what Koffield did about DeSilvo, it seemed an oddly fitting circumstance for a meeting with his en-emy—*and ally,* Koffield reminded himself. It was still most difficult to think of the man that way—but there was no doubt but that his people needed DeSilvo's help—or that DeSilvo would need theirs.

Oblivious to the thoughts of the man behind him, DeSilvo led the way into the SubLevel One conference room—itself a close copy of the conference room on the surface level. At the moment, it had been pressed into use as a dining hall. Luncheon was just about to be served by DeSilvo's robotic staff.

DeSilvo's guests had already learned that their host's ideas of proper service, as taught to the machines, were eccentric. Nor was the food remotely like what they were used to. But travelers, especially interstellar travelers, had to be adaptable, and this group had certainly dealt with greater challenges than odd seasoning on their food.

Koffield scanned the room as he took his place. The others—except Sparten—were already there. Anton Koffield sat at the opposite end of the long table from DeSilvo, considering his companions.

Felipe Henrique Marquez, captain of the *Dom Pedro IV,* the ship that brought them here. Dark-haired, olive-skinned, short, stocky, with a face that tended naturally to extremes—the fiercest scowl, the brightest smile, with no room in between. His thick eyebrows, bushy moustache, and well-trimmed beard only served to accentuate the effect. One way or the other, all the people around the table had suffered injury, deliberate or incidental, at the hands of DeSilvo. But, apart from Koffield himself, perhaps no survivor of the *Dom Pedro IV*'s journey had endured more harm than Marquez.

Marquez might still be the ship's captain, but he was, perhaps, no longer ship's master. A veritable cloud of robotic spacecraft controlled by DeSilvo had descended on the *DP-IV* almost as soon as the ship's company were aboard the lighter *Cruzeiro do Sul* and en route to the surface.

DeSilvo claimed his robots were only installing upgrades

and improvements—including, just by the way, a true faster-than-light drive—but there was no way to know for sure what he was doing with the ship, or what his real plans for it were.

Koffield looked next to Norla Chandray, second-in-command of the *DP-IV*, and the closest friend Koffield had—or had ever had. *Or would it be fairer to say "closest thing to a friend"?* he asked himself. Koffield was well aware that he was not an easy man to get to know, let alone understand. He might be flattering himself to assume that she considered him a friend.

Norla was a far from ordinary woman, for all of her ordinary appearance. She had not yet spent so much time in temporal confinements and timeshafts and relativistic velocities as to make it too difficult to compute her self-chronologic, her bio-chron age. She was roughly thirty-three, and looked it. A bit above average height, well proportioned, the privations of the last few years having burned away any excess weight—and perhaps a bit more. She had the pale-skinned complexion of many star travelers. Her hair was light brown, cut short. Her solemn brown eyes were set in a round face with a snub nose and a mouth that smiled only rarely, but did so very well.

Norla, more than anyone else, had stood by him, had kept him moving forward. He—none of them—would have gotten this far, if not for her.

Jerand Bolt, Dixon Phelby, and Sindra Chon—the last remaining crew of the *Dom Pedro IV*. Bolt and Chon were replacements. Of the crew that had started the seemingly routine journey to Solace, all those long decades ago, Phelby alone remained. All the other original crew were gone. Some had illegally jumped ship, unwilling to risk staying longer on a ship that must have seemed under a curse. Some departed legally, even honorably. Four had been killed, and at least some blame for all four deaths could be laid at DeSilvo's door.

Finally, Wandella Ashdin, the historian and expert on DeSilvo who had finally gotten her wish and met the object of her study, who she had thought was long since dead. She had been somewhat disappointed by the experience. Wandella Ashdin was old and allowed herself to look that way, with grey hair, wrinkles, and all. Her watery pale blue eyes were set in an angular, square-jawed face. She was perhaps the most disorganized scholar Koffield had ever met—but she was capable of hard and serious study as well, and her results were solid, even if her notes were often illegible, or misfiled. The journey to this place had wrought great changes in her—or perhaps merely brought forgotten, tougher-minded parts of her back up into the light. Gone was the fuzzy-minded academic, breathless at the chance to learn more about her hero. In her place sat a determined and professional scholar, dispassionately studying her subject, passionately seeking the truth.

And, not present: Yuri Sparten, witting spy and unwitting pawn of the SCO Station Security Force, assigned to watch Koffield on behalf of the SSF—and on behalf of other services, probably including Koffield's old outfit, the Chronologic Patrol's Intelligence Service. Koffield did not know or care why Sparten was not present, or what Sparten was doing.

If the lad chose to stay away from a meal or two, then it would help everyone else's digestion. He wouldn't be likely to offer much in the way of interesting or useful conversation if they forced him to attend. If he wanted to play the part of the surly teen who refused to come out of his room, then so be it.

DeSilvo took his seat and looked around the room. "Greetings to you all," he said. "Before we begin the meal proper, an announcement. The project to light the NovaSpot over Greenhouse is proceeding according to schedule. They are within a week of Ignition Day—the day they will actually ignite the NovaSpot. All seems to be going well."

DeSilvo was telling them a great deal more than he was saying. They all knew that the "report" he had received had come from one of the covert listening devices he had built into any number of facilities in the Solacian system—and that the report had been sent to him via a true faster-than-light communications system.

The FTL drive, the FTL communications system, and any number of other wonders were among the technologies DeSilvo had stolen—or perhaps, more accurately, excavated—from the wreckage of the Dark Museum, the Chronologic Patrol's storage place for suppressed technology. He was telling them all what marvelous toys he had, toys he would be willing to share—if only they all cooperated.

And he was saying more beyond even that. The Ignition Project had, after all, been DeSilvo's idea. It had been his doodle on a slip of paper that had set it all in motion, albeit a century after he had made the drawing. He had managed to remind them all of the project a half dozen times already. A reproduction of the doodle hung on the wall behind him.

It was clear that, in his mind at least, the sketch on the back of an envelope was the thing that mattered, and not the herculean efforts, or the massive engineering projects, that had made it all possible. The man had a sure instinct for claiming credit—just as sure as his instinct for demonstrating his power.

And, it would seem, a fairly good instinct for moving on when a performance was falling flat. He might be oblivious to many things, but Oskar DeSilvo could tell when an audience wasn't happy. He glanced around the table, cleared his throat, and looked down at the datapad in front of him. He went on hurriedly. "Right now I believe that luncheon is the matter at hand."

The meal went about as well as it might under such circumstances, with chitchat in low voices between various pairs of diners, very little general conversation, and no conversation at all that involved Oskar DeSilvo—or Anton Koffield. Koffield could only hope he was being excluded for somewhat different reasons than DeSilvo. He was seated between Wandella Ashdin and Norla Chandray, and he knew both of them had a lot on their minds.

There was to be a general meeting the next day, and

Wandella was supposed to do a presentation. It was a summing-up of the events that had brought them all here. Koffield had the impression that it was going to amount to a criminal indictment of their host, the man whose food she was eating, the man who held their lives in his hands. The task would be enough to leave anyone preoccupied. No wonder the woman was doing little more than toying with her food.

Koffield had considered the idea of taking on the presentation himself, but had soon realized it would be self-indulgent to do so, and bad leadership besides. If Wandella's presentation was the case for the prosecution, and if DeSilvo spoke for himself, then it was all but inevitable that he, Koffield, the group's leader, would be something between jury foreman and judge—*and executioner, too?* he asked himself with grim humor.

Besides which, quite a strong case could be made that Koffield was one of DeSilvo's main victims. That, too, made it inappropriate for him to present the case against. Certainly the group would look to him for guidance in deciding what to do. Assuming they could do anything. After all, to stretch the analogy completely out of shape, their sort-of defendant was also the absolute ruler of this place. He was their jailer, not their prisoner.

All in all, Koffield was quite happy to get out from under the duty of reciting DeSilvo's history to the group. Koffield shoved his plate away from him, barely aware that he had eaten anything. What was wrong with him, that made him fret over such trivial decisions and leadership choices? "Captain Marquez," he said, speaking down the length of the table. "You said something earlier about doing some work on the *Cruzeiro do Sul* after lunch. Could you use an extra pair of hands?"

"Absolutely, Admiral. I was going to ask for your assistance in any event. I believe the bomb you disarmed is still aboard. It makes me nervous having it there. Could you help me remove it?"

It was a remarkably offhand way to discuss a booby-trap bomb on a spacecraft, but then, in the larger scheme of their situation, a deactivated bomb in the engine room seemed a minor nuisance at best. "I'd be delighted," Koffield replied, standing up from the table. "If you'll all excuse us?"

There was a murmur of assent from the rest of the party.

Koffield looked to their host at the other end of the table. "Thank you for a splendid lunch," Koffield said. It was close to the first remark anyone had addressed to DeSilvo since the meal had started.

"My pleasure, Admiral. Please, both of you, go and do your work." Marquez stood up as well, bowed absently to the ladies at the table, pointedly did not acknowledge DeSilvo, and led Koffield out of the room.

The two of them had not gone ten meters down the hall when Marquez chuckled and turned to Koffield. "I don't know about you, but I'm going to feel more relaxed taking that bomb out than I have so far taking my meals with that son of a bitch."

Koffield smiled. "I was just thinking the same thing," he said. "Living and working with him is going to take some getting used to."

"To put it mildly. But I sure as hell don't see any way out of it."

"Nor do I," Koffield said. Even if there had been some way to escape, it seemed possible that the fate of worlds—perhaps of every inhabited world—might hinge on what happened here, now, on Glister. Koffield was willing to hand off a few presentations, but walking away from *that* duty, *that* responsibility, would be as grave a crime of omission as any that DeSilvo had committed. They had to stay, and do what they could.

Captain Marquez led the way through the corridors and walkways to the main airlock center. At Marquez's request, DeSilvo had rigged a Personnel Access Tunnel between the airlock center and the *Cruzeiro do Sul*, eliminating the need to use the personnel carrier that had first brought them from the *Cruzeiro* into DeSilvo City. There was pressure in the PAT, but, as a safety precaution, all the airlock doors were sealed at both ends when the airlock center and ship were untended.

Marquez started the lock cycling and stepped to a large viewport set in one side of the airlock center. It offered an excellent view of the lighter *Cruzeiro do Sul,* still sitting where she had landed, dead center in the middle of the domed-over landing field.

The *Cruzeiro do Sul* was not much to look at. She was a fat grey cylinder, fifteen meters high and twenty across, standing on four stumpy landing legs. She was the largest of the *Dom Pedro IV's* three original auxiliary craft, and the only one of the three to survive the visit to Mars. Now she stood at the center of DeSilvo's landing field, with any number of jacks and plugs and umbilicals plugged into her—along with the PAT. She was tied down tight, with a lid, in the form of the dome over the landing field, slammed down on top of her.

The PAT ran for two hundred meters between the city lock and the *Cruzeiro,* and was as worn-out and shabby as most everything else in DeSilvo City; cobbled together from salvage and whatever parts were at hand. It was designed to hang from suspension supports that looked like giant inverted U's. The PAT hung from the centers of the U's, the two legs holding the tunnel up. There should have been supports every twenty meters or so. Instead, there were three for the whole length of the thing.

The dome had closed over the lighter almost before she had come to rest. The dome, DeSilvo assured them, was already well camouflaged, but could and would be opened when the time came to launch the *Cruzeiro*— whenever that time might be. The earthmovers would then bury the dome to hide it even more effectively. Marquez was not in the least assured by DeSilvo's assurances that the *Cruzeiro do Sul* would fly again.

The *Cruzeiro* was in takeoff position, but he knew full well that, if need be, the landing field's automated lifters and transporters could move the *Cruzeiro* to one side of the dome in order to launch another craft—then leave her there for good. The prospect of having his ship literally shoved to one side was not one Marquez enjoyed contemplating.

"I don't like it," he said.

Koffield put his hand on Marquez's shoulder and nodded. He had no need to ask what Marquez meant. "None of us do," he said. "And the rest of us know it's worse for you in a lot of ways. He's seized your ship—your ships."

Marquez nodded without speaking. The *Dom Pedro IV* was even less under his control than the poor old *Cruzeiro*.

"For what it's worth," Koffield said, "I think at least most of the others have some idea how much that means. We've all lost our homes. But you've lost something more than that."

A bit of my manhood, do you mean? Marquez said to himself. *A captain who allows his ship to be taken from him . . .* Out loud, his words were scarcely less harsh. "But who knows?" Marquez asked bitterly. "Maybe if I'm a good little boy—if we're all good little boys and girls—he'll give me back my spacecraft."

And there's the question of what all this has cost you, my friend, Marquez thought, looking at his companion. But, as always, Anton Koffield showed very little sign of the stress and strain of his situation—or much of anything else, if it came to that.

Koffield was of average size, but his slender, well-muscled build made him look smaller than he was. His long, lean face and slightly olive complexion set off his expressive, deep-set brown eyes. Those eyes could tell you a lot—but they rarely did. Koffield kept himself under tight control. His close-cropped brown hair had thinned a bit more over the years, and even acquired a touch of grey—but for all of that he looked, if anything, younger than his years, his obvious vigor and quick, careful intelligence plain to see.

A signaler beeped over the airlock door, indicating that there was a pressure match. Marquez opened the lock door, and both men stepped inside. Marquez closed and sealed the city-side lock door, checked for a pressure match with the PAT, and then opened the PAT-side door.

If the PAT's exterior was unimpressive, one look at the inside of the Personnel Access Tunnel was doubly so. It was a worn, even shabby old thing, little more than a semiflexible plastic pipe. It was square in cross section, with the corners deeply rounded-off as a concession to the physics of pressure control. The sides of the PAT were scuffed and dirty, and the floor's rubbery hexagonal walkway grid was half–worn away, making the footing very tricky in places—especially in the stretches far away from the supports. The PAT tended to move around as one walked through it. Toward the center of the longest span, it was a little like walking on a trampoline.

"I wonder where the hell he scavenged this from," Marquez muttered as he grabbed again for the flimsy handrail and struggled to stay on his feet.

"I'm not sure I want to know," Koffield said.

Somehow, the two of them managed to stay on their feet all the way to the outer hatch of the *Cruzeiro*. Marquez examined the hatch's seals and settings carefully before he set to work opening the security locks. "DeSilvo or his robots *could* have gotten in here," he said. "He's gotten past a lot tougher security than the locks on this door. I can't swear to it, but I *think* that no one and nothing has come through here since the last time I was in the *Cruzeiro*."

He opened the security locks and bled the pressure off the lock interior. The two men entered and moved quickly through the lock chamber to the ship's interior.

Marquez looked around the cabin, checked the displays by the inside of the inner lock door, then stepped back into the lock compartment, and locked down the outer door from the inside, setting the security locks as well as the pressure seals. Then he stepped out of the lock, and back onto the main deck of the *Cruzeiro*. He sealed the lock's inner door, then repressurized the airlock chamber itself, up to 150 percent of standard. He then set the inner controls so that the lock could not be operated at all from the outside control panel.

With that much overpressure forcing the doors shut

against their seals, it would be all but impossible to open the outer hatch with anything short of explosives, or else by drilling a hole through the outer lock door to bleed the pressure. Setting the doors that way would greatly slow their escape from the lighter in an emergency, and it would make it a virtual certainty that no rescuers could get in quickly enough to be of any help.

Koffield watched what Marquez was doing, and did not say a word.

Satisfied with the airlock settings, Marquez knelt on the deck and opened the flush-mounted hatch that led to the bottom deck and the engine room. He went down into the cramped confines of the engineering spaces, Koffield following behind.

It was dark and hot belowdecks. With the ship on standby, the ventilation system was set to minimum, and there were only dim marker lights to lead the way. Marquez broke a sweat almost instantly as he led Koffield through a tight maze of installed equipment and storage lockers. At last he came to the narrow engine-room hatch. The hatch slid open and shut, the door itself fitting into the space between the engine room's inner and outer bulkheads.

The shielded hatch was heavy, and it took a good solid shove to slide it sideways out of the way. He stepped inside, and Koffield followed. There was barely room for both men at once in the cramped compartment. The ship's reactionless thrust generator took up the bulk of the space, along with the plumbing and compressors for the auxiliary rocket propulsion system.

He pulled the engine-room hatch to and used the manual clamping lever to seal it down tight. He powered up the compartment's lights and ventilation system, then switched on every diagnostic and display system, cranking them all up to full. He turned on the intercom system, but set the system into full monitor, focused on the main deck with maximum gain and an open loop circuit. If any third intercom station keyed in—or if anyone tried to tap in from outside the circuit—it would close the loop and set up a audio feedback that ought to produce a head-splitting squeal—and no sound at all from the engine room.

"All right, then," Marquez said, speaking in a low voice. "There are so many fields and circuits running now, that we ought to be jamming just about any frequency that could penetrate through the hull and the shielding on this compartment."

Koffield nodded. "Good. I was hoping you'd say that. I've been on the lookout for how we might get a chance to talk. Long ago and far away, I had some very nice pocket jamming gadgets with me—but I've lost my luggage a few times since then."

"So let's talk."

"Let's. But bear in mind he *could* still be listening in—or his ArtInts could be listening for him, more likely. The technology he's had a chance to play with— the odds are very good that he's got some sort of spy gear we wouldn't even know how to detect, let alone jam."

"Yeah, but we've done the best we could, and the odds on privacy aren't going to get any better. If what we do say offends him, screw him if he can't take a joke. So what have you spotted?"

Koffield shook his head. "What *haven't* I spotted? This place is *big*. There are at least five levels below where we were having lunch, and there could easily be more with the entrances hidden away. It's too big a place for one or two men to do more than a rough survey. Most of what I've found so far is hardware and work-shops and supply stores."

"Yeah. That matches up pretty well with what I've managed to see."

"I'm going to have one last look around tonight, before I give it up."

"Should I head out?"

"Probably not," Koffield said. "We've been at it pretty hard. One more one-man search tonight will be far enough to push our luck. If we keep snooping too long and too much, DeSilvo might not be very happy about it. I don't *think* DeSilvo is likely to have left the crown jewels out in plain sight, but I just want one last chance to see if I can come up with any interesting surprises. Which reminds me, not a surprise, but it's something odd: Half the gear I've seen looks as worn-out as the Personnel Access Tunnel, and half looks like it's never been used."

"Yeah, I've noticed that too."

Koffield nodded. "And I couldn't even tell you what half the new-looking equipment is for. I think we're looking at what his robots scavenged from abandoned cities on Glister, mixed in with whatever machines he removed from the Dark Museum, or else what he's built from Dark Museum plans."

Marquez frowned and thought for a minute. "Now that I think about it, some of the never-been-used stuff kind of looked new and old at the same time. Gear that's never been operated, but has been sitting around for a long time."

Koffield nodded. "*Most* of what's around here has been sitting for a long time. This whole place has been mothballed for a century or more. A lot of the lower sections are still powered down, no heat or ventilation. From what I can see, it all fits with the story he told us."

"I agree. Even if the story was nuts. Which brings me to my main question—is *he* nuts? What do you think— is he sane, or not?"

Koffield shook his head. "I don't even think it's a meaningful question. If sanity is having more or less the same perception of the outside universe as those around you—then no, not by a long shot. But DeSilvo isn't *like* those around him—not anymore. Maybe because there hasn't been anyone around him. He's lived in one form or another of isolation for a long, long time. He's had the power of a god for longer than that. He made a *world*—even if it's a world that's falling apart."

"And he's *still* a god," Marquez grumbled. "The robots around here do whatever he wants, almost before he knows that he wants it. He's got absolute control over this place—and damn near absolute control over us."

"He might have the power," Koffield agreed, "but I get the impression that he doesn't *use* it much. Maybe he doesn't want to use it—even doesn't dare use it."

"Why not?"

"For starters, watching all of us constantly would just take too much time, even if he handed most of the job off to ArtInts. The ArtInts would still have to report to him in some fashion—and he couldn't trust the ArtInts to know what was and wasn't significant, at least at first. These ArtInts are here to keep the machine running and the base clean. They aren't programmed for spy work, and for the most part aren't sophisticated enough to do it well. He'd have to get hugely detailed reports to be sure they didn't miss anything. It would be close to a full-time job for him just to keep up to date on the reports. Controlling us, *using* what he knows from spying on us, would be even worse. But it goes beyond that. He doesn't dare try and control us, for fear of getting us angry—or angrier, I should say. Because, on some level, he knows he needs us. He needs our free and willing cooperation."

"For what?" Marquez demanded. "*As* what? That's what I've been sweating over. To use us as lab animals, running his giant underground maze?"

Koffield shook his head. "I don't think so. I think it's to ask us our opinion of his research—and his plans, whatever those turn out to be. He brought us here so he could ask us if we think he's crazy."

"*What?*"

"Think about it—he's in worse shape to judge than we are. We just got through agreeing that he's been cut off from human society for a long, long time—and been a power answerable to no one but himself for even longer. It's enough to turn anyone's head around. If *we* can see that, so can he."

"So he needs us around just to be sure he hasn't gone around the bend?"

"Among other reasons," Koffield said. "Which reminds me, we had another reason for coming down here. I'd still like to get this bomb removed."

Marquez looked startled. "I'd almost forgotten about it. Where the hell is it?"

"Right where Sparten left it," Koffield said. "Or rather, where *I* put it back after I removed it to disarm it." He knelt and pointed to a small blue cylinder, about ten centimeters long and three wide, taped to one of the propellant surge tanks.

Marquez let out a low whistle. "It's not big, but it wouldn't have to be, right there. Set that off, and you'd blow all the propellant in that tank. Might or might split the hull, but at the very least it'd make sure neither set of engines ever fired again. Ah—you *did* disarm it, didn't you?"

"Yes," Koffield said. "But then I put it back in place, just in case Sparten decided to check on it." Moving very slowly and carefully, he reached down and peeled back the two thin strips of very ordinary adhesive tape that held it to the tank. He pulled the bomb away, and handed it up to Marquez.

"It's safe now, right?" Marquez asked, feeling nervous holding even a small amount of high explosive in his hands.

"It's a bomb," Koffield said calmly. "It's safe enough if you're careful, but it won't ever *really* be safe, until we blow it up out where it won't hurt anyone."

"Do you think he'll let us out on the surface to do that?" Marquez asked. He had imagined that they'd all be forced to stay underground for good.

"Why not? There's no breathable air. There's barely any atmospheric oxygen left. Besides, it's cold enough that all the carbon dioxide's frozen out and fallen like snow," Koffield said. "It's a dead world. He's got the only light and heat, perhaps for light-years around. Where could we go?"

"Light-years?" Marquez suddenly realized he was in the very rare position of knowing something Koffield did not. "It's not quite *that* far to light and heat. Try about seven hundred kilometers south," he said triumphantly.

"*What?* A settlement?"

Marquez had actually managed to surprise Koffield. That was a most rare accomplishment. "Bunch of diehard types," Marquez said, quite pleased with himself. "Probably buried so deep and insulated so well our scans missed their base on the way in. DeSilvo let it slip."

"Unless he let it slip on purpose," Koffield said.

Koffield stood up and held out his hand for the bomb. Marquez handed the deadly little thing back to him. Koffield carefully took it and twisted one end of it until the end cap popped free. He slipped the cap into one pocket of his trousers and tucked the rest of the cylinder into the breast pocket of his shirt. "That should make it just a bit less unsafe, anyway. But, getting back to this settlement—what more did he say?"

"Not much at all. I was at the viewport with him this morning, watching the bulldozers and earthmovers taking the outside of this place apart. I said something like it was a mighty cold world out there. And he said, 'Not all of it is quite so cold as you think.' I asked what he meant. He hesitated, like he'd said too much. Then he pointed sort of to one side of the viewport, off toward the south, and said, 'Why not tell you? That way, about seven hundred kilometers. They call it Last Chance Canyon. But I think you'll find the accommodations more comfortable here.' After that, he shut up."

Koffield leaned his back against a convenient bulkhead, crossed his arms in front of his chest, and let out a weary sigh. "Wonderful. He's been playing games with us so long, so why not play same more? Was he lying or telling the truth? Was what he said spontaneous or planned? Is it important or not? *Are* we supposed to act on it—or not? All that just for starters."

Marquez shook his head. "All I know for sure is we don't know anything for sure. But I *think* it was just a bit of trivia to him."

"So assuming the place is even there, you have no idea how many people, what they're doing there, if they know about this place—or about us?"

"I've told you all I know," Marquez replied. "I don't know if they could help us."

"Help us do what?" Koffield asked.

"Escape, obviously," Marquez replied.

"Do we *want* to escape? We just went through a hell of a lot of effort to *get* here," Koffield pointed out. "There are a lot of reasons for staying here. Besides, it's much more likely that *they* would need help from *us*. With all the equipment in this place, there's bound to be something they could use. Do we want to let them know we're here?"

"I grant all that," said Marquez, "but still we need to think it all through. We can't just dismiss the thought of leaving out of hand."

"Even if we *did* want to escape, how could we?" Koffield ticked off the difficulties on his fingers. "A habitat seven hundred kilometers away, when we don't have any transport, we don't know where it is, we don't know if they'd let us in, and we can't survive on the surface without our suits for heat and oxygen. We'd have to walk, carrying supplies that we could use without having to take the suits off for more than a few minutes at a time. Plus it would have to be all of us or none of us. We couldn't leave behind hostages. The thing's impossible in so many ways, I can't imagine DeSilvo even worrying about it."

"Granted, I suppose," Marquez said.

"And there's another issue we'd have to consider. A diehard hab that's hung on this long has *got* to be on the knife edge of survival as it is. Eight more bodies breathing air and eating food and giving off body waste and heat and sweat could easily be enough to collapse their ecostructure. We could be sentencing them to death just by walking through their front door."

Koffield frowned, and went on. "Plus, they'd know how much risk extra bodies would mean to them just as well as we do—probably better. They'd have to regard our showing up and endangering them as deliberate. We might be found guilty of attempted murder just because we arrived—and diehard habs can't afford to run nice, humane prisons. They tend toward capital punishment for most offenses, even minor ones. And they tend to be terrifyingly good recyclers. Alive, we'd be a threat to their survival. Once we were tried, convicted, and sentenced, we'd be a welcome input of fresh resources."

Marquez felt the hairs on the back of his neck stand on end. "That part I hadn't considered," he conceded. "So, we stay away from Last Chance Canyon. Fine. And DeSilvo shouldn't have any problems letting us go outside long enough to dispose of the bomb. I don't think DeSilvo will want us to keep it—and we won't want *him* to have it—not that it really makes any difference."

"Agreed. Who needs a bomb for a weapon when all you have to do is cut off food, water, and air?"

Marquez nodded, then checked the time. "We've probably taken as long as we can get away with on this. Anything else we need to cover?"

"Two things," Koffield said. "One: Everything I've seen so far tells me that DeSilvo can copy advanced technology all day long, but he can't create it or modify it. Two: There are some things that take more than two or three people to do—not one man and a crowd of robots."

"What do you mean he can't create high tech?" Marquez asked.

"I mean the faster-than-light drive, the FTL communicator, the improved temporal confinement system—the robots themselves, for that matter. DeSilvo didn't *invent* any of those things. I doubt he understands all of them completely—some of them he may not understand at all. People use tools all the time without knowing how they work, so long as they get the results they want. And what I've seen around here tells me he's got some sort of autofac—possibly a number of them, in various sizes."

"Neither of us has spotted one—and we've both been exploring," Marquez objected.

"I doubt we will see one. He'd be sure to keep any automatic manufacturer very carefully tucked away from the likes of us," Koffield said. "Still, he might have gotten sloppy. That's the main reason I want to risk having one more look around tonight: to see if I can locate any autofacs. If I can find it, and get an idea of its capabilities, we'll know a lot more about what DeSilvo can do."

"Or maybe we haven't found an autofac because there isn't one," Marquez pointed out.

"There's an indirect clue that he *does* have one. Nearly everything we saw in the Dark Museum had an autofac datastore included as part of the documentation. He'd be able to build copies of virtually everything in the museum. But, even so, an autofac *would* limit him in very distinct ways. It could do lots of things—but it couldn't let him do *everything*."

"What you're saying is that he can only make what a good autofac can make."

"Right. There must have been some sort of small abandoned landing field or service field or something here, and he built up around that. He must have an autofac, and must have used it to build everything here that he didn't already have. Subtract the equipment he found in place and reused, subtract what's obviously been scavenged from somewhere else and brought in, subtract whatever else was made in an autofac—and there's very little left over."

"So if he doesn't have the autofac documentation for a left-handed frangus—"

"He's got no other way to make one, unless he can give a robot explicit enough instructions, or else make it himself. It *must* limit him in particular ways. If he needs a bicycle, but the autofac only knows how to make a truck, then he has to use a truck instead of a bicycle. And there's more. He can't modify."

"What do you mean?"

"He isn't able to tell the autofac to change what it builds. If it knows how to build a five-liter bucket, he can't tell it to build a ten-liter bucket.

"My second point is that I think he's reached the limits of what one man can do, even with unlimited assistance from robots and ArtInts and autofacs. He can only do large-scale jobs that can be done with all-robot labor, with most of it ArtInt-controlled. I think if he's going to move forward with—with whatever it is he's doing, he going to need people—lots of them. Wandella Ashdin's been working on her presentation. She's interviewed him several times since she got here. She mentioned something to me this morning: His plan at one point, long ago, long before we came into the picture, was to bring a large staff here. The facility is certainly big enough—far too large for one man, even a megalomaniac. The place could support a staff of hundreds. Maybe we're just the first recruits."

"And I've been wondering if we were prisoners or guests. You make me think maybe we're employees—or slaves."

Koffield smiled. "Let's try and think of ourselves as independent contractors. A temporary arrangement."

"Wait a second. If he needs people, warm bodies, so badly—why not just go over to Last Chance Canyon?"

"Maybe we have skills they don't. Maybe he was lying about Last Chance Canyon, and it's not there at all. Maybe he thought they were a security risk—or were just likely to come at him with all guns blazing, and snatch everything here, if they knew he existed. Or maybe he *has* tried recruiting them, and been told no. Or maybe it's something totally different, something we haven't thought of."

Marquez shrugged and checked the time again. "Now we really have to go," he said. He powered down the equipment he had activated, set the intercom back to normal function, and slid the hatch open. Koffield followed him out of the engine compartment, and they sealed the engine-room hatch behind them. They made their way back to the upper deck, and Marquez punched a command into the airlock controls. They heard the whir of hidden pumps as the excess pressure was pulled out of the lock chamber.

Excess pressure, Marquez thought as he watched the lock indicators. *Yes indeed.* He glanced at his companion. That was something, he felt sure, that Admiral Anton Koffield knew all about.

Chapter Three

HISTORY IN THE DARK

The great looming shapes of the dormant machines slumbered in the darkness, cocooned in protective blankets that blurred their shapes and purposes. A thin layer of dust, the accumulation of a hundred long years, lay upon them, obscuring the mothballed hardware just that little bit more.

Anton Koffield trudged wearily along the labyrinthine corridors, back toward the lifts that would carry him to the upper levels of DeSilvo City, to regions of light and warmth and human contact—at least to the degree any of those commodities were available on the frozen corpse of the world that was Glister.

He had learned a great deal on his exploration of the lower regions—and yet, in another sense, nothing at all. He had seen a lot of machines, true enough. Some of the hardware he found he could identify. Some he could not, at least not with full confidence. Certainly no sign of any autofacs, but he hadn't really expected DeSilvo to leave anything that valuable out where it might be found.

The challenge was to fit what he *could* identify into some sort of coherent whole. Knowing what sort of hardware DeSilvo had should at least tell him what DeSilvo was capable of, even if it did not reveal his intent. All very sensible in theory—but the machines that he had found were so powerful, so capable of so many things, as to provide him no real clue. DeSilvo could do nearly everything with them—and therefore might be planning to do almost anything.

But Koffield had known *that* much for some time.

He was tired, dead tired. Time to go back to his quarters. Time to go to bed.

The moment Koffield opened the door to his room, before he entered, he could hear soft breathing. Someone was there, waiting in the dark, behind the door. He instantly had to fight down his old training. He knew who was in the station. Of those, there were two people who might conceivably have the motive to go for him.

DeSilvo did not have the physical courage. Sparten would have the nerve to do it, and might well have dreamed up some damned-fool reason why it was his noble duty to kill Anton Koffield—but no, he would have come straight at Koffield, not waited in ambush.

But Anton Koffield had no wish to stake his life on that sort of amateur psychology. Better to—

But then the breathing turned to a gentle snore, and Koffield caught a whiff of a fragrance he knew quite well. He chuckled to himself. He was getting twitchy.

He reached around the doorframe and flipped on the lights by hand, then pushed the door the rest of the way open. There, sitting in the room's one comfortable armchair, was Wandella Ashdin, sound asleep, a datapad on her lap.

Koffield stepped into the room, crossed to the chair, and gently tapped her on the shoulder. "Dr. Ashdin? Doctor?"

"Huh! What? Oh!" Dr. Ashdin looked around in bewilderment for a moment, then came back to herself. "Oh, for heaven's sake. Forgive me, Admiral. I didn't intend to doze off."

"It's quite all right," Koffield said.

Dr. Ashdin struggled unsuccessfully to stifle a yawn. "Just, just give me a moment, please."

"Of course," Koffield said. There were a pair of scruffy yellow plastic chairs sitting with their backs against one wall of the room. Koffield got one of them, brought it over, and sat down facing Wandella Ashdin.

Ashdin looked about the way everyone imagined the ideal grandmother would look, with a gentle face framed by frizzy snow-white hair. Her sky-blue eyes somehow made her seem constantly surprised, and that was not far off. She was far from the most organized person in Settled Space. But her work, her research, was always first-class. And, at a guess, it was her work she was there to discuss.

"What's on your mind, Dr. Ashdin?" Koffield asked.

She picked up the datapad off her lap and handed it to him. "This is," she said. "It's got my background report—basically a summary of prior events. The things that we've learned in bits and pieces here and there, put into some sort of rational order. Something everyone could read before the presentation and refer to later."

Koffield took the datapad from her. "Why is it so important that you sat up in my room until all hours of the night before your presentation?"

Wandella smiled wryly. "Because it might get us all killed if DeSilvo doesn't like it. And he won't." She stretched and yawned. "I tried like hell to tell the truth—but the truth is pretty hellish. I started out just doing a basic summing-up. I read it over tonight, and realized that it was something more like the case for the prosecution. It might go too far."

"And you want me to take a look at it before you give copies to everyone?"

"That's right. Tonight, if at all possible, so they can all have it in the morning."

Koffield nodded reluctantly. So much for getting some rest himself. "I'd be happy to," he said.

The two of them stood up, and Koffield saw her to the door.

Ashdin gestured at the datapad. "I suppose that's the first draft of the first history of all this," she said. "Very strange."

"What is?"

"To be living a part of the history that I am writing."

She tapped her finger on the datapad Koffield held. "And something else that I find odd. I have to keep remembering that practically everything in there is a secret we've uncovered. No one else knows all of what we know. History isn't usually classified."

"Or maybe it usually is—but we never know," said Koffield with a smile.

"*That* is a most disturbing idea," said Ashdin. "Good night, Admiral. And thank you."

Koffield closed the door behind his guest, then sat down in the chair she had just vacated. He began to read, not trying to take the whole thing in at once, but skimming over it, trying to get the feel, the flavor of the piece before studying it carefully.

> Just over a thousand years ago, in the year 4306 of the Common Era, someone named Ulan Baskaw wrote the first of a series of books that were of great importance to the field of terraforming. We know virtually nothing about Baskaw . . .

Not even if Baskaw was male or female, though the convention was to assume Baskaw was a woman. Koffield skipped down the columns of text, reading a bit here and there.

> . . . To oversimplify things almost to the point of absurdity, her work put forward the idea that, when terraforming a given planet, one could use a nearby world as a sort of nursery, a breeding ground for species one planned to introduce. . . . There was much more to her ideas that we will not explore here. Suffice it to say Baskaw's ideas were truly revolutionary.
> . . . between the dates of Baskaw's second and third books, the attempt to terraform Mars experienced its final collapse. A careful examination of the third volume reveals subtle textual clues that

suggest Baskaw did in fact visit Mars in the period just prior to the collapse. . . .

Her third book demonstrated not only that some terraformed worlds *could* fail, but that *all* terraformed worlds would, inevitably, fail. Again, to oversimplify to an almost criminal degree, Baskaw found that the faster a world was terraformed, the sooner it would fail.

. . . Her fourth, and, so far as we know, final work is entitled, very simply, *Contraction*. It was discovered twice, once by Dr. DeSilvo, then by Admiral Koffield—in the Dark Museum of Suppressed Technology. It therefore represents the clearest possible evidence that Baskaw's work was, at least in part, deliberately suppressed.

And they did a good job of it, Koffield reflected. Baskaw's work did not seem to have been paid the slightest attention for centuries.

. . . her first three books were discovered—and appropriated—by Dr. DeSilvo. He plagiarized her works, then did what he could to destroy all surviving references to the original. He erased the texts of her first three books from the Grand Library and claimed her ideas as his own.

Dr. DeSilvo then took these appropriated ideas and used them as the basis for a new terraforming project on the planet Solace.

. . . he applied Baskaw's techniques and completely ignored the warning in Baskaw's third book, which used a further expansion of her own mathematics to prove that the techniques DeSilvo was using would inevitably result in an unstable ecology, doomed to collapse.

And the collapse is happening right about now, back on Solace. If only that were the worst of it. Koffield read on, skimming quickly.

Dr. DeSilvo in effect suddenly had power over an entire world, indeed an entire star system. He had at his disposal a vast array of equipment—spacecraft, earthmoving equipment, massive power generators, and so on . . . he quickly established a clear pattern of "borrowing" those resources for other purposes. . . .

The resources of the terraforming project were used to pay for various medical and life-extension services for Dr. DeSilvo, to finance the DeSilvo archive in the Grand Library. . . . Dr. DeSilvo out and out stole a large number of spacecraft, artificial intelligence systems, and other major pieces of equipment.

. . . When he tapped in to the mother lode of suppressed inventions—the Dark Museum, he could not resist the chance to go further, much further. . . .

But simple information—data, schematics, plans, and so on—was not enough for the plan that was gradually forming in his mind. He would need workshops and facilities of all sorts . . .

He had to build the machines he would need to build the machines to build the machine to build the machines he wanted.

. . . In all of this, he had to work through robots, teleoperators, artificial intelligence systems, and so on. He did it all without any witting human assistants—though no doubt many unwitting ones.

. . . He wanted glory. He wanted to shower technological wonders down on a grateful and astonished humanity and bask in their appreciation. But how?

. . . Once Solace was completed, he would set himself up as a wizard of invention and dole out inventions and discoveries claiming the credit for himself. He arranged things so that, if things had gone as planned, his "workshop" would have opened for business decades after he should have died, given any sort of normal human life span.

The likely reason for that was to put several extra decades at least between himself and the "diversions" of material. He of course planned to use cryogenic and/or temporal confinement to wait out the necessary period of time.

Koffield was about to skip down a bit farther, but a line or two caught his eye, and he scrolled back up.

. . . Given what is known of Dr. DeSilvo's psychology, it is quite possible he was going to open that workshop and present himself to the outside universe as his own son—DeSilvo Junior.

That was an interesting theory. Koffield could believe it. It fit in with DeSilvo's endless rejuvenation treatments and transplants, his quest for eternal youth. But that quest was tied up with another, more morbid tendency. Did Ashdin discuss that? He skimmed ahead. Yes. There it was.

It would also fit in well with an odd psychological need—Dr. DeSilvo's impulse—perhaps even compulsion—to mimic death. Dr. DeSilvo built himself a very fine tomb on Greenhouse and arranged his own simulated death over a century ago. He spent much of the intervening time in temporal confinement. He also used cryogenics or temporal confinement to wait out other periods of time. And, he did, in fact, literally die, several times, each time being placed in powerful temporal confinements or cryostorage systems while his medical staff spent weeks or months planning how best to revive him. On some level, Dr. DeSilvo enjoyed being dead. "Returning" to life as his own son or grandson might well fulfill that peculiar need . . .
. . . Dr. DeSilvo first selected the location he wanted for his cache—a base on the planet Glister. His projections, using Baskaw's methods, were that Glister would be a dead world by the point in

time he had chosen. He would then be able to scavenge the abandoned wreckage of the world in order to build the facility he needed.

But, if he wished to *hide* his secrets in the future, he had to *reach* the future. The obvious technique would be to put his treasures in hidden storage, put himself in temporal confinement, and simply wait. But his FTL drives would deteriorate if left in untended storage for that long. Besides which, the equipment in question was quite large . . .

He decided to move his treasure out of the Solacian star system, while avoiding the use of the timeshaft-wormhole transport system.

But he then made an error—a huge error, with tremendous consequences for all those in the Glistern and Solacian star systems, and perhaps, for all of humanity.

And, for what it was worth, some pretty nasty consequences for a certain Anton Koffield. Consequences that were still being played out. He could see by glancing ahead that this was the part of the story where Dr. Ashdin really took the gloves off. He read through her account thoughtfully, concentrating on Wandella's analysis.

. . . He chose Glister of the future as the space-time point in which to build his facility, because his projections showed that Glister would have collapsed utterly by then. . . . He would make doubly sure that his treasure was safe from prying eyes if he wrecked the timeshaft wormhole that served Glister.

Part of his fleet of robotic ships he would send direct to Glister without benefit of FTL or wormhole transit—so-called slowboats. They would travel far below the speed of light, taking decades to make the journey.

Other ships, rigged for FTL travel, would take a shortcut to the future—straight through the wormholes. During that transit, they would track certain parameters of the wormhole with a precision great enough to accomplish his next goal: the destruction of the wormhole. . . .

Dr. DeSilvo claims that his plan assumed that the Chronologic Patrol Ship *Standfast* would flee the attack and not respond quickly or aggressively enough to stop all of the ships driving for the wormhole. He claims he did not intend to cause harm or casualties as he forced passage of the wormhole. He imagined the guard ship standing off at a safe distance and firing carefully aimed single shots at the attackers. Either he was monstrously incompetent or lying when he says he tried to avoid causing death or injury.

Instead of standing well off from the Intruders—as the ships came to be called—the *Standfast* went straight for them, diving in with all guns blazing, risking—and losing—the ship and the lives of all aboard in order to try to fulfill her mission. That was just the first of DeSilvo's miscalculations concerning his wormhole transit plan.

. . . When the Intruders came through the uptime side of the wormhole, they used similar tactics. The *Upholder* fought back, taking serious damage herself, her crew suffering many deaths and other casualties.

Three of the Intruders survived the wormhole transit and escaped the *Upholder*. Each carried a complete set of the information Dr. DeSilvo had diverted.

. . . the three surviving Intruders returned from Glister to the vicinity of Circum Central. Each deployed a pair of drones, then departed, returning their valuable gear—mainly their FTL drives—to Glister.

. . . They continued their attack as if the other ships were not present. The *Upholder,* though badly damaged, attempted to stop them . . . The

Upholder, with great skill and luck, managed to destroy two of the drones attacking the wormhole.

. . . Captain Koffield saw he had no choice but to destroy the wormhole. This he attempted to do—and he spent years believing he had done so, years in which every other person believed he had done it as well. People blamed him for the death of those aboard the convoy ships that were destroyed, for the loss of the relief supplies they were carrying to Glister, even, quite illogically, for the collapse of Glister itself, decades later. In truth, the loss of that convoy probably *extended* the planet's survival time. More people died sooner as a result of the relief convoy's failure to arrive, leaving fewer mouths to feed in the grim decades that followed.

. . . Captain Koffield was blamed for all of this, and much more . . . The destruction of the wormhole was not his doing; the one surviving Intruder had seized control of the wormhole and wrecked it. It would have been destroyed even if Koffield had abandoned his post and ordered his ship home.

All of Settled Space looked to Captain Koffield and saw blood on his hands. Only Dr. Oskar De-Silvo knew he was not to blame—and Dr. Oskar DeSilvo said and did nothing.

Not feeling entirely comfortable reading about himself, Koffield moved forward a bit in the text, to where Dr. Ashdin further discussed DeSilvo's motives. As if anyone could ever know them for sure. If and when the true story of DeSilvo's career got out, the debate over his motives would never end. But he was interested in what Wandella's thoughts on the matter might be.

. . . The game was not worth the candle. Even if he dismissed the harm to others from his calculations, the effort and cost needed to fly through, then destroy, the wormhole far exceeds the value Oskar DeSilvo gained from the effort. So why did he do it?

. . . there was one entity, one group, that had more power than he did. The Chronologic Patrol controlled the paths between the stars, controlled the gates that linked past and future.

If DeSilvo, working alone, could defeat or, better yet, humiliate such a powerful organization, then surely that would prove that his own power was still intact. Besides, DeSilvo had already defeated the Patrol once, by finding, penetrating, and robbing the Dark Museum.

But there was a good chance that the Chronologic Patrol was like the lion bitten by the flea: The flea celebrated his victory, but the lion didn't even know that he'd been bitten. The Chronologic Patrol likely did not know that anyone had so much as found the wreckage of the Dark Museum.

But to attack a timeshaft wormhole—to brush back the defenders, to defeat the security systems, to come from the direction no one expected, to wreck the wormhole—and to come and go traveling faster than light, demonstrating how far beyond their crude devices you have gone—then they would *have* to know they had been assaulted, been defeated.

All that damage had to be done simply because Oskar DeSilvo had to thumb his nose at the Chronologic Patrol. . . .

Well, perhaps. Koffield stopped reading there, set the datapad down, and rubbed his eyes. No explanation was ever going to be entirely satisfactory so far as he was concerned. But Dr. Ashdin had made a good start.

He would have to read through the whole report by morning, but Anton Koffield already knew he was going to approve its distribution. It was honest. It was accurate. And yes, it was angry. But cold, hard, dispassionate anger was an entirely justified reaction to all DeSilvo had done.

In any event, the danger in speaking plainly was as clear to Dr. Ashdin as it was to Koffield. As for the report endangering the rest of them . . . how much more danger could they be in? DeSilvo could kill them all at any time, for any reason, or no reason.

No. If as careful a scholar as Wandella Ashdin was prepared to speak truth to power, and do so in the stronghold of the man she was judging, then he had no right to stop her from so doing.

The question was, would DeSilvo feel he had the right, and the need, to stop her—or even all of his guests—from doing anything, ever again?

They'd all find out the next day.

Chapter Four

MIRRORS AND SHADOWS

Yuri Sparten stood in the darkness and watched the death of planet Earth. Again. Every run of the simulation model ended the same way.

"Starting to believe him?" asked Norla Chandray, looking up at the image of a ruined world hanging in the darkness. She made sure the data was stored, then reset for the next run.

"Maybe," Yuri said. "But we're still depending a lot on *his* system, his ArtInts, his programming, his initial data. I won't really be happy until we can do some runs that aren't at all dependent on *him*." He paused a moment and looked up again at the blank spot in the middle of the air, where the simulation system had shown them the Earth that was to be. "Well, not *happy*, of course—but that's what it will take to start *convincing* me."

Norla nodded. "That's about the way I figure it. But let's just say it's getting harder to *dis*believe. We already knew the terraformed worlds were in big trouble. Why should Earth be immune?"

Yuri shrugged. "Why should it?" he agreed glumly. Plainly, Earth *wasn't* immune. That was proved in every run of the model. As the terraformed worlds collapsed, their refugees descended on Earth, bringing any number of highly evolved microbes and other unpleasant things back home with them. The details of how and when it happened changed from one run of the simulation to the next, but always, sooner or later—often sooner—Earth died. In some runs, the home planet lived fifteen hundred years or more into the future. Other times, it was little more than half that long. Only rarely did it last much longer than a thousand.

But DeSilvo claimed to have found a way out. All they had to do was deal with the devil, and he would save them all. "So is it today?" Yuri asked.

"What?"

"The big meeting."

"Yes. And you should be there."

"Probably best that I wasn't," Yuri replied. "I'm really not that excited to be in the same room with *him*." After all, he had done his best to kill DeSilvo a few days before.

"You're allowed to say his name, you know," Norla said, plainly amused. "You can say 'DeSilvo' instead of—" she paused to place one hand outstretched in melodramatic fashion and put the other to her forehead—" *'him.'* "

Yuri Sparten laughed and smiled—two things he hadn't done in a long time. Up until a few days before, he'd been playing the part of a sort-of double agent, watching Koffield for the SCO Station Security Force. What he had not realized was that, more than likely, the Chronologic Patrol Intelligence Corps saw all of what the SSF saw—or that DeSilvo had been tapping the SSF's comm since well before Yuri had been born. Yuri had found out the hard way that he was not suited to such work, to the secrets and the evasions and the out-and-out lies. He was surprised to find how much of a relief it was to be exposed, to have the game be over and done with. He was discovering that he liked himself a great deal better, now that the mask had come off.

"All right, all right," he said. "I don't think it's such a good idea if I spend much time with *DeSilvo*. Better?"

"Better. But you're going to have to, sooner or later. We're all cooped up here together. And for what it's worth, I don't think DeSilvo will enjoy today's meeting much. Did you read Dr. Ashdin's background report?"

"Not yet."

"You should. She wasn't pulling any punches. It'll be worth hearing what she has to say."

"Well, maybe," said Yuri. He made an adjustment to one of the projection controls and thought for a moment. He couldn't sulk in his quarters forever—and if his whole life revolved around avoiding DeSilvo, then he had more or less surrendered control of his life *to* DeSilvo. Why should he do that? "Maybe I will be there."

"Good," said Norla. She was checking her setting, getting ready for the next simulation run. "But there's something else. Something the admiral heard from Marquez."

"What?"

"Marquez said that DeSilvo told him that there was a diehard colony not all that far from here," Norla said.

Yuri looked up at her sharply. "What?"

"Diehards. About seven hundred kilometers away. Sounds like DeSilvo was talking as if he knew all about them."

Yuri's insides froze up hard as the ice on the surface of Glister. Whatever good mood or marginally less hostile attitude toward DeSilvo he might have had died in that moment. Everyone knew about diehards—the saying was they might die hard, but the way they lived was harder. They might hold out two or three generations, in whatever wreckage was left behind when the main population left, but there were limits to how much could be scavenged, how completely supplies could be used and recycled, limits to how long the machines vital to their survival could be kept running, how often they could be repaired. And two or three generations was long enough for inbreeding to be a problem, or for any system of succession to the leadership to collapse. From what Yuri had read, it was political problems as often as starvation or life-support collapse that did in diehard colonies.

"What's he done for them?" Yuri asked, already knowing the answer.

"So far as Marquez could tell, nothing."

Yuri looked at Norla. Her expression was carefully neutral. Yuri couldn't help but wonder why she was telling him this, and telling him now.

"This place could support hundreds of people indefinitely," he said. "And in all this time he hasn't lifted a finger to help starving people when he could fly a food drop to them in two hours?"

"Hold it. Hold it. We don't know they're starving."

"Ever hear of an overweight diehard?"

"Ever hear of a diehard who didn't shoot first and ask questions later—or maybe not ask at all? And besides, think about it. DeSilvo was in temporal confinement for something like a hundred years. He was still in it up until a few days before we landed—and we've only been here a few days. I can't even see how he'd know they were there. We did an infrared-signature search from orbit, and *we* didn't pick up anything. What sort of detectors has *he* got?"

"He could have anything," Yuri said. "Stars alone know what he pulled out of the Dark Museum."

"But he couldn't know for sure they'd be there unless he had some sort of vast network of ArtInts scanning the planet for the last hundred years, or unless he started looking for diehards the second he came out of temporal confinement."

"Seems like a lot of trouble to take either way," Yuri conceded. "But keeping sensor equipment running that long in this environment without human maintenance would be close-on impossible. Probably a lot easier to search for the diehards once he woke up."

"Agreed. But *why* would he search for diehards?" Norla asked. "Seven hundred kilometers away makes it a pretty wide search radius if he's just trying to secure his perimeter or some damn thing. And why would he make it known he found them? Either he just accidentally let it slip to Marquez, or else he had a reason for doing it. And I don't think it could be an accident."

"Why not?"

"DeSilvo's done nothing but plan for our arrival since before you were born. He's a planner, a schemer. He's not the sort who does things impulsively."

"So what would his reasons be?"

Norla shook her head. "I don't know. But unless he's

even more out of touch about human behavior than I thought, he'd *have* to know that Marquez would repeat the news—and that sooner or later, probably sooner, the word would get to you—the son of Glistern refugees, *and* the man who tried to kill him a few days ago. So why would he do that?"

Yuri shrugged. "Maybe whatever plan he's got can't be affected by what I do."

"Or maybe it absolutely *depends* on you."

"So, what? Should I do exactly the opposite of what I'd do if I did think it was just by chance that he mentioned it?"

Norla smiled. "That's got so many conditionals in it I'm not even sure I followed it the whole way. But maybe that would be a good idea—if we knew for sure what he expected you to do—and if we knew for sure that we *didn't* want his plan to succeed."

"But we haven't the faintest idea what sort of plan he has!"

"Or even if the diehards are there. Maybe he's just plain been alone too long and has a tendency to babble. Maybe he was just making conversation. Or maybe he was lying. Maybe there isn't any diehard colony out there—but he wants us to think there is."

Yuri groaned. "I thought I was out from under all this," he said. "No more spying, no more cover stories, no more secrets." A few minutes before, Yuri had felt lucky to be unexpectedly free of the land of secrets, out of the forest of mirrors. Truth and lies, right and wrong, honor and deception had become mere reflections of each other, each reflection reversing the original, before being reversed again in some further mirror. Now he was thrust back in again, his return as involuntary as his departure.

"Sorry about that," Norla said. "But I think De-Silvo's put us all back into the game."

Yuri nodded and returned to his work, setting up the next run. "Yeah," he said. He worked silently for a moment, and spoke again. "I'll be there for Dr. Ashdin's presentation," he said. "I have to look at him, see if I can get some sort of feel for what he's doing."

Have to. The words echoed in his head, for they were all too true. He had no choice in the matter. *And who was it who took away my freedom to choose?* Yuri knew the answer to that one all too well. He was already doing what DeSilvo wanted, his motions and gestures as utterly controlled, as involuntary—and as meaningless—as the motions of DeSilvo's reflection, a shadow forever trapped inside a mirror.

They met in the usual conference room. Koffield got there a bit early and watched as the others came in. DeSilvo arrived last, his expression completely neutral, a chessmaster's face, carefully arranged so as to reveal absolutely nothing.

The rest of the party having assembled, Koffield nodded and looked around the table. "Shall we begin?" he asked.

"If we must," DeSilvo said. "The tone of Dr. Ashdin's written report was far different from what I expected it to be. It was my impression that it was not to be anywhere near as accusatory as it seems to have become. I thought Dr. Ashdin's written report was simply to gather together a coherent narrative of past events."

"Yeah—so we maybe we can figure out better what you got wrong and what you got right—this time," said Jerand Bolt.

DeSilvo glared at the source of the interruption. "If you please, Bolt, I would appreciate if we could maintain a level of discourse on a professional, if not scholarly, level." The fact that Bolt had saved DeSilvo's life a few days before clearly did not earn him much license.

"Right," said Bolt. "I'll do that."

"I'd appreciate it," DeSilvo answered smoothly. He looked past Bolt to Wandella Ashdin, who sat between Bolt and Koffield's place at the far end of the table. "Dr. Ashdin. You're a scholar, not an advocate. Surely you agree that this need not be an adversarial proceeding."

"I agree that I do not *wish* it to be adversarial, and it was not my intent to make it so. But I fear I can see no way to avoid that result completely. We are here to review and consider what has already happened, with the goal of deciding what to do next—and also to decide whether or not we should be guided by your ideas of how to proceed.

"You yourself said that we must draw our own conclusions, because you felt you could not entirely trust yourself or your data. Indeed, *you* brought us to this place in part for the purpose of examining the situation and providing you with our views. And, needless to say, *you* caused most of what happened, and it was, ultimately, *your* actions that brought us to this place, and these circumstances. How can we judge the matters before us without, in some degree, judging you and your actions? Tell me how to square that circle, and I will do it."

She paused briefly, but was greeted with nothing but silence. "There is no law here, no social restraint on you. You control our access to light, food, air, water, warmth, our ability to leave, and virtually everything else. There can be no middle ground. We must have the courage to judge our jailer, knowing he could, at a whim, be our executioner, or else we must speak so as to please you—in which case there was no point at all to bringing us here."

DeSilvo did not answer at first. He looked around the room. His fingers twitched for a moment, as if he were about to start drumming them on the table, but then he brought his hand under control. "Your points are all well taken, Dr. Ashdin. I do not agree with them—but my situation is strange, as well. In order to get what I want from you—your honest evaluations and true opinions—I must accept certain *other* honest and true thoughts. I reluctantly withdraw my objections."

Koffield was fascinated. He had thought they had been brought there because DeSilvo was a sane man who knew he might have driven himself mad, cut himself off from humanity and humanness in new and strange ways. But he was starting to understand that DeSilvo *knew* he was mad and wanted them all there to push him back to sanity. DeSilvo, indeed all of them, teetered precariously, balanced on the point of a knife. Tilt too far one way or another, and it would be all over.

The only safety, the only way forward, was in the extremely narrow middle ground, where madness and sanity stood in judgment of each other.

There was no safe way to say any of that. But then, there was no longer any safe way to say or do anything. "Perhaps it would be best if we got started," he said. "Dr. Ashdin?"

"Thank you, Admiral." She stood up and looked around the room.

"I will begin by amplifying a few points made in the written background report," she said. But another voice cut in before she could go on.

"Excuse me, Dr. Ashdin," said Dixon Phelby. "Before you begin, I have a question regarding one point in the background report. If Baskaw's work was suppressed hundreds of years ago, why wasn't DeSilvo stopped from using it when he started talking up the terraforming of Solace?"

"I think I can answer that," said Koffield. "It seems as if it was my old outfit, the Chronologic Patrol, that did a lot of the suppressing. Five or six hundred years is a long time for an institution to remember a certain thing. More than likely, they simply lost track of what they had suppressed, and failed to monitor properly for a fresh outbreak of the same idea. Once an idea gets past them, and there is public knowledge of something they want to have stopped, it's too late. The genie is out of the bottle and can't be stuffed back in. By the very act of successfully making Baskaw's ideas public, DeSilvo had defeated them."

"And 'suppress' doesn't necessarily mean 'wipe out' or 'erase,' " said Norla Chandray. "It can mean 'slow down' or 'delay.' After all, they did manage to keep Baskaw's ideas from getting out for several centuries. We saw lots of things in the Dark Museum that had been suppressed five hundred years ago, but are now in common use. What happened to Baskaw's work is just more of the same."

"Does that satisfy you on that point, Mr. Phelby?" Ashdin asked.

"Yes, pretty much. Please forgive the interruption."

"Not at all," Ashdin replied. "It was a valid point. Now then." She paused and looked about the room. "I will begin by touching on certain events after the horrific Second Battle of Circum Central. After surviving that disaster, and a journey of tremendous hardship, Captain Koffield got his ship home. However, because his ship could no longer use the destroyed timeshaft wormhole, he and his crew arrived home eight decades into their own future. The *Upholder* and all aboard her were home, and yet marooned, trapped in their own future, prevented from returning by the very laws they had enforced."

Something in her shifted as she began to speak. She stood taller, her voice became louder and stronger, taking on the tones of an academic addressing her classroom. No longer a refugee-scholar wandering the starlanes, she had become a university professor again, dispassionate, and yet impassioned, speaking with the confidence of one who had mastered her material—and wanted her class to understand that she was planning a most challenging final exam.

"Koffield had followed his orders and done everything he was supposed to do, and done it splendidly. He had protected the past against an assault from the future. His superiors promoted him, decorated him—and put him up on a very high shelf. The political climate made it impossible for him to command another ship. Officially, he was a hero. Realistically, his career was over."

Koffield knew that the others in the room were looking at him, but he kept his gaze fixed on Ashdin, who addressed the gathering as impersonally as if he and De-Silvo were long dead rather than in the room, close enough for her to touch. But what was he supposed to do? Burst into tears? It was no particular effort to keep his face impassive.

"The shelf they put him up on was a meaningless and vaguely defined assignment to the Grand Library. In the eighty years that had passed since his departure, the terraforming of Solace had been declared complete—and final collapse of Glister had *not* occurred.

"Both of these events were significant to another man then resident in the Grand Library habitat—Dr. Oskar DeSilvo.

"I wish to put his actions at the Grand Library in broader moral context. To do so, we must first turn to what DeSilvo's fleet of ships did when they arrived in the Glister system. The three surviving FTL craft were programmed to rendezvous with the slowboat fleet, and this they did. They transferred their cargoes and their datastores, and configured themselves for the final assault on Circum Central. Each of the three FTL craft took a pair of attack drones aboard, flew them to the vicinity of Circum Central, released them, then departed before the attack even began. They returned to the slowboat fleet, then about a hundred astronomical units outside the Glister system.

"Even from that vantage point, it was plain that Glister had not yet collapsed. Though his contingency planning had not been all it could have been in other ways, at least DeSilvo had allowed for the possibilities that his eighty-year projection might be inaccurate. In such a circumstance, the fleet was programmed to put itself in a long, slow orbit of the planet, tens of billions of kilometers out from the orbit of Glister itself, and wait for the inevitable—vultures circling in the darkness, waiting for the victim to expire.

"Like all good scavengers, DeSilvo's ships didn't hesitate to hurry the victim along just a bit by wrecking the wormhole and making transit to Glister far more difficult. Consider: The slowboats were programmed to deal with the contingency of Glister still being populated. They simply went into a distant parking orbit. But the FTL ships, part of the same fleet, faced with the same contingency, *went back and wrecked the wormhole anyway*. I should also note that DeSilvo had enough confidence in his prediction of Glister's collapse to create the whole huge project I have described. But *never once did he make any effort to warn the Glisterns*. All his efforts were engaged in a plan to take advantage of the catastrophe's aftermath.

"Let us turn to the other event—DeSilvo's encounter with Koffield at the Grand Library. Here too, I believe, is an insight into DeSilvo's mind. Four ships were utterly destroyed at Circum Central, and one other damaged beyond repair. Thousands were either dead already, or in peril of their lives because the relief supplies were lost. All that, thanks to DeSilvo's actions, actions for which he allowed Koffield to be blamed. But all that was far away, remote, far from DeSilvo's personal experience. He made no effort of any kind to make restitution or to compensate for any of the losses he had caused.

"But he *saw* Koffield, face-to-face, at a cocktail party. He *saw* the man he had injured, and the insult and humiliation that Koffield suffered. I think Admiral Koffield would be the first to agree that his own emotional distress was the least of the injuries caused by DeSilvo's actions. But the difference was this: DeSilvo *witnessed* that distress. He tried to make amends, even if the amends were ludicrously inadequate. Later, as we shall see, DeSilvo went to a great deal of trouble to cause Koffield harm once again—*after Koffield was safely out of the way,* where DeSilvo could not see or hear him. Later still, DeSilvo arranged for a way to confess his crimes to Koffield from light-years away.

"This fits a pattern of DeSilvo hiding away, keeping himself removed, acting at a distance. He is capable of inflicting terrible harm on others, so long as they are far away—but he cannot bear to see suffering he has caused, no matter how slight.

"In any event, DeSilvo met Koffield and took misplaced pity on a man who needed no pity at all. DeSilvo then made another of the greatest mistakes of his career. He offered Koffield a chance to work in the DeSilvo Institute, where they were preparing a history—actually, more of a DeSilvo hagiography—of the Solacian terraforming project. This simple act was DeSilvo's undoing.

"While working at the DeSilvo Institute, Koffield discovered a reference to Baskaw's work, then discovered that the works themselves had been erased. He tracked down surviving copies of the text. He studied them in detail and realized that they proved, very clearly, that Solace would fail in a manner similar to Glister's failure. He put a rush message, containing his preliminary results, aboard the *Chrononaut VI*, the next ship outbound to Solace, then spent several frantic weeks refining and expanding his work. Meantime, he booked passage aboard the *Dom Pedro IV*, bound for Solace. He planned to deliver a warning in person.

"Koffield studied Baskaw's antique mathematics and made a terrifying discovery: It was not merely Solace that would fail. *The problem was systemic to all terraforming procedures:* The faster a world is terraformed, the faster it will fail. *All* the terraformed worlds—which is to say, every inhabited world but Earth—would, eventually, fail.

"But DeSilvo discovered what Admiral Koffield was doing. Telling himself that he was acting to prevent needless panic on Solace, he sabotaged the *Dom Pedro IV*, reprogramming its navigation system to travel direct to Solace without any use of timeshaft wormholes. In effect, he converted the *Dom Pedro IV* into an interstellar slowboat. As a result of this, the crew was kept in cryogenic sleep nearly five decades longer than intended in the flight plan. Two crew members died as a direct result—and, of course, the ship and ship's company were suddenly stranded one hundred and twenty-seven years in their own future. Thus, DeSilvo had time-stranded Koffield twice, for a total of more than two hundred years.

"By then, of course, Koffield's warning was far too late. The rush message he had sent aboard the *Chrononaut VI* had been read and ignored, and the disappearance of the *Dom Pedro IV* had become a minor local legend. The story was barely remembered nearly thirteen decades after the fact.

"In the meantime, DeSilvo was busy being dead again—a favorite refuge for him. During the time Koffield was still doing his research at the Grand Library,

DeSilvo entered temporal confinement while his medical staff grew a new heart for him.

"After he was revived, he did not focus on Baskaw's work, and, I suspect, found many reasons to do anything, everything, but. It was not until years later that he began to reconsider his actions. It was something close to ten years after the departure of the sabotaged *Dom Pedro IV* before DeSilvo finally looked once again at Baskaw's work and applied modern mathematics and analysis to it. He reached the conclusions that Baskaw had been right when she warned that a Solace-style terraforming was inherently unstable, and that Koffield's warning had been legitimate. However, DeSilvo convinced himself that it was already too late to warn Solace, that to do so would do more harm than good."

Wandella Ashdin paused a moment and looked about the room. "So far, my account has mainly been a cataloging of what Dr. DeSilvo did *wrong*. Now we must come to what he did *right*. He acted hesitantly, cautiously, and made sure to insulate himself from consequences as much as possible. But, in all justice, Dr. DeSilvo had the courage to see that his past projections had been spectacularly wrong. It would be rash indeed to have faith in further predictions without some testing of his methods, comparing predictions against interim results—and it could take decades to gather that data.

"He thought long and hard about how best to make use of those decades and how best to maintain, expand, and finally make use of the tremendous resources that he still controlled.

"So, at last, he began to make substantive moves, to do more than pour a token thimbleful of water on the forest fire he had so carelessly ignited.

"It seems highly likely that this was the first time he sat down and read Baskaw's fourth, and, so far as we are aware, final work, simply entitled *Contraction*. This was the book he found in the Dark Museum, one that Anton Koffield later discovered as well.

"The contraction of the title is, of course, the contraction of interstellar civilization, the inevitable withdrawal back toward the Solar System and Earth, as the terraformed planets fail, one by one.

"Dr. DeSilvo began to run increasingly more detailed and sophisticated simulations of the fates of the various worlds and their interactions with each other. He modeled the effects of back-migration, economic destabilization, population pressure, and the psychological effect on the population as the knowledge of the coming collapse spreads. He also applied terraform modeling to study biological contamination.

"The results of his simulations were bad—indeed they could hardly be worse. Once his data and models were reasonably refined, he discovered that every test run ended the same way: not with the Earth as the last surviving world after the Interstellar Contraction was complete, but with Earth overwhelmed by population spikes of incoming refugees, political upheaval, and perhaps war, and, worst of all, by biological back-contamination and crossbreeding. Plagues sweep the planet. Hybrid microbes, viruses, molds, spores, and worse infest everything, eat everything, choke off food supplies for native species. By the end of every run, humanity—indeed all vertebrate species—are extinct. Contraction goes as far as it can, all the way down to zero.

"This was the data he could not bring himself to believe, the predictions he could not trust after all his other predictions had failed.

"He suddenly found himself in a position to answer a question he hadn't thought to ask himself for decades, perhaps centuries. *Why* were certain inventions suppressed? The Chronologic Patrol's core task, after all, was to protect the past from the future, to prevent any form of time travel that might threaten causality. The Dark Museum should have been full of machines and devices related in some way to time travel; inventions that might threaten causality. But many, if not most, of the suppressed inventions were related to star travel and terraforming.

"Dr. DeSilvo suddenly saw the Chronologic Patrol's technology suppression policy had been aimed at slowing, and, if possible, stopping, any improvements in interstellar travel that would make going from one star system to another too cheap, too fast, or too easy.

"He studied the cultures of Earth looking for clues, looking for patterns—and finding them.

"He saw ways of doing things, attitudes, traditions, that were enshrined in law, habit, and custom. He saw infrastructure—empty roads, unused power service, overbuilt food production systems, transportation networks with capacity for ten times the traffic, half-vacant cities with the vacant places carefully maintained.

"He saw population and family policies that resulted in a steady decline in the population long after it had dropped below the calculated 'optimum' range. He saw governments and other institutions that placed tremendous reliance on artificial intelligence systems that had been installed and programmed centuries before—ArtInts fully capable of working, of guiding and shaping subtleties of policy, and even of tradition, decade after decade, without losing interest, without changing their minds.

"In short, he saw that Earth had, for centuries, been quietly preparing herself for an influx of refugees. He saw that the Chronologic Patrol had likewise been suppressing advances in terraforming and discouraging new projects. In that they had been completely successful: No new terraforming projects had been started since Solace. Terraforming was turning into a historical science, an activity no longer performed. The logic behind this was plain: The fewer planets that were remade, the fewer planets that would inevitably collapse.

"In short, slowing and preventing expansion, and preparing for eventual collapse and contraction, were the hidden long-term policies of the Chronologic Patrol and of Earth.

"But DeSilvo's simulations showed that even with all of these preparations factored in, the ecology of Earth would still fail—a bit later, and a bit more slowly, perhaps, but just as completely. It seemed unlikely to him that Earth and the CP would focus so much of their time and energy toward the far-off goal of keeping one last dying world alive for an extra hundred years.

"But, perhaps that was too narrow a view. If the best possible outcome was to keep the race alive an extra century, to allow two or three more generations a chance to live, to let perhaps billions live and love and think and feel, to stave off, even for just a little while, the prospect of an Earth covered in a dreary, malevolent crust of mold and matted algae—no, that was very much worth the effort.

"Or perhaps—perhaps—there was some other truly long-term goal Earth and the CP were working toward, something that would take so long that keeping Earth alive a year, or even a day, longer, might tilt the balance. Or perhaps DeSilvo's simulations were inherently flawed—an error he worked desperately to find, but could not.

"None of these answers were really plausible or satisfactory. So why were Earth and the CP merely working to prepare Earth to accept a massive influx of refugees and slowing outward expansion? Why were they following a policy of contraction management?

"Clearly, someone must have performed some sort of projection or analysis well before the policy of contraction management was established. Just as clearly, the policy had been in place for centuries. Therefore, their projections must have been done using the mathematical and simulation tools of that day.

"Based on his examination of the models, data, and predictive tools they would most likely have used, it was all but certain that the scholars who had done the original work had stretched their tools too far. The odds were excellent that they had not been able to make a sufficiently long-range forecast, or one that was reliably accurate. Their work would have failed to predict Earth's collapse—or might even have made the positive—though false—prediction that Earth would survive.

"It was decision-makers informed by these flawed forecasts who had set policy—and programmed the Art-Ints to keep following that policy, long after their human masters and clients had likely forgotten the matter altogether. That is one danger of suppressing important knowledge—restrict it too completely, and the odds increase to near certainty that the knowledge will be lost altogether.

"But all Dr. DeSilvo knew for sure was that he did not know for sure. There seemed no doubt that all the other worlds would, sooner or later, fail. And there seemed at least a strong possibility, perhaps a high probability, that Earth herself would die, probably somewhere between a thousand and fifteen hundred years from now.

"There was no way to act publicly, directly. If he called a press conference and announced his findings, at best he would simply not be believed. Worse, he would likely be killed, or locked up for good, or wind up with his mind 'adjusted' in some way. Nor could he have really blamed the authorities for doing so. If the collapse was inevitable, speaking of it publicly could only produce panic and might even hasten the end, for example by inspiring people to back-migrate sooner rather than later. Besides, he could not even be sure of his own conclusions. He did not wish to cry wolf.

"There was also the small matter of the impending collapse of Solace. There could be little argument that he, Oskar DeSilvo, was directly responsible for that. On a smaller scale, he had to make some sort of amends to Anton Koffield, and to the others he had wronged.

"Dr. DeSilvo decided to deal with the situation he faced—a situation largely of his own making. It would take decades for him to be able to confirm even the beginning of the trend lines his simulations predicted. The *Dom Pedro IV* would arrive at its destination in ten-plus decades. He decided to let that be the baseline for his data collectors.

"However, Dr. DeSilvo, as always, was still unable to deal well with authority or with being proved wrong. He found the chance to tweak Admiral Koffield's nose a time or two more, even as he confessed and sought to recruit Koffield to his work. At the same time, Dr. De-

Silvo's fondness for puzzles and tricks perhaps got the better of him.

"But there was also a certain degree of logic behind the way Dr. DeSilvo worked. In effect, he set Koffield and his party off on a scavenger hunt, so that each clue they—we—found led them forward to the next clue. Koffield and his party were made to *see* things—the nightmare landscape of Mars after the Great Failure of that first terraforming attempt, the beauty of Earth, the customs of Earth's people, the state of terraforming research, the half-empty cities, the Dark Museum itself, and many other things besides. You were all there for at least part of the journey, and some of you for nearly all of it. That part you know. We were led to this place, and to the choices we now face."

She paused, then turned to face Koffield directly. "So there we are," she said. "And, let us face facts—there *you* are. We will not be ruled by you in these matters, but it would be pointless to suggest we will not be *guided* by you. I have presented what I believe to be an honest and balanced statement of the events that brought us here. That it came across as an indictment of Dr. DeSilvo, I do not doubt and do not deny. To report the facts is to report his crimes. Now we must ask—and must ask *you*—what are we to do now?" Ashdin sat down, and the room was silent.

Koffield frowned. Blast the woman! He had not expected this. To be asked to consider the matter, yes—but she seemed to be asking for his own, personal, immediate snap judgment. He knew, instinctively, that even a moment's hesitation on his part would be fatal. He had to speak, and speak decisively, at once, to maintain credibility as their leader.

"What we do is believe him," Koffield said, after a pause of less than a heartbeat, not sure of his own reply until he had made it. And perhaps that had been Ashdin's goal—to force him to give them his gut feeling, his unexamined first reaction. The rest was easy from there. "We believe him when he tells us he thinks he has found a way. It is no trick, no fraud. He might be mistaken, but if so, the mistake is sincere, and not some gambit within a gambit, no mirror in a mirror."

"Why do you say that?" Yuri Sparten demanded.

"Because he has allowed all this to happen," Koffield said, deliberately speaking as Ashdin had, pretending DeSilvo were not there. "Consider what drives Oskar DeSilvo—and then consider what Dr. Ashdin's report has *cost* him. Think how humbling, how humiliating, this presentation has been for the man who could command our deaths at any moment—and remember this is a man capable of convincing himself that virtually any action that suits his needs is of great benefit. He sincerely believed that all his acts were for the greater good."

"He managed to *convince* himself they were all for the greater good," Norla Chandray objected. "That's not at all the same thing."

"Granted," Koffield said. "But if so, how could he convince himself that this proceeding"—he was very careful to avoid calling it a trial—"was to his benefit?"

No one answered that.

"I think your failure to answer is answer enough," Koffield said. He gestured to DeSilvo, at last acknowledging his presence. "The actions that Dr. Ashdin have described were acts of megalomania, of madness. But Dr. DeSilvo's willingness to subject himself to unexpected humiliation and accusation here, now, in order to serve the greater good—and the *later* good—is, I suggest, strong evidence of sanity. That he doubts himself enough to bring us here is further evidence that his megalomania is at least somewhat under control.

"We must accept that his present actions are at least to some degree altruistic, and also meant to make sort-of amends for past deeds. Those are sane motives. He may have further agenda—I would be surprised if he did not. But that's as may be."

"So you trust him?" Yuri Sparten said, plainly unconvinced and unmoved.

"Not in the slightest," said Koffield. "I trust his *motives*, to some extent. But he might be mistaken as to his conclusions. I could have it wrong about his being sane at present—he might be delusional but utterly convincing. But on balance, I think the most likely circumstance is that he is more or less sane and trying to do the right thing—perhaps while benefiting himself. But that merely leads us to the next question—*is he right*? Are his predictions reliable?"

"That is the question you were to answer, Mr. Sparten." It was DeSilvo, speaking for the first time in a long while. His voice was gentle, respectful. "You, above all, have the least reason to trust me, and the most reason to hate me. But it has fallen to you, and to Officer Chandray, to judge the value of the predictions I have made."

"We haven't had enough time to make a complete analysis," Yuri objected.

"No, of course not. You have had only a few days to consider data that took many years to accumulate. But surely you have made some progress, reached some sort of initial findings."

"Well, yes. But we're nowhere near done."

Koffield spoke. "Mr. Sparten—there can always be surprises, some unexpected factor that changes everything. But there also comes a point when you get a *feel* for the data. You have had enough time to judge the basic quality of the work—the data, the models, the procedures—and probably enough time to set up alternate models and procedures as a check. Am I right?"

"Yes, sir."

"Then report to us on what you have found so far."

Sparten hesitated, looked to DeSilvo, and frowned. "It seems all right," he said, the anger as plain in his voice as in his face.

Koffield had wondered why the devil DeSilvo had leaked word of the diehard outpost. Maybe this was why. Maybe it had been to bring Sparten's hatred to the boiling point, then call on him to report on his analysis. If Sparten, seething with rage, still had to report that DeSilvo had gotten it right, then that could only lend credence to a positive report. Maybe there was no Last Chance Canyon outpost. Maybe DeSilvo had made the whole damned thing up for the sole purpose of setting Sparten off.

But after so long alone, the man was so detached from human behavior that it seemed unlikely he could anticipate anyone's reactions that precisely. He had put Sparten into a homicidal rage with a casual remark just a few days before. Would he really risk playing that game again so soon—or try something as elaborate as planting a false story with Marquez, trusting that the story would reach Sparten?

Koffield shook his head. That was the trouble with paranoia. It could make any story almost plausible, until the truth was buried under a whole forest of fictions that seemed more believable than the facts. But facts, not guesses or emotions, were what they needed. "You're going to have to give us a little more than 'It seems all right,' Mr. Sparten," he said gently. "This is a most important issue, and we need a useful summary of your results to date."

Sparten looked again from DeSilvo to Koffield, and his expression shifted. He blushed, a schoolboy caught out in poor behavior in front of his most respected schoolmaster. "Yes, sir. Excuse me, sir."

He paused, took a sip of water from the glass in front of him, and spoke again, in careful, professional tones. "The results of our examination showed Dr. DeSilvo's predictions are more than all right. They are highly reliable. We have tested the model by using alternate data sets, as extracted from the copy of the Grand Library on board *Dom Pedro IV*. We have tested the data by constructing our own predictive model system. Our model was of course much less sophisticated than Dr. DeSilvo's. His took months or years to create, and ours was something we put together in less than a day—but it was elaborate enough to provide a check, a comparison. We then used our model and the Grand Library data—in other words, a complete independent check, none of it based on Dr. DeSilvo's work. The results weren't precisely the same as Dr. DeSilvo's—they couldn't have been, since we were using different algorithms and data and models—but they were highly similar. They satisfied every statistical check we could make."

"No outliers?" Koffield asked. "No data runs that were completely outside prediction?"

"Two," said Norla Chandray. "But they told us nearly as much as the other runs. One was just the randomizers happening to set most of the possible initial variables—political instability, disease virulence, speed of technical innovation—up toward the bad-news end of the scale. That gave us our shortest run—Earth only lasted eight hundred years. And we did one run where we deliberately forced all the variables to the good-news end of the spectrum. Earth survived so long we thought she was going to make it, but then she crashed hard—very hard, the fastest collapse of any run once it did come. The end came at about thirty-one hundred years. And *that* was forcing all the news to be good."

"But we can't predict the future!" Sindra Chon protested. "We can't know for sure that such and such will happen if you set some arbitrary artificial variable to this or that level."

"No one is *saying* we can predict the future," said Dixon Phelby. "We don't know what's going to happen in the next five minutes, let alone three thousand years. But if you examine a large enough system, with enough actions, and at least some sort of understanding of what the rules are—even if you don't understand *how* the rules work, or why—then you can get damned good estimates. Maybe you won't be able to predict to the millimeter how much rainfall you'll have ten years, three days, and two hours from now next—but maybe you *can* say the odds are 90 percent you'll have between three and six centimeters of rain in a given month ten years from now."

"Which means there's a 10 percent chance you *won't* have that much rain," Sindra countered. "There are reasonable odds that you'll have more, or less, or none."

"True enough," said Norla. "But the results we're getting would be more like saying that for the period from five to ten years in the future, there's a 99.999 chance that it will rain at *some* time. The odds are about that high that some variant of the collapse will come. Would you want to gamble that Earth will survive if you were on the other side of *those* odds?"

The room was silent, until at last DeSilvo spoke again. "Let us return to the main point at hand," he said gently. He stood up. "Mr. Sparten—do you believe my results? Do you now think that Earth, and all the other living worlds, are likely to die, from the causes we have discussed—sometime in the period between eight hundred and three thousand years from now?"

Again, silence, until, at last, Yuri Sparten spoke. "Yes," he said, with infinite reluctance. "We need to keep digging, keep studying, keep refining, keep getting data—but that will merely confirm that all the worlds, including Earth, are going to die."

DeSilvo nodded. "Thank you," he said. "Those words would be difficult for any of us here, but I know that they were hardest for you, because of who I am. But—I am pleased to say that is not the whole story. Yes, all the worlds, including Earth, are going to die—unless we, here, those of us around this table, act." He paused dramatically. "For, you see, I have the answer."

The room was deathly silent at first. DeSilvo looked around, surprised. He plainly had been expecting an excited, enthused reaction. The silence held a few more seconds, then was broken by derisive snorts of laughter.

Koffield looked to Ashdin, and she at him. She shook her head and shrugged, as if to say *What else would you expect?*

And Koffield could have answered *Very little else.* De-Silvo had as much as promised them some such magic answer, back when they had arrived, a few days ago, in what already seemed another lifetime. *We've just gotten through agreeing you're a megalomaniac,* Koffield thought as he watched DeSilvo. *And now you say that only you know how to save all the living worlds?*

"Perhaps—perhaps that was not the best way to put it," DeSilvo said—inspiring a bit more disrespectful laughter, led by Marquez and Bolt. "Please!" The room quieted. "I know, very well, how mad my claim must seem. For what it's worth, I do not imagine we can do it *all*. But we can demonstrate a possibility, show it to others."

"A possibility of what?" Jerand Bolt demanded.

"A possibility of—of hope," DeSilvo said, seeming to flounder a bit.

Koffield watched DeSilvo closely. He looked very much like a man who had expected to electrify his audience and had failed utterly—a man who knew he had best get offstage quickly, before anything else could go wrong.

"I will say little else about my plan at present," DeSilvo went on, speaking a bit faster, "save only this: We'll need Greenhouse as a base of operations. There are resources there that are available nowhere else. But, ah, as chance would have it, the attempt to ignite Greenhouse's new SunSpot—NovaSpot—is almost upon us. Much depends on how well that effort succeeds, and I would prefer to delay saying anything else until we know more."

Koffield got the distinct impression that DeSilvo had been casting about for some reason to stall—and had found it in Ignition Day.

"I have plans to cover all the likely results of the Ignition attempt," DeSilvo went on, still talking fast. "Failure, success, various degrees of partial success. We *can* proceed if Ignition fails, but only with difficulty, and only in a manner far different from what we otherwise would do. The range of possibilities is great—but it will be, ah, greatly *reduced* once we know the results of the attempt at Ignition. In the meantime, Mr. Sparten, Officer Chandray—get back to your studies. Continue your efforts to prove me wrong."

He stepped back and walked to the door. He paused before leaving, and turned to face them. "After we know about Ignition there will be time enough to consider the unhappy chance that I am right," he said. He bowed to them. "Until news of Ignition, then," he said, and left them all, making an odd and hurried exit.

The room was silent for a moment. Then Jerand Bolt laughed again. He stood up in front of his chair, leaned forward a bit, just as DeSilvo had done, and gestured just as DeSilvo had, reaching up with his right hand to rest his palm on his chest. "For you see, *I* have the answer," he said, with an exaggerated theatricality that really wasn't all that much more overdone than De-Silvo's had been. He laughed again and dropped back into his seat. "Can you *believe* that guy?"

"Yes," Koffield replied sadly. "Yes, I can."

Bolt was taken aback. *"What?"*

"His performance just now might not have been much, but his data's all been good," said Norla. "Bad acting doesn't mean he's done bad science."

"You're not really going *along* with him, are you?" Bolt demanded. "Him and his 'answer'?"

"Everything leading up to his 'answer' checks out. What have *you* got?" asked Sindra Chon. "Anything better?"

Koffield spoke before Bolt could reply. "*Someone* had better come with an 'answer,'" he said. "Otherwise, humanity's doomed. So yes, we're going to wait until he's ready, then we'll listen." He gestured around the room, and DeSilvo City besides. "What else have we got to do?"

It was some hours later, after Koffield had turned in for the night, and was lying awake in bed, unable to sleep. There was something he had missed, a movement, half-hidden in shadow, that had put his subconscious on guard, even if his conscious mind had missed it. Then it came to him. He remembered, and put the pieces together.

"What else have we got to do?"

Koffield's gaze had fallen upon Yuri Sparten as he had asked that question. Koffield remembered Sparten's expression at that moment.

A tight, angry little smile, almost a smirk—as if Sparten had an answer to that question—an answer that Koffield felt sure he would not like one little bit.

And *that* was a notion that banished any thought of sleep for a long, long time.

Chapter Five

MEMORY'S REACH

Elber Malloon backed himself into the far corner of the tiny kitchen compartment, making room to let his wife Jassa open the cupboard and get down a bowl for their daughter Zari's breakfast, hot cornsoy porridge from the pot on the cooktop. Elber struggled to keep half an eye at least on the view panel set into the wall opposite as two-and-a-half-year-old Zari unfolded her chair from the wall and sat down, happily singing to herself. Jassa closed the cupboard, pulled the table panel out, and set Zari's breakfast before her. Zari set to work with a will, proudly eating by herself at the grown-up table.

Jassa put the porridge pot in the cleaner, carefully folded the cooktop up out of the way, then snuggled into Elber, wrapping her arms around him.

Elber, still holding coffee in one hand and soytoast in the other, had all he could just to avoid spilling coffee on Jassa, or smearing her with jam. He smiled to himself. It was a pleasure to have such minor problems. He popped the last bite of toast into his mouth, wiped his hand on a borrowed corner of Jassa's apron, set his coffee down on the pull-out table, and hugged his wife properly. "Good morning to you," he said.

Jassa looked up at him and smiled. "We've already said good morning," she objected.

"I know—but it *is* a good morning. A very good one. Good enough to say it twice." He pointed at the viewscreen. "From what they say, it's all on schedule. They've got the system tests done. The NovaSpot is all set, the *Lodestar VII* is in position, and they'll be ready when the day comes. It'll work."

"Do you really think so?" Jassa asked. She always had less faith in the authorities than Elber, and didn't hesitate to express her doubts about what motivated the uppers to do whatever they were doing. "Is it really going to bring Greenhouse back to life? Will Greenhouse really save us?"

"I don't even really know if we need saving," Elber said playfully. "We're safe here."

Safe. That was something to think about. They had lost everything—home, farm, their firstborn child Belrad, their neighbors, their whole way of life. They been forced to start over from nothing in this strange, cramped, inside-out urban jungle of a giant space station. But somehow, in exchange for all that had been taken away, they had been given *safety.* No famines for Zari, no mobs, no floods. The trade seemed more than fair. Except for the loss of little Belrad, at the start of their troubles. That was a scar—no, an open wound—that would never heal. But still, they were here, and moving forward, moving upward, and *safe.*

"I hope you're right, Elber," Jassa said.

"I am," Elber said, startled by how sure he sounded, how sure he *was.* "Things will keep getting better."

Jassa laughed. "Not if you lose your job, they won't. Now hurry, or you'll be late."

Elber checked the time. "You're right," he said. He kissed her good-bye, then knelt by his daughter and was rewarded with a porridge-coated embrace. He glanced up at the viewscreen again. He would have loved to stay home and pull up a more detailed report, but the job came first. Besides, they were merely getting ready. Nothing exciting to watch.

Elber stepped to the apartment's cramped bathroom and washed the porridge off his face. He looked in the mirror and laughed. What was the old saying? *Life is what happens while you're doing something else.* They were preparing to remake a world out there—but he had to get his daughter's breakfast off his face and go to work.

Elber left their apartment and started his walk through the maze of corridors and elevators and stairways that made up the low-rent districts of SCO Station's Aft End. Not so long ago he had dreaded stepping out of their door, for fear of getting hopelessly lost—again. Now he followed his usual route to work without a moment's hesitation, finally getting clear of the Aft End econoflat complex and on to the larger corridors.

After a few more minutes' walking, he stepped across the threshold into Ring Park. As always, his heart skipped a beat as he did so. Elber walked through the park every workday morning and evening back and forth between his family's small apartment on the Aft End and the cubicle he shared with three others in shipping operations on the Forward End. But no matter how many times he made the brief transit of the park, that sense of shock was always there.

Once, not so long ago, he had been a refugee in the big Collapse Panic, a squatter, a gluefoot, stuck on SCO with no place to go. And he had lived in Ring Park, in the open air—or as close as one got to open air on the station.

And now, he didn't live there. He had a proper job, and his family had a proper place to live.

These days, long after the crisis was over, he could almost bring himself to believe that he had a right to be on Solace Central Orbital Station, that he *belonged* there. But then he would cross into the Park, and walk past the very spot—long since relandscaped and all prettied up again—where his group of refugees had set up camp and torn up the trees to burn campfires in a futile attempt to keep themselves warm. Even now, Elber's cheeks burned with embarrassment when he thought of that, and of how pig-ignorant of stationside life they had been to try such a thing, how totally unaware of how the station's thermal control system worked. They might as well have drilled a hole through the outer hull to let in fresh air.

But now he knew better. He was nearly, if not quite, a station man. He had learned fast in his new job in the shipping office. But for all that he had learned his new job, and even if he wore a grey tunic and blue trousers and clean dress shoes and carried a datapad, there was much about him that still said "farmer."

He was tall for his people, about 180 centimeters, with long gangly arms and legs, and a slim, wiry build that made him look taller. His hands were hard and calloused still, though far less so than they had been on arrival at SCO Station. Shut away from the sunlight, here inside the station, his farmer's tan had faded as well, and his blond hair had turned several shades darker. At times, his dark blue eyes, oval face, and habitual shy, slight smile made him seem almost childlike, though what he had been through should have hardened him long ago.

Elber walked past the smoothed-over lawn where the gluefeet had tried to bury their dead in the ten centimeters of topsoil and gravel that were all the living soil the Ring Park had, and remembered that, as well. When Station Security took away the dead for what they called "proper disposal," things had teetered on the knife edge of riot before calming back down.

And then—then, after a half dozen provocations had failed to produce an explosion—then the explosion came, for no good reason. For no reason at all, bad or good, other than Zak Destan.

The gluefeet men were bored, they were restless, and they had been pushed around long enough. When Zak had led a bunch of the lads out to have a drink on the Long Boulevard, all it had taken was an argument with an aggressive bouncer to set them off. But it was Zak who had led them that night, and it was Zak who had gone looking for trouble.

Elber had been part of the group. He had run for the camp in the Park at the first sign of trouble, and had never quite decided, even deep in his own heart, why he had done it. Was it cowardice? Prudence? The instinct to be with his wife and child, to protect them when trouble was brewing? Had he done the right thing, or the wrong one? Either way, had he done it from good motives, or bad? Did it matter now, and had it ever?

He stepped through the Forward portal of the Ring Park, and onto the Long Boulevard. There, too, where the riot had started, and done its worst damage, all was clean and tidy again. The sidewalk cafe where Zak had picked a fight was still there, although under new management, and, of course, every stick of furniture, every glass and every bottle in the place had had to be replaced. Elber felt a completely irrational twinge of guilt over the damage every time he passed the place. He had, after all, been just about the only one there who *hadn't* joined in the destruction.

But the riot didn't matter anymore, either, and nor did who had done what. Not anymore. That was the clear message that came in from every corner. The claims had been paid. The investigations had all ended—or, more accurately, had all unraveled after learning very little that everyone didn't already know. The last of the gluefeet had been dealt with—shipped back down to Solace, nearly all of them, with a small handful, like Elber, staying aboard SCO Station and finding work. Everything and everyone swept away or tidied up, the scars hidden discreetly under the new-planted trees and the fresh coats of paint.

Elber smiled to himself as he turned off the Long Boulevard and entered the elevator that would carry him to Station Level Six, where the shipping operations center was. Things changed so fast. Now, in his present job, one of his duties was checking the insurance status of every outbound cargo. Six months ago he hadn't fully understood the concept of insurance, and now he was documenting premium payments, checking risk assessments, and comparing actuarial tables.

He arrived at the shipping office and made his way to the large, crowded, cramped back room that he shared with thirty other shipping clerks. He elbowed his way through to his cubicle, smiled a greeting at Fredor and San—Jol, his fourth cubicle mate, had not yet arrived—sat down and set to work.

He looked to his datapad, brought up the first file in his docket, and frowned at the words that jumped out at him. *Risk assessment revision.* He had seen those words more and more often in the last few months—and they never meant that the assessed risk was going down. And when the risks went up, the premiums went up.

But it wasn't all the travel routes that were suffering risk spikes. The pattern was there, as clear as day, and this one fit in with the others. The cargoes outbound for Greenhouse and the orbital habs all arrived without unusual mishap. But the cargo going the other way, from Greenhouse and the habs through SCO to Solace—well, cargo that landed on the planet had a nasty habit of not getting where it was going. It was getting chancier and chancier to ship anything on the surface, through the countryside. He scanned through a whole series of reports. *Lost in transit, damaged in transit, incomplete inventory on arrival, pallet listed on invoice not delivered, shipment did not arrive.*

There were a lot of names for it, but it was plain to Elber that a lot of cargo was vanishing. And yet, no one seemed willing to use the word *theft.* Which in turn suggested to Elber that people on the reporting end were afraid.

Elber glanced around the roomful of clerks, and, in his mind's eye, at the huge spinning station full of people beyond. There were, he knew, merely a handful of people aboard who had any recent extended experience of life on Solace. Most of those aboard had lived in space for years, on SCO Station or elsewhere. A fair number had been born on the station, and had never once left it. And, as things onplanet got worse, there was less and less incentive for anyone to visit the surface. Of those who *did* visit, few would stray outside the upper-class areas of Solace City.

In other words, it was unlikely that there was anyone else aboard SCO Station who knew the first thing about the countryside of Solace and also knew about the shipping business.

What the pattern of thefts told Elber was that the reivers were back. Or perhaps they had never been shut down in the first place, despite all the pronouncements from Solace City, years ago. Come to think of it, it did seem to him that the government had announced their eradication more than once. If they'd been completely wiped out, why would anyone need to kill them again?

The reivers used techniques that stretched back at least to the near-ancients, based on the principle that it is easier to run a criminal gang in places far removed from the central governments, and in places where the locals are at least willing to tolerate you. And the best way to ensure that they did tolerate you was, of course, to buy them off, while being careful to do it in a way that let them at least pretend to keep their dignity.

Make a gift of a new water purifier to the village elders and slip the mayor some cash to pay for its installation— ten times more than the job would really cost—and who's going to ask the mayor what happened to the rest? Fix up the old school, and the parents will be grateful enough that it will be thought bad manners to ask if the building materials were stolen. Show up at local weddings and festivals and hand out lavish gifts often enough that people come to count on them as a normal part of the celebration.

See to it that slightly bad things—or even very bad things—happen to people who object, or who ask questions. Keep at it for a while, and the villages will resent the hell out of the Central Police who come and try to shut down the local benefactor. A nice man like him couldn't possibly have committed that murder, or robbed the bank in that town a hundred kilometers away, or run that smuggling ring—and even if he did, well, the people who got hurt were outsiders. *Our* reiver watches over his own people. Besides, he is so strong. We couldn't fight him even if we wanted to—so why not enjoy the wealth he offers us in exchange for just a little silence?

Elber knew the story from the inside. He had grown up listening to romantic adventure stories of the reivers, told in the village inn or around campfires. Robbing the fat upperclassers who got what they had by squeezing the peasants, using the booty to stop the widow's farm from being sold away from her or to save the village girl from a marriage she couldn't abide. Propaganda, they'd call it on the station. Or, perhaps, marketing.

Child and adult, he had played along. There had been a grand gift of two healthy cows and a store of hay at his wedding, and a wad of cash as well. Elber had been pleased, but not surprised. It was part of the natural course of things.

So when the Center Cops finally did make a move that meant something, and dragged away Smit Sarten, the local reiver king, Elber had been as hurt and confused and resentful as anyone. And, somehow, the way the Center Cops rubbed the hard evidence of robbery, murder, and smuggling in the locals' faces made them angry at the cops, not at Sarten. The old crones still had a warm place in their hearts for him. He was just a mischievous boy, not a cold-blooded murderer.

But, even so, for a time, at least, the cycle had been broken. Until, just recently, it started up again. It was a lot to read from the cautious phrasing in a few insurance claims, but Elber knew his people, knew the way rural life worked on Solace.

But who could he go to with his warning? What did he have, except for vague suspicions? He might be able to talk to Beakly, his department head. But what could *she* do, except pass it up the line? What would be the final result? They'd raise the premiums, perhaps, but they were doing that anyway. And if Elber could read the return of Smit Sarten's sort from as far a remove as claim reports on SCO Station, no doubt the Central Solace Police Service could do so from closer in and with far more information.

But even if he could or should do nothing, it was worrisome. The reivers didn't come out when times were good, or stable, when the government was strong, and people had faith. Things were getting worse.

Rumors about graver, deeper problems planetside had been floating all over the station for months. If the Central Cops could no longer keep a lid on the reivers, that made Elber that much more willing to believe the situation was still deteriorating—and faster than they were being told. His confident prediction to Jassa that morning, his promise that things would keep getting better for his family, suddenly sounded horribly false.

Elber's own village had been caught in surprise spring floods that had never receded. His village was still underwater, and the last Elber had heard, the local officials had finally given up pretending that the waters would ever recede—and that was far from an isolated incident.

But even if things might be bad, and getting worse, back on the planet, there wasn't a thing he could do about it. Besides—it was nothing to do with *him*. Not anymore. Elber shook his head and tried to focus on his risk evaluations.

"Elber Malloon?"

Elber looked up sharply. It had been a long time since anyone in the office had addressed him by name. He wasn't of high enough rank or sufficient consequence for it to be worth their while to learn his name. But he saw as soon as he looked up that this was not someone from the office who had taken a sudden interest in low-level functionaries. People who worked in the shipping office did not wear the uniform of the Station Security Force.

Elber suddenly realized that the entire office had gone silent. Everyone was looking at him, and the SSF officer. "Ah, yes, that's me."

"Come along," said the SSF cop. "You're wanted downstairs."

Elber stood up uncertainly, his heart pounding. "Ah, ah, all right," he said. "I'll have to clear it with my supervisor."

"She knows all about it," the officer said, casually gesturing in the direction of Supervisor Beakly's office. Sure enough, she was watching along with everyone else. She nodded once at Elber, her expression puzzled, perhaps a bit worried.

And in that moment, Elber saw the ruin of his world in her face. All his endless efforts to work hard, show good faith, earn the trust of his superiors—all of it was gone in a blink of an eye, the turn of a frown. If they had come for him at home, perhaps it could have been all right. But not now, not after arrest in front of the whole office. Why would any of them have the slightest reason to take a chance on him now? His hopes and plans for a comfortable future for his wife and child, a safe future here on the station, had vanished like a soap bubble stuck with a pin. It was all over.

He gathered his things and meekly followed the officer out of the room, not looking back, looking no one in the eye, refusing to hear the murmuring tide of voices that swelled up behind as he passed through the big room.

It was not until they were out of the shipping office, and in the corridor, that it even occurred to him to wonder why he had been arrested. Even then, it never entered his head to ask the SSF officer. Elber had lived his whole life in a world where no good could possibly come from questioning an authority figure.

So Elber said nothing, asked nothing, as the SSF man led him to a waiting open-bodied free-runner car. He took his seat and did not even listen as the policeman spoke to the car and told it where to go. The car turned itself on and rolled off down the labyrinthian corridors.

The policemen spun his seat around so that he faced Elber in the backseat. He smiled at Elber, and seemed to expect him to have something to say. But Elber still kept silent. "One of the quiet ones, huh?" the policeman said, and shrugged. "Suit yourself."

The free-runner whizzed along the corridors, rolled itself onto a cargo elevator, and decanted itself just off the Long Boulevard. It instantly started off again, heading back toward the Aft End and Ring Park, retracing Elber's journey of the morning. The car threaded itself neatly through the busy vehicular traffic. Soon it was at the bulkhead opening that formed the entrance to the Park itself. It rolled inside, then turned off the main road onto a side path.

Elber saw the cop watching him. Elber had lived in the Park, squatting with his family on that patch of ground right there, not twenty meters from where the car was rolling. And the copper knew, and knew that Elber knew. He wanted to see Elber be embarrassed, or ashamed, or just plain scared.

Elber felt reflex take over, turning his face impassive, unreadable. A smart peasant didn't let cops know when he was worried. The clerk, the desk worker, the station man was already vanishing, exposing the lost and bewildered peasant dirt farmer underneath, bringing the old habits and survival skills to the surface.

The free-runner came to a halt beside a low building set into an artificial hillside inside the Park. There were a remarkable number of people coming and going from the place, from all corners of Ring Park.

With a shock, Elber realized what the "building" was. It looked very different than it had when he had lived in the Park. Then it had been surrounded by guards in olive-green assault fatigues, the grass had been burned off and blackened by an accidental brush fire, and the landscaping around it had been chewed into a muddy brown pulp by marching feet in combat boots and the comings and goings of severe black command cars that seemed to drive everywhere but on the designated roadways.

Now the grass was a lush green carpet, the vehicles were free-runners painted in cheerful pastels, the pedestrians were civilians dressed in stylish, brightly colored office wear, and everyone kept politely to the paths.

Elber and his sort had never gotten within a hundred meters of this place, or the others like it. The guards had been there for the express purpose of keeping gluefeet away. It was one of the entrances to DeSilvo Tower and the Gondola, the massive structure that hung off one side of the spinning station. DeSilvo Tower was actually three giant glass-and-steel towers that formed the legs of a massive tripod, topped off with a six-sided office building, generally known as the Gondola. It held the poshest, most grand homes and offices on the station.

They had expended endless effort to keep his sort out of the Tower and the Gondola. And now Elber was being taken there whether he liked it or not. And he most decidedly did not.

They shot down an incredible glassed-in elevator car with a view of the wheeling, gleaming exterior of the station and the shining world of Solace far below, then dropped into the six-sided jewel that was the upper side of the Gondola proper. Elber stumbled a bit as he exited the car, half from shock and half because he suddenly weighed more, so much farther out from the station's spin axis. The cop led him along to another elevator— no ornate glass box that looked out on wonders but just a simple steel lift. The doors shut, and Elber watched the floor indicator on the forward display count down. *Upper Level, 5, 4, 3, 2, Lower Level.* Then the display went blank, and Elber was alarmed to see that the car kept moving, as if it were dropping down past the bottom of the Gondola, headed straight into space where—

Then the car did stop, and the door opened. The cop gestured Elber to step out. He did, onto a greyish silver floor. Something in the floor was *moving.* He glanced down and realized that the movement lay *beyond* the floor, outside. He was looking down at Solace, spinning past, dimly seen, beneath his feet. At last Elber realized where they were, and knew that they were as far "downstairs" as anyone could get at SCO Station. He had read about this place. Everyone on the Station had.

They were in the famous commander's office, at the very base of the Gondola, a room with a smartglass floor and smartglass walls that looked out into space and let one watch the universe roll past as the station spun on its axis and orbited the planet below. A grand view, but a supremely distracting and disconcerting one, so much so, the news stories said, that the commander usually kept the walls and floor opaque.

Or at least, thought Elber as he watched the planet wheel out of sight and dim stars come into view, *the commander tried.* The smartglass was supposed to dial down to perfect opacity, but Elber had read in the same somewhere that the smartglass all over the station was beginning to wear out, the opacifiers no longer reacting as quickly or as fully as they were supposed to do. Even there, in the commander's office, it would seem the smartglass was not working as well as it should.

"Elber Malloon," the SSF officer announced. Elber

looked up and realized for the first time there were other people in the chamber. Two other people, and he recognized both of them at once. The dark-skinned bald man with a seemingly permanent frown sitting behind the big desk was Karlin Raenau, the station commander. Elber had seen his picture often enough to recognize him without trouble. The other man was standing by the desk, wearing an SSF uniform. He was short, burly, olive-skinned, black-haired, with a beaklike nose and hard grey eyes under bushy black eyebrows. Elber had seen him in person, plenty of times, commanding the crowd-control squads against the gluefeet. It was hard to imagine a gluefoot not knowing Captain Olar Sotales, director of Station Security. Elber's own little daughter Zari still had nightmares about being chased by the Sotales monster.

Elber's bewilderment transformed into utter shock. These were the two most powerful men on the station. What in the name of dark devils could he have done that was bad enough that it could bring him before them?

"Glad we finally found you," Sotales said. "We've been looking for a while now."

"Do you know where you are?" Raenau asked. "Do you know who we are?"

Elber felt as if he were in fact a gluefoot, rooted to the floor. He nodded without speaking and swallowed nervously.

"Good," said Raenau. "So we can get started. The situation is getting serious, and we need to do something."

What was getting serious? Do something about what? Why were two of the greatest and most important men on the station concerned with Elber Malloon? What could make *him* that important?

More out of bewilderment than anything else, Elber finally worked up the nerve to speak. "Sir? Please—if it wouldn't be too much trouble, can you please tell me why I was arrested? I mean, what the charge is? What am I accused of, I think you call it."

"Arrested?" Raenau asked, apparently surprised. "You weren't arrested. You were invited to answer a few questions and to see if you could help us with a problem. That's all."

From some part of himself he barely knew, formed more from fear than nerve, Elber Malloon found the courage to contradict the man in absolute authority over him. You never dared argue with a copper. But sometimes—sometimes—you could appeal to the big uppers, the sort who assumed their cops and overseers treated the lowdowns as nice as nice and were surprised when things weren't like that.

"Sir, I'm sorry, sir, but, well, sir—this officer came to my workplace during business hours, spoke to my supervisor before looking for me, had her point me out to him, then told me I was 'wanted downstairs' in front of all and everyone."

Raenau frowned thoughtfully. "I see. That makes it sound bad for you. Is that how people get arrested back home?"

Elber nodded stiffly. "Pretty much, sir. Everyone in the office thought I was being arrested. *I* thought I was. My boss thought so."

"We'll make sure they know it was a mistake," Raenau said.

"Well, ah, sorry sir, but—I saw the look my boss gave me, sir, and I *know* I've lost my job already. I'm cooked. Fired."

"But you're *not* being arrested. Why would they fire you over answering some questions?" Sotales demanded.

"They has a thing they says," Elber answered, half-conscious that his speech patterns were drifting back from station man to the phrases of a lowdown peasant. " 'If it smells bad, it is bad.' They don't like things that don't *look* right in my office. My boss always talks about not wanting scenes and scandals. There's lots of confidential info we see, and they don't take chances on their people. If they aren't sure of you all the way through, you're out—and my boss can't be sure of me at all anymore. Maybe some uppers—uh, higher-ranking people—might get a second chance, but not people like me." The speech astonished Elber himself. He had never dreamed of saying so many words, or words so blunt, to the big boss.

Sotales looked toward the cop who had brought Elber in. "Is his account accurate?"

"Um, well, yes, sir. You just told me to bring him in to answer questions, and I didn't think—"

"Obviously you didn't. Stars and devils, Jentens, if this man loses his job, why the hell should you keep yours?"

Jentens opened his mouth and shut it again, and he seemed to decide he couldn't do himself any good by saying more.

Sotales glared at Jentens, and somehow that one look was worse than the worst shouting-down Elber had ever had. Sotales muttered something very unpleasant under his breath, then gestured toward the elevator. "Get out of here," he said. "I'll deal with you later."

Jentens turned beet red, then saluted, spun on his heels, and stepped back into the elevator car. He pushed a button, and the car lifted itself back up out of the strange room. The opening through which it had come irised shut in smooth and perfect silence, leaving only the thinnest circular scribe on the ceiling to show from where the elevator had come.

Sotales turned his attention back to Elber. "Sit down, son," he said. "Let's see if we can work this thing out."

Elber stepped forward and perched uncertainly at the corner of the big and expensive visitor's chair, and found himself looking up at Commander Raenau, seated in majesty behind his enormous desk, and at Sotales, standing at his side, the loyal and powerful lieutenant ready to do the great leader's bidding. A part of him knew the furniture had been chosen and arranged to make the effect happen—but knowing didn't stop it from working.

"I don't know if there is that much to work out," Raenau said with a crafty smile. "The plan always was that we'd take care of Mr. Malloon. Now he just has a bit more incentive to help *us* out."

"I—I don't understand," Elber said. Even in his confused

and terrified state, the thought *good cop, bad cop* flitted through his mind. They were both being good cops, and letting Jentens be the bad one. He realized it had all been a performance, a show. Jentens was more likely to get promoted than fired for the day's work.

Elber knew how it worked, knew they were pushing him around, trying to trick him. But even though he understood it was a trick, he knew the trick was going to work. They could do with him whatever they liked, and there was nothing he could do to stop them.

"Help us," said Commander Raenau. "Help us, and we'll help you."

"With what?" Elber asked.

"Not so much with 'what' as with 'who,' " Sotales answered.

He handed Elber a datapad. It was looping a security camera recording, showing the very start of the Long Boulevard riot, of the moment when Zak Destan brought a wine bottle down on top of an enforcer's head and touched off all the trouble.

Zak. Zak Destan. Now, at last, Elber was beginning to understand. An enhancement grid locked on to one scared-looking, blurry face at the edge of the action and brought it into sharp focus. It was his own face—dirty, half-starved, terrified, Elber at the absolute worst moment of his entire life.

"We had the faces," Sotales said. "But no names, no I.D.s. We got lucky when we checked station records. We want to talk with you about Zak Destan."

Whatever tiny shreds of hope Elber had begun to feel were swept away. Suddenly, once again, the future was nothing but blackness. Elber had done nothing wrong that night, but Zak had done plenty—and in the world of the lowdowns, association was all that it took to draw a guilty verdict—and a long, unpleasant punishment.

In Elber's soul, that punishment had already begun.

Part Two
IGNITION DAY

Chapter Six

CURSES IN THE DARKNESS

ALONG THE MISTVALE ROAD
WILHEMTON DISTRICT
THE PLANET SOLACE

By the light of the burning police cruiser, Zak Destan walked back from the road and surveyed the scene with satisfaction. The two dead bodies, facedown in the road, marked a significant victory. No one—not even the local groundcop force—*especially* the local groundcops—was going to shed a tear over Watch Officers Walzen and Teglen. Of course, the groundcops would investigate, but that would just be for form's sake. They wouldn't really *need* to investigate. They would know, forty-five seconds after they came on the scene, who had done it. He *wanted* them to know it. He was going to make *sure* they knew it. And they, and everyone else, would know why. Copies of Walzen's and Teglen's discipline files, along with certain other highly informative documents, would arrive the next morning at every mayor's office and news service and police department in the district. Everyone had always known the two of them were dirty—now everyone would be astonished to learn just *how* dirty. With the whole district bleeding to death, the two of them had just kept squeezing harder for more. A little honest graft between friends was one thing—but cops running a protection racket, and upping the rates, on farmers with starving kids—that was crossing every line there was, and maybe a few that hadn't been thought of before.

"Let's wrap it up, boys," Destan called out into the darkness, and his troopers started to put a move on, gathering up the loot and the weapons they had pulled from the cruiser before setting it alight.

Destan stayed where he was for the moment, savoring the moment. Even though he had just done the local groundcop commander a favor, even though the commander would know it, and be glad to be rid of the pair, that wouldn't matter. They would have to go after him, and Destan knew he would get the jolt for this one if they caught him. It didn't bother him. They had evidence enough against him to do plenty already—if they caught him. How many times could they execute one man?

He had done the local commander more than one favor, come to think of it. Not only had he weeded out the two worst crooks on the force—he had given all the others a very strong incentive to play the game straight—unless they wanted to end up like the two in the road.

His troopers finished packing the guns and gear they'd stripped from the cruiser, and started hauling it toward the two camouflaged aircars they had used to spring the ambush.

The weapons Destan would keep, but the satchelful of cash and the other goodies—that was blood money. That he could not keep, and still be thought of well by the villagers—or by himself. Besides, the two dead cops had been good enough to keep detailed records of their shakedowns and other enterprises. It would take some care, and some doing, but quietly, carefully, their victims would be compensated from the stash, as best Destan could manage it.

There was a muffled *boom* and the flames flared up for a moment. It was time to go. They had a lot to do yet. Everyone would be watching the Ignition Day doings. It was as if the Planetary Executive herself had arranged a gigantic diversion for Destan's Reivers, drawing all the world's attention away from them. Zak Destan was determined to make the most of it.

He headed toward the lead aircar, and their next objective. He'd planned a busy night for his boys—and for the cops.

ABOARD *LODESTAR VII*
IN ORBIT OF THE GAS GIANT PLANET COMFORT
SOLACIAN SYSTEM

Neshobe Kalzant stood on the narrow platform in the rear of the large compartment, ignoring the busy people at the command consoles below. Instead she studied the huge display at the far end, the forward end, of the compartment. She glared at the display, at the numbers slowly ticking away toward a zero that would arrive in just over an hour. The big screen was subdivided to show a half dozen different views at the moment. Her gaze shifted to the image of the small world Greenhouse—then to the image of the SunSpot, the artificial sun that was about to die. Last, she looked on NovaSpot, the still-dormant artificial star that orbited Greenhouse. If all went well, SunSpot would die giving life to NovaSpot—giving life to all of them.

Neshobe could feel sweat trickling down the small of her back, and wished once again they could do something about the heat—but she knew better. There were simply too many nervous people and too many overworked machines in too small a space. The ship's cargo-zone cooling system hadn't been designed to handle the load. It had taken some doing to build the command center into what had been the cargo hold of the *Lodestar VII*, but they'd managed it. Barely. And so the heat built up. Never mind. The people working there were concentrating on somewhat larger climatic problems.

From behind her came a voice she was already thoroughly tired of hearing. "On my mark," the voice said, "Final Sequence start in one hour—*mark*."

As if she, or anyone else, needed to be told. The moment

of Ignition had been chosen—or perhaps *preordained* would be a more accurate term—years before.

Ignition would generate a hellfire of radiation, a spherical blast wave of gamma rays, X rays, and heavy particles that would sterilize any living world or habitat unlucky enough to be caught in its path. Therefore Ignition had to be timed for a moment with very particular conditions of planetary alignment, such that not only the planet Solace, but all the spaceside habitats, were well out of harm's way. Those alignment conditions would obtain very soon—but once the window was closed, they wouldn't come back for another dozen years. Even then the alignment would be far less satisfactory, with several orbiting habitats in the danger zone and requiring evacuation.

Not that it would matter, twelve years in the future. By then, nearly everyone in the Solacian system would have been evacuated—or would be dead.

Unless—unless a lot of things. Starting with whether the Ignition worked. All else depended on that. Neshobe Kalzant had bet nearly everything and everyone on it working. A high-risk gamble—but then, it was the only game in town. There were no other options. Depending on one's point of view, it was therefore most fortunate, or disastrously unfortunate, that Neshobe was a gambler. She had to be. She was utterly convinced that to play it safe in their current situation would be the same as playing dead.

"In just under one hour's time," the announcer droned on, "the final sequence will begin, culminating in the Ignition of NovaSpot, successor to the aging SunSpot. NovaSpot will, of course, be the largest and most powerful artificial fusion reactor in all history, larger than any ever seen in any sky, with a maximum potential output four times more powerful than the original SunSpot was at maximum output. That's more than ten times the SunSpot's *current* output. The excess power output capacity was engineered in to permit centuries more power at optimum capacity."

The announcer's console was at one corner of the

narrow platform, affording him a fine view of everything that happened down below. Just incidentally, it put him but a few meters from the spot where Neshobe Kalzant and a few other notables had been invited to observe the proceedings. Neshobe was not grateful for the proximity. She turned toward him, and her face was caught in shadow for a moment. The curses she thought at him from the safety of darkness should have been enough to turn him to stone then and there. But there was no justice in the universe. Her bitter maledictions had no effect whatsoever.

"Once, the SunSpot was powerful enough to light an entire hemisphere of Greenhouse, from pole to pole," the announcer burbled on. "But for more than a century, the SunSpot's power output has been diminishing, and the light from the SunSpot has been concentrated down into a tighter and tighter beam, in order to conserve power and protect the SunSpot's aging machinery. For the last fifty years, that light has been directed only onto the equatorial zones of Greenhouse, literally leaving the higher latitudes in the dark.

"Now, all that ends. NovaSpot will operate with sufficient power to permit illumination once again from pole to pole, thus providing a day-night cycle over the entire surface of Greenhouse for the first time in many generations.

"One hour from now, the Final Sequence leading toward Ignition will commence, and a new era will begin in the history of Greenhouse—indeed in the history of the entire Solacian system."

If it works, Neshobe told herself.

"At my mark, fifty-five minutes until Final Sequence start. *Mark.* This is the voice of Ignition Control."

Neshobe felt her hands balling up into fists. She wasn't going to be able to tolerate much more of the endless chatter. She felt a great desire to stomp off to her private quarters and watch the show from there. But she was going to *have* to stand it, at least for a little while longer.

One of the great disadvantages of being the Planetary

Executive was the need to endure the foolishness of ritual and ceremony. Her part of the job of making Ignition happen, the political job of arm-twisting, backslapping, promising, lying just a little, had been over for months, even years. There was no work for her here. Nonetheless, retiring to her quarters at this crucial juncture would look too much like abandoning her post.

She could have, perhaps should have, stayed safely home on-planet, on Solace, along with everyone watching from there. After all, part of a leader's job was to ensure continuity of leadership, to avoid getting killed when getting killed would produce a crisis.

But staying alive in the event of disaster didn't matter so much in the present case. If things went terribly wrong, if, for example, the NovaSpot ignited just a trifle too soon or a bit too energetically—well, then, they would all soon be dead anyway. Leadership would be able to do no more than point the way to the graveyard.

Greenhouse was merely the rocky outer moon of a quite ordinary gas giant planet in the outer Solacian star system. But everything—everything—depended on Greenhouse, to the point that there had been serious discussions about the possibility of renaming the little satellite "Lifeboat." After all, the little world's little sun was dying, and now a new sun was about to be born. Those were profound changes—certainly profound enough, it was argued, to be marked by a change of name. And if the old name had accurately described the use to which the world had been put, then surely the new name should do the same thing.

Neshobe had vetoed the idea. The name change idea was apt—too apt. Morale was bad enough without indulging in a surfeit of honesty. Besides, Neshobe herself could not help but wonder if this particular lifeboat would have spaces enough for everyone. Changing the name would only make it more likely that others would think to ask themselves the same question. In her more superstitious moments, Neshobe worried that a name change might even be bad luck, tempting fate. For all that she cited various political reasons, and the needless time, effort, and confusion that would be produced by the effort to change the name in all the books, charts, histories, and so on, that had been the *real* reason she had refused to make the change.

Neshobe Kalzant had no desire to bring down further curses on Solace and Greenhouse and the rest of the worlds of the Solacian system. They had been under a curse, many dark curses, for far too long already.

"The timing of Ignition is of course absolutely crucial," the announcer volunteered to no one in particular. "In the first hours after Ignition is initiated, a lethal blast of radiation, more powerful than any other radiation burst ever produced by humanity, will roar out from the NovaSpot. That initial radiation blast will bloom out in all directions, until NovaSpot's power shields can be brought on-line to control and focus the power output and dampen the radiation.

"All the inhabited places of the Solacian system must be shielded from that first blast, either by simple distance, or, better still, by being behind some massive body. At the moment chosen for Ignition, the planet Solace will be on the farside of our sun, and, for good measure, the gas giant Comfort will stand between Greenhouse and the sun. This is a relatively common alignment, but it is rare indeed that it coincides with a set of planetary alignments that also serve to shield the major outer-system habitats. It will be many years before such a moment comes again, and even then . . ."

That was enough for Neshobe. If she could not leave the room, she could at least escape that damned low, soothing drone of a voice. She turned and walked to the far end of the observation platform and made her way down to the main level of the command center. She wasn't really supposed to go down there, but who was going to stop her?

She looked around the command center and spotted Director Drayax. The director was, arguably, every bit as useless as Neshobe, just at the moment. Berana Drayax had already made her strategic decisions and commands. Now she, like Neshobe, could do little more than watch and see what happened as those commands were carried out. Not too long from now, once the final sequence began, she would once again have real work to do, guiding the minute-by-minute, second-by-second details of the operation. But for the moment, she could stray at least a few meters from her console.

Neshobe caught Drayax's eye and walked over to the older woman. Drayax was tall and slender, with snow-white hair done up in a braid, pale skin, and a calm face that fell easily into a calm smile. The fact that she looked like a kindly grandmother had not hurt her in the least during the hard-charging times leading up to this day. The unforgiving deadlines, the technical challenges, the political battles, the fights over funding, staffing, supplies—all those should have drained the life from her. And yet here she was, cool and poised in a formal business suit, the picture of confidence, looking for all the world as if she were hosting a cocktail party reception for visiting business associates.

"What the devil do we have to hang around here for?" Neshobe asked Drayax, in a voice that would not carry, a very sincere-looking and quite artificial smile on her face. The press would be watching, and so she had to play the game. But at least they would not be listening. So long as her facial expression had nothing to do with her words, she could say what she liked. She refused to worry about lip-readers. "Hell of a day, Berana. Please, tell me again why the hell we couldn't have just come a day later and had it all over with by now, one way or the other?"

Berana Drayax was every bit as practiced as Neshobe in the obscure art of speaking words that did not match her expression. She knew as well as the PlanEx how many cameras were around. She smiled warmly and said, "Why hurry? We'll find out if we're all dead soon enough, Madam Executive."

"That's not exactly the optimism I've heard from you before," Neshobe said, genuinely taken aback behind her cheerful smile. Drayax wasn't much given to gallows humor. "Has something happened that I need to know about?"

"Probably, Madam Executive—but what? This is one of the most complex engineering tasks ever attempted— comparable with setting a timeshaft wormhole. Something is *bound* to have gone wrong—something we haven't detected yet. If it's critical, if it's something we haven't got a redundant system for, or if something else we haven't thought of takes us by surprise from out of nowhere—the later in the game we are, the higher the odds on a possible system failure where we wouldn't be able to do anything except sit back and watch the disaster."

"I know. You've told me all this before—though not with quite so much drama. But you don't know of any *particular* problem right now, do you?"

Drayax shrugged. "There's one sensor problem that's got me a bit worried. I suppose it's just a dramatic moment, with a lot of dangers just ahead—and maybe I've done just a little too much pretending everything is fine and nothing can go wrong. It's too late for pretending, don't you think?"

It was impossible for Neshobe not to note that Drayax's false smile remained where it was and seemed just as real as it always did, even as she spoke those words.

Neshobe suddenly understood. Drayax was scared to death, more scared than Neshobe—and yet it was absolutely impossible for Drayax to show the slightest niggle of worry. Venting at the Planetary Executive from behind a frozen smile was her only possible release.

So who do I vent at? Neshobe asked herself, knowing full well that answer was "no one." That was one of the other problems with being Planetary Executive.

"Now coming up on fifty minutes until NovaSpot Ignition," said the announcer's voice. Down off the platform, Neshobe was far enough away from the announcer's desk not to hear him directly, but that did not stop his voice from pursuing here, booming down from a speaker directly above her head. Was there no escape from his endless repetition of what everyone already knew? "Final preparations are now under way for refocusing the power beam of the original SunSpot," he went on, "to be followed by the power-surge transfer to the Timeshield Generator. Those aboard the *Lodestar VII* and other close-in command, control, and observation craft are now starting their final safety preparations before those events."

A gong sounded, and another voice cut in. "All nonessential personnel to preassigned strap-down locations. All nonessential personnel to preassigned strap-down locations."

"That's my cue, Madam Kalzant," said Drayax. "If you'll excuse me?"

Neshobe Kalzant nodded and watched Drayax head back to her console. Neshobe had been at any number of official events where she was required to put in an appearance, remain for a politically appropriate amount of time, and was then permitted to escape. That sense of relief when the blessed moment came was always intense, but never before had it been so powerful.

At last there was something to *do,* even if it was nothing more than going to an assigned seat and strapping herself in. Not that there was much point to the exercise, insofar as safety was concerned. Nothing was going to happen aboard the *Lodestar VII.* It was the SunSpot that was going to be called upon to go through a complicated sequence of targeting and refocusing operations.

Granted, there was a small chance that the SunSpot could malfunction spectacularly while so doing—but if so, being strapped down ahead of time would do but little good. If the SunSpot blew up, the *Lodestar VII* would doubtless be torn apart by blast debris, shortly after all those aboard absorbed a lethal dose of nuclear radiation, all while being incinerated.

The real reason was to get Neshobe Kalzant and all the other useless Very Important People out from underfoot so that Berana Drayax and her people could concentrate properly on their jobs at a crucial moment in the process. So be it, so far as Neshobe was concerned. Anything that would occupy her mind and keep her from *thinking,* at least for a few moments.

But even so, Neshobe could not help but find it intensely irritating that the damned-fool announcer wasn't among those being herded out of the command center. She, the leader of the planet Solace, the *de facto* ruler of the entire Solacian star system, was "nonessential." The endlessly blathering announcer was not.

There was probably a message in there somewhere. If so, PlanEx Kalzant chose not to go looking for it. She started heading for her cabin, in the forward end of the *Lodestar VII.*

Chapter Seven

A SHIELD OF WORLDS
AND TIME

Berana Drayax watched PlanEx Neshobe Kalzant and the rest of the dignitaries depart her command center with what she hoped was well-disguised relief. For the moment, at least, the political side of her job was over. She let the smile drain away from her face, little by little, as she turned toward the status screens and increased the volume on her earphone. The tiny speaker was concealed inside an earring, and her comm speaker was hidden inside her necklace. It was ridiculous that she had to disguise the tools of her trade as gewgaws, but so doing allowed her to do her job of operational commander while still playing the part of charming hostess.

The cameras were still there, watching her every move. But so be it. Even the most muddled viewer at home would expect her to get serious, to focus, to let her face display concentration, even worry, this close to the moment. And it helped that they were only broadcasting pictures, not voices. She hoped. No, strike that. She didn't care. If they *were* running voices, too bad. She had to do her job, and doing it included talking about bad news. There was still that sensor that had been worrying her. She activated her mike. "SunSpot Power Shunt, this is Project Director. Are you in the loop?" she asked.

"SunSpot Power Shunt here. We're in, PD."

The voice on the other end didn't seem shy or worried about talking to so exalted a person as the Project Director. Good. That's why they had been trained to address her by her job title or its abbreviation, and not Madam Project Director Drayax or some similar nonsense. It made her just one more voice in the loop, unintimidating enough so they could actually report bad news. "What about that ground station alignment problem?"

"We're still working it, PD. Groundside Power Reception isn't quite sure yet, but they now think it's a blown sensor and not a real problem."

"They don't have much time to decide. We've got fifty-three minutes and twenty seconds left before it's too late to call a wave-off for power transfer."

"Believe me, PD, we're watching that clock, and so is Groundside Power."

"Well, don't be shy about cutting into the loop if you get some news."

"Copy that, PD."

Berana stared at the fault display, willing it to go green. No doubt, somewhere down on Greenhouse, someone was frantically pulling out a spare sensor, while his or her sweating team member burrowed down through the cables and conduits and shielding of the huge power receptor station built specifically for this job. Someone else was checking a schematic and shouting instructions through an access hatch, or rigging an improvised piece of test equipment, or checking the ops manual to see how to run a realignment by hand since the autos had packed it in. What showed here as a simple red panel that should be green, what SunSpot Power Shunt saw as a blown sensor, was in reality a collection of sweaty, half-frantic junior engineers getting their hands dirty and their clothes ruined as they crawled around the innards of whatever machine had failed.

They knew, she knew, everyone knew, that, if absolutely necessary, they could abort this first try, and come back again in twenty-seven hours, once the SunSpot and NovaSpot had completed one more orbit and arrived back over the target. But twenty-seven hours from now, the planetary alignments would already have started to deteriorate. Facilities that were shielded now would not be so then.

A one-day delay would thus force more emergency evacuations, and force others who were already evacuees to stay in their shelters longer. Emergency supplies would get used up. Evac shelters would be forced to operate longer, leaving more time for systems to fail, leaks to develop, tempers to shorten. People would stay on watch too long. Machines would stay untended for longer than planned. Those who took ill would be kept away from medical attention that much longer. Almost certainly, someone, somewhere—maybe a lot of someones—would die as a direct result of the delay.

But all that was as nothing compared to what would happen if she called a wave-off, and they tried again the next day—and then failed at the *second* attempt. Never mind that all the problems produced by the first waveoff would be worse than doubled. By the time the next window rolled around, twenty-seven hours after the second attempt, the planetary alignments would have deteriorated drastically. The problems would multiply as the various planets, satellites, and artificial structures moved around in their orbits. With each day that passed, the available time windows for starting the Ignition Sequence would shrink—and even the best of those windows would decay further, starting from a point that was barely acceptable. Both the number of settlements and the total population that would be exposed to massive doses of radiation would ratchet higher every day. Every day would come the choice between killing thousands now, or thousands more the next day, in the gradually fading hope of saving millions later on.

And all those nightmare scenarios started small, with the failure of a part that cost half a starmark, a failure that forced a wave-off on the first attempt.

And now it seemed that the failure might—*might*—be a failed sensor putting out wrong data, with no relation to the actual state of the equipment at all. Berana Drayax had not thought to add *that* extra layer to the fears and doubts she had imagined. But then, life always did find ways to make itself more interesting.

Drayax stared straight ahead at the red light marked GROUND STATION ALIGNMENT on her board, willing it to turn green, begging the seconds in the countdown clock to run more slowly.

Neshobe made her way up two decks to her private compartment. Along the way, her security team rematerialized from wherever they had been hovering discreetly, and formed up around her—one in front, three behind. They were all big, tough, and dedicated. They were all absolutely focused on their duty—a very good thing, the way Neshobe's life was, these days. Once, she had been able to travel with only a minimal security detail, or even, impossible as it might seem, with no protection at all.

Those days were gone. As PlanEx, her primary duty these days was to preside over a mounting series of crises and disasters, none of which she could prevent, and most of which she could do little to make better. It did not make her the most popular of leaders. There had been attempts on her life—a lot of them. She had the idea that there had been more tries than her security team was willing to report, perhaps out of fear of hurting her morale.

So be it. So far, her security people had had 100 percent success in not letting her get killed. She had no reason to question how they did their job. If they wished to be silent as well as invisible, she would not argue. Still, there were times when she was taken aback to realize how much she took them for granted. More than once, she had started to disrobe for the bath while her security team was in the room, simply because she had ceased to be aware of their presence.

Today, however, there was no forgetting them for long. The *Lodestar VII* was a big ship, and there were a lot of people aboard, and no matter how carefully all of them had been vetted, there was no telling who might be nursing a grudge these days. The endless disasters had cost too many people family members, or property, or fortunes, or status. The security team kept close to her anywhere outside the ultrasecure areas, such as the command center.

They arrived at her cabin, and Neshobe obediently waited in the corridor while two of the team did a careful sweep of it, the other two standing guard over her in the corridor. After a bit, one of the team inside emerged, and signaled the all clear to his fellows.

She entered the cabin and took her place in the crash chair in the center of the room. She made no move to strap herself in. She had learned the hard way, long ago, that there wasn't any point. Hands more skilled and less gentle than her own adjusted the belts and clips, tugged and pulled to test the restraint. One of the team sealed and locked the hatch from the corridor, while another checked over the hatch to the cabin's escape pod one last time, then climbed in to check the pod's status board. The first check had been for bombs and assassins hidden in the pod. This check was to make sure the pod itself was in good working order, ready to save Neshobe if need be. The agent nodded in satisfaction and climbed back through the hatch. Apparently all was well. And never mind the fact that there was no good place to escape to, if the ship failed.

Confident that she was properly strapped in, that the door from the corridor was locked, and the escape pod was functioning, the four security operatives strapped themselves in, then vanished from Neshobe's consciousness. So far as she was concerned, she was alone. She used her seat's controls to bring up the countdown display and the image of the worlds outside. The world the *Lodestar VII* orbited, and the world that world orbited . . . Wheels within wheels, worlds around worlds. That was the way of it, the essential truth of the situation, written in orbits and in geometry.

Lodestar VII orbited Greenhouse, and Greenhouse was a medium-sized moon orbiting the gas giant Comfort. Comfort orbited the star HS-G9-223, officially named Lodestar. There was a sort of symmetry about the ship called *Lodestar VII* orbiting the object that orbited the object that orbited the star called Lodestar. In name, at any rate, the least came round to meet the greatest. It was a notion that appealed to the stratified, neofeudal worldview of rank-conscious Solacian society.

Other worlds circled Lodestar, of course—most significantly, a world called Solace, that poorly terraformed and swiftly failing more or less Earth-like planet. As the display showed, Lodestar was at present behind Comfort as seen from Greenhouse, and Solace was behind Lodestar as seen from Comfort. Put another way, the four bodies were, momentarily, lined up like unevenly spaced beads on a string, thusly:

Greenhouse, Comfort, Lodestar, Solace.

But vital as that alignment was to the Ignition Project, it was not the natural worlds, but artificial suns, that were the central issue.

SunSpot, simply put, was an artificial sun that orbited the small world of Greenhouse once a day, every 27.3 hours—precisely the same period as a Solacian day. The new NovaSpot was circling Greenhouse about eighty kilometers behind SunSpot in the same orbit. Once it was ignited, it would quite literally be a nova—a new star—in the skies of Greenhouse.

As Neshobe Kalzant worked to strap herself in, SunSpot and NovaSpot were already between Comfort and Greenhouse. In something like twelve hours and forty-five minutes, the minor outer planet Alloy, home to the mining stations Goldrush Alpha, Goldrush Beta, and Goldrush Gamma, would move behind Greenhouse as seen from the NovaSpot. In other words, the bulk of Greenhouse itself would serve as a radiation shield for Alloy. Shielded by Greenhouse, Alloy would be safe. Similar alignments would shield the other major outer-system population centers.

A handful of smaller free-flying stations had been forced to change orbits, or evacuate for the duration of the Ignition Project, but aside from those trivial exceptions, it was the alignment of the worlds themselves that would serve as natural shields against the hellish blast of radiation that would be part and parcel of igniting NovaSpot's fires. The engineers and physicists all gave strong assurances that, assuming all went well, NovaSpot's output of hard radiation would settle down to barely more than the local background of cosmic rays and stellar wind within a few hours of primary reaction initiation.

All the inhabited worlds and stations would be shielded by the bulk of Comfort, or the lesser but still quite adequate mass of Greenhouse, or by Lodestar itself, during those hours.

All the worlds save one: Greenhouse itself, the aptly named moon that was the center for terraforming and climatic-repair operations for the entire Solacian system. Without Greenhouse's expertise and storehouse of diverse genetic material, held in the form of living plants, animals, and microbes, Solace would have collapsed years before, indeed would never have been terraformed in the first place.

Greenhouse was dotted, from pole to pole, with endless domed habitats. Once, long ago, during the main Solace terraforming project, virtually all of them had been operational at the same time, nurseries and genetic labs for the thousands of species that were to be adapted, and then introduced, onto Solace. The domes of Greenhouse had been bursting with life.

But before the Ignition of the first SunSpot, nothing at all was alive on the surface. The original SunSpot had been ignited *before* the domes were even built, let alone populated with living things. Indeed, the SunSpot was lit before there was much of anything alive anywhere in the Solacian system. The blast of killing radiation produced by the SunSpot's Ignition hadn't been much of a problem, simply because there was nothing much for the blast to kill.

The original terraforming plan had seen Greenhouse as an interim home for the living things that were to be transplanted onto Solace. It had been expected that the SunSpot would serve its purpose and that the last of the domes would be shut down—or simply abandoned—

long before the SunSpot guttered down to die, its fuel expended. But it hadn't worked out that way. Solace had never lost its reliance on Greenhouse.

An ecosystem could be considered closed when it received no significant outputs from the outside, aside from raw energy. Earth was a closed ecology, completely reliant on itself, except for the Sun's light and heat. In hindsight, at least, it was clear that the Solacian ecosystem had never really been "closed" at all, even after the planet had been officially declared to be terraformed. It had always been an open ecosystem, dependent on outside sources, mainly Greenhouse, for substantial biological inputs, such as additional populations of a plant species that had died out, or additional biomass in the form of raw organic material to serve as foodstock for bacteria, or even new species. Whatever Solace needed to meet the ecologic crisis of the moment, Greenhouse provided. Greenhouse still did so, down to the present day.

But the SunSpot was dying. The engineers had performed miracles to keep it going—but even miracles could only do so much. They had run out of tricks, run out of ways to stretch its dwindling output of light and heat.

And that led directly to the current crisis and the present mad plan of action—a plan of action suggested centuries before by Oskar DeSilvo himself, before his supposed death.

DeSilvo. We're actually here, getting ready to do what DeSilvo says again. That was the heart of the madness, so far as Neshobe was concerned.

DeSilvo, hero to all those who knew half the story, and devil to the very few who knew it all. DeSilvo had led the effort to terraform Solace. That much, everyone knew. Everyone also knew that the failures, the things that had gone wrong, were all bad luck, or the fault of sloppy management, or a failure to follow properly the plans that DeSilvo had left behind.

One man had learned more only quite recently, and informed Neshobe. At her direction, what they had learned was being kept very, very quiet, for fear of touching off stars alone knew what sort of unrest. Neshobe now knew that DeSilvo was, at the time he was terraforming the planet, *in possession of incontrovertible proof that the terraforming attempt would inevitably fail.*

Neshobe had spent many a night wondering: Did DeSilvo fail to *read* the evidence—or did he fail to understand it, or refuse to believe it? Or did he read it carefully, understand it perfectly, believe it completely—and forge ahead anyway?

Neshobe's thought flitted briefly to Anton Koffield, the man who had discovered the fraud, the man who had come to warn Solace, who had been cruelly tricked and punished for doing so, the man who had discovered that DeSilvo had faked his own death and was likely alive, the man she had sent off in pursuit of DeSilvo.

It had been nearly two years since Koffield had departed on his mission to find DeSilvo. There was no word of him since a sketchy intel report, now over a year old, that had him leaving Earth's Solar System. Nothing since. It was not time to give up hope—but it was just about time to stop *expecting* Koffield to return.

Hell's bells and damnation, she thought. *It's past time to expect anything good to happen.*

The countdown display caught her eye, and she focused again on the matter at hand, on the marvelous irony that they had turned to DeSilvo's century-old scribblings on the backs of envelopes for a solution to the problem.

The core of the conundrum came down to this: No matter how cleverly they made use of planetary alignments to shield the other worlds, it was impossible to ignite a replacement for the SunSpot without releasing massive amounts of radiation, twenty times more than enough to sterilize an entire hemisphere of Greenhouse—indeed, something more than a hemisphere, as the replacement SunSpot swept overhead in its orbit. And if they killed that much of Greenhouse, Greenhouse could no longer supply the biomass and living things needed to keep Solace's ecology creaking along.

DeSilvo had seen the answer to that problem—but he'd seen it generations before technical advances made it possible to do the engineering that made the answer practical.

Temporal confinement had made interstellar flight vastly more convenient—once the equipment for it became cheap, light, and powerful enough to be widely useful. Generate a spherical temporal confinement field, and time inside the field would slow down by whatever factor you wished—if you pumped sufficient power into the field. Slow time down enough, and a hundred-year-long passage between the stars would seem to last only weeks, days, or even minutes.

Electromagnetic radiation passing through a temporal confinement field did not slow down, but instead experienced Doppler-shift effects, slipping down the electromagnetic spectrum, becoming far-lower-energy radiations. Beam gamma rays and hard X rays into a 15,000,000:1 temporal confinement field, and sensors inside the field would detect nothing more malign than easily managed infrared, visible light, and ultraviolet radiation. Visible light would be detectable only as radio waves.

DeSilvo's back-of-the-envelope solution, little more than a doodle or two of a planet with a circle drawn around it, a crude representation of the SunSpot, and a few scribbled numbers alongside, had become one of the most famous graphic images in the Solacian system over the last few years. It had been endlessly reprinted, and used to illustrate innumerable news reports about the Ignition Project. There was a reproduction of it hanging on the port-side bulkhead of Neshobe's cabin. She turned to glance at it. The legend under the doodles said it all:

Use Sunspot Output & Put G-house
in Temp Confine Field.

Simple enough in concept—but almost impossible in execution. In theory, and given modern temporal confinement technology, draining the remaining power output from the old SunSpot would provide more than adequate power to run the confinement—but how to store, then channel, that much power that fast? Besides, a confinement had to be powered from the *inside,* and the whole point of the operation was to keep the old and new SunSpots on the *outside* of the confinement. Beyond all that, no one had ever attempted to create a temporal confinement field a tenth, a hundredth, a thousandth as large as would be required to shield Greenhouse.

And that was only the start of the list of problems— the big, obvious problems. There was an endless series of others. For example: Was there any point in attempting to evacuate the hemisphere of Greenhouse over which Ignition would occur? Thousands lived in domes near the target area.

If the Ignition attempt failed, after the last of the SunSpot's power had already been drained, Greenhouse would descend into the cold and dark that was the natural environment of a small world in the outer reaches of a star system. No living thing on Greenhouse would survive for more than a few days, except for places with their own power sources. Besides, there simply were not the ships, crews, places of refuge, or other resources to evacuate the satellite before a failure, let alone after, when the job would be far more difficult. The cold-blooded analysis said that anyone remaining on Greenhouse after a failed Ignition attempt was dead anyway.

In the end, that whole murky debate was resolved by looking not at what was desirable, or necessary, but what was possible. Neshobe Kalzant knew better than anyone just what resources were available, and what could and could not be done. Time and treasure spent on an evacuation plan that merely made people feel better was a luxury they could no longer afford, whatever the political advantage there might be to running an evac.

There were a thousand such choices, large and small, mixing science, engineering, logic, politics, and the rawest of emotions, that Neshobe had been forced to make. Never had she been able to make them based on complete information or even a solid idea of the risks. It seemed as if nothing was solid anymore.

And always, in the back of her mind, was the story Wandella Ashdin had told about Glister, a world in a nearby star system that been wrecked by a similar series of disasters.

The Glisterns had met a series of worsening setbacks with a series of "all-out" efforts. Every "all-out" effort had drained resources and diverted them from other uses where they might have done some good. Worse and worse climatic disasters were met by "all-out" responses that grew weaker and weaker, until the disasters were so vast, and the remaining ability to respond so weakened, that Glister collapsed altogether.

Neshobe had diverted vast resources to ignite the NovaSpot and save Greenhouse. With every authoriza tion of time, materials, ships, equipment, people, or money, she had asked herself *what will be left?* When the next bad news came—and it would come—would the cupboard be bare?

In a sense, the answer didn't matter. Greenhouse was vital to the long-term and short-term survival of Solace. If they didn't save Greenhouse, they were all dead any-way, and there was no need to waste time worrying about what they could and could not afford.

Time. Neshobe blinked and came back to herself. She had been staring, unseeing, at the countdown clock, and yet had completely lost track of how much time there was left. She refocused her eyes and her attention. *Twenty minutes, fifteen seconds.* Not very long—but long enough to keep worrying.

But no, she thought. *The displays would show it. We'd know already if anything was going wrong. Wouldn't we?*

She was appalled to find herself suddenly missing the soothing tones of the voice of Ignition Control. Still, she resisted the temptation to turn up the sound.

After all, she told herself with a smile, her security team might have turned invisible, but they weren't deaf. No point in letting that damned voice drive *them* mad.

Chapter Eight

LIGHT FROM A SUNSPOT

Twenty minutes, ten seconds until Ignition Sequence Start, Drayax told herself, as if she didn't know. But only two minutes left to call a wave-off, if need be. And that damned red light was still on. She debated calling Power Shunt again, but then she changed her mind. All they could do would be to call Power Reception down on Greenhouse and relay her queries. There was no time for such niceties. She had to cut out the middlemen. She set her comm to call Power Reception directly.

"Reception, this is Control. Drayax speaking. We need—I need—your best guesses, your best call. Are we going to get that sensor swapped out in time?"

"We're—we're, ah doing, doing our best, Madam Drayax—Control."

Plainly they were rattled as hell down there. They needed a little backbone enhancement. "Never mind all that, Reception. Just answer the question. Can we get that sensor repaired or replaced in time? Yes or no?"

She heard a drawing-in of breath on the other end of the line, and she imagined the young technician whose name she did not know, whose face she had never seen, standing a little straighter, throwing his shoulders back just a little. "No, Control. I do not believe we can."

She had thought as much—but she needed them to admit it as well before they could go to the next step. "Very well," she said, speaking slowly and calmly, struggling to ignore the way the countdown clock was shedding seconds at an alarming rate. "I need your best, your very best estimate, based on all your experience with your systems. Do you have a sensor failure, or a good sensor reporting a true misalignment?"

Silence on the line, and seconds melting away. Then, at last: "Control, I would put it at 85 percent likely we have a blown sensor sending bad data."

"Very well." One last question to ask, and she had to phrase it in neutral terms. "Again, based on your experience with the systems involved, and the last reliable data you received, please report on your opinion: What do you believe is the alignment status of the reception grid?"

More silence, more seconds draining off to nothing, and at last a strained, quiet voice, struggling to keep itself calm. "Control, *if* the sensor is in fact bad, based on last good data received, I would say there is a 95 percent probability that we still have a good alignment."

The silence was at her end, now. She had the best data she was going to get, and now it was up to her to decide. *So, an 85 percent chance of a 95 percent chance,* she thought. *What did that work out to?* Work the numbers and they had a hair over 80 percent confidence that the grid alignment was still within tolerance. The kid was telling her he thought it would work, but he couldn't be sure.

She checked the clock. One minute, fifteen seconds remaining during which she could call a wave off.

"Thank you, Groundside Power Reception," she said. "Stand by for initial power shunt sequence." She switched over to the general comm channel. "This is Ignition Control." *Not the "voice" of Ignition Control,* she thought to herself. No flacks, no public affairs officers for this. *I'm the only one who can say this.* "We are go for Ignition. All systems showing green, or have red status overridden by me. No wave-off. Repeat. We are go. There will be no wave-off."

She stepped back from her display panel and folded her arms in front of her chest. She herself wondered if it was a gesture of finality, of determination—or whether she was subconsciously putting her arms up to protect herself, to shield herself, and hold on tight through whatever was to happen next.

She flipped to the public affairs channel and listened in as that damned "voice" calmly talked them all through it as the last of the seconds smoked away.

"That was Project Director Berana Drayax providing the final approval for the Ignition Sequence to start. That sequence will begin in twenty-five seconds, as the old SunSpot powers down to 5 percent of capacity, then refocuses and retargets its light cone for the Power Shunt operation."

He makes it sound so simple, Drayax marveled. She knew how much work had gone into planning that one sequence, into rebuilding the SunSpot controllers to make it possible, into surveying the ground target precisely, into constructing Groundside Power Reception, into rehearsing and simulating everything, over and over again.

"On my mark, Ignition Final Sequence begins with SunSpot power-down in fifteen seconds. Mark. Minus fourteen and counting. Thirteen. Twelve. Eleven—"

The soothing voice faded into the background as Drayax stared at the main display screen. The graphics and simulated images were gone, replaced by a split view, with the daylight surface of Greenhouse as seen from space on the left and a shot of the SunSpot on the right. Even an elderly SunSpot put out a hellacious amount of light energy, of course, and the image adjusters had accounted for that, so that what was really a blinding flare of light appeared in the screen as a comfortably warm yellow bloom of luminance.

"Five. Four. Three. Two. One. *Mark,* Sequence start."

That comfortable warm bloom of light suddenly began to dim, guttering down to a faint red glow. Drayax knew better than to trust to the corrected images, however. It was impossible to control all the biases. The auto-adjustment system would inevitably try to make the light look the way the adjuster's algorithm thought it ought to look rather than as it was. Far better to go by the meters and sensors, the numbers. She flipped that view onto a side display, and nodded to herself as she watched the numbers change, saw the graph line move down the intended path.

The world that had been lit, at least in part, by a still-bright torch was now illuminated by a dying ember. She looked toward the image of Greenhouse and watched the surface of the planet, or at least its equatorial regions, fade, not quite to black, but down to a dark grey-black red. The landscape was cast in dim yet lurid tones darker than blood.

Darkness. The final blackout. That's where we're all headed, if we're not careful—and lucky. Drayax thought.

In a disturbingly short span of time, the blazing light of SunSpot had guttered down to a weak red glow. But massive power still lurked inside the truncated sphere that was the heart of the SunSpot—power that was going to come out, sooner or later. Either it would be released under control—or else the damping fields would give all at once, and the SunSpot would flashover in a heartbeat, and for a few brief moments would outshine the local star, Lodestar. Unfortunately, those aboard the ship named for that star, *Lodestar VII,* would not have time to admire the phenomenon, as they, and the ship itself, would be vaporized milliseconds after the lightblast reached the ship.

Drayax checked the telemetry from SunSpot, and was relieved to find the damping fields appeared to be in good health.

With the SunSpot safely powered down, the next task was refocusing and retargeting the SunSpot's light cone, tightening it down to as small a focus as possible and aiming it as precisely as possible at the Power Reception Array that was still showing a red panel and serious misalignment.

If the Power Reception Array wasn't precisely aligned as it tracked the SunSpot in its orbit, either the SunSpot's tightened light cone was going to melt large portions of the Array—and the hopes of survival for everyone in the star system—down to slag, or else the Array simply would not receive enough power for the job ahead. Drayax was tempted to call into Power Reception Control again, but she knew it would be pointless at best, and likely counterproductive. They were doing everything they could down there, and another call from the boss could do nothing but distract them.

Now it was out of her hands, out of human control altogether. The next part of the Sequence was in play, the automated fusion controllers and beam focusers taking over.

Seconds, minutes, passed. Drayax watched the surface of Greenhouse as the light cone was tightened down.

Generations ago, SunSpot had been bright enough to light an entire hemisphere of Greenhouse, providing the whole world with a reasonable approximation of a day-night cycle. As the SunSpot's power had ebbed, the beam had been focused down, and focused down again, until it was merely a broad oval cross section, centered on the equator. The poles were left in darkness, the higher latitudes received far less light and heat, and even the equatorial regions received fewer hours of light than they once had. Now that broad oval of light had become nothing more than a dark red glow that spanned much of the visible face of Greenhouse. And then Drayax saw something that made her heart beat just a little faster. Something was *happening* to that dim and angry glow. Something that whispered that maybe, just maybe, it was all going to work.

The light cone was contracting, focusing the beam down tighter and tighter. As it shrank, the dim red oval of light on the surface grew brighter, as the SunSpot's minimum power input was focused down onto a smaller and smaller area. The spot of light on the surface shifted its shape, rounding into a perfect and steadily shrinking circle of light, the SunSpot aiming an ever-smaller, ever-brighter spotlight down onto the planet.

The point of light began to shift color as well, as SunSpot Control shifted the output frequencies upward in preparation for the next phase. The bright red dot turned orange, then yellow, then blazing white, even as it shrank down past the point of visibility.

But Berana Drayax knew the SunSpot's light beam was still there, even if she couldn't see it from space. One of her displays switched itself to the feed from one of a series of groundside cameras, this one atop a three-hundred-meter tower, built a kilometer from the planned ground track of the light beam.

The beam was very definitely visible from there—a blazing hot circle of brightness, a hundred meters across, and still contracting as the targeting system in orbit swept the beam forward, and it made its final approach to the Power Reception Array.

The surface of Greenhouse was in theory a vacuum. In practice, the barest trace of atmosphere—some small fraction of the gases leaked and purged from domes over the years—remained near the surface. That residue never quite dissipated altogether, with the result that there were at least detectable amounts of oxygen and nitrogen. Still, any human caught outside a dome without a pressure suit would not have gained much by trying to breathe the stuff in the few moments left of his or her life.

Though the intense human activity over the centuries had produced the trace atmosphere, it had never been enough to matter, never enough to signify, let alone generate, weather.

But then came the moment when the concentrated power of the SunSpot's light beam struck in one spot. Power enough to light half a world, however dimly, suddenly smote the earth in one small patch of ground. Smoke and dust boiled up out of the superheated soil, the land itself exploding, rocks and soil suddenly blown up into the sky by the violent outgassing. In the blink of an eye, there was atmosphere, and a lot of it, and it was very active, at least locally.

The light beam marched across the landscape, and as it moved, the heat of its passing boiled all the volatiles out of the soil. Every bit of moisture, every stray organic

chemical that had ever bonded with the sands and rocks
and dirt of the surface of Greenhouse, was abruptly
cooked out of the mix, boiled off into steam and smog.
Jets of dust and grit were blasted up out of the surface
and kicked kilometers high. The dust and debris were
caught in the light beam, making it visible, a flame-
bright sword slashing down out of the sky, cutting deep
into the vitals of Greenhouse.

The dust cloud weakened the light beam, absorbing
much of its power before it reached the ground. But
even the attenuated beam was a fearsome thing—and
the clouds of dust would not trouble it for much longer.
The beam was approaching the start of the guide path, a
perfectly paved, arrow-straight, jet-black roadway a
hundred meters wide and ten kilometers long.

It was there to provide the beam with a dust- and
debris-free final approach to the Power Reception Array. The guide path thus protected the Array from being
damaged by falling debris, but, just as important, it prevented the Array from losing 20 percent of its effective-
ness because dust chanced to settle on the receptors, or
because too much dust was suspended in a puff of temporary atmosphere over the Array.

As she watched, the view shifted to a camera alongside the far end of the guide path, looking down its
length at the beam as it marched straight toward the
viewer.

Drayax had ordered that the guide path be built, then
ordered it doubled in width and length. She had done so
more because she was worried about the near certainty
of dust contamination if they took no precautions and
less because she feared a one-in-a-million strike by an
improbably large chunk of back-falling debris.

The simulator teams all assured her that there was little need for the guide path, and certainly no need to
make it so large. But no one had ever done anything remotely like this before—so how could she know how far
to trust in simulations? Nor were they going to get a second chance at this if they got it wrong. Better to build
better, bigger, and stronger, just to be sure. They were

going to need the Array to absorb every watt of power it could, and Berana Drayax was damned if she was going to go down in history as the woman who allowed the Solacian system to die because she economized and did not defend against a few cubic meters of dust.

The beam struck the forward edge of the guide path and continued its steady march toward the Array. The dust and debris whirled away into the darkness, and all that was left was the beam of light on the guide path, marching straight down its centerline toward the Array. Then even the beam itself faded away as the finest of the dust and the last of the trace gases blew off into the surrounding near vacuum. The guide path blocked any further generation of gas and dust, and thus the beam turned as invisible as any other light ray in vacuum. Only a sun-bright disk of orange light remained, slowly crawling down the center of the path.

But being lost to sight did not mean the light beam's power was diminished—quite the contrary. Drayax shifted her gaze from the remote-imaging cameras to the telemetry from the thermal sensors built into the guide path. That jet-black surface was absorbing a hellish amount of power—several percentage points above projection. She glanced back at the camera view and was startled to see a spot on the guide path showing a dull and angry glow of red. The guide path was made of material that could absorb and diffuse tremendous amounts of energy. The SunSpot would have to be generating significantly more power than projected for the guide path to show any outward sign of heating.

Good. They would need all the power they could get. But then Drayax frowned. Or was that true? They had spent precious little time worrying about what to do with too *much* power. They had worked up some contingency plans, but they had not been rehearsed more than a few times. *Too late now,* she told herself. *Besides, it's a better problem to have than too little power.*

Assuming they got far enough along to worry about that problem. The GROUND STATION ALIGNMENT light was still glowing red. Was it an instrument problem—or was the Reception Array off axis, and off by enough to cause problems—or a disaster? *Too late now,* she told herself again. Her fists were clenched, and she could feel the sweat trickling down the small of her back. There was a cold, dark pit in her gut, down where her stomach had been a few minutes before. But some part of her knew that she was showing even less outward sign of stress than the guide path. She knew she looked as calm as if her gravest worry were running short of orange crumbbake bread for the reception. Good. That was the way she wanted it.

The main viewer switched to a camera with a good view of the Ground Reception Array itself, and the ranks of deep blue hexagonal receptor plates, each angling over toward the light beam, an endless field of weirdly identical robotic flowers, all pointing themselves precisely at the rising sun.

Precisely. That was the key word. The receptor plates used a system of collimated microlenses, so that their surfaces, when viewed up close, resembled nothing so much as the eye of an insect. The microlenses focused and concentrated the infall of light, and greatly improved reception efficiency—at a price. They could absorb energy from nearly any angle, but their efficiency was vastly better if they were aimed precisely at the power source. That improvement had meant the difference between success and failure in all the simulations. But if the alignment was off by so much as two-tenths of a degree, the microlenses would lose a quarter of their efficiency—and that severe a power loss would mean the game would be over and lost. There simply would not be enough energy to generate the necessary temporal confinement field.

The light beam slowly tracked into the center of the Receptor Array. It did not touch any of the receptors as it moved, but instead moved down a narrow continuation of the guide path. The beam was focused too tightly to allow it to strike the receptors. The receptor panels would not have absorbed its energy but merely vaporized or exploded.

At last the beam came to rest in the precise center of the receptor. The SunSpot itself was still low in the east as seen from the Receptor Array, not far at all above the horizon. Drayax watched her displays and nodded as they confirmed that the beam-aiming system aboard the SunSpot had locked on to the center of the Array. It should be able to hold that lock for at least ten hours—which ought to be long enough for the Receptor Array to accumulate the power it needed—if, if, if all went well.

Having made a good lock-on, Beam Control prepared to widen the beam back out from a few meters in diameter to a full kilometer across and to crank up from 5 percent back up to full power. At full power output, even when spread over that far larger area, the light beam would be ferociously intense.

Once the SunSpot had lit half a world. Even now, decrepit as it was, it packed more than enough power to turn a few square kilometers into a hell-hot nightmare.

Drayax frowned, and wished the term *nightmare* had not come to her so easily. That red light was still glowing—and there were thousands of other problems that could still happen, flaws and faults that were not so kind as to warn of their existence through the diagnostic systems.

This was the moment, as the SunSpot's power beam bloomed outward and struck the Receptor Array. Now they would know if the alignment *was* actually off—or if the sensor and telemetry systems had been giving them all needless fits.

Drayax switched her displays to show a new set of data reports. No more need for beam-transit trajectory. Now she needed to know power input, Array temperatures, accumulator status. The beam jumped from ten meters across to a thousand in less than a heartbeat, and the SunSpot's power level began its climb to maximum output. She watched the charts and numbers spike from nothing at all to nearly off the chart.

There was a sudden noise behind her, a high roaring noise she did not recognize at once. She looked up, startled, to realize it was the sound of people cheering, of every person in the room clapping and yelling as the accumulators successfully engaged.

Berana Drayax did not allow herself to take part— not at once. That one red light was still on—even if it was in disagreement with every other display on her board. All the other numbers were good, very good, showing the power receptors working at peak efficiency, the madly complicated system smoothly draining off the SunSpot's remaining power, precisely as intended. She flipped her comm system. "Groundside Power, this is Project Director. We're showing good power accumulation across the board, but my board still shows a bad alignment. Do you have any updates for me?"

"Project Director—we're showing the same thing. With the power shunt in progress, I had to pull three engineers back to their operations-monitoring station. That leaves me with only two people working the problem directly. They'll do their best, but there are no new data yet."

"But we're showing good power accumulation," Drayax objected.

"Yes, ma'am. For now, we are. It all looks good—but we've got to get through the whole power shunt process. And we *still* don't have hard numbers on alignment itself. If the Array starts to drift, we could have problems later."

"I thought you said it was an instrumentation problem," Drayax said.

"I said 'probably,' " the voice in her ear replied. "But we have to work on the *assumption* that it's *not* the instruments and the alignment system is slightly off somehow. That's why I need to start working contingencies, working on ways to run the alignment manually if the automatics do fail."

"You're not making me happy, Groundside Power," Drayax said.

"No, ma'am. That's not my job."

"I'm coming to understand that, Groundside Power. Keep me informed." She switched off.

It's never straight and smooth, she thought. *Never simple or direct.* Just as she had never really considered the possibility of an instrumentation failure forcing a wave-off, it had not occurred to her that the status of the Power Shunt alignment might still be uncertain even after they had started. It should have been either/or, fail or succeed, live or die. But no. Once again, it was the fretful doubt of the middle ground.

And even if this all works—if the accumulator does its job, and the timeshield works, and the NovaSpot and the SunSpot both behave—if, if, if—then what? What have we bought ourselves?

A little more time. Perhaps that was all. Berana Drayax was privy to the inner secrets. She knew that the planet Solace was well along a path of irresistible decline. Nothing could stop the crash—but perhaps, with a little more time, they could soften the blow, save a few more lives, or perhaps a few more million lives. Perhaps the best they could do would be to add a day, a month, a year, to some unknown number of lives. *If,* because of their efforts, a million people all had six months more of life, then that would be a victory—of sorts. And time, after all, was hope. Buy the people of Solace six months, a year, five years—and there was no telling what might happen.

And no telling if it would be good news—or further disaster.

Berana Drayax settled in, along with everyone else in the Solacian system, to wait out the SunSpot's orbital pass over the accumulator.

Chapter Nine

POWER STRUGGLES

Neshobe Kalzant tried to think about how her day had started, but she could not remember that far back. She stared down at her coffee cup, trying to figure how long she had been awake, how many cups of coffee she had drunk. But all things blurred together. She had been on the *Lodestar VII* forever; she would always be on it. She had spent all her lifetime waiting out the SunSpot's pass over the Power Reception Array; she would still be waiting until the end of her days.

She could not clearly remember the all clear call after the SunSpot had been safely reaimed and refocused. She had a vague notion of her security team unstrapping her, but that seemed so long ago that she could not truly believe it was all part of the same day. She must have returned here at some point, drawn, like everyone else on this platform, back to the central point, to the control center, where their joint fate would first be known. If she really concentrated, she could remember the short walk from her quarters.

She could even remember at least some of the polite, meaningless conversations she had had with various politicians. None of the pols had anything larger in mind than the prestige of being seen with the Planetary Executive on this all-important day. Assuming civilization held together long enough to allow it, there would be a whole series of virtually identical new still images:

Neshobe smiling and shaking hands with Mayor Blank on Blank's wall, with Habitat Executive Dash on Dash's bulkhead, with Representative Dot in Dot's newsletter, and on and on and on. She did not know whether to marvel respectfully at the way Blank, Dash, Dot, and all the others could focus on the trivia of political gamesmanship at such a moment, or else whether to stand aghast that such powerful men and women had so little imagination and understanding, appalled that they were actually capable of functioning at such a time. Their worlds, their lives, were balanced on a knife edge, and still the buffet table did a steady business.

But even as the day lasted forever, time was running out. Each minute, each second, seemed to pause forever, and then lurch clumsily into the past, shoved aside from behind by the next lumpen fraction of time that would tarry too long, then leave too soon.

The magnificent starscape gleamed down at her from the command center's main display screen. Inset in the four corners of the screen were numeric displays of one sort or another, showing various parameters and statistics and projections that were no doubt of great importance to the technicians on the main level below. The two numbers Neshobe understood were in the upper-right corner.

CURRENT POWER RECEPTION PROCESS DURATION: 08:51:13
CURRENT POWER STORAGE LEVEL AS PERCENTAGE OF
REQUIREMENT: 82.97%

The two numbers kept moving, and no doubt they mattered greatly, but it was the center of the display that demanded her attention.

The satellite Greenhouse floated there, its cratered surface shrouded in gloom, lit in half phase by its distant sun. Dimmer light, reflected off the surface of giant Comfort, lit part of the dark side, forming a band of lighter shadow.

The huge habitats that made the world important were barely visible, tiny gleaming dots of light in the greater darkness, gathered in clusters here and there.

One spot of perfect blue-white gleamed from the darkened surface of the world—the Power Reception Array—soaking up all the light energy that the SunSpot could deliver, a few square kilometers of power receptors greedily absorbing all the power meant to light a world.

There was something terrifying in the fact that the Reception Array was large enough, bright enough, to be seen so easily from space. That much power, in so small a space, was deeply unnerving to contemplate. Someone had told her that the SunSpot was beaming as much power as would be produced by a constant series of small nuclear explosions, one every five seconds.

And this is just the banked embers of SunSpot's former power, she told herself. *This is just a tiny fraction of the energy we'll unleash once we light NovaSpot.*

She wondered, only for a moment, if she and her people ought to be trusted with such power. But the mere need to ask the question brought its answer: *Of course not.* It took but a glance at the shambles they had made of Solace to answer that one. No human beings ought to have such power; none could be trusted with it. But "ought" didn't matter anymore. This was survival, and the most immoral act Neshobe could possibly choose would be to take no risks, take no action, have her people do only what they ought—and then watch their worlds die.

Just over an hour to go. Power storage crept up over 83 percent as she watched. She glanced down at the lower-right-hand corner and saw that the history graph confirmed what she had thought: The rate of increase had slowed to almost nothing over the last hour or so. But the power was still going in. That much was plain.

"This is the voice of Ignition Control," said the announcer, speaking from his station in the farthest corner. "We are coming up on the nine-hour mark of power accumulation. Though the nominal period for power reception is ten hours, we anticipate approximately one and a half additional hours during which the SunSpot will actually be in effective line of sight of the Power Reception Array. SunSpot will then move past the point in the sky, as seen from the PRA, beyond which the individual receptors in the Array cannot be pointed. We are anticipating accumulation of the last 17 percent of required stored power during that period. This is the voice of Ignition Control."

Neshobe Kalzant was starting to develop a strained sort of respect for Ignition Control's calm and understated voice. All of what he said was true, and yet it was wonderfully misleading. He made it sound as if all was as it had been expected, that everything was going exactly according to plan.

Neshobe Kalzant knew otherwise. Receptor efficiency had started high, but had begun drifting lower almost at once. The power storage level should have been well over 90 percent by now, perhaps higher. The mission plan called for reaching 100 percent at about the ten-hour mark, with the last half hour before they lost line of sight spent in banking reserve power.

But the voice of Ignition Control misled in another direction as well. No one really knew how much power they would really need, and no one had really known ahead of time how much they could get. The target of 100 percent by the ten-hour mark was almost completely arbitrary, merely setting down two round numbers that were reasonably close to the rough estimates.

The question marks were on the Groundside part of the operation. The SunSpot's orbital period was, of course, known down to the microsecond, and likewise its engineers knew everything about its power curves and output signatures. However, there were tremendous uncertainties as to the behavior of the Reception Array and the power storage system. The design had been tweaked and tuned and refined over and over again, maximizing its efficiency at all cost. That had been absolutely necessary. Various engineering restraints meant it would be impractical, or even impossible, to make the Array larger than it was. Even so, the initial simulations had all come up short of the required power levels. So the tweaking and upgrading and fine-tuning had started. The designers had promised the power levels would improve—but the numbers at the moment were almost exactly where the pretweaking simulations said they would be.

But we're only pretending we know what the required power levels are, Neshobe reminded herself. No one had ever created a temporal confinement this large before, or even anything remotely as big. There had not been time to run the integrated simulations that would have given them a precise figure—or at least a better guess—of how much power was required. If the actual power level required was lower than thought, all might still be well. If it was higher—then they might as well shut down the whole operation and head home now, so the crew could wait out the coming end times with their families.

Neshobe gave up all pretense of doing anything but staring at the image of Greenhouse. Greenhouse, now a world of murk and shadows, with but one tiny, bright gleam of hope aglow upon its surface, and that gleam fading slowly but steadily all day long.

She stared until her neck ached, stared until she realized the pain in the palms of her hands was made by her own balled fists, by her nails digging into her own flesh, stared until she could make nothing meaningful at all of the images she saw, until the globe of Greenhouse was a dark and monstrous eye, a blaze of light for its pupil, staring back at her, pulling her into its soulless gaze. The voice of Ignition Control said something more, his tones booming and echoing in the background, but the words were nothing but pleasant, meaningless noise to her.

At last, by sheer effort of will, she tore her eyes away, turned her back on the huge images, and looked down at the command center, at the people laboring to save the world she could no longer bear to look upon.

As Planetary Executive Neshobe Kalzant looked down, Project Director Berana Drayax looked up. Drayax looked worn down. Her hair, perfectly coiffed at the start of the day, was now in disarray, strands drooping to frame her face. Her clothes were rumpled, her skin pale and drawn, nearly ashen. Their eyes met, but

Neshobe could read nothing there. Drayax could not even manage an insincere smile.

And *that* scared the devil out of PlanEx Kalzant.

Somehow, Berana Drayax had felt Kalzant's gaze on her, and known to look up. Kalzant looked worried, worn-out—as well she ought. *She's lucky,* Drayax told herself. *She doesn't know what's really going on.* Thank the stars the PlanEx hadn't ordered status reports every five minutes, or some such damn-fool thing. "Groundside Power Reception," she said to the open air, and into her hidden microphone, "is there any change in status?"

"Nothing, ma'am. We've replaced the bad sensor but the replacement unit shows there is an actual slight misalignment. But even accounting for that, efficiency is still trending down, just barely—but the slope is still getting steeper. And we still don't know why."

Drayax looked at the power storage indicator, stuck at 83.01 percent, willing it to climb higher, faster. "Very well," she said. "What are our manual control options at this point?"

"High-risk," the voice replied, his tone flat and unequivocal. "I've—we've—figured out how to configure the control system so we can do it, at least in theory—but there has been no way to test it."

"I know," Drayax said. "Not enough time before today—"

"And no chance to try during the day," Groundside Power agreed.

"And no reason for trying tomorrow," she said. *Unless there was . . .* "What about doing a wave-off?" she asked. "A wave-off now, as we are, with the power store nearly full? We let the SunSpot set while we sit on 83 percent of the power we need, plus whatever we can pull in on the rest of this pass. Then we wait for the SunSpot to rise again tomorrow, pull in the last 10 percent or so, plus whatever power we need to make up overnight losses."

"Ma'am, it won't work—or at least I'd strongly advise against risking it. Our current lead theory is that we've got multiple problems, not just on the receptor alignment that bad sensor was masking. We think there are several additional faults masking each other. There's something wrong at the storage end too. We're getting a much faster power drain-off than expected."

"We knew we'd lose *some* stored power," Drayax objected.

"Yes, of course. That's inevitable. Second law of thermodynamics. But we're getting a much bigger loss than we thought. We're pouring water into a leaky bucket. The bucket's filling, because we're pouring water in faster than the leak is draining it out—but it might be that the leak is getting bigger. Once SunSpot sets, and we're not pouring anything more in, the leak will take over. We might not even have 50 percent power tomorrow morning—and the power storage system loses efficiency every time it drains power. It might not even accept any additional power beyond what it's retained overnight.

"Besides all that, the Array took a hell of a beating today. We've put a massive amount of energy through it, and it's deteriorated somewhat. Again, that's more or less inevitable. Plus the Array is *hot* right now, but it's going to get cold overnight. If we heat the whole system up again, with another shot from the SunSpot, something will be bound to give out. And I'd be willing to bet the SunSpot control team wouldn't want to try the whole thing twice from their end. I'm sure they've got the same sorts of problems. And the timing of the orbital alignments for shielding will be way off if we—"

"All right. All right. You've made your point." Drayax shut her eyes and tried to shut out the outside world, if only for a moment. *Why in the hell did I take this job?* she asked herself. She had more than half expected Groundside Power to say what he had said, but that didn't make it any less frustrating. There had to be some sort of way out.

She opened her eyes and stared at the figures on her center screen.

CURRENT POWER RECEPTION PROCESS DURATION: 09:00:35

CURRENT POWER STORAGE LEVEL AS PERCENTAGE OF
REQUIREMENT: 83.10%

To come so far, to be so close . . . Her gaze slid down
to the big red button, front and center, in the middle of
her console. She could see it through the clear safety
cover. The button that would light the NovaSpot. The
button wasn't activated—not yet—but when it was, and
if and when she chose to push it—well, whatever happened, would happen. No ArtInt control, no cutouts or
countdowns or second buttons that someone else would
have to push. She had ordered the system to be set up
that way, so it would be her immediate, personal, final
choice. However things turned out, people would know
who had done it—or who had chosen not to act.

"Groundside Power—best estimate—how much more
time will you have the SunSpot usefully visible?"

"Our estimate is sixteen degrees above the horizon,"
he replied. That works out to one hour, twenty-one minutes from my mark—*mark*. But the closer to the horizon, the tougher it will be for the receptors to make the
angle. We'll be less and less efficient with every minute
that passes."

"Understood." The receptors could track on the
SunSpot, but only within limits. And the closer to the
horizon, the more one receptor would tend to crowd out
another, the western receptors literally casting a shadow
over the eastern ones. "You were talking about just
barely keeping up with the power loss. When's the
break-even point? When are we just treading water, taking in just as much as we're losing?"

"Ah, I can't give you anything exact, but, say, ah,
about four minutes before we reach that sixteen-degree
point."

"Can you get me more stored power or less by jumping over to manual control?" Drayax asked, still staring
at that big red button.

"Ma'am?"

"We're running out of time, and we're not going
to reach 100 percent. Will we get closer with manual or

automatic?" There was silence on the line. "Well? Which is it?"

"Please, ma'am. Just—please. Let me think for a moment."

Silence again, and then the young man's voice again, subdued and hesitant. "It's—it's nothing anyone can answer absolutely," he said. "It's guesses, probabilities, how much power input we could lose in the changeover, how long the changeover would take, what might work, what might break . . ."

His voice drifted off. Drayax spoke again. "I need an answer," she said, her voice as flat and hard as she could make it. "I need it now."

The briefest of pauses, then—

"Manual," he said. "If I were a betting man, I'd put my money down on manual."

"Well if you weren't a betting man before, you are one now. Do it. Get me the power I need. And tell me the *instant* we start losing instead of gaining. Now go do it."

"Understood, Program Director." The voice was scared, no doubt—but also resolute. "Going off comm now to carry out your instructions. Groundside Power out."

The line went dead. Drayax felt her heart pounding and wished she had not felt that the leader needed to be seen always standing, directing, upright, and alert—in other words, that she had instead designed her own console with a place to sit down. She desperately needed to rest, to shut her eyes, to make it all go away. No, that wasn't it. She needed it all to stay with her, to stay together. That was what this was all about—holding it together, as long as they could, buying time for Solace, as much time as they could, buying decades, years, months, even weeks or days, at any cost, in the slender hope that it would be enough time for miracles to happen.

Villjae Benzen was halfway across Groundside Power Reception's control room almost before he finished signing off. He'd been worried about the autoalign system for months, and had spent many a sleepless night fretting over how to configure for manual control in a hurry.

But Villjae hadn't considered the possibility of autoalign packing it in this late in the game. His extremely sketchy contingency plans had all assumed they would discover a major autoalign failure two days before Ignition, or at the very worst, just after the SunSpot had begun beaming down power. The one saving grace was that they'd all been watching the autocontrol system flaking out all day long, and therefore knew there was a good chance they'd have to override. Villjae had had time to think it through, work out some sort of hashed-together procedure.

"All right," he called out to the controllers at their stations. "You heard the director. We've got to pull this one out, people!"

"I wish I could get my hands on the genius who designed this system," Ballsto Vaihop growled. "Buran Rufdrop got all the medals for design. I wish to hell he could see how nice all his pretty systems are working now."

"Me too, but he's too busy being dead," Villjae replied.

Villjae could not help but think that, if an exhausted pilot hadn't killed himself and Designer Rufdrop and half the rest of the trained staff in a lander crash three months before, then perhaps they wouldn't have been in this mess. Or perhaps they would be anyway. Villjae had started to have doubts about Rufdrop, and Rufdrop's design, since the day he had been tapped to take over the section.

"Ballsto, get on panel three and bring up Subroutine Gamma-Two. Curthaus, I need you to get down to the power distribution panel on Downlevel Baker. Panel 343. Get the safety cover off, stay on comm, and stand by. Beseda, you cut panel one's power off, then breathe down my neck. I'm going to need more hands than I have hooking up the test-stand controller. Ballsto, got that subroutine up?"

"Yah," Ballsto Vaihop answered. "Should I run it now?"

"No! *No!* That might scramble the whole system. We don't run it until *after* we've got the manual control plugged in. Wait for my say-so. Somebody, get the hand-controller module and roll it in here. Fast!"

Beseda Mahrlin cut out panel one using the command console at her station and hurried after him. The two of them shoved chairs out of the way and knelt in front of the main control console. Villjae popped the cover off and peered into the gloomy interior.

"Handlight!" he called out, and one appeared at once, offered from behind him. "Hold it for us," he said to whoever it was who had produced the light. He didn't have time to look behind and see who it was. He heard a rattling rumble off to one side and saw the battered old wheeled utility table that held the hand-controller lash-up being rolled into place.

"Okay, point the light over toward that corner a bit. Okay. Good. Beseda, start handing me hookups from the test-stand controller."

The test-stand controller, a three-way hand-controller scavenged off an old remote operator system, was the one piece of hardware in the control center that could be used to control the pointing of the Receptor Array directly, without any computer input. They'd used it during the final phases of construction and during the few dress rehearsals they'd managed before today. Mainly it had been used to simulate a deflection or impose a misalignment to see how the system would respond. Now the very shabby-looking old industrial joystick bolted to a rollaway table was the one thing left that might get them out of this.

"We should have flipped to manual two hours ago," Villjae muttered as he started hooking the leads up to the panel's innards.

"We weren't scared enough to do it then," Beseda replied. "And they weren't scared enough to give the order."

"Well, we're all plenty scared now," said Villjae. He

pulled his head out from under the console's access panel and scooted backward on his hands and knees. "Okay, Beseda, double-check me. Are those all the leads? Are they in right? One chance only on this one."

Beseda Mahrlin took the handlight and checked each connection carefully. Villjae resisted the temptation to shout at her to hurry. He had picked her to check him because she was the most thorough, the most careful. "Check blue-four," she said.

Villjae grabbed the light and stuck his head back in. Sure enough, there was some sort of crud between the hold-on clamp and the board. He pulled the clamp and wiped it on his none-too-clean shirt. Well, if the residue from sweaty lab clothes prevented good comm contacts, not a damn thing in the whole place would work. He hooked it back up again and scooted out from under the console, then stood, moving carefully as he moved around the hand-controller's table so as not to disturb any of the connections they had just made.

"Okay, Beseda, cut all main path net linkage to console one, then give me local power." Beseda pulled the links, then flipped the local breakers. In theory at least, console one was no longer part of the command center net, but electricity was again running through it—and, for what it was worth, the hand-controller hookup wasn't throwing sparks in all directions.

"Somebody get me a chair," he half whispered as he stood in front of the controller. Suddenly a chair was right behind him. He sat down, pulled himself up carefully, and with as much reluctance as if he were expecting a massive electric shock, reached out his right hand and took hold of the controller. With his left, he started powering up panel one's displays, now routed through the hand-controller hookup.

"Okay." Suddenly, not one but two alarming thoughts popped into his head. "Oh, damn. I didn't think of it in time." Now that he had hold of the controller, he didn't want to let go of it. Villjae knew the state of the aiming system's net-link hookups. The thing looked finished with the panel doors shut and the nice shiny covers in place, but inside, it was a mess of temporary hookups turned permanent, test clips, bridge wires, jumpers, and every other bad practice Rufdrop could have left to his successors.

Villjae should have torn it all out and started over months ago, but there hadn't been time for that, either. Which left the small but real possibility that there was some forgotten cross-connected diagnostic line, some backdoor patch-link still connecting console one to the rest of the net. If he took his hands away from the controller, and the controller sagged to the left the way it did sometimes, it might be received as some sort of low-level command input to the aiming system—and the aiming system didn't need any more problems.

But Villjae didn't dare remove his hand for another, and far more basic, reason: He didn't know if he could work up the courage to reach for it again if he let go. He was already thinking too hard about how the fate of worlds depended on the hash-up he was making of the control room.

In any event, it would take three hands at least for what came next, and he was coming up short. Left hand working the panel, right hand still on the controller, he looked behind him and saw Bosley Ortem, holding the handlight. "Bos—I don't want to let go of this thing. Reach into my breast pocket and pull out my datapad." Villjae had worked long hours to get his datapad to do receive-and-repeat of the data the hand-controller would need during the switch to manual. He had worked it all out ahead of time, except for the last detail of getting the damned thing out of his pocket while his hands were busy.

Bosley did as he was told, plainly feeling most awkward about pawing about in the boss's pockets. He came out with the little pocket-size datapad and looked to Villjae. "Now what?"

"Flip to screen three. It should be showing remote repeaters of the aiming data."

"Ah, yeah. Yeah, that's right."

"Okay. Now fish in my pocket again. There should

be a data cable there. Pull it out and jack it into port two on the datapad."

"Uh, okay. Hang on. Ah, sorry." After a moment of apologetic fumbling, Bosley found the slender cable and plugged it in. "Now what?"

Villjae nodded toward the hand-controller settings panel. "Jack it into the test port there. The one up in the corner."

Bosley did as he was told, and suddenly the hashed-together beast they had frankensteined out of console one, the hand-controller, and a datapad configured as a data repeater came to life, information flowing in alongside the electricity. They could have fed the aiming data direct from the system, but Villjae was not interested in taking chances. Using the datapad as a repeater prevented any premature feedback to the main system.

Villjae worked the console-one display settings with his left while he kept his right steady on the hand-controller. He ordered up graphical symbol-logic displays of the ideal and actual alignment, and swore to himself when they appeared. Things were drifting even more than he had feared. "Beseda, I can't do this all from here. Give me an overlay of my current weighted center. Once we're on manual, I'll need you to work from console two and keep me tracked on it."

The Reception Array was big enough that the aim-angle for the receptors on one side was going to be slightly different from the receptors on the opposite side. The pointing system was designed to compensate for this; but in order to run the calculations, it needed to be told which single receptor would be treated as the center point. As the SunSpot moved in its orbit, the optimum center point, the weighted center for the whole Array, moved as well.

The system allowed them to choose any single receptor as the center, keying all the pointing corrections off that position. Along with everything else, that selection was supposed to be automatic—so automatic, so supposedly reliable they had barely monitored it after the initial start-up procedure. But also along with everything else, the weighted center autoselect was very slightly off. Worse, the history chart showed an error that had been gradually increasing all day long. Villjae could see it the moment Beseda brought up the displays.

"God damn it all," he swore. "Why the hell did Rufdrop have to make this thing so bloody *sophisticated*?" The supersophisticated aiming and pointing systems, and all the rest of the cutting-edge stuff, were part of an attempt to squeeze every last drop of power from the system. But there hadn't been time to test it, debug it, tune it, and find any tiny systemic biases. They should have gone for something solid, something simple.

They were left with a delicate, finely tuned system that, in theory, would produce maximized power—*if* conditions were perfect. Rufdrop had built them an overbred and nervy Thoroughbred intended for blue skies and dry tracks, when what they needed was a strong, stolid plow horse that could still haul the cart no matter how thick the mud.

It was becoming plainer and plainer to Villjae that each overtuned subsystem was introducing its own errors, and the errors were amplifying each other, not canceling each other out. No wonder the damned thing was underproducing. "Beseda, you were right—we should have gone to manual—but we should have done it five minutes after we switched on. Or maybe five before." Villjae checked his displays and nodded. "All right, that's about as good as I'm going to get this. Beseda, how's your panel?"

"I've got you slaved and matched with real time," she said.

In other words, his hand-controller would go active "knowing" the precise pointing of the Array at the moment of switchover. Now all they had to do was make the switchover without crashing the whole system. "Curthaus," he called out to the comm panel. "You with us?"

"With you," Curthaus Spar's voice replied from the overhead speaker. "I've got the cover off 343. Standing by."

"All right. Now, everybody, listen up. Ballsto, make sure I'm feeding to everyone's comm. Am I?"

"Ah—you are now. Go."

"All right. Everyone, listen up. The Project Director ordered us to switch to manual power. I think what we're about to do will work, but I don't know. Okay, first off, I'm going to talk about what we're going to do. Don't anyone *do* anything right now. Clear?" There was a muffled chorus of assent. "Right. I've talked about some of this idea with some of you, but not much, and mostly I've just worked it out in my head. The pointing hardware, the system actually driving the motors and actuators, is programmed to ride out a five-second loss of signal from the aiming system that does the computation and direction, then hand that off to the pointing hardware. If it regains signal within that five seconds, and the protocols are all right and so on, it accepts the signal as legitimate and just moves on.

"If there's more than a five-second lapse, it assumes the aiming system has failed or been sabotaged, locks out further input, and drops back to a pointing routine that directs the system based on past inputs from the aiming system—and since the aiming has been off, that backup system is going to be way off from the start, and only get worse. We *can* get back control once it locks us out—there are written procedures, and some of you were here when we rehearsed it." *The others who were here all died in that crash, but never mind.* "But that's a complicated procedure, and it takes *time*. We don't *have* time. So we're going to do a complete control transfer, autoaim to manual, in less than five seconds."

Another murmur of voices. "We can do it," Villjae said, with maybe 10 percent more confidence than he actually felt. "I know how. Beseda knows the control links better than anyone, and she believes it will work."

Villjae glanced at Beseda and prayed that no one else saw her hold her hand up, palm down, and wiggle it back and forth. Villjae felt a momentary annoyance. What was she doing signaling a "maybe" when he needed a "yes"?

No. She was right. What he needed wasn't cheerleading, but honest assessments. It was the lack of such assessments, along with a few other bad habits, that had gotten them into this mess. Rufdrop had always tended to assume that "automatic" meant "accurate," for example. And Rufdrop had not appreciated it when Villjae had told him otherwise. The desire not to be like Rufdrop washed away all traces of his resentment toward Beseda. She might think the idea was a maybe—but she was still in on it, trying to make it work. That counted for a lot.

"Okay, now, nobody *do* anything yet. We're just talking. Here's the plan. Curthaus—there's a main breaker for the pointing-aiming comm loop down there. Don't touch it yet. Do you see it?"

"Yeah, right in front of me."

"Okay, good. Here's what's going to happen once we go. Curthaus is going to give us a countdown, and then open that breaker when he gets to zero. He's going to keep counting, and we're going to work to the count. We've got five consoles live, numbers two through six. We need number three to run a special subroutine, so it stays on. It's the only console without a hookup to the aiming-pointing comm link. When Curthaus says *one,* we need four fingers on four buttons, shutting the other consoles off. When he says *two,* Beseda will power up *my* console, and the patch-through to the hand-controller. At *three,* Ballsto will run his subroutine off console three. It copies itself to console one, shuts off console three remotely, and does a hard restart on the aiming-pointing comm loop, getting all input from console one. The subroutine should make the actual switch in about a tenth of a second.

"So, one, two, three. We need to do all that within *four* seconds, because 4.5 seconds after he opens it, Curthaus is going to close that breaker again." He looked around the roomful of worried faces. "Is that clear enough?"

There was silence for a moment, then Beseda spoke. "I think it needs rehearsal."

For one brief and irrational moment, Villjae thought

she meant he should practice his speech a few times. But then he understood her properly. "She's right. We're going to run through it a couple of times—but we have to do it *fast*. We don't have much time."

As if anyone needed to be told that.

Berana Drayax certainly didn't need to be told. Time was the only factor that mattered—until they activated the temporal confinement. Until then, she would do anything—everything—she had to do in order to make all their gambles worthwhile. There was almost no price she wouldn't pay at that point—if need be, she even would make a small down payment in lives. And it might come to that.

"NovaSpot Control, this is Project Director. Do you copy?"

"Project Director, this is NovaSpot. We are on schedule and on track for a nominal Ignition Sequence."

"Glad to hear, NovaSpot, but I don't think that's going to happen. Stand by. I'm patching in Temporal Confinement Groundside Control. Groundside Temporal, this is Project Director with NovaSpot Control in the loop. Do you copy?"

"Project Director, this is TC Groundside Control. Understand NovaSpot Con is in the loop. Go ahead."

"Thank you, Groundside TC. We've got a serious power problem at Groundside Power Reception. They might not reach the power levels listed in the operations specs, and they also seem to be experiencing a serious power storage drain. Right now they're working to shift to manual control in order to up their power inputs. *If* that works, maybe they can do something about the power drain—but I doubt they'll have time and bodies enough to do much before the SunSpot sets."

"The hell you say—uh, I mean, copy that, Project Director." NovaSpot Control just barely managed to get her voice under control.

"Copy, PD." Temporal Confinement Control sounded almost as unnerved. "So is this a wave-off? We reset for tomorrow's window?"

"Negative," Drayax replied, quiet steel in her voice. "The situation will only be worse—a lot worse—tomorrow. The systems are deteriorating. We're going to have to go today—and maybe go early."

"Say again?" Both controllers spoke the same words at the same time, which surprised Drayax not at all.

"We're throwing out the operations plan," she said. "We are not going at the start of the optimum shielding period—we're going the moment Groundside Power tells me they have the maximum power they're going to get. If they're at 95 percent, or 101 percent, or 112, we go when they say. The latest that might come would be just as SunSpot sets, but it's likely to be something on the order of twenty minutes before that time. Based on what Groundside Power told me, I would estimate the earliest possible moment would be an about an hour and fifteen minutes from now—about 16:02 hours. But when they tell us the power storage is at max—we go."

"Project Director—we can't do that!" NovaSpot Control protested. "There are people in unshielded habitats on Alloy. If the NovaSpot ignites before it moves around behind Comfort as seen from Alloy—"

Then people on Alloy will die. But she could not speak those words. Instead she brought up a textcom window on her console, typed in a few words, and sent off a message. "I've just sent a text communication shelter alert to Alloy, and we'll resend that, and voice alerts, every two minutes. The first alert will reach them at least an hour and fifteen minutes before we ignite NovaSpot." *See? I typed three little sentences, and solved the problem just like that.* Somehow, her interior thoughts were taking on something like a hysterical tone, bright, grim, unfunny little jokes, even as she kept up her tough but sensible exterior. *So which one is really me? Which one should I pick?*

"You know as well as I do they don't have enough shelter space out there! That's why Ignition had to wait until Comfort eclipsed NovaSpot for Alloy in the first place."

"Understood, NovaSpot Control." *Who would you like to kill instead of the miners on Alloy?* "But we're down to hard choices. Comfort will eclipse for Alloy at 16:43:05—one hour, forty-one minutes from now. If we *can wait* until then, we will. But we can't wave off. It's do it now, maybe a little early, or never." *And if it's never, it's never-never time for all of us.*

There was silence on the line for a moment. "Do you copy, NovaSpot Control?"

"We copy. I sure as hell don't like it, but we copy."

It's not my favorite idea either, Drayax thought. "Temporal Confinement Control—do you copy?"

"We do—but we're not too happy either."

"No one is, but we've run out of good choices," Drayax replied. "But I need to know from both of you, all other issues aside—can you be ready to go, at your last programmed hold before initiating, at 16:02 hours?"

"Stand by on that, Project Director. NovaSpot Control out."

Was NovaSpot's controller going to consult with her technical people, or was she just sitting there, comm off, taking her soul out and taking a good hard look at it?

Never mind. "Temporal Confinement?"

"We're at Power Shunt standby now. All we have to do is link to the Groundside Power's energy store, charge the initiators, and induce the field. The whole sequence should take three minutes, maximum. No problem."

"Copy that." *Was Temporal Confinement's controller that much more cold-blooded? Or just so wrapped up in playing with his wonderful toy that he wasn't willing or able to think about radiation deaths on Alloy? Or does he figure that it's NovaSpot Control's problem? Or is he a more or less decent person doing what you're doing, dearie—trying to stay professional on the outside while his insides want to scream?* "But there's another problem—power levels," Drayax went on. "You've had the chance to power up to standby and evaluate your integrated system efficiency. What's your floor, the dead-minimum power level you need for the confinement to work at all?"

"No real problem there, either, Project Director, if

things hold together. We can at least initiate a field with a power level of, say, 75 percent of rated storage capacity. We're there now, and then some. The question is, then what? With 75 percent, we couldn't hold that field for more than ten minutes, external—and it would be far less intense than we'd want. The good news is that inducing a field this big is the power hog. Once the field is there, maintaining it doesn't take nearly the power."

"What can you give me at, say, 86 percent?"

"Half of Greenhouse burned to a crisp," the disembodied voice said briskly. "*If* everything works just right, it's going to take at least seventeen hours before the NovaSpot's under enough control to block hard radiation. Probably closer to twenty hours. At 86 percent, we *might* be able to hold together a minimum field for, say, ten hours—and that's a field that's just barely intense enough to redshift out the heavy radiation. But ten hours in, even that field would die."

"Go at it the other way. With what you know about your hardware right now, what's the lowest level that would let you go the whole way?"

"Stand by." A moment's silence. Drayax was learning to get used to careful pauses—but she was also learning to hate them. But it was another voice that spoke next.

"This is NovaSpot Control, back in the loop. We have those figures for you now. We cannot initiate Ignition until—"

Don't say it yet, Drayax thought. "Stand by, NovaSpot. I'm waiting on a reply from Temporal Confinement. TC, do you have anything yet?"

"Ah, yes, yes we do. Our projections say we'd really need to have 91.2 percent to provide minimum full coverage. Anything less than that, and at least part of Greenhouse gets some sort of dose of heavy radiation."

"Understood." She herself paused—and hated it. Then she spoke, choosing her words carefully, very much aware that NovaSpot Control was listening as well. Even if she was addressing Temporal Confinement Control, she needed both of them to get the message. "Understood, TC. You need 91.2 power to provide minimum protection. Thank you for that input. But be aware, Temporal Confinement, that if we max out at under 91.2 percent power, if we only get to 86 percent—*we are still going.*"

She kept talking, struggling to keep her voice under some semblance of control. "We went into this trying to save lives, and that's still what we're about. But unless Groundside Power Reception can pull out a miracle, we're down to buying lives tomorrow with deaths today. It's too late to wave off. Groundside Power won't be able to regroup in time, and I don't think the SunSpot is in much better shape. If we don't go today, we don't go— and *all* of Greenhouse dies when the SunSpot goes dead. After what it's been through today, the SunSpot can't last more than a few more weeks or months at the outside. If Greenhouse goes, it takes Solace down with it, probably a year or two from now. If Solace goes, so does every habitat in the system, sooner or later. Save a few lives today, and *everyone* is dead five years from now." She paused again. "Are we clear?"

Silence on the line. And then TC Control spoke. "We copy, Project Director."

"Thank you for that, TC Control. NovaSpot, we're ready for your report now."

"Ah. Hold off on that just a second, Project Director."

Lose your nerve, NovaSpot? Feeling a bit less noble? If the situation had been a bit less grim, Drayax would have been tempted to laugh. She *knew,* knew to a moral certainty, what had happened.

Drayax didn't know NovaSpot's on-duty controller well, but she did know *Haress Bevard,* NovaSpot's chief engineer. He was a peppery old sort, given to picking his ground and standing on it. All very well when it was an engineering issue, something he had studied and worked on for years, and he truly did know the One Right Way to do things. People quite properly deferred to him at such times.

But the old boy had a tendency to assume that he was due that deference in all things, from the right amount to tip a waiter on the rare occasions he picked up the check in a restaurant with human service—nothing if service wasn't perfect, and make damned sure they didn't try to tack their tip onto the bill—to the proper form of address when speaking to the Planetary Executive—no honorific, just "Kalzant"—*he* hadn't voted for her. He could be irritating as hell to deal with, but his engineering skill gave him a certain degree of license.

At times, however, when he realized he had gone completely over the line, he was the very picture of a sincerely repentant little boy, his eyes downcast, his booming voice suddenly low and apologetic. It could be most amusing—or heart-wrenching—to watch the puffed-up little man visibly deflate right in front of you.

Drayax *knew,* absolutely *knew,* that Bevard had sputtered with indignation at the very idea of going early and endangering Alloy. He had pulled some high-and-mighty engineering reason out of thin air that made it impossible to move up the moment of Ignition. The controller on duty had been about to report that, put it on the record, when Drayax had stopped him—and stopped him just in time.

And, now, as she waited, she knew that her words had reached Bevard, actually made him stop and listen. Even he could understand that sometimes there were no good choices, or even right choices.

But there wasn't time for handholding and making people feel better. She needed the answers she needed— and she needed them at once. "NovaSpot Control, we are very much on the clock. Can you now advise as to earliest possible time we can begin the Final Ignition Sequence?"

"Stand by one more minute," the controller said. Before the mike cut off, Drayax could hear muffled voices for a moment, the sound of a hurried and heated conference. In far less than a minute, the controller came back on-line. "Project Director, this is NovaSpot Control. We'll need a few more minutes to give you an absolutely precise figure, but if we scratch two programmed holds we don't expect to need at this point, we can press ahead to minus three minutes in our countdown, and get to minus three as of approximately 16:08. We can hold at minus three for at least twelve hours, so we've got a lot of flexibility at that moment. That gives us first possible Ignition start as of 16:11 hours, assuming three to four minutes' notice." There was another moment's silence, then the voice came back. "We here would like to emphasize that is an estimate based on purely *technical* grounds. We still urge delay until 16:43:05 hours and Comfort eclipsing for Alloy if at all possible."

Drayax allowed herself a sigh of relief. That was as close to a "yes" as she was ever going to get. "Thank you, NovaSpot Control. You are ordered to scratch unneeded holds, press ahead to minus three minutes, and hold at that point in your count. I promise to do everything I can to hold off until eclipse for Alloy. Project Director out."

She cut her mike and stared at screens full of information she no longer had the will to read. That promise to do everything she could would be an easy one to keep; there was as near nothing as could be that *anyone* could do. Everything, *everything,* was on the shoulders of the well-intentioned, far-too-young, hopelessly inexperienced team at Groundside Power Reception.

Berana Drayax hoped to hell they didn't have time to think a great deal about how much was up to them.

Chapter Ten

THE LEGACY OF RUFDROP

"All right, then," Villjae asked. "Have we got it straight?"
This time the chorus of agreement was far stronger and
more confident. Going through the procedure two or
three times had helped, even if all they were doing was
pantomiming, holding their fingers over the buttons and
pretending to push them. "Good," he said. "Because the
next time is for real. Curthaus—are you ready down
there?"

"Absolutely. Just tell me when to do it."

Villajae glanced over at Beseda. She shrugged. "Now
would be about right," she said.

Villjae shrugged. That was about as direct as Beseda
was likely to be on that or any other subject. "So let's do
it. All right, everybody. Be ready on my mark. Get ready.
Get set. Curthaus, start countdown on my mark. Mark!"

"Minus *Ten*—nine—"

Villjae felt a cold sweat pop up on his forehead and
instantly wished that he had told Curthaus to do a
countdown from five instead. You needed the countdown to get people focused, to get them into the rhythm
of the sequence, but starting from ten just gave everyone
more time to get nervous, distracted—

Distracted! Villjae blinked and came back to himself.
They were trying to save the world, and he was letting
his mind wander. How much of the countdown had he
tuned out on? Was it too late already? Had he missed—

"Five—four—three—"

No, it was all right. He'd only missed a few seconds. But it was amazing how fast your thoughts moved when you were panicking. *Stay on it. Stay focused.*

"Two—one—ZERO!—Breaker open—plus *one*—"

"Console off!" four voices shouted in unison.

"Two—"

"Console one on!" Beseda called out.

"Three—"

"Subroutine running—complete!" Ballsto called out.

"Restart confirmed!" said Beseda, almost at the same moment.

"Four—half—breaker closed!"

"I see a normal comm loop between the aiming and pointing systems," Beseda announced. Everyone—everyone but Beseda and Villjae—cheered. Beseda just sat there calmly, without so much as a smile, and Villjae frankly stared at her. *Not that there was a normal loop,* Villjae thought. *That she saw one.* There was something just a trifle creepy about the way everything turned oracular around her. Villjae blinked and came back to the moment. *You're drifting too much,* he told himself. *Too long with not enough sleep. Which is just too bad, because you need to hang in there a while longer. The job's on you now.*

"All right, all right," he said. "Let's settle it down. I still have to steer this damn thing." He checked his displays and saw that Beseda had somehow found the time to fiddle with the presentation. The numeric display was still there, but now, alongside it, was a multicolor symbol-logic display. The actual position track showed in an unpleasant throbbing yellow, while the optimum track appeared in a steady line of pleasing blue. The position set by the hand-controller feedback was marked by crosshairs, at present locked on to the front end of the actual position track. Villjae's job was to move the crosshairs over to the optimum track, but to do it by moving them slowly and gently enough so as not to stress already overheated and overworked hardware to the breaking point.

There had been no time to work in any sort of buffering or overload safeties into the manual system. Yank down hard on the controller, and all the receptors in the Array would attempt to move just as hard and fast—and likely burn out and jam their positioning motors in the process.

He confirmed that the track-and-feedback system was reporting normally, reset his right hand's grip in the controller, and reached for the hand-controller's sync button. The sync button took whatever control coordinates the hand-controller was putting out and passed them on to the aiming system.

The button had a safety cover over it, of ancient and simple design. It was spring-loaded, so it could either snap open or snap shut, but would not stay in any intermediate position. Villjae flipped the cover up, pressed the button—and realized the mistake he had made, they had all made, a split second too late. A split second after that, the safety spontaneously snapped itself shut, mashing down on Villjae's left index finger, in effect catching it in a miniature vise.

He cursed vigorously, but resisted the temptation to pull his finger out. He had realized, a heartbeat after he had done it, that he dared not release that button at all. It was a momentary-contact switch, the sort that went on when you pushed it, and went off as soon as it was released. It was the right sort of switch for the controller's original purpose. It had been designed as test equipment, to impose an aiming error on the Array and see how well and quickly it corrected itself. Use the hand-controller, move the crosshairs to where you wanted to start the simulated error correction, mash down the button to blip the data to the system, and release the controller.

But to let go of the button now, even for an instant, would be to cut off the continuous two-way flow of aiming and pointing data, possibly scrambling it in some unforeseen way, sending a truncated data packet the system would misinterpret, and then—then the stars alone knew. Not worth risking it. Just as his right hand would have to stay on the controller, and just as he dared not take his eyes off the tracking display, he would have to keep his left index finger on that button for the remainder of the run.

"For star's sake, someone get that safety cover off my finger."

Bosley was there in an instant, and flipped the cover back. "Thank you," Villjae said gratefully. "Damn, but that hurts. Now get some heavy adhesive tape and strap that cover open, or find a pair of pliers and pull it off the board."

"You can't take your finger off," Beseda said, looking down at him with her owlish eyes.

Villjae could not quite tell if her words were an observation, a question, a command—or maybe even a curse. Having Beseda around had made spending the last thirty-six straight hours awake just that little bit more surreal. He promised himself to spend less time with her in future. "You're right," he said. "We forgot what kind of switch was under that safety cover. I don't dare take either hand off the controls."

"Might as well use them, then," Beseda replied.

"Huh? Oh, right." Villjae had been concentrating so hard on not perturbing the pointing system, he had almost forgotten the whole point was to make things move. But how hard and how fast could he move? He needed some sort of feedback.

"Bosley, Beseda, somebody. We still have console three live. Use it to bring up a general average strain meter reading on the Array, and rig some sort of way to get that display to where I can see it."

"Ah, okay," said Bosley. "Gimme about five minutes to rig it."

"Make it three," Villjae said. "Meantime, I'm going to work without it. We've got to get started." With infinite care, he pulled gently back on the hand-controller, and watched the screen as the crosshairs drifted slowly, oh so slowly, toward the blue optimum line, pulling the throbbing yellow line along with it. It was working. It was actually working. He glanced at the power accumulation display and was delighted to see the rate line twitching up by just a trifle. Not only was manual control working, it was doing what it should. More power was getting to where they needed it.

In more than three minutes, but far less than five, Bosley propped up yet another repeater-configured data-pad on the top ledge of console one, where Villjae could see it easily. Villjae was further pleased to see that the strain meter levels were well within tolerance. He could move a lot faster toward where he needed to go. Still moving with great care, he pulled the hand-controller back just a little more. The crosshairs sped up their motion toward the optimum line. Villjae watched his other gauges. The power absorption rate climbed noticeably higher, but the strain meter reading barely moved at all. Much sooner than he would have expected, he was able to bring the throbbing yellow line over the steady blue— and was rewarded with a lovely glowing green when the two merged.

It was working. It was *going* to work. Assuming he could keep his finger on the button.

Villjae breathed a sigh of relief. "Beseda, get the Project Director on comm. Tell her we have achieved manual control and significantly improved power input. And, ah—Bosley—could you scratch my nose?"

Berana Drayax was glad to receive the news, but by the time she received it, she scarcely needed it. The incoming telemetry was telling her everything she needed or wanted to know. They were getting more power—maybe not enough more to make everyone happy, but enough to at least make Ignition possible—and maybe enough to keep them from having to choose which people to kill. That was more than enough to put a smile on the face of the Project Director, at least for the moment.

She flipped on her comm. "This is Project Director for NovaSpot Control and Temporal Confinement. Request you watch the numbers coming in from Ground-side Power and update your time and power estimates based on new data. PD out."

It was *her* turn to send the good news that the recipients already knew from the displays. It made for a nice change from what she'd mostly been doing so far.

Maybe, just maybe, they were going to pull this thing out after all.

Curthaus Spar wandered up the stairs from the lower level. It had been a hell of a long day, and they'd all been sweating the work like mad things. But now even his console had been darkened, shut down altogether. With all the weirdgear Villjae and Beseda had strung together, there wasn't even room for him to go in and *sit* at his console. So he was out of a job, for the moment. Fine with him. He was dead tired. He deserved—they all deserved—to get some *rest*. Maybe he could find some dark corner, maybe fish one of the cots out of the back storeroom, unfold it and get some—

"Curthaus! Good!" It was a voice from behind his back. "Glad to see you. I need you on something."

Curthaus knew without turning around. It was Villjae, of course. And it was impossible to say no to Villjae. The man worked harder and longer than anyone. He'd saved the day by hacking together the manual system—and now he was literally stuck with it, forced to stay on that console for fear of cutting the links if he twitched. Curthaus forced a smile on his face and turned to face the boss—and the music.

"Yeah, Villjae?" he asked, walking over to stand over the hackwired remains of console one. "What have you got?"

"Power leaks," Villjae said without looking up from his screens. "We're still getting way more drain from the stored power than we should be. I was sitting here thinking: The auto aim-point system had so many bugs in it they were masking each other. We were looking for one big problem. We didn't find out we had twelve little ones until we shut down the whole thing. That gave me an idea on the power leak side. Start cutting power. Any system we don't need right now—shut it down. Simplify the power net. See if you can clear out enough things that are superfluous right now that you're able to spot the mistakes, the stuff that shouldn't be drawing at all."

"What don't we need right now?" Curthaus asked.

Villjae shrugged. "Lights and vents to the lower level. Hell, cut back our cooling up here—we can sweat for an hour if we have to. Backup systems for jobs we've done. Cut all power consoles we pulled out of the loop. Get creative—but be careful you don't shut down the stuff we do need—"

"Like *your* console. Got it. Can I borrow Bosley? He's good at this kind of stunt. Probably be safer if we double up and watch each other for mistakes."

"I was just about to volunteer him for you," Villjae said with a grin, and nodded back and toward the right. "I think he's sort of passed out over there. Give him a poke and get to it."

Curthaus found Bosley right where Villjae's nod had said he would be—in the nice dark corner Curthaus had been planning to filch, racked out in the cot Curthaus had hoped to use. "Great minds think alike, I guess. I hope," he muttered to himself, and gave the side of the cot a poke with his kickboot.

"Ah! Huh? What?" Bosley sat bolt upright on the folding bed, nearly sending it toppling over.

Curthaus felt a certain dark pleasure, but also a twinge of guilt, in rousting Bosley—but if he couldn't rack down, why should Bosley? "Come on," he said. "Work to be done."

Unfortunately, whatever satisfaction Curthaus derived from waking Bosley was short-lived. The kid was the sort who woke up fast, and alert—and he *was* good at the sort of job they had drawn. Ten minutes after Curthaus had put his kickboot in, Bosley was doing scans of all the power buses, querying Curthaus as to what was all right to power down, and moving on to the next item almost before Curthaus could respond. Groundside Power was a big place, built to house many more people than were there at present. Just cutting out unneeded life support— without leaving those present choking in the dark—was a complicated enough job to keep them busy.

Then there were all sorts of other things—the landing field was powered up in case they needed to evac, which they didn't. Down went lights, radar, comm links, transit tunnel services.

Thanks to some crazy in project planning being too damn clever and not smart enough six months earlier, the operational plan called for the fabricator line for receptors to be kept at standby, just in case they needed to build more receptors *after* the SunSpot started beaming power. How the hell was anyone supposed to go up topside out of the bunker complex and hook up spare receptors without being incinerated? Down with the fab line. Two or three other examples added together were enough of a power drain to be borderline-significant even on the grand scale of the Groundside Power Array. Maybe enough to add two- or three-tenths of a percent—maybe even half a percent—to outputs. As close as they were cutting things, even that much might matter—a lot.

Curthaus was starting to realize how much they were still paying for that crash, months before, and, if he had nerve enough to speak ill of the dead, still paying for drawing Designer Rufdrop as their fearless leader, way back when.

He was starting to wish Rufdrop had done some better operational thinking before he checked out. The station design as a whole was first-level, lots of big machines pointed at one big job. But no one had really sat down and figured out how the machines should fit together, how they ought to *run*.

If there had been time before Ignition Day just to sit down and run through the power process in detail, that would have been *something*. If Rufdrop had just managed to turn down even one of his "politically essential" cocktail parties and seminars and publicity events, he could have held that power management meeting he had always been promising. They might have had a chance to catch some of the worst errors.

"Hey, ah, Curthaus—this one's really off chart."

"What have you got there?" he asked. He stood up and looked over Bosley's shoulder at the screen he was working.

"That," said Bosley, pointing. "Should the guide path preheater still be running?"

"The *what*?"

"The guide path pre—"

"Yeah, I heard you. I just couldn't believe it's on the screen." The guide path had been made of the most thermal-shock resistant material available for the job—so naturally some committee had started worrying about protecting it from thermal shock. Every test had shown the path would be able to go from subzero to temps high enough to boil lead without any problem, but even so, the decision was taken to run enormous electric resistance coils down its length to bring it up closer to operating temperature before the beam from the SunSpot struck it, thus protecting it from the thermal shock that wouldn't affect it in the first place.

"Well," Bosley went on, "do you think it should be running now?"

"Of *course* it shouldn't be running. We don't need the guide path anymore. I don't know if we *ever* needed it preheated, but we sure don't need it *now*. How many watts is it pulling, anyway?"

Bosley pointed to a number on the screen, and Curthaus cursed eloquently, using a few words and phrases that Bosley probably didn't even understand. "That's the whole mud-sucking power deficit right *there*! If *that* had been powered down when it should have been, if it had never been powered *up,* then we'd be in power surplus right now!"

"Should I shut it down now?" Bosley reached casually for the controls.

"No! Not yet. And not all at once. The power surge could trip every breaker in the system. We need to figure out where that power's being routed to and from and make sure we cut it gracefully. And this is such a honking *huge* mistake we gotta check and make sure it isn't on *purpose* for some crazy reason." He sat down in the seat next to Bosley. "You keep scanning for other possible power-downs. I'll put the preheater thing in work."

Ninety seconds later, he had a better trace on the

power routing. The preheating system was designed to work off its own quite substantial auxiliary power store, charged off the local grid. But somehow, the preheater system had read its own normal shutdown as an emergency cutoff, and done an autoshunt off main bus C to maintain operations. And bus C was bridged straight through to the main power store.

The main consoles would show no power to the preheaters, because they were watching drains from the preheaters' own power store. And since the cutoff to the heaters happened just as the main SunSpot beam was starting to dump power to the Array, the power leak would be there from the first go. *That* made it look like a fault in the power store's ability to retain a charge, not a power drain. The leak couldn't have done a better job camouflaging itself if it had been designed to do it.

"Curthaus," Bosley asked, "did you find anything?"

"Yeah. A hulking huge damned bloody *mess,*" Curthaus growled. "Bosley, you might have just saved the world. I gotta go run this by Villjae, just in case, but he's *gotta* say this is a screwup. *Can't* be on purpose. Meantime, you start working out some way to turn those heaters off gently so we don't punch an overload and blow every circuit in the joint."

Villjae's arms were aching. His right hand felt as if it had been welded to the controller. His left hand felt as if the welding tech had decided to keep the job simple and had just used a hammer and nail to attach Villjae's index finger to the button. But it was the ache between his shoulder blades that had his attention. It was a throbbing knot, a silent shriek of straight-ahead pain that just kept going and going.

He was doing his best to focus on the aim-and-point system, struggling to keep the crosshairs where they should be, keep the green line from splitting off into yellow and blue, but it was far from easy. He longed to dedicate his whole attention to the thought of *moving* again, to revel in the mad impossible fantasy of taking his hands and fingers off the controls. To scratch his own nose, to rub his eye, or to reach for a drink seemed the very heights of hedonistic delight, and the very depths of betrayal. *Sure, go ahead. Take your finger off the button. Your shoulders will stop aching—but maybe the whole aim-point system will crash, they'll have to abort Ignition, and you'll doom everyone in the whole damned system. But so what? Your finger won't be sore.*

He blinked, trying to bring the data screens back into some sort of focus. It was a constant struggle to keep alert, to keep his mind from drifting, to keep his eyes where they needed to be. He didn't dare send Beseda for more coffee, or for anything else that might help keep him awake. Matters regarding liquids were critical enough as it was. He had already decided that if it came down to a choice between his dignity and the fate of humanity in the Solacian star system, then dignity would lose. If the price of keeping his finger on that button was a puddle under his chair, so be it. But so far things hadn't gotten quite to that point. So far.

He blinked, shifted in his seat as much as he dared, and tried to concentrate on his work. After a moment, he became aware that there was someone—Curthaus—standing in front of his console. He didn't dare shift his eyes far enough from the screens to look up, so he addressed Curthaus's blue-checked shirt instead. "Curthaus!" he said, trying to sound cheerful. "What have you got for me?"

"A pie in the face. But maybe a good-news pie. You know anything about why the guide path preheaters are still running at full power?"

That was enough to get his attention, almost enough to pull his eyes off the screens for half a moment. "*What* did you say?"

"The preheaters are still running full blast. It's so crazy I wanted to check with you before I pulled the plug, but it's got to be unintentional. It looks like the breaker sequence was set wrong, and the heaters have been drawing bus C power since the millisecond the Array started drawing power."

"Bus C! But that means—"

"We just found our power leak. Is there some completely bizarre reason this is on purpose?"

"No way. Just more of the same," Villjae said bitterly. "More top-flight project planning from beyond the grave, that's all." He shook his head.

"Scary, isn't it? I wonder if we'd be better off right now if Rufdrop had lived."

"Worse off," Villjae said. It was uncharitable of him, but the ache at the base of his neck was throbbing worse than ever. "We'd have to tiptoe around his ego for half an hour on every one of these glitches. He'd have to make sure we all understood it wasn't *his* fault—"

"And we'd all have to pretend we didn't know that it *was* his fault—"

"Before we could get anything done. Go shut the damn heaters down—without blowing a surge through the whole storage system."

"Bosley's working on that side of it now," Curthaus said. "I tell you, I keep wishing this was that all-out simulation we never got. Think how slick this thing would have run if we knew all this crap before we started."

"It's crossed my mind," Villjae said with a smile. "Go get started on that power-down. And find Beseda or someone, and have them relay to Drayax what you two found."

"Will do. Except Bosley found it. Not me."

"Good on you, Curt. He'll get the credit—but we *all* found it," Villjae said. "The same way we all missed preventing it before it happened."

"Ouch. Right. Okay." Suddenly it was a quiet, even private, moment, a pause before the next big rush. Curthaus glanced at the wall chrono and let out a sigh. "Not much longer," he said.

"Yeah," said Villjae as a stabbing pain worked its way up his motionless left arm. "Not much longer. Just forever."

A few minutes later, the power accumulator displays twitched and quivered, then moved smoothly, gently, upward, coming to rest dead center in the middle of the green zone, exactly on the numbers they should have been showing all along. Thirty-five minutes from the predicted end of run, all the inputs and levels were finally where they were supposed to be. All the numbers except the one that mattered most. Total stored power was still only at 94.2 percent. *It will have to be enough,* Villjae told himself. It *would* be enough. After all they had been through, it was inconceivable that a miserable 5 or 6 percent power deficit would be enough to stop them. They were too close to give up, even if what they had wasn't enough.

And that's the whole problem, Villjae realized with a start. It was going forward even when they weren't ready that had got them into this mess. The pressure to go for it, to be ready by Ignition Day, had bulldozed all of them into reaching too much, stretching the possible too far. The whole history of Solace was the story of doing it now and fast, instead of later and right. It had come close to killing them all today—and it still might do them in if some other section had even half the problems that Groundside Power had fallen into.

Next time—if they survived long enough for next time to arrive—they might not be so lucky.

"Dammit, my back and arm hurt," he growled.

Thirty-five minutes. That span of time seemed to stretch and compress for Villjae. He would catch himself losing concentration again and force himself to focus on the displays and the hand-controller—and the ache between his shoulder blades. Then he would blink, look at the time display, and discover that five minutes, eight minutes—or maybe no time at all—had passed. *But thirty-five was just an estimate,* he would remind himself. *We don't really know how steep a view-angle the Reception Array will accept.*

And then he would try to keep himself alert by working out the geometry of the situation in his head. He played with the numbers, assuming the receptors lost efficiency at this rate or that rate, that the manual control would or would not allow a steeper point-angle than all the safeties on the automatics would allow.

He was trying to keep alert, keep focused, keep—
don't let your finger slip! Villjae was seriously starting to
wonder if they'd have to amputate his left index finger
after the job was over.

Part of his mind knew that was ridiculous, that the
worst he might have would be a sore finger, and besides,
they'd stopped amputating somewhere back in the near-
ancient period; but the melodrama of the idea appealed
to part of his psyche. He imagined himself with a look of
noble suffering on his face, the admiring whispers behind him as passersby told each other of his heroic sacri-
fice—which was going to be a whole hell of a lot less
heroic-sounding if it was a burst bladder instead of a
chopped-off finger. He shifted on his chair again and
checked the time. Twenty-nine minutes left.

The rest of the team was gradually assembling in the
main control room. Whatever jobs they had been doing
were all completed. It suddenly dawned on Villjae that the
Groundside Power Reception Array had been the whole
focus of his existence, all that he had worked on, thought
about, or related to, for the last two years of his life. In—
what?—twenty-four minutes now—all that would be
gone. He couldn't quite imagine what he was going to do
next, aside from taking a shower and sleeping for a long,
long time. He risked a glance up at the others in the room.

He noticed with a start that everyone else was looking
at him. No, not at him—at the work he was doing. All of
what *they* had done came down to what *he* was doing, to
his hand holding steady on the control, to keeping his finger jammed down on that damned-fool button. How did
so much importance come down on doing so little?

If he *could* do it at all. The shooting pain in his left
arm was more or less continuous by then. And his damn
finger hurt so much that he was starting to think they
wouldn't have to worry about amputation. The damn
thing would fall off by itself.

"This is the voice of Ignition Control. We are coming up
on five minutes until the predicted cutoff for power
reception at Groundside Power. Earlier concerns about

accumulated power levels have now eased significantly. We are currently showing 96.7 percent of predicted power accumulation, well within the limits set for safe operation."

The hell you say, thought Neshobe Kalzant, staring daggers at the announcer. Ever since it had become clear 100 percent wasn't going to happen, they'd been getting an unending stream of assurances that whatever amount of power they happened to have at that moment was going to be enough. As if anyone knew what the minimum levels for "safe" operation were.

At least the voice, too, was starting to look worn-out and disheveled. The stress and strain of the day showed on his face, if not in his words.

Neshobe looked down at the main level of the big control room. Drayax was the face to look at to learn what was really going on. The Project Director's ability—or perhaps merely her willingness—to conceal her feelings had fallen by the wayside in the past hour or so. *Maybe she figures it doesn't matter anymore, one way or the other,* Neshobe thought. *Or maybe she is just too tired to give a damn anymore.* Whatever the reason, it had gradually become possible to learn something by watching her. And it looked as if the news was just possibly, provisionally good. Given how bad things had looked not so long before, that had to rate somewhere near a miracle.

For Berana Drayax, at the moment the power accumulator leak ended, life began again. In that moment, when the power they needed stopped draining away, the use-it-or-lose-it dilemma was suddenly gone. She would not have to choose between going early or not at all, choose between exterminating the habitats on Alloy now or allowing the collapse of everything in the Solacian system later. She did not have to choose whom to kill. She could wait until Comfort eclipsed for Alloy, and harm no one by so doing. Never had she received a greater gift.

Now things were simpler, without any such horrible moral choice hanging over mere questions of engineering. They had done their best. Either Ignition would work, or it would not. Either the temporal confinement would work, and hold together long enough, or it would not.

Any number of things could still go wrong, and people, lots of people, could die. But if they did, they would do so because Drayax and the Ignition Project had tried and failed to save them, not because they were forced into a deliberate choice to kill.

"This is Project Director to all controllers," she said into her comm unit. "Here is an update of current status. SunSpot is getting close to the horizon as seen from Groundside Power. We're already seeing substantial drop-off in power input as the angle on SunSpot starts to lengthen and Array panels start casting shadows on each other. Obviously, that was as expected.

"Groundside Power is going to try and stretch their run as far as they can on manual, but we don't know if that's going to work. So we are at present looking at end of power accumulation in approx five minutes, nominal cutoff at 16:31:35. Groundside Power will attempt to continue after that time, and will advise when they have done all they could.

"While their power storage leak seems to be solved, it still seems wise to go for Ignition as soon as possible. We are therefore moving NovaSpot Ignition up to 16:43:05, the first moment allowed under the standard safety rules. NovaSpot is currently holding at minus three minutes. Last poll of all controllers showed all systems ready for Ignition at that time. This is Project Director out."

"Three minutes past nominal," Bosley announced, as if no one else were watching the clock.

Villjae was the only one *not* watching it, but he didn't need to be told either. He was fully aware of every second beyond nominal cutoff. He had known it wasn't the real, absolute, definite cutoff all along, of course, but it had been the measure he had used to keep himself going. But the moment had come and gone, and nothing changed. There was still power they could get, and they had to get all they could. That was all that mattered.

Beseda was working up a variant on standard receptor-angle management, seeing if she couldn't get the easternmost receptors at least somewhat out of the shadows of the westernmost. The gimmick might be good enough to draw a few thousand more amps. If stretching it another three minutes, four minutes, five minutes, bought them another half second of shielding, then maybe that half second would be just enough to save one more life.

"Four minutes past nominal." said Bosley. "We're really getting an input decline now. Losing the angle."

Villjae nodded. Both his arms felt as if they had turned to stone, and the stone had turned to fire. But that didn't matter. They were getting it done. Done.

"Four minutes thirty. Okay, Villjae. We're seeing the tail-end curve signature."

"All right," Villjae said. That had shown up in every simulation they had managed to run. It was a sure sign that the Array had reached its maximum usable look-angle.

"Four minutes forty-five." A pause. "Five minutes. Five minutes five, six—showing final tail-off—seven seconds—and we're under minimum threshold. That's it. Power it down."

Done, Villjae told himself. *Done.* The others cheered and applauded, but somehow, even though he was aware of it, he didn't really hear them.

He lifted his finger off the button and let go of the controller. He had imagined this moment a thousand times in the last hour or two—his moment of triumph, of release, of victory—and now there it was, and he was simply too tired to feel much of anything about it. He just wanted to sit there, close his eyes, and feel the weight lift off his shoulders. "Give me a minute," he said to the others, but he spoke so quietly he could barely hear himself. "Just a minute, then I'll be okay."

The job was done.

It was time for great things to start.

Chapter Eleven

TO LIGHT A SINGLE CANDLE

"Once we clear the three-minute hold, there's nothing that can stop Ignition," said NovaSpot Control. "You understand that, TC, right?"

Drayax sighed as she listened to this latest debate. She was weary to her bones—and *now* they had to come up with something new to hash over.

"We copy, NovaSpot," Temporal Confinement replied. "But our power projections tell us we can't afford to run three spare minutes of confinement just to be sure we're covered. Safer for us just to start our power-up sequence at minus thirty seconds, just before NovaSpot Ignition. It should take no more than twenty seconds to go from a cold start to establishing the field. That gives us a solid ten seconds of full coverage before Ignition."

"But if your field *doesn't* form, Greenhouse will be incinerated."

"We show 99.99 plus certainty the field *will* form properly, NovaSpot. But with the power available, we show only 90 percent certainty that we'll have sufficient power to provide full shielding during the danger period. If we burn up three or four extra minutes of shielding on the front end, certainty drops to 75 percent. That's one in four that the shield will fail while you're still pumping hard radiation at us."

"But if it *does* fail to form—"

At long last, Drayax lost her patience. There was

letting your subordinates talk through issues and there was pointless bickering. And it was easy to see the heavy hand of Chief Engineer Haress Bevard pushing everyone into this latest spat. "This is Project Director Drayax," she said, deliberately adding her name to the title, in hopes of adding that little bit more authority. "NovaSpot Control, TC Control. This is Project Director. We have to move on. Each of you has reported to me on what you believe is the best way for your section to proceed to Ignition. I don't think I need remind either of you that we don't have the luxury of unlimited time for discussion." *Or would that be a curse?* she asked herself. "I have to make the decision, and I have to make it *now*. So we're going to run NovaSpot the way NovaSpot wants it run—and we're going to do the same for Temporal Confinement." In other words, she was letting Temporal Confinement win—but she had phrased the ruling so it sounded like a tie. She could do that much to keep Bevard more or less happy. "Please confirm on that point."

"We copy," said the cheerful voice of Temporal Confinement. *They* knew they had won the point.

After a slightly too-long pause, NovaSpot Control checked in, in far-less-happy tones. "Received and understood, PD."

"Good." Perhaps it had dawned on Bevard that, short of refusing to start NovaSpot's Final Ignition Sequence, there was nothing he could do, anyway. And this close to time, it was hard to imagine his refusing to play with the biggest, loudest toy he had ever had, or ever would have.

"It's now 16:35:00, *mark*. We go in eight minutes. NovaSpot, commence Final Sequence at 16:40:05, for Ignition at 16:43:05. Temporal Confinement, initiate temporal field at 16:42:35—and we'll see you on the other side."

"And we'll be looking younger than all of you, PD. Temporal Confinement out."

Drayax had to smile at that. TC Control was literally correct: During the eighteen or so hours of external time it would take to get NovaSpot's radiation output under control, time would all but stop *inside* the confinement. Only a few minutes would pass. Temporal Confinement was also eager to play with its new toy.

The eagerness was in her, as well. They were close, so very close. "Very well, TC Control. But just remember, those of us out here will get a chance to catch up on our sleep." She switched her comm to the all-points link, and spoke more formally. "This is Project Director Drayax. We are go for Ignition at 16:43:05. All stations reporting go for Ignition in approximately seven minutes. All stations, recheck all radiation protection procedures and secure for Ignition."

Villjae had promised himself something a long time ago, and now he was going to make it come true. He was going to see it—and see it by himself. Curthaus and Beseda and Bosley and the others were nice enough folk, but Curthaus was too flip, Bosley too shy and awkward, and Beseda just too damned weird to make a suitable companion at such a time. None of the other members of the team seemed any more suitable. Nothing wrong with any of them, but they weren't what he needed just then. He had had enough of being the levelheaded leader, of dealing with personalities, of being forced to be the reasonable one because everyone else was so strange. He wanted to experience the event itself, by itself—not experience the event while feeling the need to make conversation, not be distracted from it by the need to handle someone's delicate ego.

A quick trip to the refresher, a brisk wash-up in lieu of the shower that could come later, and a few stretching exercises, and he felt remarkably better. His arms, hands, and neck were still all sore, but not painful.

He was tempted to grab some sort of hand meal out of the dispensing machines, but he wasn't absolutely sure there was even time for that. Not with everyone else likely to be hungry and heading for the dispensers at the same time. He wasn't going to risk missing a spectacle his grandchildren would likely want to hear about—and *would* hear about, from him, whether they liked it or not—just because there was a line at the extruder.

No. Best to get to where he needed to be, fast. In aid of that, days before, he had written a quick little systems command for the base-control ArtInt and stored it in his datapad. He pulled it and ran it. Then he headed, not for the main lift, but the auxiliary service lift, farther on down the corridor. The lift car was waiting for him, naturally. He punched in the special access code that made sure it wouldn't leave without him, just in case someone else had the same bright idea.

The doors closed, and he rode the car up. There was something oddly pleasant about that ascent to the surface. It was private, it was quiet—and it *wasn't* special. Nothing about it would decide the fate of worlds or form a lifelong memory. It was his first ordinary moment in a long time. He rode up, massaging his left hand with his right, then his right arm with his left, trying to work the knots out, not worried about anything.

The door opened, and Villjae stepped out into the north construction operations center—a grand name for what had been built as a place to store and patch up the robots that had built the Array. The building system detected his presence, and dim yellow lights in the ceiling bloomed into halfhearted life. The ops center was a windowless, bunkerlike structure. Four cargo-sized airlocks lined the south side of the building. Broken-down machines hulked in the far corners. Roller-bots, built for the sole purpose of installing the receptors into the Array, were parked in neatly lined-up rows facing the airlocks. They were a little worn and scraped here and there, but otherwise perfectly serviceable. Except, of course, the job for which they had been made was over. Perhaps some use for them would be found. Or perhaps they were as useless as their bent and broken brethren in the corner.

Villjae crossed the room, threading his way through the bots, his feet crunching on the grit and gravel the bots had carried in on their wheel treads from the dead surface of Greenhouse. He reached a rickety metal staircase on the south side of the building and climbed three flights up. It felt good to use leg muscles that hadn't been exercised much in recent days. The stairway ended in the ceiling of the top floor. A steel-mesh hatch was set into the ceiling, and Villjae swung it open and climbed out to stand in the ops center's observation dome. He was careful to close the hatch after him. He hadn't come this far just to fall down a stairway.

The dome itself sat on a cylindrical base a bit over waist high. The dome that sat on the wall was hemispheric, a perfectly transparent clear plastic bubble about five meters across. Villjae looked south out over the strange and silent landscape. The huge bulk of Comfort loomed up over the western horizon, as it always did from this spot. Greenhouse's rotation was tidally locked relative to Comfort. Everything else in the sky might change, but Comfort would always be where it was.

It was cold, deathly cold, in the dome. Slightly warmer air was starting to bloom up through the mesh openings in the hatch, and the vent system had kicked in, drawing the cooler air down through smaller grilled openings around the edge of the dome, but it would be a long time indeed before the dome *seemed* warm. Outside the dome the land was airless, lifeless, cold, and forlorn, lit only by the gloomy long-shadowed light of Comfort.

The Array itself was about two kilometers away, affording some sort of safety margin between the ops center and the burning heat of the SunSpot's power beam. As the ops center had not been melted down to slag, apparently the safety margin was sufficient.

Villjae knew that the ferocious amount of power beamed down onto the Array surface had raised the surface temperature by at least several hundred degrees in the immediate vicinity of the Array. From where he stood, there was no visible sign of that heating. It still *looked* cold.

It was strange to see the Array at all. For all the endless hours he had spent working on it, Villjae had spent precious little time *looking* at it. There had been a sort of orientation hike, when Rufdrop had ordered the team into their pressure suits, walked the construction site, and watched the roller-bots bolting the receptor panels into position. Villjae had been fascinated by the tour and had always meant to go out again. But he had never again gotten closer than he was at that moment.

The blue-and-silver hexagonal panels that made up the Array were still angled over toward the west, as if still reaching for the last watts of power the SunSpot might offer, or perhaps seeking in vain after power to be drawn from Comfort. But the SunSpot had set, and Comfort offered virtually no power at the proper wavelengths. The Array had done its job and sat as useless as the roller-bots down below. Perhaps the panels could be salvaged and reused somehow, but they had been designed to draw energy from highly concentrated light beams. It seemed unlikely anyone would ever need their specialized capability again. *Not until NovaSpot dies a few hundred years from now, and we have to do all this again,* Villjae thought. He hoped they would manage to archive all the notes and procedures from this time out, so maybe those in the future could learn from present mistakes.

All of it over with, all of it no longer needed, all of it cooling down, shedding the last of the heat of the SunSpot's last powered pass. *All of it about as useful as me, right now.* Villjae knew he could find other work, that he would go on to other things—but it was hard to avoid a letdown after such an intense period of work came to such a sudden end.

But none of that was what he had come to see. Villjae pulled a pair of high-powered binoculars out of his pocket, turned them on, and hung the strap around his neck. It was going to be in the west, moving straight down, almost exactly through the centerline of Comfort's disk. It would be very dim, very hard to see—

There! He had spotted it. A tiny grey disk, just barely above the western horizon, trailing the SunSpot in the same orbit. The SunSpot had set for the last time as it had been. The NovaSpot was about to set—and would next be seen as it had never been.

It was very close to the horizon. On a world with any appreciable atmosphere, it would have been lost in the ground haze. He lifted the binoculars to his eyes, centered the grey disk in the view, and set the binocs to maximum tracking, stabilization, enlargement, and enhancement. Suddenly the little grey disk filled the view of the field glasses, standing out bright and clear against the dim bulk of Comfort. The image broke up just a trifle, and the enhancement routine put a little bit of fuzz and hash into the background, but that didn't matter. He was *seeing* it. Perhaps he would be the last man to see NovaSpot this way, as a dim grey dot floating quiet in the sky. Soon, very soon, it would look quite different indeed.

He watched through the binoculars until the NovaSpot touched the horizon, and kept watching as it slid quietly out of sight.

Villjae stood where he was, looked to the sky, and waited.

Neshobe Kalzant accepted instantly when Drayax conveyed an invitation to view the next phase from the command deck. She made her way down from the observation platform, followed by the aide who had brought the invitation. It was a very different Berana Drayax who welcomed her, compared to the poised, perfectly coiffed woman she had seen all those hours before.

"We're nearly there, Madame Executive," said Drayax with a weary smile. "I think we're going to make it. For a while, I was just about convinced we wouldn't."

"I was starting to worry myself," said Neshobe. "Your face was getting so unreadable that I almost didn't want to know why. Then I *could* read it—and I didn't want to."

"It's nearly time, Project Director," the aide said in a quiet, almost apologetic tone of voice.

"Good," said Drayax. "Let's get things started—then

let the next shift take over. They've had a hell of a long rest. I don't know why I assigned my shift team to take the whole pre-Ignition Sequence."

"I do," said Neshobe, and nodded toward the big red button in the center of Drayax's terminal. The one button, the only button, that could start everything.

The smile faded away from Drayax's face. "You've seen through me, then."

"Why did you wire it that way?" Neshobe asked, although she thought she knew the answer.

"So no one will ever be able to wonder who did it," Drayax said. "For good or ill, no one will ever be able to say that it was miscommunications, or a software error, or some murky system failure like the ones that almost did us in at Groundside Power. Everyone needs to know that a human being had to push the button in order for Ignition to happen. The final choice has to be a *decision*—not the result of some algorithm that a committee of ArtInts has chewed over."

Neshobe nodded. She understood, better than most people would. It was important for people to know, really *know,* where responsibility lay. But Neshobe knew something else as well—that Drayax's ability to choose whether or not to push that button was in large part illusory. She had already made too many choices. Too much had been invested for it to be realistically possible to turn back.

If news came, that instant, that Ignition would certainly fail, then Drayax would have the courage to keep her finger off that button. But there was next to no chance of absolute knowledge about anything. It was far more likely Drayax would be confronted by some terrifying last-minute *maybe*—not new knowledge, but new doubt. Would she have the wisdom to choose quickly and correctly, and, if need be, the courage not to go?

Let's hope we don't have to find out, Neshobe thought. She looked Drayax in the eye. Drayax nodded, and it was hard for Neshobe to avoid thinking she had read the same thought in the other's mind.

"How close are we?" Neshobe asked, not quite

knowing where to look on Drayax's display for the main countdown.

Drayax smiled. "Quite close. I'd estimate we'll be ready to try for Ignition in about six months." Then she pointed to one of a half dozen countdown displays running on her board. "But we've got just about three minutes and twenty seconds until that goes to zero, and I have to push that button. That will send the final command to start the Ignition Sequence. And precisely three minutes after *that,* all hell breaks loose. Nothing will be able to stop it."

Neshobe nodded, and her throat suddenly felt very dry. Her stomach knotted up. If they had made a mistake, if there was something they had missed—suppose the NovaSpot somehow consumed all its fusion mass at once, a three-hundred-year supply going up in a flash? Would even the sheltering bulk of Comfort be enough to protect them? Suppose nothing at all happened? Suppose the NovaSpot just *sat* there in orbit, an unexploded bomb that didn't go off as planned—but still might?

"This is the voice of Ignition Control. We are coming up *mark* two minutes and counting until start of the final three-minute activation sequence. Now coming up on one minute and forty-five seconds in the count to—"

"*Turn that damn thing off,*" Drayax said to her aide. "This is supposed to be the one place in the Solace system you *can't* hear that man."

The sound shield masking sound from the upper level came back on, and the voice of the Voice cut out in midword. Somehow, the tension in the control center seemed to ease as well. Neshobe smiled. Maybe that was the whole idea. If the voice of Ignition Control was irritating enough, it would keep your mind off everything else.

Now there was silence, and nothing to do but watch the clock. Two minutes. Ninety seconds. Neshobe Kalzant had been present at countdowns beyond counting. Spacecraft launches, docking sequences, demolitions, and all sorts of other highly important technical events. Always the chant began, everyone counting down together, as time drew to a close, and everyone watched the clock.

But somehow, this one was different. Maybe it was that someone should have started the chant days ago, years ago. A minute or two was not long enough. They stood in silence and watched the numbers fade away.

Berana Drayax stepped closer to her control panel, flexed her right hand, and flipped open the safety cover on the big red button. Then she pulled her hand back, unwilling to have any part of her close to that button before time.

But it nearly *was* time. Neshobe resisted the urge to count down, to say the numbers. Somehow it was important that it all happen in silence.

The moment came. Drayax's finger reached out and stabbed down hard on the button, holding it down for what seemed a long time, but must have been only a second or two. A green light came on over the button, and she lifted her finger off it. Drayax looked at Neshobe, then turned to look at the roomful of people watching her.

"Very well," she said in a quiet voice that carried to every corner of the compartment. "Let's see what happens next."

Now she is where I have been, Neshobe thought. *Between the order and execution, between choice and consequence.* Neshobe had spent years in between saying yes to NovaSpot and the explosion that was about to happen. Now, at last, Drayax was there too. There was that strange old word—*schadenfreude*—"pleasure in the misfortune of others." *What sort of people would need to invent that word?* Neshobe wondered. But it didn't matter. She took no pleasure in the moment—only empathy. She knew, better than anyone else, what this time must be like for Berana Drayax.

"Coming up on ninety seconds," someone said, breaking the silence at last. "They start forming the temporal confinement in one minute."

"Or trying to," said another voice, speaking in much lower tones.

And suppose the confinement *didn't* form, and NovaSpot *did* ignite? *"Nothing will be able to stop it."* It was hard not to hear those words again. Without the confinement to protect it, "nothing" was what would be left of the surface of Greenhouse. Everything would be incinerated.

The next sixty seconds seemed to rocket past. "Nova-Spot Control reports nominal Final Ignition Sequence so far," said one of the voices behind her.

"Coming up on Temporal Confinement Initiation," said the other. "Make it work, dammit."

Neshobe turned her attention to the big display screen, showing Greenhouse as seen from *Lodestar VII*. It hung in darkness, eclipsed for the sun by Comfort, and lit only by the dim, watery light reflected off the nightside of the gas giant. Probably even the murky view they had required image enhancement. A small, pock-marked world, thinly peopled, lightly dotted with habitat domes. And carrying all of their futures.

"Thirty seconds to Ignition. Temporal Confinement Initiation—now!"

But nothing happened. A thick, hard boot of fear kicked Neshobe in the gut, and her fists clenched tight. *We are all going to die.*

"It takes twenty seconds!" Drayax said. "Not yet. The confinement field should cut in about ten seconds before "

But suddenly Greenhouse wasn't there anymore. A perfect black disk, a hole neatly punched out of the sky, was there instead. It happened too quickly to see, all at once, with no intermediate phase. Neshobe knew that it was a sphere of black, and not a disk, but her eyes told her differently. All the visual cues said it was a perfectly flat disk. There was no limb-darkening, no highlighting or shading, to give the utter darkness any sense of three-dimensionality. It was only the absence of stars that defined the hole, the dot, the disk, the sphere, where Greenhouse had been.

Where Greenhouse still is, Neshobe reminded herself.

Still there, and safe inside that time-blocking, redshifting sphere.

There were muffled shouts of surprise, and a hesitant cheer or two, but there was hardly time to react. The main screen switched to another view, from the farside of Greenhouse, centered on two dim dots of light. The closer one was SunSpot, guttering down to nothing, the last of its energies spent, its tight power beam defocused, casting hardly any light at all. But next to it, just starting to glow, just starting to flare up into light and power— there was NovaSpot, seconds, mere seconds away from its grand destiny—or the doom of them all.

They watched, and waited, for those final seconds to die. And then—

A flare of light, and Fire and Glory shone out upon the face of the deep.

Chapter Twelve

NEW WORLDS AND OLD WAYS

That part, Villjae did not see. From where he stood, in less time than the blink of an eye, the universe simply turned utterly dark. The sky vanished, the stars vanished, Comfort vanished. The confinement field had come alive, drawing on the power that his team had captured.

The darkness was all but absolute. The only light remaining was the glow coming up from the stairway and the interior of the dome, and even that was so dim it took his eyes several seconds to adjust enough to detect it. But for that light from below, he would have had no vision at all. He was suddenly glad that he had closed the steel-mesh hatch. In darkness this complete, it would be easy to become disoriented. The fear of falling down the stairs could have been enough to paralyze him. Knowing that he *had* closed it—or at least fairly sure he had closed it—he wasn't afraid—or all that afraid—to shift his stance, or turn around.

He had expected the darkness, of course, but somehow, he had not expected it to be so complete. There should have been guide running lights around the Array, safety beacons here and there—but then he remembered. He himself had ordered them all shut down to save power.

There was something altogether unnerving about looking out into so open a blackness. There was nothing but a transparent dome between himself and the sky—

but no light at all showed from that sky. Absolute darkness reigned.

Time stands still, Villjae thought. *In the time it takes for me to think that thought, how many hours have passed?* He knew enough that it was all but impossible for there to be a clear answer to that question. The confinement field was variable in intensity, and it would take a little time for it to be throttled up to full power. They would begin at a temporal compression of about a thousand to one, then move higher as fast as possible, toward a maximum compression of at least a hundred thousand to one, and far higher if the power was there. Between the first beat of his heart and the second since the confinement came on, a few tens of seconds might have passed. Between the second and the third, a minute or two. If all went well, it would take several minutes, a half hour, an hour or more of outside time for each subsequent beat of his heart.

By now, out there, the Ignition had begun—or not. The new sun was aborning, or had met with some terrible failure, or not worked at all. Strange. They were right next to the most powerful explosion ever touched off by humans in all history—and yet there was not the slightest clue that it had happened at all.

Villjae smiled. That was, after all, a good thing—and the very thing he had spent the last two years of his life ensuring.

But he would have liked to see it, all the same.

NovaSpot did not rival the local sun, Lodestar—it overwhelmed it, altogether. Everywhere that NovaSpot could be seen, it lit the sky in a new and brighter day—and yet, fortunately, precious few witnessed the spectacle directly.

The timing of Ignition had, of course, been chosen to keep as many as possible from seeing it. To see that star aborning was to die, roasted by the onslaught of hard radiation. Here and there in the wide expanse of the Solacian system were a few such luckless souls: those who heard all the warnings and ignored them, those who meant to get to shelter in time but failed to do so, those on urgent errands who took one risk too many, and even those who, incredibly, never got the word that Ignition was coming, despite the endless reporting, the endless broadcasts and alerts. These few did witness it, and died.

But all the rest were shielded by the mass of a planet or satellite, by Lodestar, by heavy radiation shielding. And nearly everyone watched through the remote cameras positioned everywhere that might afford a useful or interesting view. But the sight could be as fatal to lenses as to humans. The cameras were expendable, and a good number of the closer-in ones vaporized mere seconds after transmitting the first views of NovaSpot's Ignition. It was the radiation-hardened long-range cameras that provided the best view.

Those cameras revealed NovaSpot as a featureless, incredibly bright point of light, hard by the utterly black and featureless void that was Greenhouse. The small world was doing a fine imitation of a black hole, though of course it was no such thing. The actinic blue-white pinpoint of light had no outward effect on Greenhouse or its shielding, but the gas giant planet Comfort was hit, and hit hard. Its upper atmosphere was bombarded with every form of hard radiation and heavy particle, setting off massive auroral effects, sheets of blue and red and green fire that flared and glowed on the nightside of the planet. The lower atmosphere was suddenly subjected to light and heat a thousand times more powerful than usual. The sudden influx of raw energy set the atmosphere roiling, churning with power that upset ancient wind patterns, and destabilized weather systems centuries old. Massive lightning strikes exploded in all directions, and the cloud layers boiled over, redrawing the entire face of the world. Those who had seen the planet up close every day of their lives would find it unrecognizably changed within a few hours.

The unspeakable power of the initial blast faded slightly after a few minutes, then subsided gradually over the course of the next few hours. NovaSpot was still a monster newly unleashed, but its initial fury faded rapidly.

The engineers of NovaSpot Ignition Control set to work, tapping the massive energy of the beast they had created and using it to tame the beast, tamp down the power output, and suppress the hard radiation and heavy particles. Slowly, patiently, they worked to bring their new sun under a semblance of control, steadying it down, making it safe to be near.

It was painstaking work, but they dared not be too slow about it. No one could know for sure how intense the Greenhouse temporal confinement was, or how long it would last. No one had ever created a confinement this large, this powerful—or exposed it to this hostile an environment. They took what readings they could, and took heart from the optimistic results, but dared not have faith in them.

But perhaps Groundside Power Reception had absorbed all of the Ignition Project's bad luck, as well as all the power of the SunSpot. Everything in the post-Ignition Control Sequence went according to plan, or even a little better. Well before time, NovaSpot was, if not completely tamed, at least brought to heel, its power, radiation, and heavy particle outputs well inside safety limits, though still above the final target levels. NovaSpot had been born, and come to life as a seething and violent star.

By the time it had completed three-quarters of an orbit around Greenhouse, NovaSpot was close to being the sort of calm and gently warming sun that would suit the purposes of any greenhouse, of whatever size.

Villjae stood there in the darkness, darkness as thick as velvet, as absolute as the inside of a cave, and waited to see what he had come to see.

He was getting to the point where he would be eager to see anything at all. The darkness, the blackness, was more complete, and having a more profound effect, than he would have expected. His eyes strained to make something, anything, of the darkness. He held one hand, the other hand, both hands in front of his face, and wiggled his fingers vigorously. His senses strained harder still to know something of the universe around him. He found himself becoming disoriented, unsure of where he was standing or which way he was facing—or even exactly which way was up. He found himself convinced that he was standing right by the edge of the steel-mesh hatch— and not at all convinced that he had in fact closed it.

He knew perfectly well he was a good meter and a half from the hatch, and he could remember quite clearly that he had swung it shut. But the all-enveloping darkness was the breeder of fear and doubt. It whispered that things could move in the dark, that he could have shifted his stance without noticing it, that the whole room could be moving about.

He felt as if he were standing on an angle somehow, about to fall over. He put his two hands out in front of him and shuffled forward as carefully as he could, until his left hand touched the dome. He reached forward with his right and discovered that the dome was out of reach. Somehow, he had gotten turned at an angle to it in the dark. He swung the right side of his body around and was greatly relieved to touch the dome with his right hand as well. He slid both hands down, until they came in contact with the top of the solid cylindrical wall upon which the dome sat. The join was made so that a narrow ledge, about ten centimeters wide, sat between the edge of the wall and the dome itself. He laid his hands flat on the ledge and found that his left hand felt as if it were five or eight centimeters higher than his right, though of course that could not be. The ledge between wall and dome was perfectly flat and level.

He leaned his head forward until it thumped gently against the dome. He pressed his forehead against it and felt the solidity of the cool hard plastic. He braced his feet, a bit apart from each other. He closed his eyes. By all logic, that shouldn't have made any difference, but it made him feel better, somehow. The world was *supposed* to be invisible when your eyes were shut. He forced himself to concentrate, to reorient himself, to make himself know for sure where down was, where up was, where he was.

It seemed to help. The sense that he was about to topple over, that the world was half on its side, seemed to fade away. With the world now steadier under his feet, Villjae felt calmer, better able to think about what came next, and when it would come.

But how long, in his own subjective time, *had* it been since the lights went out, since the temporal confinement was activated? The featureless darkness, and the all-but-absolute silence as well, gave him no way to judge. Three such meaningless minutes? Ten? Twenty? A half hour, or more?

In theory, a temporal confinement could be made self-sustaining, self-powering, drawing energy from the temporal distortion itself, though no one had ever managed it. Suppose that had happened, somehow, and Greenhouse was to be trapped forever inside this pinched-off bit of frozen time?

Absurd ideas. But in the midst of such silence, such darkness, on a day when so much physical power was set to so many remarkable purposes, what was truly impossible?

Villjae opened his eyes and pulled his head back from the coolness of the dome. Still he kept his hands on the narrow ledge, and still he kept his feet well apart and firmly braced. He knew where up and down were now, and that was at least a start, something at least that he could build on.

And he was, after all, there to *see* something. Something that had not happened yet. He could wait there—would wait there—unmoving, in the silent darkness, in the strange long moment outside time, until that something came to be.

So he stood, staring out at the darkness.

In the space between heartbeats, the temporal confinement ceased to be, and Greenhouse rejoined the outside universe. The sea of utter darkness gave way all at once, and light was upon the face of the world—

Dazzling, brilliant, eye-stabbing light that was too much to see. Villjae had of course known how bright it would be, but he had chosen not to do anything about it. What was the point in being the first to see the world of Greenhouse lit by its new star if one saw it through filters or glare glasses or attenuators? He wanted the sensation of the honest, real, raw light of a new sun, a new day.

And now he had it, blinding bright, painfully bright. But then, at last, his dazzled eyes adjusted. There was the land before him, lit with a brilliance it had not known for generations. Still a land of greys and browns, still lifeless—but the light was a promise, and an opportunity, and life was never long in arriving once there was the chance for life. With eyes still dazzled, with patches of haze and color still sparkling in his vision, he could see new habitat domes springing up, old domes, long abandoned, but newly reborn, cool blues and greens to come, replacing the burned-out, frozen-over wastes of the Greenhouse that was.

He looked up into a black sky that seemed far less dark than the one he had seen not so long before. There it was. NovaSpot, shining down upon its world. Judging by its position in the sky, high in the east, something like eighteen hours had passed. When the confinement cut off, NovaSpot had appeared, full-blown, well into the first morning of a new day for Greenhouse.

It hurt too much to look at it for more than a moment, but a moment was all that Villjae needed. He had seen it. There it was, and if he was not the first to see it from the surface of Greenhouse, then certainly he was among the first. He dropped his eyes from the skies and again surveyed the landscape around him. He stood there a long time, imagining what would be, through eyes no longer dazzled.

After a while, he heard some small sound down below, footsteps crossing the open room garage, coming closer. He paid them no mind, but instead looked upward to the roiling turmoil that was the surface of Comfort. The face of a world remade—there was proof of the power humanity had set to work that day. It seemed an appropriate image. After all, the remaking of worlds was what this was all about.

The footsteps came closer, and he heard the sound of someone on the stairs below. The steel-mesh hatch swung open and banged down onto the floor of the dome. There in the hatchway was Beseda Mahrlin, peering up at him.

"I thought you might be here," she said, and came up through the hatch. She knelt, lifted the hatch, and swung it back down into place. She stood up, dusted off her hands, and joined Villjae in his contemplation of the new-made world.

"So there it is," she said.

"There it is," Villjae agreed. "We did it. We lit a new sun and saved Greenhouse."

"No," said Beseda. She was silent long enough that Villjae thought she had finished, but then she spoke again. "All we've done is bought some time. Time we needed, yes—but that's all."

"What are you talking about?" Villjae said.

She gestured out into the bright-lit landscape. "It's necessary," she said. "But not sufficient. We needed to do this, yes—but it doesn't solve the core problems. The ecosystem on Solace is still in very bad condition. There are still refugees, and floods, and bandits and schemers."

"Well, yes—but still, this *was* necessary, and important. We needed to fix Greenhouse so it can help rebuild Solace. And we did it."

"Just barely," she said. "You know that much, better than anyone. When they pin a medal on you for saving the day—and they will, and they should, because you did—consider why the day needed to be saved."

Villjae was almost speechless in his confusion. The day marked what would likely be the greatest accomplishment of his life, and here was Beseda, talking in more and longer sentences than he had ever heard before, saying that it wasn't good enough! "It needed saving because Rufdrop got himself killed before he could complete his design."

"If Rufdrop had lived, they'd have had to wave off,"

Beseda said flatly. "No Ignition. His designs were all wrong for the job—fancy, not strong. Pretty, not robust. But he was a symptom, not a cause."

"What are you talking about?"

Beseda gestured again toward the landscape, then at NovaSpot, and then waved her hand dismissively. "This is small," she said. "The smallest part of what we have to do to save Solace and all the people who depend on Solace—such as us. And we barely got through it. Rush, improvise, go before we're ready, hold it all together with hacked-out ArtInts and spare cables, trust to luck. We *can't* trust luck anymore. Never should have. Not when we've lucked into the mess we have. Barely made it, and getting here wore us out, used us up. We'll need to rest, all of us. Used up treasure, too." She gestured out toward the Reception Array, and down at the building, and the massive bunker complex, below them. "Look at all the fancy hardware we needed, that we can't use again. Think what we *could* have built, if we hadn't had to build all this instead. Can't afford to do that anymore."

"We had to rush! The planetary alignments—"

"We knew when the alignments would be right way back when DeSilvo was in diapers," Beseda said snappishly. "We just didn't worry about it until it was nearly too late. Then we rushed too fast, spent too much, tried too hard. *That's* the Solacian way."

"What is?"

"Look in the history books. Always the same. Big delays, then the quick fix, the rush job. That's how we started. DeSilvo spent forever telling everyone he'd found a way to terraform fast, lost time getting ready— then cut enough corners to say he got done on time."

She shook her head and looked out on a landscape that seemed to hold far less promise than it had before. "We can't go on this way," she said. "Have to change. But I don't know. Might be too late. Maybe the way things are, the way *we* are—maybe we find out that we just plain can't go on at *all*."

She was silent for a while and stood with him at the

railing, looking outward. "Mmmph," she said at last. "Well, there it is. See you downstairs."

Beseda turned, knelt, opened the hatch, and started down the stairs, carefully closing the hatch behind her, leaving Villjae wondering what the hell she had come up for in the first place.

After she was gone, he stayed there a long time, looking out on a new world that suddenly seemed a very different place than he had thought.

Part Three
HUNTERS AND THE HUNTED

Chapter Thirteen

SLEEPING DOGS
AND TETHERED GOATS

CHRONOLOGIC PATROL INTELLIGENCE COMMAND
HEADQUARTERS
(CHRONPAT INTCOM HQ)
KOROLEV CRATER
LUNAR FARSIDE

Kalani Temblar stood in the airlock, willing the inner door to open sooner rather than later. She desperately wanted to get out of her pressure suit—and, for that matter, just plain get *out*. Of course, they could never let her go. Not after what she had already found. But still, a girl could dream.

At last the inner door slid open, and she lumbered through it into the ready room and slapped the seal-door button behind her. She sat down on one of the curved benches spaced around the walls of the compartment, unlatched her suit helmet, and set it down next to her on the bench. She leaned back, setting the back of her head against the cold metal wall of the ready room, and closed her eyes. The trip out to the asteroid belt and Ceres, largest of the asteroids, had been nothing, no effort at all—especially compared to the trip to Mars and back. She shuddered just thinking about that one. But even if this last trip had been far easier on her than that one, she still felt exhausted.

Rest. If I can only rest for a little while, that will help so much . . . It was not her body that was tired, not even her mind—but her spirit. She had put all she had, and all she was, into the Chronologic Patrol. But even before she had started on this case, she had started to wonder if the organization was moving in the right direction. After what she had learned—on Mars, on Earth, at the Grand Library, at Ceres—her niggling doubts were edging closer and closer to becoming unpleasant certainties.

But it was cool and quiet there in the ready room. No duties to perform, no one to interview, no files to study, no leads to pursue, no spacecraft to pilot. Just a few minutes of quiet, by herself, and then maybe she could—

"There you are! I was out on the surface. Saw you put down. Very nice."

Kalani did not open her eyes. She did not have to. She knew it was her commanding officer, Burl Chalmers. She kept her eyes shut. She heard him moving closer, felt the bench shift slightly as he sat down next to her. Judging by the sound of stiff, creaking fabric and the metallic clicks and clacks as he set himself down, he was still in his pressure suit. Burl in a pressure suit, Burl being out on the surface—for that matter, Burl being out of his *office*—was an odd enough occurrence that she was almost tempted to open her eyes and actually see it.

No, better to imagine it. Would he somehow have managed to get gravy stains on the front of the suit, the way he had on every shirt he owned? If she opened her eyes, she would find out it wasn't so, and that would spoil everything. Life was so much more pleasant when you could keep your eyes shut, and not see what you didn't want to, and imagine things to be the way they ought to be.

"Good morning, sir, Lieutenant Commander Chalmers, *sir,*" she said without moving, putting a brisk parade-ground tone in her voice.

Chalmers chuckled. "*That's* a strangely official form of address, considering you didn't salute me," he observed placidly.

"I only have to salute you if I see you," she said with a yawn. "I don't see you."

"Yeah, well, I'm not really all that worth looking at,"

he said. She heard him shift on the bench again, and felt a pat on the shoulder. "But we do need to talk. Soon. Very soon. It is now exactly 1103 hours, mark. Grab a shower, get some coffee and something to eat, and be in my office in one hour, max."

Kalani groaned. "I couldn't get you to make it ninety minutes, could I?"

"It's only because I'm taking pity on you that I didn't make it twenty minutes. Seriously. One hour. And be ready for real work."

Eyes still shut, she gestured out behind her, at the landing field and her scout ship, and all the worlds she had visited. "What was all that?" she asked. "A warm-up?"

" 'Fraid so," he said. "Now you have fifty-nine minutes. Use them well."

The bench creaked again, and she could hear him standing up and leaving the compartment.

With infinite reluctance, she stood up, opened her eyes, and started peeling off the suit. Shower first, food second. Maybe the shower would wake her up enough to have an appetite.

Kalani was somehow annoyed with herself for feeling so much better when she arrived in Burl's office—a full one minute and forty-five seconds early.

His office didn't look any better than the last time she had been in it—or the time before that, or the time before that. It had been said of his working habits that there was untidiness, and then there were archeology sites. Burl Chalmers's office was definitely in the second category.

At least the food stains on his shirt hadn't gotten any worse. Kalani recognized one tomato-sauce splash pattern that had not faded at all since the last time he had worn the shirt. One story had it that Chalmers had chosen the Intelligence Service so as to avoid wearing uniforms. He certainly didn't treat his civilian clothes very well.

Burl was reading as she came in, intently studying a datapad. She knew better than to interrupt him. Instead she picked up a familiar stack of papers off the visitor's chair and set it on the floor. She had noted the migration of that particular stack of files about the office over the last few months. It had been shifted from the floor to the desk to the table to the chair to the top of the file cabinet to the floor to the chair, and on and on and on, over and over again. To her all-but-certain knowledge, no one had ever consulted any of the papers in that particular stack since Burl's very tidy and organized predecessor had left them for him in the precise center of his desk two and a half years ago.

She turned to the one spotlessly clean area in his office—the coffee service on the chest-high table just inside his office door. She poured herself a cup of the superb fresh-brewed coffee that was always there, sat down, and waited. It surprised her not at all that he looked up from his work at precisely 1203, the exact moment he had ordered her to be there. "So," he said, tossing aside the datapad he had been studying so intently, as if it were no more interesting than a ten-year-old obituary. "How was Ceres?"

"Weird. Creepy. Marginally useful. Tracked the two crewmen who jumped ship off the *Dom Pedro IV* from the Grand Library. Both still there. Both more or less safe and comfortable, but not so comfortable they weren't just a little afraid of ChronPat Intell. They talked, but they didn't know much we didn't know. Confirmations. And on the second matter, I was able to confirm that DeSilvo *wasn't* on Ceres any of the times his bios say he went there."

"So?"

"So line up the dates he was supposed to go, and the orbital positions, and what his ship could do, and where we have confirmed records of him before and after when he was supposed to be on Ceres—well, it boils down to that he pretty much had to have been on Mars at those times. Only place he could have reached that wouldn't have produced some kind of record of his visit."

"But we knew he got to Mars."

"Now we have a better handle on when, and how often. Besides—" Kalani pointed straight down at the floor, the universal gesture for Intell Central Command at

ChronPat Intell HQ. IntCentCom was buried deepest under the lunar surface. As the duller wits of Intell were fond of pointing out, Command was literally beneath them all. "—Yeah *we* knew. Did *they*? Did they *want* to know?"

"We had evidence."

Kalani shrugged. "Now we have more—and we've eliminated all the possibilities that could explain it away. And we have the Mars angle confirmed in case any of the brass in the bunker don't want it to be true. We can stick their noses in it if we have to."

"Point taken," Chalmers said. "But let's remember you said it, and I didn't."

Kalani snorted. Chalmers stuck his neck out a lot farther than that, a dozen times a day. "We can now show definitely DeSilvo was on Mars, at specific times—and also show additional evidence he was probably there at other times."

"You've done a lot," Chalmers said. "No doubt about it."

"Yeah," she said bitterly. "*I've* done a lot. Burl, from what I know, the thefts from the Dark Museum represent the single gravest threat to, to, I don't know what—to interstellar civilization, I guess—since the Chronologic Patrol was founded. I couldn't understand why some of it was suppressed—but there were some pieces of hardware where even I could see why the Patrol has sat on them. If it all got loose—I don't even want to think about it. But the Dark Museum angle is just *part* of this case."

She set down her coffee on a small clear spot on the edge of his desk and leaned forward, elbows on knees, hands clasped together, staring at Chalmers, intent on what she was saying. "The bunker brass ought to be in full-blown panic mode, pulling investigators off every other case and putting them all *over* this thing. Instead they've got a field rookie like me out looking for clues, a few favors called in from places like Asgard Five, and you doing what you can to cadge research and tech support out of headquarters." She leaned back in her chair again, slumping against the cushion. She gestured behind her, at the big room they called the bullpen, and the clusters of workpods, an investigator in each pod. "Meanwhile you've got sixty officers working full shifts every day checking to make sure all the tariff rules are being obeyed! What the hell is with the priorities around here?"

Chalmers looked at her sadly and was quiet for a long time before he spoke. "If it will make you feel better, I can tell you they *are* panicking down below," he said at last. "They're just doing it very quietly. The split second they heard that you'd found connections between the *Dom Pedro IV,* DeSilvo, and the Dark Museum, Central Command—not Intell Central Command, but the *real* Central Command—decided this had to be kept very, very, quiet—and I agreed with them. They considered the danger from leaks so grave that they toyed with the idea of not investigating at all, of letting sleeping dogs lie."

"Who are they keeping it from? DeSilvo? Are they that afraid he'll find out we're after him? And *what* danger? What kind of danger?"

"You said it yourself," Chalmers replied in a chillingly calm tone of voice. "The gravest threat ever to interstellar civilization. And it's not DeSilvo they're afraid of. It's your colleagues in the bullpen. It's you. It's me. I know more of the big-picture story than you do, and the big brass knows more than me—a lot more. And what they're scared of is that one of us will find out everything *they* know—maybe *more* than they know. They're scared someone will talk. They fear that the danger of the story, the *whole* story, getting out to the public, might well be greater than the danger of letting DeSilvo do whatever the hell he's trying to do."

Kalani frowned and knitted her brow. "Wait a second. We know—we *know*—he's had access to some of the most dangerous and powerful technology in history. And they think it might be safer to let him do whatever he wants with it because the ultimate results of a possible investigative leak might be *worse*?"

Chalmers nodded. "That, Lieutenant Temblar, is an excellent summing-up. Exactly right."

"Stars in the sky," Kalani said. Suddenly her heart was racing. "That's for *real*?"

"For real. That's why it's just you out there. A compromise between no investigation, and the all-out effort you're talking about—which is what a lot of the War Council wanted."

"They called a *War Council*?"

"Yeah. It's that big." Chalmers stood up, collected her cup, and walked across the room to the coffee service. He poured her a fresh cup and made one for himself, heavy on the cream and sugar. He handed her coffee to her, then padded quietly back to his own chair. "Let's pretend that last part of the conversation didn't happen," he said. "Otherwise, we'll both go nuts. Okay?"

"Okay." Kalani held her cup in both hands and stared down into the dark, steaming liquid. What else was there to say? How could anyone deal with something that size?

"Good. Real good," Chalmers said, nodding vigorously at nothing at all. He set down his coffee without so much as taking a sip. "So. So—give me a sum-up of what else you got," Chalmers said, leaning back in his chair. He put his hands behind his head, cradled his head in them, and looked at her, frowning thoughtfully. "Shopping list of evidence in hand."

"Ah, yeah. Yeah." Kalani gave herself a moment to force other matters from her mind and focus on the investigation itself. "We've got my reports on events at the Grand Library and the Permanent Physical Collections, the action reports I pried loose from Interdict Command, the arrival and departure times of the 'Merchanter's Dream,' which is a 99.99 percent probable match with *Dom Pedro IV*. We've got statements from people who talked to people who were all but certainly our friends when the subjects were in Berlin, Rio, Haiti. There was another *Dom Pedro IV* crew member who went over the side in Rio, but we haven't found him yet. I don't want to try any harder than we have, just yet. I don't think he could tell us much new—and we don't want to attract attention. And we're still waiting on interrogation reports on Hues Renblant, the officer of the *Dom Pedro IV* who was left behind at Asgard Five."

"Nope. That came in while you were gone," Chalmers said. He leaned forward, reached over, picked up the data-pad he had discarded earlier, and handed it to her before resuming his previous position. "Glad we didn't send you all the way the hell out *there* just to get his statement. Asgard Five's station manager was only too glad to help us out by asking friend Renblant a few questions. Read between the lines, and you'll see Renblant isn't exactly winning popularity contests up there. He's been stranded there since the *Dom Pedro IV* left him—and he has not been enjoying himself. Read it later. It's got a few tidbits in it—but not many."

"Can you give me the short version?"

"Oh, he's the hero and the victim, the *Dom Pedro IV* was crewed by archfiends, and Koffield was the worst. He, Renblant, knows the whole story and has just been aching for someone to ask him. My read is Koffield and company sat on him pretty hard—and probably paid him a reasonable amount—to keep quiet when they dumped him. It's taken until now for Renblant to get bored and angry and frustrated enough to break his silence contract—or maybe he just stopped being afraid of whatever they threatened him with to keep him quiet."

"So Renblant confirms that the 'Merchanter's Dream' really was the *Dom Pedro*—and that Koffield was aboard?"

"Those were the tidbits," Chalmers agreed. "Beyond that, his statement fleshes out a few things, gives us details on the back story, but doesn't really tell us anything directly on topic that we didn't know from other sources. And, oh, by the way, the station manager took the hint—Renblant's going to be stranded there a while longer."

"How far can we count on the station manager?"

"He's retired Chronologic Patrol and still a true believer. Drew the job on Asgard Five because he likes his peace and quiet. Psych projection is about 98 percent that he wouldn't spread the story around, even if he got the chance. We're about as safe as we could hope to be on that end."

"Same thing other places. We've gotten lucky on keeping it all quiet, so far."

"It's those last two words that worry me," Chalmers said with a frown. "But, anyway." He pulled one hand from behind his head and pointed down, then put his hand back behind his head. "Pretend I'm one of the leaders of the brain trust down there. Sum up. What story do all the findings tell us?"

Kalani shook her head. "All I know for sure is that we don't know all of it. Here's the real fast version of what we're pretty sure on: Something like 150 years ago, and maybe long before that, while he's still working to terraform Solace, DeSilvo breaks into the Dark Museum on Mars and starts stealing hardware, and, we're pretty sure, making copies of lots of datasets—on how to build this or that gadget. Probably a lot more data than actual hardware. He keeps that up for a long time, making lots of trips to the Museum and probably working via remotes and teleoperators for a lot of it. He builds himself a whole operation down there.

"There's no sign of his ever *using* any of his new toys—until one fine day, when the terraforming project is winding down—a very weird fleet of ships that gets to be called the Intruders hits two of our ships and wrecks the timeshaft at Circum Central. Anton Koffield commands the surviving Chrono Patrol ship. He limps back home and provides a lot of evidence that suggests the Intruders were using a faster-than-light drive, which, of course, everyone knows is impossible. Except that the Dark Museum seems to have had at least two or three FTL drives tucked away down there. Burl, do you have any *idea* what sort of suppressed technology the Patrol has filed away down there?"

"No," he said flatly. "And I don't want to. That stuff's classified kill-yourself-before-reading-further."

"*That* makes me feel better. Anyway, Circum Central is the first connection between Koffield and DeSilvo."

"*If* we assume it was DeSilvo running the Intruders."

"That's the way Occam's razor would cut. Otherwise, you need to come up with real alien intruders, or else have someone *else* steal or invent FTL—and show a penchant for using robots and ArtInts to do everything.

Those ships were almost certainly uncrewed. Plus there's another, admittedly much weaker link—Circum Central is—was—in the same part of the sky as the Solace system. Not next door, but not too far off."

"I agree the odds are very high that Circum Central was DeSilvo—but the big shots might have some reason for wishing it were otherwise. You might have to be ready for that. Go on."

Be ready for that when, exactly? Burl hadn't told her everything yet. "So you've got the file on how they meet again, later—but still a long time ago. Something like 130 years ago. Koffield does some research for De-Silvo, and then, for some reason, sets off for Solace on the *Dom Pedro IV.* The ship never gets there. Listed as missing, then lost. Very sad, but it happens. Except the ship shows up—120-odd years or so late for the party. Turns out the ship was sabotaged in a very particular way. There's no hard evidence that DeSilvo did the sab-otage, but, again, there are no other likely suspects, and he would have had means, motives, and opportu-nity.

"Anyway, Koffield pops up in the Solace system and starts warning everybody that he can prove a collapse is coming. He gets sent to some terraforming center on Greenhouse—that's a satellite of a gas giant in the So-lace system. While he's there, he visits DeSilvo's tomb, of all things. He finds something that we don't know about that must be pretty amazing—then starts a crash pro-gram to lead an expedition to the Solar System—appar-ently to look for DeSilvo.

"Something he found in the tomb convinced him that DeSilvo was *alive*—and maybe even waiting for Koffield to show up. *There's* a relationship I don't understand. De-Silvo attacks his ship—though Koffield doesn't know it's DeSilvo doing the attacking. Then DeSilvo hires him to do some research. *Then* Koffield charges off to warn every-one that the world DeSilvo made is going to crump, De-Silvo sabotages his ship, then, best we can figure, more or less leaves a trail of bread crumbs for Koffield. Koffield follows that trail through the Grand Library, through sev-

eral cities on Earth, through the Dark Museum on Mars—
and then off again for parts unknown." She let out a sigh.
"And that's just part of what's got me thrown."

"What do you mean?" Chalmers asked.

"We know a lot about what both of them did—but
not the least idea in the world *why* they did those things.
We know that something big is up, but we don't know
what. We don't know what this case is *about*. I spent the
whole run back from Ceres staring at the bulkheads, trying to come up with some sort of logical motive that
would explain it all."

"Maybe throw out that part about logic," said Chalmers. "Just because someone does a thing on the grand
scale, that doesn't mean he's thought it all the way
through, or planned it all out very sensibly. And motiva-
tions aren't carved in stone. The reason you're doing
something will change as you go along."

"I know, I know," Kalani said wearily. "But I can't
even make a *start* on the why and wherefore on these
two. And I can't get much further without it. I've run out
of meaningful leads to follow. God knows where either
of them went off to."

"If God knows, he's not the only one," said Chalmers,
unable to repress a smile.

"What do you mean?"

"I mean, we've got ourselves a lead—and you got it
for us. You got images of some weird plaques in the
Dark Museum. These." He reached into a pile on his
desk and pulled out a color print. It showed two
plaques, each about ten centimeters by twenty-five.
Each had a yellow background, with a blue line drawn
around the border. The lettering was in red, and the type
was raised. They were very much meant to be seen. The
first read

$$\models (\upsilon s k d @ (\forall X \ni X \neq A \upsilon))$$

and the second

$$\rightarrow (\forall X \ni X \neq A \upsilon)$$

He handed them to her. Kalani took them and shook her head. "I took the pictures, but I never could make heads or tails out of the plaques. Math formulae?"

"Don't feel bad. It took our crypto people a lot longer than it should have to figure them out. They cracked them just after you boosted away from Ceres. I had to wait until you were here to tell you about it—the big shots are so paranoid they forbade any electronic communications on this matter. Turns out the plaques aren't mathematical formulae, exactly. More like mathematical puns. And it would help if you were conversant with pre-near-ancient dramatic literature as well."

"Sorry. I must have been out sick that day at school."

"Yeah, me too. Anyway, if you parse through the math symbols, *and* read part of it as a sort of shorthand for De-Silvo's name, *and* read the last part as a chemical symbol, you get something like 'Belongs to Oskar DeSilvo at the set of all values of X such that X does not equal gold' and the second would be something like 'Go to the set of all values of X such that X does not equal gold.' "

Kalani beetled her brow at Chalmers and chortled. "Yeah, terrific. Real breakthrough."

"It is if you brush up your Shakspur," Chalmers said loftily. "Or was it Sharkspar? Some name like that. Anyway, some hotshot managed to remember a quote that said something about not everything that glitters is gold—except he got it kind of wrong. The right quote is 'All that glisters is not gold.' "

Kalani's eyes lit up. "If you go to the place that is not gold—you go to Glister."

"Right. So that's where we're going. Tomorrow."

"*What?*" There were too damned many surprises in this conversation. "Why tomorrow?"

"Because they can't prep a ship in time to leave today," Chalmers said. "If you were asking why so fast— the top brass has spent every minute since crypto cracked this wondering what the delay was. They would have launched me alone and had me intercept your scout coming back from Ceres if it would have saved any time."

"You're getting me very nervous, Burl," she said. "And no offense—but why *you*? When was the last time you did any field work?" She had been about to ask when he had last left the base for any reason, but that seemed too untactful, even under the current circumstances.

"Let's just say it was within your lifetime and leave it at that," Chalmers said evenly. "As to why me—they had to send somebody. One person can't fly an interstellar ship alone. Two can barely do the job. I agree that I'm not exactly the Chrono Patrol's action hero poster boy—but this whole operation is all about need-to-know. If they brief someone else with what I know, that's one more person who knows. But if they send me, that's one *less* person—and it gets us *both* well away from civilization. If we go to Glister and spill the beans, who are we going to tell? The ice?"

"Maybe the frozen corpses," Kalani said. "It's not supposed to be a nice place."

"No, it isn't," Chalmers said.

"What are we supposed to do when we get there, anyway?"

"Not much. Find DeSilvo, find Koffield, see what they're up to, and stop them doing anything they shouldn't."

"That's all?"

"One other thing. We're supposed to make sure Central Command knows about it if we get killed. We're supposed to send back regular messenger pods. Lots of them."

M-pods were basically miniature timeshaft ships, programmed to fly back through the timeshafts, carrying urgent information. "I thought they were being paranoid about security. M-pods aren't exactly the most secure form of communication," Kalani objected.

"These won't carry information, of any sort. That's a direct order from on high. We send them back with nothing but date, positions, and the message 'We're still not dead yet.' " Burl frowned, stared at the wall for a moment, and spoke again. "Let me make it sound even better. We're going to be the tethered goat."

"I don't know that one."

"It's an old idea. If there's a wolf causing you trouble—don't go hunting for the wolf. Set out a nice fat goat on a good strong tether, hide in the bushes, and wait for the wolf to sniff out the goat and come to you. If you can kill the wolf *before* he kills the goat, that's a nice bonus—but you can always get another goat."

"You don't have to keep trying to make me feel better, Burl." It wasn't much of a joke, but it was all she had left.

"Sorry, Kal, but that's about where we are. If we get ourselves killed, but they know when and where, that'll tell them what they need to know—and then they'll mount the full-scale operation—a military operation, not just an investigation."

"An operation to do what?"

"They'll decide when they get there. It depends on what DeSilvo's doing—and we haven't the faintest idea about what that is. Whatever DeSilvo's up to, he's simply accumulated too much hardware. He's dangerous—dangerous enough that he might be able to take on a full military assault. Part of the idea in sending in such a small team is to keep the stakes from getting that high. Send in an invasion fleet, and you'll probably start a war. Send in two cops to snoop around, and probably you won't. And if you lose the two cops, but in exchange you prevent a war—well, that sounds like a pretty reasonable bargain, even to me. How's it sound to you?"

"I don't think I want to answer that question," Kalani replied. She was surprised she was even able to speak that clearly. Things had come at her too fast, from too many directions. She was scared, more scared than she had ever been in her life. Even more scared than she'd been on Mars—and only someone who'd been down there could understand how scared *that* was. "Burl?" she asked. "What do I *do*?"

"Get some rest, Kalani," Chalmers said gently. "Tomorrow's going to be a hell of a day."

Chapter Fourteen

TO CATCH A LOWDOWN

Solace City Spaceport
Solace City Transport Complex
The Planet Solace

The rain roared down, beating on the landing field, slapping at Elber as he stumbled out of the orbital transport and onto the upper platform of a set of mobile stairs. Elber Malloon breathed in the air of his native world for the first time in nearly a year, and almost drowned in the process, as the wind blew the storm right into his face. He was none too pleased to be back.

The rain was hard enough that he could scarcely see the bottom of the stairway. Holding tight to his travel bag, he moved as quickly and carefully as he could down the steps, leaning into the wind as he forced himself forward toward the waiting ground shuttle.

He lunged inside the vehicle and climbed up into a seat, gasping for breath, feeling half-drowned. He could not have been out in the weather more than thirty seconds, or traveled more than twenty meters, but still he was soaked to the skin and chilled to the bone. He had been the first off the orbital transport, but the other passengers were right behind him, staggering up the stairs and finding themselves places to sit.

"Not so bad this trip," said a friendly voice from over Elber's shoulder.

He turned to see a drenched, but cheerful, young woman, pale-skinned and clear-eyed, smiling at him. Her blonde hair was bedraggled, and her clothes were as wet as Elber's, but none of that seemed to bother her.

"What's not so bad?"

"The rain," she said. "Every trip, the locals tell me that it comes and goes—but it never goes when I'm down. *They* can tell you all the exact dates when it didn't rain in the last three months. But never when I'm around."

"And it gets worse than this?"

The woman shrugged. "Well, maybe this is a *bit* above average—but it sure as DeSilvo was heavy last time. The landing pads flooded out so bad they had to shut down the spaceport right after we landed. Water was ankle deep."

"Oh," said Elber. The water hadn't seemed to be much shallower than that when he went through it, but his new friend seemed to be the sort to look on the bright side, no matter what.

"So this is your first trip down?" she asked.

"Ah, no, actually. I was born on Solace. But it's been a while."

"So what brings you here now?"

Elber was far from being a suspicious sort, but somehow this woman seemed a little *too* friendly. Why had she singled *him* out? Why was she taking so much interest in him? Perhaps it was just old-fashioned warmth and openness—or perhaps it wasn't. But his mission—and his situation—were already delicate enough as it was. And, come to think of it, he didn't remember seeing her on board. It was possible he had missed her, or that she had been on another deck—but Elber was usually pretty good at remembering faces. His own instinct, born of a lifetime lived down on the farm, was to be just as open and friendly as she had been—but it was no time to trust to instinct. "Business," he said, and left it at that.

"What sort of business?" she pressed.

It was not hard to imagine a very slight change in her

tone, to hear a little bit more steel in her voice and a trifle less silk. "Nothing particularly interesting," he said. "Just a few matters that have come up, now that they're done with NovaSpot's Ignition. I have to sort out some details for supplies on a new project on Greenhouse." It was a bald-faced lie, from top to bottom. Elber was astonished at himself for being able to invent it on the spur of the moment. "What about you?" he asked the woman.

"Me?" she asked, plainly not ready for the question. Her smile suddenly seemed fixed, forced, as if she were determined to keep it in place no matter what. "Oh, nothing interesting at all. Just—just a small shipping operation, that's all."

"Oh. Well, good luck with it." Elber smiled blandly and calmly turned forward again in his seat, but his heart was pounding. Maybe he had just been rude to a very nice lady. Or maybe someone was working very hard, and very fast—if not all that skillfully—to find out what Elber had been sent to do.

Another group of sopping-wet passengers rushed aboard the ground transport, one of them carrying a large and awkward package. Elber took advantage of the moment to move "helpfully" out of the way of the package, then shift to a seat as far away as possible from his new friend.

He caught a glimpse of her expression as he sat and saw that her smile was gone, replaced by a hard and determined frown. Either he had been a lot ruder than he thought, or her mask had slipped completely away.

The ground transport's ArtInt seemed to decide that no one else was going to get aboard. It closed the passenger door and started the drive toward the main transfer terminal, the rain sheeting down on all the half-fogged windows.

The transport pulled up inside a roofed-over vehicle concourse, and the passengers stepped out. The concourse led toward the air/sea/land terminal proper on one side, but on the other three it was open to the weather—and there was a lot of weather. The wind had picked up, and was managing to drive the cold rain nearly sideways, right into the faces of the passengers. Elber staggered inside with the rest of them and paused just inside the entrance to catch his breath. Elber stood under one of the powerful hot-air blowers angled down from the ceiling for a minute, but it didn't do much good. It got him a bit warmer, but it would take something more than that to get him remotely dry.

He suddenly noticed that his friend from the ground transport had vanished as mysteriously as she had arrived. Did she have a flight she had to catch in a hurry— or was she already reporting in to—well, somebody? Elber shrugged and forgot about her. There was nothing he could do about her, and he had plenty of other troubles to deal with.

He looked around. Once away from the puddles and streaks of mud and sodden floor mats by the entrance, the terminal was clean, warm, dry, well lit, dotted with well-behaved, well-dressed travelers. *A little different this trip,* Elber could not help thinking. The last time— for that matter, the only other time—Elber had been at Solace City Spaceport, he had been with his wife Jassa and his daughter Zari, and they had been part of a mob, swept up in the panic that had seized their village and most of the rest of the planet's rural settlements.

He remembered those days. The muddled, conflicting stories came up out of nowhere: The spaceport would be shut down, the planet abandoned, they were evacuating uppers from the cities but leaving everyone else behind. The wild ride on whatever transport would get them to the spaceport, the scramble to force themselves onto a ship, any ship. Then, as now, the driving, endless rain. The shouts. The screams. The smell of fear and filth and unwashed bodies and blood. The crushing weight of the boost to orbit—and their confused, terrifying arrival at SCO Station. It was a wonder his family had managed to stay together. And now, SCO was home, and his wife and daughter were still there. Captain Sotales had not exactly said they were hostages to Elber's good behavior—but then, he didn't need to. No matter where Elber's thoughts started, it seemed as if they always ended up with Jassa and Zari.

He forced himself back to the problem at hand. He had been here before, but his experience of the place wasn't going to do him much good. You don't learn how to hire surface transport while part of a rioting mob. It didn't help matters that he had only the vaguest idea of where he needed that surface transport to take him. Nor could he seek advice on the topic. He could scarcely wander up to the traveler's advice booth and ask the best way to travel to the hidden camp of one of the most wanted men on the planet.

Well, half the reason Sotales had recruited Elber was that he and Zak Destan were from the same district—and Reiver Destan was widely reported to be active in that area. Plainly, the best thing to do would be to return to his old hometown—or what was left of it—and ask his way from there.

A confused hour later, Elber, reunited with his baggage and laden down with maps, receipts, tickets, transit transfers, schedules, seat checks, and a whole stack of other bits of paper he could not readily identify, found himself all alone in a private top-class compartment, aboard a sleek, fast, levtrain as it pulled smoothly out of the transit terminal and gathered speed for the run south. Elber had never been on any sort of train before, let alone in top class, and he was not entirely certain what he should do, or even what he was allowed to do.

He sat at the edge of one of the luxuriously wide armchair-style seats, trying to take up as little room as possible on the upholstery, for fear of getting it wet. The train was already climbing up Parrige Mountain toward Long Tunnel before Elber noticed a printed card lying on the small table under the window compartment's door. It listed the services available.

Apparently Elber was not the first traveler to come aboard soaking wet. He was delighted to find a complete, compact, private refresher behind a small door at the rear of the compartment, including a pocket-size autolaundry. There was even a warm full-length robe for him to wear while his clothes were being washed and dried.

Elber locked the door, opaqued all the windows, and set to work. He gloried in the shower and shaved carefully. Then he put his sodden clothes in the laundry chute, pulled on the splendid robe, and sat down in the other still-dry armchair, feeling warmer and drier than would have seemed possible to him an hour before. He flipped the view window back to transparent just as the train was diving into the darkness of Long Tunnel. Two minutes later, the train burst forth into a blaze of sunshine and blue sky on the other side of Parrige Mountain.

Some years back, Elber had read somewhere, without fully understanding it, that Parrige Mountain was in large part responsible for the seemingly endless rain in Solace City. Something about a "rain shadow," whatever that was, and an abrupt shift in weather patterns that had shifted a persistent low-pressure air mass and left it parked for good over Solace City.

The train began the long run down the other side of the mountain, and Elber read over the service card more carefully, with an eye toward what to order for lunch. Ten minutes later, a server-bot wheeled itself in and delivered one of the best meals of Elber's life. Things were looking distinctly up.

They stayed that way all through coffee, and until after the server-bot cleared away the dishes and left Elber to himself. He sighed contentedly and leaned back in his chair, snuggled deep in his robe, watching magnificent scenery roll by as the train flew onward, down into the low plains of the continental interior.

It might be his last chance to review his briefing material for a while. Elber had been quite pleased to receive a new, highly sophisticated datapad from Sotales, with full data on Zak Destan already loaded in. Well, *nearly* full data. Elber had done some data-cruising of his own, pulling down insurance claim reports, district tax receipt reports, police incident files, and a number of other information sources. His time in the insurance office had taught him the value of pulling data from lots of places, how to keep from getting swamped in the data, and the importance of mastering the file, studying it in detail until you understood all the pieces and could really make them fit. He didn't have *all* the pieces yet—but he was starting to see the picture. Maybe more of the picture than Sotales had intended him to see. Elber wasn't entirely sure, just yet, that he wanted to see quite so much.

But it was hard *not* to see. And once he saw, it was harder still to avoid acting.

Elber thought back to his conversation with Raenau and Sotales, the lords of creation, with the power to do what they wanted to him and with him. How big a chance did he want to take on going past what they had intended, on doing more, on donig better? *They* had pushed him into this, poked and prodded him to do their bidding—and they hadn't had to poke very hard. But would it really be safe, or wise, to exceed his instructions?

The one bright spot was that they didn't seem to suspect Elber of any crime—but Elber had no faith in that, either. Not after his time in Commander Raenau's office.

"We got a job for you," Captain Sotales had said then. "We want you to contact the character in the middle of the pictures. Zak Destan."

"Except these days," Raenau had put in, "Zak is respectfully addressed as *Reiver* Destan—or even Bush Captain Destan—even Bush Lord Destan. He's done all right for himself since we booted him off the Station and dumped him back on-planet."

Sotales nodded and went on. "We got reports from the planet-side cops that Destan has been leading raids and stirring up trouble—enough trouble that he has to be dealt with, rather than ignored or destroyed. Some of the planet-side cops think Destan's criminal gang is trying to turn itself into a semipolitical group. Do that, and all of a sudden his gang of crooks turns into—what did they call it?" He had glanced at a piece of paper "—'the core cadre of what might well become a powerful paramilitary organization.' Fancy words they use," he said, and dropped the paper. "They figured it might help if they could talk to him, establish a dialogue, or whatever the hell they call it. They checked his file, saw he was part of the Big Run up to SCO, and they called us. So we're doing a favor for the planet-side cops, trying to help them establish a backdoor contact with Destan— through you. Set a thief to catch a thief."

Sotales laughed at his own joke, noticed that Raenau was not smiling, and forced his expression into a bad imitation of a solemn frown. "But that's only half-right," he went on. "Right, Elber? You're no thief."

Elber had received *that* message loud and clear. Sotales couldn't have made it plainer. He could invent crimes for Elber to be guilty of just by waving his hand.

By the time the scenery stopped being quite so magnificent Elber's former happy mood had collapsed altogether, turned as dried-up and blown-away as the world outside. The train rushed along through the flat, featureless plain, and with each kilometer that passed, there seemed to be fewer trees, scrubbier grass, and greyer skies. High water had been there recently and debris was still caught in the trees, caked mud was still stuck to everything, and the landscape was dotted with pools of standing water left behind by the receding flood. This was Elber's part of the world, and it was in bad shape.

Again, his thoughts flitted back to Jassa and Zari. He could bear it, or at least try to bear it, if he were cast out of SCO Station and sent back down here, so long as they were safe. But what about them? Things on-planet were plainly much worse than they had been before, and things had been bad enough then that their first child Belrad had died. If Mistvale had gotten hit as hard as the landscape he had seen so far, then life was very hard there. Hard enough maybe to kill his wife and daughter. He was almost glad they had been kept behind to serve as hostages to his behavior. At least it meant they were out of harm's way. The land he was traveling was no place for a mother and a toddler.

He dared not fail. Not when Sotales could send his

family back to this place. Or someplace worse. And if he was not to fail, he was going to have to go beyond what Sotales had wanted—and do what Sotales needed.

The sights outside the window and the fears in his heart were enough to put Elber in his place. He'd been playing the part of an upper ever since he strapped himself into the shuttle for the ride from orbit down to Solace, ever since he took a job in an office where his hands stayed clean and his muscles didn't ache at the end of the day. But that was just pretending, things on the outside. Deep inside, he still was what he always would be—a lowdown dirt-poor peasant farmer.

The train slowed and came to a halt at a small-town station, a tired, mud-caked place where everything seemed used up and worn-out. Elber could spot a dozen things that told him the high water had been there many times in the last few years and that the town had long since given up any serious attempt at holding it back.

And then, with a start, Elber recognized the place, a split second before he read the name off a sign. Brewer's Station, two stations up from Mistvale. He had been there as a boy, going along with his father on a business trip as a special treat. The journey was more than a hundred kilometers, an impossibly long distance from home. Brewer's Station had seemed a huge and sophisticated city to him then, after a life on the farm.

He had returned to Brewer's Station a time or two as a teenager, and he remembered walking the streets of a clean, well-kept place. By then he had known enough to realize the big city of his childhood was really just a little town.

The two images of the place had remained fixed in his mind, side by side. But there was nothing left that was remotely like either the big city or the small village he carried in his memory. This Brewer's Station was more than half a wreck, with no sign that it was ever going to recover itself.

Brewer's Station had been the central receiving point for all the valley's farmers, the depot through which all finished products came, and it had always prospered off trade. If Brewer's Station was like this—what could his own little village of Mistvale be like?

The train pulled out of the station. The next stop was Wilhemton, the closest station to Mistvale.

Elber stood up, opaqued the window, and pulled his cleaned, dried clothes out of the autolaundry. He shed the splendid robe and pulled on his own plain clothes once again. He smoothed down the fabric and wondered how plain his outfit would appear to the Mistvale farm folk. Would these clothes that now seemed very ordinary to him seem very fancy and special back home? No point worrying about it. Clothes like these were all he had anymore.

Moments before, he had been enjoying all the pleasure of life as an upper, soaking up all the top-class goodies. But one look at Brewer's Station was all that was needed to remind him where he came from, and what he really was. That place had been way up-class from where he came from, and what he had been. Now it had been brought low, and here he was, coming back, looking grand while everyone else had gone poor. Rubbing their noses in it. Putting them in shame. And what did that make him but lower than lowdown?

Not long after, he disembarked from the train at Wilhemton, and then had a lonely two-hour wait. Wilhemton was smaller and even more decrepit than Brewer's Station. The sun beat down there as hard as the rain had struck him in Solace City. Elber knew he had to be far from the first person to wonder why something could not be done to bring some of the sunshine to one place and some of the rain to the other.

Wilhemton was all browns and greys, little more than a collection of shanties. He did not see a soul while he waited there. Were they all hiding behind the shutters of their houses, fearful that the man in the spaceside clothes was there to cause trouble somehow—to take the last of what they had left? Or, worse, were the houses truly empty, abandoned? He couldn't bring himself to go and check, to peek in the window of a building that seemed cast aside. What if it just *looked* that way, and the occupants—a man, a woman, worst of all, a child—caught him peering through the glassless window and understood what he was expecting to see? Better, far better, not to look, not to know.

At long last the local ground bus—really just a mid-size delivery van—came around the corner, bumping along the washed-out road. It came to a jerky stop and pulled up to the bus stop right in front of him. Elber was not surprised to see the bus did not have an ArtInt driver. Instead, there was an actual human being behind the controls. The door swung open, and Elber looked inside.

The driver was a wizened old man, his deeply tanned face lined and worn, a three days' stubble on his face, and two or three teeth missing from his wide and friendly smile.

The driver sat at what appeared to be an old wooden chair out of someone's kitchen. It had been bolted to the floor of the bus. The enclosure for the ArtInt driver had been ripped out, and a complicated set of hand controls, plainly built out of whatever spare parts had been to hand, had been installed in its place. Elber recognized a pump handle and a couple of old doorknobs, but nothing else on the jury-rigged control panel was readily identifiable—though it looked as though the driver operated the brakes by pulling on a rope that went down through a hole in the floor.

"Hello to you!" said the driver, climbing down from his perch and coming out the door. "Lucky day for you. I don't come by here more'n twice a week. Usually just fetching and carrying packages from the depot here. Packages, not people. That's the workaday of this bus. Then I got word on th' link we had us an actual transfer *passenger* off the train today. Didn't hardly believe it, cause no one's gone up to City from here for a while—so *couldn't* be no local coming back. Figured it was likely a mistake. But no it weren't, and here you are." The driver stuck out his hand and smiled again. Elber offered his hand, and the old man shook it vigorously. "I'm Sandal Abbleman."

"Hello," Elber replied, glad the torrent of words had subsided. "Elber Malloon. Call me Elber." He had forgotten that part of it, the neighborliness that was instinct, reflex—and sometimes, relentless. Knowing all about each other, about all your neighbors, and all their neighbors—that was survival in a place like this.

And the bus driver *had* to be the most neighborly—the most nosy, if you wanted to put it that way. In Wilhemton and Mistvale, the bus driver would also be the main conduit for news, for rumor. He would hear all the stories first. He would know, would *have* to know, who was feeling poorly, who was behind on their bills, who was visiting whom. Every now and again—when a shut-in's mailbox just kept getting fuller, when he saw a little boy he knew on a road far from his home, when he knew the Reivers were about to stir, it would be one of the tidbits of news or gossip that he heard, his knowledge of the habits and routines of all his customers, that saved lives.

Not that Sandal Abbleman would ever think of it in those terms. Such things just came with the job. "I'll do that, Elber," he said. "Don't get many City uppers coming down this way." Abbleman cocked his head and looked thoughtful. "Malloon. That's a name we hear local-like. Not a City name."

"Born twenty kilometers from here," Elber said proudly.

"Elber—Elber Malloon . . ." Abbleman looked out into the middle distance for a moment. Then his eyes brightened, and he pointed a gnarled finger at Elber. "You're Eli and Suza Malloon's boy! You lived over near Mistvale."

Elber grinned. "That's right. But Father and Mother passed away a long time ago."

Abbleman nodded. "I 'member the funeral. I don't get over that way much—no reason to, that's the sad thing. But I don't think I've heard news of your folk—since—since that, uh, Big Run about a year ago."

Elber grimaced. "Yes, we—my wife and child and I—got caught up in that." Not something he was very proud of, but there it was.

"Yeah," Abbleman said, drawing the word out sadly. He patted Elber on the arm, trying to comfort him. "Things was bad when you left, but they've gotten worse. The old Mistvale folk like to say the mists are twenty meters deep in places. Half the land is flooded. Including your old place, I'm afraid."

"I know," Elber said, and thought, for the thousandth time, of his little boy Belrad, dead, buried in back of the house, his grave drowned forever by the water that had never receded. "Things must have gotten mighty hard around here."

Abbleman nodded thoughtfully. "Yes, sir. Yes, sir, they have, and that's the truth." He paused, then smiled suddenly. "But let's not fret about that now. They say, now that that Greenhouse and NovaSpot business is all done, maybe the uppers on Greenhouse can do something to fix the problems around here. So maybe they's hope. And you're *home,* that's the main thing. They'll all want to hear your story, back in around Mistvale."

"Yes, well, but I'm just here for a vis—" Suddenly Elber stopped short. Suddenly he saw it, saw how he was going to make contact with Zak. He had been looking at the whole thing all wrong, looking with City eyes, with SCO Station eyes. He had been trying to come up with a way to track down a well-hidden, well-protected Zak in the middle of his well-hidden territory. He had come up with nothing better than a vague idea about trying to search out old friends who might to be able to connect him with Zak—an idea that seemed unlikely to work, to put it mildly.

Suddenly, looking at it with Mistvale eyes, he could see that all was completely unnecessary. If Zak Destan—*Reiver* Destan, Bush Lord Destan—wanted to stay hidden—well, no one was going to find him. But if, as Captain Sotales seemed to think, Reiver Destan wanted to talk with someone from the outside, wanted to get a message sent—then Elber Malloon had already finished all the work he needed to do.

People talked about each other back here. Someone coming back from the Big Run had to be Big News. Every friend of Sandal Abbleman would know about Elber's arrival by nightfall—and every one of them would pass it along as well. It would be impossible for Zak not to hear word of his arrival—and Zak would know perfectly well, better than any of the locals, that no one came all the way from SCO Station just to call on the old neighbors in Mistvale.

"What were you about to say, Elber?"

Elber blinked and came back to himself. "Sorry. I just thought of how to do something I need to do. I said I'm just back here for a visit."

"Well, that's fine. Bet you're hoping to see all the folk from the old days."

"Oh, yes," said Elber. He looked to the east and spotted a fat dot of light low in the sky, rising quickly up into the gathering twilight. SCO Station, swinging around the world on its orbit. Jassa and Zari were up there. Probably just sitting down to dinner. Probably praying for him. "Yes indeed," Elber said again. "I'm hopin' that harder'n you could ever know."

"Well, help me tote the coming-and-going cargo off and on the bus, and we'll get there all the sooner."

Elber grinned and nodded. "Glad to do it, Mr. Abbleman. Just like the old days." He followed the old man back toward the clapped-out shed that served as the Wilhemton transit station.

SCO Station
Orbiting Solace

Captain Olar Sotales smiled broadly at the soon-to-be-former prisoner, and pushed the release form across the table at him. "Once again, Mr. Brantry, my apologies. It was all such a terrible misunderstanding," he lied.

"Sure it was," Brantry replied, snatching up a pen

and scrawling his name across the bottom of the paper.

Sotales cocked his head to one side and shrugged, very slightly. That was the way the game got played sometimes. He knew that Brantry knew that Sotales knew that Brantry knew the charges had been deliberately invented. But still the scene must be played. And, in a sense, justice had in fact been done, for Brantry and his friends *had* been guilty—though, perhaps, not of the crimes with which they were charged.

Brantry jabbed his thumbprint down in the ID box and shoved the paper back across the table. Sotales added his own careful signature—no need for him to apply his thumbprint; only the prisoner had to do that— then looked to Brantry again and gestured down at the table. "Both copies, if you please, Mr. Brantry. You'll want one for yourself."

"Yeah. I really want a souvenir. Something to help me remember the last two months." Brantry snatched at the second copy, and, if possible, signed it with an even poorer grace, and even more illegibly, than the first, and stabbed his thumbprint down with even more violence, hard enough to shake the table.

Sotales took the second form, signed it, and slid it back across the table. "You're free to go," he said with a smile. He made no attempt to stand or to shake the man's hand. There would have been no point. Brantry scooped up the paper, snarled at Sotales, and stomped out, slamming the door behind him.

Good. That was the end of that. So far as Sotales was concerned, the release of Brantry marked the formal end of his own very private effort to support the NovaSpot Ignition Project. Sotales had detained a good two dozen troublemakers on SCO Station and made arrangements for three times that number to be detained on-planet, and in other habitats. Any or all of them could have stopped or delayed the project—and, of course, given the rigid deadlines and technical requirements, delay would have been the same as outright cancellation. The public was by no means aware of it, but the Ignition

Project had succeeded by the narrowest of margins. One more featherweight on the wrong side of the balance, and it would have failed.

Sotales unlocked the file drawer of his desk, picked up the paper Brantry had signed, and carefully filed it with the others. He thought for a moment, then pulled out the complete file. It seemed a good moment to review the whole operation—an operation of which there were no computer records, no ArtInt storage, no datapads, nothing except this file and the far more detailed and far-ranging records Sotales kept in his head.

Brantry was one of the featherweights that Sotales had kept out of the Ignition equation. In the case of Brantry and his cargo company, it was simple corruption, overbilling and undershipping. Brantry had played that game just a trifle at first, and then gotten more and more greedy. A trumped-up morals charge had taken him out of circulation—and also sent a very clear message to his competitors. The rest of the cargo support operations had proceeded, not honestly, but at least with a level of theft and fraud that was kept within the bounds of reason.

There had been others who threatened Ignition one way or another—factory owners who jacked up prices, leaders of worker groups who tried to renegotiate one time too many, politicians who thought to gain fleeting advantage in some other game they were playing by holding some part of the Ignition Project hostage for a while in this committee or tangled up in that appropriations measure.

Though in theory Sotales was merely commander of SCO Station's Security Force, in practice his reach extended much farther than that. SCO Station was the center of trade and commerce in the Solacian system, and Sotales had followed in the tradition of his predecessors, leveraging the station's economic clout, using it to enhance the SSF's own power, assisting other habitats with their security needs, even cooperating with planetside security to the point where it wasn't precisely clear where the Solacian Planetary Police Force ended and SCO SSF began.

By Sotales' rough calculation, for every Brantry he had fined or jailed, or even merely threatened or blackmailed, Sotales had managed to discourage fifteen or twenty from getting out of line in the first place. But the most artistic part of it was that no one knew what he had done. Brantry was one of the few he had dealt with directly. All the others had been managed from a distance, by this or that subordinate on SCO Station, or through some colleague on-planet, or even a few private citizens who owed him favors.

He shoved the drawer smoothly shut and locked it carefully. He hadn't added or subtracted anything to the file beyond adding Brantry's release form, but that didn't matter. He knew what came next without looking at bits of paper. And that was just as well. There wasn't even a paper file for what he intended next.

The long and the short of it was that he planned to do what he could to support the restoration of Greenhouse. He was no engineer, of course, no scientist. But the director of the most powerful secret police force in the Solace system could still do his share, quietly, behind the scenes. In large part, he expected his role to be a continuation of his effort in the Ignition Project—using manipulation, misdirection, threats, bribes, encouragement, and, if and when necessary, plain old-fashioned violent force to keep the jackals at bay and the project on track.

Sotales also had a longer-range goal in mind. Greenhouse was important—everyone knew that—but Sotales had his own opinions as to *why* it was important. The official line focused on how a revived Greenhouse would mean a revived Solace. With Greenhouse back in business, it wouldn't be long at all before the whole Solacian ecosystem was back in working order, and all was lovely in the garden once more.

But Sotales had seen the most secret versions of the reports on the Solacian ecology, and those reports made it plain that there was no hope at all.

It took very little effort on Sotales' part to understand what the effort to revive Greenhouse was actually in aid of, and not much more to confirm his theory with a few very quiet inquiries. Greenhouse was to be the way station for the eventual evacuation of Solace, a place of refuge until more permanent places could be found in other star systems. There simply was not enough transport capacity available to move everyone off-planet and directly out of the star system quickly enough. There weren't enough ships, the ships weren't big enough, and the ships weren't fast enough.

Even once they were out of the Solacian system, it was far from likely they could dump that many refugees in any one inhabited star system—Solace had learned that lesson the hard way when it had absorbed most of the surviving population of Glister—and the population of Solace was far larger than Glister's. Other worlds had seen how much upheaval the resettlement of the Glisterns had caused—and some were of the opinion that the collapse of Solace had been caused by the sudden arrival of so many new mouths to feed. For those reasons, it would likely also be politically infeasible to resettle the Solacians quickly out of system. And then, of course, there was the question of how much money the operation would cost.

But Greenhouse could be the holding tank, potentially supporting the entire population of Solace—though in very spartan quarters. With NovaSpot making thousands more habitat domes available, Greenhouse could hold out for years, perhaps even decades, until the political situation made it possible for people to be resettled more gradually on other worlds.

And so Sotales had set himself the additional task of *guiding* Greenhouse's revival, seeing to it that more time and money went into building and restoring more and bigger habitat domes, and less into research facilities that were just for show and would likely never see use before the coming crises swept over them. Leave enough in the way of research facilities to serve as window dressing, and nothing more. That was Sotales' goal, his ideal. He doubted he could reach it, but it was useful to have something to aim at.

He knew that it would be far more difficult to steer

construction policy from this far off than it had been to squash inconvenient station- and planet-based corruption, but there were several things working for him. Chief among them, he had not the slightest doubt that Planetary Executive Kalzant was working toward the same goal, though she couldn't admit it openly. He was going to try to ease the way for the goal the most powerful person in the whole star system wanted to attain. That *had* to help.

But Sotales had more agenda than those two in play, and not all his schemes and plans involved such long-range, long-distance do-gooding.

It was essential that the existing social patterns, with the uppers still on top, and the lowdowns and peasants still down below, be maintained as long as possible, simply because that was the best way to keep order. Maybe he was just thinking like every secret policeman in history, but he believed order was going to matter a great deal more than justice in the days to come. The peasants had many legitimate complaints, but what point in land reform or building schools or fixing roads when the whole planet was about to be abandoned?

The trick was to keep the lid on the existing social order for as long as possible, and, somehow, at the same time, to find a way to keep the pressures on it from building up to explosive levels.

Sotales did not know or care if the reivers and bush lords were a source or a symptom of social pressure. All he knew was that they were destabilizing the situation, and needed to be shut down, or, better still, co-opted, before things got completely out of control.

Friend Malloon was a part of that project—a bigger part than he knew. Sotales switched on his secure hardwired datapad, the one that was literally chained to his desk. The actual physical data cable—a heavy-duty, multishielded cable—was snaked through the links of the chain and vanished into his desk. His datapad neither sent nor received any sort of data via radio or any other form of electromagnetic frequency. Sotales' people had snooped—and cracked—enough supposedly "secure" wireless datapads that he knew not to trust them. His hardwired pad was immune to such problems—though he also knew no data channel was ever absolutely secure. There were always ways to get in. Even so, his secure pad was as close to safe as it was practical to get.

He endured the pad's retinal scan and thumbprint check, and the rest of the biometrics, and at last got to what he wanted to see: Elber Malloon—or more accurately, what Malloon was seeing, and hearing.

The implants had gone in during Malloon's premission medical checkup—and in fact putting them in had been the whole point of *doing* the checkup. Simple, really. They had him come in the night before the physical check, under the pretext of monitoring what he had eaten and drunk for twelve hours beforehand. Once he was already asleep, they anesthetized him and injected the nanotaps beneath the skin—two vision taps at his temples and the audio taps at the base of each earlobe. Each was about the size of a smallish grain of rice, and somewhat rubbery in consistency. The mike heads and lenses themselves were about the diameter of human hairs, and protruded no more than a millimeter or so through the skin. The implants were colored to match Malloon's skin and hair, and, once properly implanted, they were virtually undetectable.

Two slightly larger units, a primary and a backup recorder-transceiver, were likewise implanted into Malloon's upper arms. All the units powered themselves off body heat.

The taps did not attempt anything so complex as actually hooking into his nervous system. They were merely very small mikes and cameras, tied in to even smaller transmitters with a range of only about thirty centimeters, just enough for their signals to be received, recorded, and relayed by the transceivers in his upper arms. Nor was the sound quality or the visual resolution particularly good—but then, they only had to be good enough.

The transceivers were able to record audio and visual

data during periods where it was impossible to transmit, and then do "burst" transmissions when such were possible. The implant transceivers in Malloon's upper arms were also of severely limited range, of only a few tens of meters. The system could only work if a larger transceiver was nearby, ready to receive data and pass it on. The exterior unit also had to be able to detect snooperscans, and shut them down before getting caught. And then, the subject of the taps had to be induced to carry the exterior transceiver along with him.

That part hadn't been hard. They gave Malloon a bright and shiny new datapad, a very stylish pen, and a wristaid with more functions and displays than most commerically available datapads. Any or all of those, or any of the other exterior devices he was unknowingly carrying, could manage the dataflow from the nanotaps. They all worked in concert with each other, sharing the data storage and transmission loads, encrypting the datastream, storing it, then passing it up the line through the existing radio datanet until it was beamed to SCO Station.

Sotales—or rather the ArtInt monitoring the transmissions for Sotales—would see and hear *everything* that Malloon saw and heard. Most of what the system detected, would, of course, be crashingly dull. The ArtInt would edit the raw inputs down to something worthy of being watched by Sotales—and even most of that would likely be drivel.

But, with any luck at all, there would be diamonds he could sift from the dross. If Malloon managed a face-to-face with Zak Destan—what couldn't be learned about his Reiver band from that? And Sotales had watched and studied long enough to be sure Destan's Reivers were the alpha group down there. They were the key to the whole reiver crisis. What Destan did, the others would do. Manage Destan and he would manage all of them.

And all he had to do was sit and watch.

Sotales' secured, hardwired, snooper-proof datapad came to life, playing realtime sound and images direct from a human being who had no idea he was transmitting. Sotales felt a real moment of triumph. It was all going to work.

At the moment, it appeared that Elber Malloon was looking through the grimy front windshield of some sort of rickety vehicle, reminiscing with the driver about some long-ago outbreak of corn spore blight.

Not the most vital or up-to-date intelligence—but never mind. Sooner or later, Sotales would get what he was waiting for.

And then the rules of the game would change.

Chapter Fifteen

LAST CHANCE TO SEE

DeSilvo City
(aka Base Glister)
The Planet Glister

It was dark in the cargo transfer center, and cold, and quiet. There was a little light from the one viewport by the main cargo airlock, cold fingers of sunlight just fading behind the far-off hills as the local sun set. Not that outside day or night mattered inside the burrows and tunnels of DeSilvo City. Oskar DeSilvo ran the place on a standard Earthside twenty-four-hour clock that had no relation to Glister's own day-night cycle.

You could see out from the cargo transfer center, but from few other place. There were only a handful of topside structures in DeSilvo City, fewer still with viewports, and it was rarer yet for anyone to bother looking out the windows. There wasn't usually much to see, and what there was was infinitely depressing.

Soon there would be even less chance to see out, once DeSilvo's robots set to work burying and camouflaging this entrance, along with all the others.

Two figures stood in the center of the big, shadowed compartment, the air cold enough that their breath came out in puffs of fog. Neither was dressed warmly enough, but then, neither intended to be there long.

"All right," Norla said, "we're here. Tell me what you've got, from the top. And tell me how you found it."

"What's the point of how I found it?" Yuri demanded.

"If you want to get yourself a pilot, there's plenty of point," Norla replied. It was bad enough that she was listening to Yuri Sparten, spy, as he claimed the moral high ground. Worse still, she found herself almost agreeing with him and with his plan. But she would be damned if she was going to let things get so bad that she let herself be hurried into a plan like his without being *sure*. "Tell it to me again. Starting with how we'll even be able to get out the door without being stopped."

"First off, DeSilvo can't possibly be watching everything."

"No, but his ArtInts could be—and they are."

"And then they pass it all on to him, and nothing is done unless he decides to do it. The ArtInts can't act on their own. This place is a totally top-down operation. Nothing gets done unless he tells the ArtInts to do it, either with a standing order that covers a period of time or else with a specific order to cover a specific event. And they haven't received standing orders on how to handle us."

"And how the hell do you know that?"

"Simple. I asked some of the ArtInts—and they answered me. He hadn't given them any directives that said something like 'Don't talk to strangers.' They answered all my questions very fully and clearly. They have almost no security programming. They're here to maintain DeSilvo City, and to cook and clean for De-Silvo, and to build whatever damn-fool machines he orders up. They're watching—but they aren't briefed to react in any way. If Ashdin was right about the original purpose of this place, then it was going to be populated by DeSilvo's loyal and trusted employees. It wasn't designed as a prison, and the ArtInts aren't programmed to treat us like prisoners who'll likely try to escape."

Unless the ArtInts who told you that were programmed to lie about it, Norla thought. But no sense pursuing that sort of paranoid reasoning, or they'd be paralyzed by fear of imaginary dangers. "Point taken. DeSilvo might have decided not to bother programming them for that kind of work. After all, where, exactly, would we run *to*?"

"Right. Besides, if we do get caught, what's he going to do? Lock us up? We *are* locked up. He hasn't said we can't leave—he's just let us assume it."

"*You're* assuming he's going to feel the need to play fair," Norla said. "Even if he's left the rules fairly loose so far, he *is* the absolute ruler here. He could be completely arbitrary about it. Why should it matter to him whether or not he said we could leave? Why is he going to be bound by your splitting hairs about what he has or hasn't said? He can punish us arbitrarily at any time for anything—or for nothing at all. Who's going to stop him? Who are we going to appeal to?"

"Granted—in theory. In practice—*he needs us*. All of us. For what, I don't know yet, but I do know he needs us. Does he really believe that he could get Admiral Koffield's willing cooperation after torturing us for trying to escape?"

Norla nodded. It was a reasonable argument—but it depended on DeSilvo's acting rationally, and in his own best interest. How hard did she want to gamble on that?

"What about our people?" she asked. "If we ask Admiral Koffield about this, he'd say no in a heartbeat."

"I'm not so sure he would," Yuri said. "But you're right that he might well say no. So we don't ask his permission."

"That sounds closer to being childish than being ethical," said Norla. "That's not the sort of game I want to risk playing with the admiral."

"You mean *Retired* Admiral Anton Koffield? Or is he even *retired*? He must have been declared legally dead once the *Dom Pedro IV* was listed as lost with all hands. Either way, he's not on active duty and has no legal authority to command, even in the Chrono Patrol. Besides, *you're* not *in* the Chronologic Patrol. You're an officer on a civilian vessel. Show me how he has any legal authority over us, or any legal right to dictate our behavior."

"If I was worried about legalisms—and maybe I should be—I'd be talking about what Captain Marquez would have to say about all this."

"As far as Marquez goes—we're not aboard ship, we aren't standing watches, he has assigned us no duties and given us no orders. He doesn't even control his own vessel anymore. DeSilvo controls it. Plus, the ship's current registration is under the name 'Merchanter's Dream' with *me* as the captain—all fraudulent, plus it lists Marquez as my first officer under an assumed name. He's in six kinds of violation of the law. What's *his* legal authority to control us?"

"I'm not sure," Norla admitted. "But if we decide to act on our own this way, and we get away with it, we'll show the rest of the crew that there are no consequences to their actions. Our people are under a lot of pressure right now. If crew discipline gets pulled too hard, crew cohesion is going to start unraveling—and that gets us killed, lots of ways. We'd have come all this way, and been through all that's happened, for nothing. Do you really want to risk that?"

"I don't *want* to risk it," Yuri said. "But I *have* to. If there really is a diehard habitat out there—hell, for all I know, they're family! It could be. Even if they're not blood relations, they're Glisterns, and so am I. The only difference between us is that my family managed to get out in time, and theirs didn't."

"If they even exist."

"If they exist," Yuri agreed. "But if they do exist, and they're that close, and we could help them, and we don't—the group, the colony, the habitat, will die out, sooner or later. You know what it's like for diehards. If they exist, they've been hanging on for something close to a century, fighting every day of every one of those years just to survive. If they exist, they're second, third, maybe fourth generation by now. If we *don't* help them, then all of what *they've* been through will be for nothing."

Norla looked at him thoughtfully but did not answer. He was speaking with far greater eloquence than she had ever heard from him.

"If they exist," he repeated. "Let's find out, one way or the other. Maybe they were never there at all, and DeSilvo's just playing games with our heads. If so, we can call him on it. Maybe there was a colony, and it died out forty years ago. If so, there was nothing we could have done—but we'll have tried, and we'll know. Or maybe they *are* there, and we can find out how many of them there are, and what kind of shape they're in, and what they need. *Then* we can go to the others with real information," he said. "Let's go find out."

Norla looked at him and sighed. She knew Yuri had won. It would be impossible for her to say no.

Yuri played one more card. "This could be our last chance, our only chance, to go see and find out," he said. "Once DeSilvo tells us what the grand plan is, my guess is we're going to be busy. Way too busy to slip away without someone stopping us. Maybe we'll even leave Glister, and never come back."

"All right, all right. Let's leave all that for the moment," she said. "Show me how you found it."

Yuri pulled out a datapad, set it down on the top of a waist-high equipment locker in the center of the room, and started showing her imagery. "I started with the name, and what DeSilvo said about the location. Last Chance Canyon, seven hundred miles south of here. We brought down copies of most of our data files from the *Dom Pedro IV* when we landed—including the imagery from our planet scan."

Norla nodded. Upon arrival, the *Dom Pedro IV* had gone into a close-in polar orbit of Glister, such that the ship tracked over a different swatch of the planet with each orbit. They had spotted DeSilvo City easily—mainly because Oskar DeSilvo had done everything he could to make sure the place was noticed. But they had scanned the remainder of the planet, just to be sure.

"So, anyway, here are images of the area due south of us, centered on a point seven hundred kilometers from here." Yuri brought up pictures of a frozen and all-but-featureless wilderness of ice, snow, and bare rock. "What I've got here is the integrated data from all of our overflights—the infrared, the visual, everything, merged into one set of image files. Now, we didn't get anything at all on infrared of our scan of the area in question," he said. "Nothing at all that looked anything like a non-natural source. At first I thought that meant there was nothing there. DeSilvo was just messing with us when he said there was a colony. But then I realized that heat would be the *last* thing diehards on Glister would waste. They'd be very well insulated and use every kind of co-generation system they could to squeeze every last bit of energy out of heat sources. There'd still be some waste heat, of course—second law of thermodynamics. But where would it go?"

"Maybe there was no infrared signature because there was no waste heat because there was no colony producing it," Norla said.

"Or maybe we just didn't see it. Don't forget the *Dom Pedro IV* isn't a spy ship or anything. It's got pretty good sensors, not top-of-the-line stuff. We had to do some adapting just to configure them for the planet scan."

"Fair enough. But still, we were *looking* for that size of installation. And even a smallish settlement would throw a lot of heat, no matter how efficient it was."

"I know," Yuri conceded. "I knew about all that, but then I got to thinking. I've read up a little on diehards. They usually work pretty hard to keep a low profile. They hide as much as they can. So they'd hide their waste heat output as much as they could, design things so that would happen. So—what would dissipate heat energy very quickly, and continuously, so that it wouldn't have a chance to accumulate and raise the temperature enough to register on a medium-grade sensor scan from orbit?"

"I don't know. Magic, maybe. Yuri, all this isn't looking for the colony. You can't see them because they're not there, not because they've got some superadvanced high-powered cooling system."

Yuri smiled. "But that's what I was going to tell you. They *do* have that kind of cooling system. It's called 'wind.' " He worked the datapad and brought up the images he wanted. "I told myself, if they're in a canyon, they must be there for a reason. They'd have picked a spot that had some sort of advantages for them."

"Unless they just stayed wherever they wound up by chance and remained there because they felt stubborn."

"I doubt it. As I said, I've been doing some homework on diehards these last few days," Yuri said. "There have been studies. The groups that survive are the ones that do something sensible about their situation. They might be crazy enough to stay behind deliberately after an evacuation, or unlucky enough to get themselves stranded—but from then on they're sensible enough to do some real engineering, hunker down in temporary shelters while they scout locations and build themselves a permanent base. So my guess is they found a place that would do them some good, one way or another. Like this one."

The image on the datapad zoomed in on one area, centering on a canyon system shaped like an upside-down capital "T," with the horizontal arm running almost exactly east–west, and the vertical arm pointed due north. "It took me most of last night to find it," he said. "That formation is 720 kilometers southeast of here. That's a good enough match with DeSilvo's description that I was a little suspicious of it at first."

"So what good does a T-shaped canyon do them?" Norla asked.

"The prevailing winds average about thirty kilometers an hour, due east," said Yuri. "Canyon effects would probably amplify that quite a bit in the upper reaches of the east–west arm of the canyon, and give you a lot of turbulence in the region where the two arms meet. The part of the north–south arm farther away from the east–west arm would have much gentler wind conditions and be well out of most of the heavier weather generally."

"So what good does all that do?"

"Wind power," said Yuri. "Inexhaustible, always-there power. The wind generates electricity, and you can store or use the electricity however you want. Low-tech, maybe, but a lot easier to maintain than other power sources. The same wind can blow away your waste heat through radiators. If they placed their habitat in the shallower part of the north–south arm, they'd get direct sunlight coming in from the south. That gives you a chance to hang solar power collectors, plus you have shelter from the prevailing winds."

"Sounds great," Norla said. "So why can't we see them?"

"We can," said Yuri. "If you know what to look for, and you look hard enough." He zoomed in closer to the central area of the canyon. "There. This is from the day-time pass images. Very regularly spaced shadows being cast on the canyon floor. Each one like a dandelion—a long stalk, a fuzzy head. I read those as windmills. Rapidly spinning vanes supported by a central pillar." He flipped to another image. "This melt pattern in the ice downwind of the north–south canyon. I didn't see anything like it in any of the other canyons, but it's very prominent. There's a flow pattern, as if something were melting the ice, and it was refreezing almost at once. The wind is doing the cooling, obviously—but what's causing the heating? Note the pattern of very dark spots just *above* the melt pattern. Waste heat dumps? Trash dumps? And there. Right in the center of the north–south canyon, right where there's maximum exposure to direct sun—there's a very regular pattern of hexagonal shapes, right in the best spot to aim solar collectors. You can see that the hexagonal shapes are all distorted in the same way. It looks like they're tilted, down and to the left, each by the same amount. Work out where the sun is above the horizon, where the *Dom Pedro* was, figure the angles, and tilt a regular hexagonal by the resulting amount—*that's* the shape you get!"

"You lost me," said Norla. "What does all that mean?"

"It means those are regular hexagonal panels aimed straight at the sun!"

Norla looked carefully at the images, then, just as carefully, looked at Yuri Sparten. She honestly couldn't tell, from either examination, if he was for real. She could, if she tried just a little, imagine that she saw what *he* saw in those images, and she could even allow that his interpretation was more or less reasonable. But it could just as well be flaws in the detectors, artifacts of whatever image enhancers he had used, natural patterns that chanced to look like something regular and artificial, or maybe even something less than that—random noise on the images, with just enough chance regularity that the human eye could force into the patterns it wanted to see. Or maybe he had spotted something, real structures, made by human beings—but made before Glister collapsed and having nothing to do with imaginary diehards.

"You can't tell for sure, can you?" Yuri asked, studying her face as closely as she was studying his. "You can't say for certain whether or not I'm imagining the whole thing."

Why deny it? she asked herself. "No," she said. "No, I can't."

Yuri nodded. "Which leaves us back at *maybe,*" he said, his voice quiet and intense. "Suppose we leave it at that?" he asked. "Then what?"

"What do you mean, then what? That would be the end of it."

"I suppose," he said. "But it might not." He tapped his fingers on the datapad. "How soon would it be until you started wanting to see these images again, just to get another look? Just to be *sure* there was nothing? And how sure would you be then if you aren't sure now? And suppose maybe DeSilvo *does* lock things down tomorrow. Or maybe he packs us all aboard the *Dom Pedro IV* and hauls us off somewhere. How will you feel when you want to see the images again, even though there won't be any chance to do anything about it?"

She stared at him, eyeball-to-eyeball, then blinked, literally and metaphorically. "All right," she said. "We'll go. Just this once I let you play mind games with me. Try it again, and you lose. Clear enough?"

"Clear."

"We go out. We do a flyover. A careful flyover, in case they don't like strangers and don't mind shooting them down. *We don't land.* If there are five hundred freezing diehards right below us, and we have five hundred blankets, *we don't land*. We don't get curious and change our minds over the site. If we can't tell for certain if anyone is alive, just from a flyover, but we see a hatch we could open and check, *we don't land*. We get information. We bring it back and tell the people here about it. No heroics. Is that all clear?"

Yuri grinned. "Yeah, sure. All clear."

But she could tell that he was only hearing the words he wanted to hear, just as he had only seen on the images what he wanted to see.

"All right," she said. "Now show me this aircar you found."

"It's over here," he said, setting off through the dim recesses of the big chamber. Yuri led her off through the jumble of machines and vehicles that crowded the floor of the cargo center. "Here," he said at last. "This is it."

Norla didn't speak. She walked around the stubby little craft, studying it carefully. Judging by appearances, the aircar was a Glister precollapse model that had been swept up in some general salvage run made by one of DeSilvo's larger land transport vehicles. It *seemed* to be intact, but that was a long way from a flying vehicle she'd be willing to trust her life to on a fourteen-hundred-kilometer round-trip flight. "Yuri, this thing has to be at least a hundred years old. Literally."

"I know," Yuri said.

"And it must have been sitting in some pretty rough weather for a long time, too."

"Yeah, I know," said Yuri, staring at the beat-up old craft as if he had never seen anything so beautiful. "But what's it matter? Either it works, or it doesn't."

"I can tell you right now, it doesn't work," said Norla. "*Something* has to have given out on it since the last time anyone flew it. And it's not either-or. Suppose it *sort*-of works—and then sort-of breaks down, halfway back from our flyover?" But still, she had to admit, at least to herself, it did seem to be in fairly good shape—and aircars were built to last. And the idea of flying

again, of getting out, of seeing the landscape, was starting to appeal to her.

Besides, she reminded herself, the aircar had been in a
deep freeze for something like a century. She had been
kept in cryostorage a lot longer than that when DeSilvo
sabotaged the *Dom Pedro IV,* and *she* was still in working order. More or less. It might be about time for her to
have her head examined, for example. Instead, she
found the release latches on the car's forward access
panel and popped it open. She peered inside and nodded
thoughtfully. Not too bad, really. "We're going to be on
this job for a while," she announced. "Maybe a day or
so. We'll need tools. And let's go get some warmer
clothes on before we start."

It was closer to three days before Norla slammed the last
access panel shut and stepped back from the aircar, at
last satisfied with the vehicle's state of repair.

"We're done," she said. "Give it a try."

Yuri climbed into the passenger compartment and
flipped the main power switch. The display board lit up
smoothly, all systems green. "Nice work, Norla," he
said. "Very nice work indeed."

"Not bad," she allowed, wiping her hand on a rag.
Not only had the job taken longer, but they also had to
avoid attracting attention.

All of them—Koffield, Marquez, and the rest—were
marking time, waiting for word of how the issue of Ignition had been resolved, one way or the other, on Greenhouse. All the ship's company had been through a lot in
recent times, and fortunately, Marquez saw no reason to
assign a lot of busywork. Everyone had a light work
schedule. But even if they didn't have much in the way
of official work to do while DeSilvo was in semi-
seclusion, they still had to show up at mealtimes and
make an appearance in the evenings, and do so without
obvious signs of having spent half the night sweating
and cursing over a recalcitrant levitation unit.

After getting a few quizzical glances and odd smiles,
it dawned on Norla that some members of the group

had noticed that the two of them were both missing for hours at a time, and that at least some of them had concluded that she and Yuri were carrying on a torrid affair. Her first reaction was to blush violently in embarrassment. Her second thought was to wonder what Admiral Koffield would think. Yuri was so much younger than she was! But her third thought was that it made an excellent cover story. The etiquette of space crews was to be very respectful of privacy. The others would not ask any awkward questions. Better still, no one would dream of looking for them, or trying to find out what they were doing.

And so she had left it alone, not even telling Yuri what she suspected. He would want to burst in at the next meal and deny it all at the top of his lungs, and that would spoil everything. Better to let it alone. The way that she probably should have left the aircar alone. But it was too late now.

"So let's go," Yuri said.

"Not just yet," Norla said. "One: We need some sleep first. It'll be a long flight. Two: We need to make sure we have provisions enough for the trip, plus a good flight plan so we can get there and back. Three"—she gestured toward the window—"it's the middle of the night out there. We have to wait for daylight."

Yuri's face fell as he looked out the window, but even he had to concede the point. "All right," he said. "But we leave as close to first light as we can."

"We will," Norla said. "We will."

Norla was thinking ahead to the end of the flight, toward the end of the day. She had no desire to try to find DeSilvo City in the dark.

For that matter, she was far less sure than she had been that she *wanted* to find Last Chance Canyon, whatever the lighting conditions. But she was committed. It was far too late for such worries.

On the other hand, she told herself, *it's never too soon for regrets.*

"In the morning, then," she said. "Let's get some sleep."

Chapter Sixteen

A MATTER OF FACT

Somehow, Glister looked even colder from in the air. It didn't help that the aircar's heating system wasn't all it could have been. They weren't freezing, but they weren't exactly breaking into a sweat, either.

And there could be no doubt that the world outside looked colder when *you* were cold. The view that scrolled past them down below—ice, snow, frozen rock-strewn wastes—was spectacular, but far from inviting.

Norla checked her displays. They were doing all right, so far. The biggest challenge had been getting the cargo transfer center's vehicle airlock to cooperate. Norla had been worried that opening it manually would set off all sorts of security alarms. That hadn't happened—at least so far as they knew—but it had never occurred to her that simply cranking hatches built to handle vehicles far larger than their aircar would take a lot of muscle power.

Now that they were airborne, and already several hundred kilometers from home, she had thought of a whole new worry: DeSilvo's robots were still hard at work, hiding the exposed sections of DeSilvo City under rock and dirt and ice. Suppose they got around to burying the cargo center airlock before she and Yuri got back? *That* would be a lot of fun to deal with if they were delayed en route and were making final approach just after sunset.

Never mind. There was nothing they could do about

it anyway. Not anymore. The best they could do was to continue forward.

She shifted in her seat and flexed her shoulders, trying to relax, trying to keep from getting stiff. They were flying in their pressure suits with their visors open, and the suits were really too big and bulky for the cramped interior of the aircar. Norla had insisted on the suits, mainly to keep them warm in case the aircar's heating system went out. But there was also the chance that they would be forced to land and get out of the aircar to attempt repairs or signal for rescue, or whatever. If so, they'd need the pressure suits for more than heating—there was precious little free oxygen in what passed for air out there. Still, the aircar's cabin was awfully crowded, and getting damned uncomfortable.

Suddenly the aircar was jolted violently from side to side as it banged into a patch of turbulence. Norla held on to the controls for dear life and fought the vehicle back to a stable heading. Turbulence stopped, as suddenly as it had begun. She hadn't done much atmosphere flying in a long time. She had forgotten how *different* it was from space flight, how the surprises came at you in a whole different way.

Yuri sat beside her on the right, staring endlessly down at the ruined landscape. She could barely imagine what was going through his mind as he looked down at the planet from which his people had come. Nor, to be honest, did she want to ask him about it. She knew Yuri could turn theatrical at times, and she had no desire to invite a display of histrionics.

Yuri had seemed to grow *younger,* more immature, in the last few weeks, but Norla thought she understood that as well. He'd been playing the part of a spy, pretending as hard as he could to be harder, tougher, more determined than he really wanted to be. And then his cover was blown, and he was free to be himself again, to do and feel as he wished, and not as he thought a seasoned intelligence agent should act. It sometimes seemed to Norla as if all the emotion that he had been bottling up all that time wanted to rush out all at once.

She checked her navigation system—a grand name for the crude lash-up she had rigged up by wiring together an inertial tracker, the aircar's onboards, and a datapad. It *seemed* to be running with a reasonable degree of accuracy. "We're getting close," she said. "Get ready with the cameras and recorders."

If theirs had been any sort of real reconnaissance mission, they would have had every sort of high-resolution sensor built into the aircar, an ArtInt busily managing all of them, aiming and focusing the cameras, recording the data, shifting scan frequencies, and so on. Not on this operation. All they had was whatever cameras they could scrounge while hoping no one would notice they were missing. Yuri had worked out a series of mounting brackets so two cameras could peer through the front windshield, while he worked with a third, handheld camera. If all went well, they would get at least some sort of general visual and infrared coverage, and Yuri could use the handheld to get detailed images of specific areas.

Unfortunately, the jury-rigged camera mounts were so awkward and took up so much room in the cramped passenger compartment that it would have been all but impossible to leave them in place for the whole journey. Yuri had to spend a thumb-fingered five minutes fumbling around with the clamps and brackets before he had the thing even halfway set up. Then he got out the handheld camera and powered it up. "Ready," he announced.

"We'll see," said Norla, not entirely convinced the bracket wouldn't fall down. "I make us about five minutes out. We ought to be coming up on the western end of the east–west canyon. I want to do a flyover straight east, flying just south of the canyon. That ought to give the best view out the right side of the aircar. All right?"

"All right."

Norla peered ahead through the windshield at the cold, hard landscape down below. There! That looked a hell of a lot like the jumbled ice pileup Yuri had shown her from the orbital scans, and the improvised navigation system was in close agreement. She came about to fly due east, brought their airspeed down to about 100 kph, and took them in lower.

She had more or less expected to see it all turn into nothing, to discover all the things Yuri had seen in his scans to be imaginary, a colony willed up out of nothing at all.

But Norla found out fast just how wrong she was. They came in low and slow, the sun high and behind them. They could see everything sharply and clearly. They spotted the first cooling shaft about two kilometers out from the north–south arm of the canyon. A thin wisp of steam curled up from the dark shaft and twisted lazily higher before getting caught and cut to ribbons by the winds in the upper reaches of the canyon. And there was another, and another. A thick glaze of ice had formed on the downwind side of each shaft, frozen waves forever pouring down and forever locked in place.

They passed still another shaft, and another, then one that seemed broken, collapsed, walls of dark and dirty ice engulfing the heat output, plugging it up all but completely.

But then they were at the junction of the two canyon arms, and there was the solar power array that Yuri had half seen, half imagined. Hard by the array, they had just the briefest glimpses of a low round building that had to be an access to the main habitat below. Warm yellow light glowed from the windows of the structure. Norla resisted the urge to slow and turn the aircar to get a better look. She had a very strong gut feeling that they needed to see all of the canyon, from end to end.

The aircar moved on, past the north–south arm, then right past the wind farm that Yuri had imagined he saw on the scans from orbit. The reality was so like what Yuri had divined from the murky images that for one mad moment Norla wondered how he had summoned it into being.

The wind towers—far too grand and powerful to be called mere windmills—marched proudly across the landscape, the massive blades of the rotors turning purposefully, steadily. Any doubts Norla might still have had were banished. Last Chance Canyon was there, and real, and very much still alive.

Yuri was bouncing in his seat with excitement, so much so he was barely able to operate the handheld camera, and Norla was every bit as enthusiastic. This was a find. This was history. When was the last time any of these people had seen outsiders? They had been cut off from outside civilization for generations. Perhaps they had even forgotten the outside world, as it had forgotten them.

"Give me another pass!" Yuri was saying.

Norla blinked, came back to herself, and realized she had been so excited by their discovery that she had flown clear past the end of the wind farm, almost to the end of the canyon.

"Sorry," she said, and began banking them around. "Let me come about."

"Come on, Norla! Turn us about. I want another pass over the whole thing before we land!"

That brought her up short. Her sense of excitement was suddenly overtaken by fear as she remembered some of the stories about diehards . . . She stopped the turn and left the aircar at its present heading, off to the southeast. She brought it straight and level. "No landing, Yuri. We can't take the chance. That was part of the deal."

Yuri said, "But—but that was before we *saw* the place," he protested. "Turn us around! Now we know—we can see—"

"We can see that there must be people still alive down there," she said. "That's all. We don't know, we *can't* know, what sort of shape they're in, or how they feel about strangers."

"We don't *know* that they're dangerous!" Yuri protested.

"Granted—but we also don't know if we can trust them. And if we blunder in now, without preparation, without a plan, without reporting what we've found first—then we'll likely not only get ourselves killed, we'll have made things much worse for the diehards. They'll be in a trigger-happy mood, and our people will walk right into that when they come looking for us." *If they come looking,* she reminded herself. Koffield and the others wouldn't have much idea where to start looking, and might well take the very cold-blooded decision that it was not worth risking the living just to search for the dead. "Besides, we don't have much in the way of provisions with us."

"We're not going to stay long," said Yuri.

"We wouldn't *plan* on staying long. But supposing the landing went wrong, and we couldn't take off again? Or suppose they grabbed the aircar and searched it, and decided it looked like we were planning to live off them? The diehards might not feel much like sharing. So no landing. I need your agreement on that. I can't take any chances that you might try some piece of idiocy like grabbing the controls. I need you to give your word, or else I turn this thing around and head straight home right now. Understood?"

There was silence for a moment, broken only by the hum of the aircar's levitators and the quiet hiss of air through the vent system. Finally, he spoke. "Yes, ma'am. I give my word that I won't do anything to try for a landing here."

"All right then," Norla said. She resumed her turn, arcing about in a long sweeping S that brought them back on the reverse of their previous course, until they were moving west to east, back down the canyon. Norla slowed their airspeed until it seemed they were scarcely crawling across the sky.

"Lower," Yuri said. "Lower."

She brought them down to about two hundred meters up, holding course just south of the canyon's edge. She could see the first windmill just ahead, coming up slowly. It was a tall, proud thing, the fifty-meter blades of its rotor gleaming in the sunlight.

But then it was as if Norla blinked, and a veil

dropped from in front of her eyes. Suddenly, she was seeing, really *seeing,* what was there.

The windmill's rotor was not turning. Lines of rust and dirt streaked down the blades, and down the tower itself. One rotor blade was pointed straight down, parallel with the tower, and a long red crack ran half its length. It looked as if some sort of scaffold had been started, in an attempt to reach the crack in the blade, but the scaffold had slumped over and leaned against the tower. Ice was caked thick over the scaffold; it was plain that it had been abandoned a long time ago.

Then they were past the first windmill, and approaching the second. It at least was turning, but now that she was looking for such things, Norla could see the signs of wear and tear and piecemeal repairs. Of the ten remaining windmills, only six were in operation at all. Three of the nonfunctional ones were plainly as far past hope of repair as the first. One had lost all three rotor blades. They lay in a broken heap at the base of the windmill tower. Norla couldn't see any visible damage to the fourth nonworking windmill. It might have severe damage somewhere in its inner workings, or it might be down for some trivial repair. But Norla was starting to get the feeling these people couldn't afford to forgo a single watt of power generation. Nothing as vital as a power source would stay out of service a moment longer than necessary.

They came up on the north–south canyon, on her side of the aircar, the left. Norla resisted the urge to fly up through it. A tiny voice whispering at the back of her mind told her it would be far wiser not to get too close. She slowed their forward progress to almost nothing, and Yuri leaned around her as best he could to get the handheld camera aimed out her side window.

Norla could see clearly enough, but she wasn't sure she wanted to.

Something like a third of the solar array elements weren't tracking the sun properly. Some of the defective units were simply pointed the wrong way. Others had snapped off their supports, or were half-buried in snow and ice. And now she could see that the central structure, the one with the lights still gleaming from its interior, was only one of a dozen or so buildings. But at least two of the smaller structures had suffered roof collapses, and most of the rest were all but completely buried by the drifting snow.

There was enough damage obvious to almost every human-made object, even from this far off, that Norla was starting to wonder if they had it wrong. Maybe this place *was* dead, and the lights they had seen were what was left on after the last of them had died, half an hour or half a century before.

She peered about, seeing if she could see any sign of graveyards—but then her insides tightened up as she remembered that diehards would never think of wasting all the organic material that went into a corpse. They didn't bury their dead; they *recycled* them.

Just as she had realized she wasn't going to see any sign of the dead, she saw signs of the living. There was movement—*human* movement—out on the surface. Even before she could focus clearly enough to see them, her hindbrain told her she was seeing, not robots, not the wind moving snow, but humans in motion. There! Three tiny suited figures, just coming out of the lighted structure, gesturing at each other, pointing at the aircar, practically parked low in the center of their sky.

Norla had seen enough. She turned the car hard to the south and throttled up hard, gaining speed and altitude.

"There were people!" Yuri cried out. "We have to go back and—"

"And what?" Norla asked. "We have nothing to give them, but a lot they might want to take." *Like our bodies, for example,* she thought, reflecting again on why there were no diehard graveyards. "Too many risks, not enough benefit," she said.

She waited until they were ten kilometers south and a kilometer high, before coming about, pointing the aircar toward the northwest, on a direct bearing for DeSilvo City. "We've got what we came for," she said again, before Yuri could protest. "We know they are there, and we have proof of it in the cameras. The longer we stay around, the bigger the risk that—"

BLAM! BLAM!

The two explosions lit up the sky, one on either side of the aircar. Norla's reflexes tried to jump her out of her seat, but her seat belt held her in place. The aircar twitched and shuddered through the sky, half as a result of the shock waves from the blasts, and half from Norla's reaction. She forced the car back on course, and held it steady for a good fifteen seconds before heading into a slow, steady turn toward the west, until they were headed straight toward the setting sun.

"Norla! Put on some speed! Go evasive!"

"Quiet!" she snapped. "Quit your damned second-guessing. We fly smooth and easy, so they can track us accurately and won't hit us by accident if they fire more warning shots. Those were *aimed shots,* deliberate misses that bracketed us exactly. If they can put two in the sky exactly a hundred meters apart with us smack in the middle, they can put one right where we are. This aircar's no supermaneuverable fighter craft, and it's a hundred years too old for me to want to stress it too far. They just told us 'Go away and don't come back.' And I'm tempted to do just that. We're going to fly west at a nice steady rate of speed for as long as we can, so maybe they'll think we're from over that way instead of from the northwest. We'll just have to hope they'll stop tracking us before I have to change course. I should have thought of that before we came in, and flown in and out from some other direction than straight from home. Too late now."

And even Yuri Sparten could say nothing in reply to that.

They flew on in silence. Norla couldn't help but wonder what sort of reception would greet them on their arrival. They would surely have been missed. Somehow Norla couldn't help but worry over—and dread—what Anton Koffield would say. Silly, really, when it was *De-Silvo* who could punish them, severely, if he so desired—

and Captain Marquez who would be more or less *obliged* to punish them, if only to demonstrate that he still held authority over them. But it was Anton Koffield she did not wish to face. It was absurd, but she felt like a teenage girl who knew damned well she was going to catch hell from Daddy for staying out too late.

But deep in her heart, she knew that her subconscious was stirring up such minor concerns as a distraction from the real worries, the real issues.

Last Chance Canyon was *real*. People lived there. The place, and the people, were both in bad shape, no question. The amount of visible damage suggested they were near a point of collapse, or perhaps already past it. If they got help, enough help, the right kind of help, and got it soon enough, it might make a difference. But if not, well . . . they wouldn't last much longer. Not much longer at all.

Norla timed her turn back toward DeSilvo City carefully and brought the aircar in for a landing just as daylight was fading. It wasn't much of a homecoming. An annoyed-looking Jerand Bolt was there, waiting inside the airlock, when they arrived. Bolt escorted them to the main conference room, where Marquez and Koffield were waiting, and left it at that.

The meeting didn't take long. Marquez ordered Yuri restricted to his quarters while off duty for five days, all meals to be eaten in quarters, alone. Norla, as the senior officer who should have known better, drew a full week of restrictions, and accepted them meekly—even, it seemed to Yuri, gratefully. Maybe she had meant what she had said about discipline and authority.

Koffield, oddly enough, merely looked amused. Had he been *expecting* them to try something?

Marquez at least took the data from the cameras when Yuri offered it, though Yuri was careful to keep a copy for himself. They had proof, and he was going to make sure it didn't vanish.

Twenty minutes after their return, Jerand Bolt was escorting Yuri to his quarters. Bolt opened the door and hooked his thumb toward the interior. "And stay there," he growled as Yuri went inside. The door slammed behind him.

There were no locks on the doors, and there were no physical barriers to Yuri's taking off again. But there were intangible barriers that did the trick just as well.

Yuri's basic defense was that no one had *said* they couldn't go off on their own. Well, he didn't have that anymore. Marquez had told him, in graphic and degrading detail, exactly what he *was* allowed to do, then explicitly banned all activities he didn't list. Leaving his quarters, except to attend to his duties, without permission, was very clearly *off* the list.

Yuri stared at the door for a moment, then sat down at the edge of his bed. Well, Norla had warned him: A childish excuse would get him treated as a child, and it had come to that. He'd been sent to his room. Yuri could see that. The best he could do for himself—and, perhaps, for the people of Last Chance Canyon—would be to take it like a man. His own self-respect would keep him in quarters, holding him as firmly as any prison bars.

He lay back on the bed and sighed again. Tomorrow, during duty hours, he would face down DeSilvo and demand that the old tyrant do something. What, exactly, he wasn't sure yet. He had no idea what the Last Chancers most needed. All he really knew for sure after the day just ended was that they *didn't* need target practice.

Tomorrow then. Yuri started to prepare for bed, not in the least sure he'd be able to sleep. But that didn't matter, he told himself as he peeled off his clothes and stepped into the refresher. He had won.

After all, their host had made lots of noises about wanting to help, about wanting to make some sort of restitution. Well, Yuri had proof now, of people urgently needing help. DeSilvo, guided by his own principles, confronted by the evidence that everyone now knew about, would *have* to help the Last Chancers. Yuri smiled as the water jets played down on the back of his neck.

He had DeSilvo right where he wanted him.

It was only a day or two later, after everything he knew had been turned most thoroughly upside down, that Yuri had time to think again.

Only then did it dawn on Yuri Sparten: Oskar De-Silvo had undoubtedly gone to bed that same night feeling exactly the same way about *him*.

Chapter Seventeen

A MATTER OF CHOICE

Truth be told, Oskar DeSilvo did not know whether to be grateful to, or angry at, the two adventurers. Even on the morning after their return, he was not sure. On the plus side, of course, their disappearance had provided an ironclad excuse for him to delay his speech a little bit longer. And, unquestionably, Yuri Sparten had played right into his hands. Now Sparten would want, desperately want, to support the plan DeSilvo had in mind.

On the minus side, their little jaunt had demonstrated that he did not have the base anywhere near as organized or controlled as he had allowed them to believe.

Their departure had been discovered almost at once, of course, and Koffield and the others had all demanded that DeSilvo tell where they were—assuming, perhaps understandably, that he would know.

DeSilvo, however, did *not* know. But, once queried, his ArtInts' reports were enough, more than enough, to tell DeSilvo where the two had gone. Overcoming his own instinct for secrecy in all things, DeSilvo had even passed the information on to Koffield—via intercom. For DeSilvo had elected to keep himself in seclusion as much as possible for as long as possible. He was not used to people. Not yet. Dealing with their moods, their emotions, their reactions—dealing with their *hatred* of him, hatred he knew he had done much to earn—it was all more than he could handle.

But today, now, at last, he would *have* to handle it, confront it, force his way past it. Today was the day that he would have to tell them. Today was the day he would reveal his plans. Today, the schemes he had started to shape more than a hundred years before would be accepted—or laughed out of existence.

But there was one last arrangement to make. There were two players in the game who might well listen more sympathetically if they knew certain things ahead of time. A bit of theater, a bit of drama, and perhaps two enemies could be pushed along, if not into friendship, at least toward friendly neutrality.

At first Captain Marquez was tempted to tell DeSilvo what he could do with his request for a private conference in the cargo center, especially as he was also requested to drag Sparten along. On reflection, however, he concluded that there were already enough feuds and arguments and mortal insults going back and forth to keep them all busy enough for quite some time to come.

And both his pride and his curiosity were piqued by the invitation. Not one but two of them had been asked. That confused Marquez. If it was some bit of punishment DeSilvo wanted to inflict, or if he wanted to lecture the malefactors in the presence of their captain, why hadn't DeSilvo asked for Norla Chandray as well? She was the senior officer of the two miscreants. If it was a question of discipline, then she ought to be *more* involved than Sparten, not less. And if it *wasn't* a question of discipline, then why ask for Sparten and himself? But DeSilvo offered no explanation for why he wanted a conference with them, particularly. The location DeSilvo had chosen was likewise intriguing. Why the cargo transfer center? He decided to go.

At 1000 hours the next morning, Marquez escorted the prisoner down to the cargo center with as much bad grace as he could muster. While there wouldn't be much point in his aggravating DeSilvo, he had no such view concerning Sparten. The kid—and Marquez had come to think of Yuri as just a kid—had caused nothing but trouble for everyone. Always for good and noble reasons, always high-minded, never for his own benefit—and always trouble. Marquez didn't literally pull Sparten along by his earlobe, but he more or less imagined himself doing so.

In reality, both men walked to the lift and rode down in dignified silence, but Marquez entertained himself by thinking up all the hard-edged, biting comments he could have made to Sparten. Sparten, meantime, was scowling straight ahead at the lift door. At a guess, he was thinking of all the acid remarks he didn't dare make to Marquez.

The lift doors opened, dissipating the angry silence, and the two men stepped out into the cold darkness of the massive chamber. The aircar Sparten and Chandray had used was still parked just inside the airlock entrance.

But it was the sight of the world outside, visible through the viewport by the airlock, that drew their attention. DeSilvo was standing by the viewport, watching the show. His earthmoving robots were hard at work, burying the outer wall of the cargo center. "Good morning to you both," DeSilvo said, glancing at them over his shoulder before returning his attention to the bustling activity outside. "I wanted you both to see that this—you especially, Mr. Sparten."

"I see it," Sparten said. "I understand. You don't want us to get out again. You're burying us all alive to make sure we know this is supposed to be a prison."

"On the contrary," DeSilvo replied, turning his back on the window and looking straight at Sparten. "It was never my intention to hold anyone here against his or her will. I wanted you to come here and see that that is still true."

Marquez was watching DeSilvo's face carefully as the man spoke. DeSilvo was solemn, sincere, respectful—but Marquez had not the slightest doubt the man was lying. And yet, at the same time, Marquez felt quite sure that *Sparten* believed DeSilvo—for the show of sincerity was only intended for the younger man, aimed at him; it was also *tuned* for him. DeSilvo was so focused on Sparten that it almost seemed he wasn't even aware that Marquez was there. "Come," said DeSilvo, taking the young man by the arm. "Look. I very much want you to see this."

It wasn't just the words, but the way DeSilvo said them, the tone of his voice, the gentle way he touched Sparten and guided him along. Sparten, plainly baffled, allowed himself to be led toward the viewport. All his anger suddenly seemed to have nowhere to go. Marquez could almost see that cloud of rage evaporating, fading away to nothing.

Marquez followed along behind, watching the interplay between the other two as much as he was looking at the scene outside. It seemed plain to Marquez that DeSilvo must have begun to remember some of his old politicking skills.

"Yes, Mr. Sparten, we are burying ourselves alive. We can, after all, expect that, sooner or later, someone from the Solar System will follow you. That was inevitable from the first. So we must hide—but that does not mean that we must imprison ourselves. Look out there. See for yourself."

Marquez saw it too. A huge reinforced concrete pipe, about three meters high and thirty meters long, jutted out from the side of the station, just to the left of the viewport.

"That tunnel section was just installed this morning. It butts up against the exterior door of the cargo lock," said DeSilvo. "The earthmover robots will bury it at the same time they cover this part of the station—but the far end of the tunnel will remain open. You'll always have a way out. We will of course cover over and camouflage the tunnel exit, but we'll be able to come and go at will."

"Good," said Sparten, plainly wanting to be convinced but not quite there yet. "That's something, I admit." He stood up close to the viewport and watched the robots working. "But you know where I want to go," he said, still looking straight ahead.

"Oh, yes, of course," DeSilvo said with a smile. "I

was very interested to see your pictures of it. Would you like to see mine?"

Sparten turned suddenly and looked at DeSilvo in surprise. "*What?* When did—what do you mean?"

"Come this way," DeSilvo said. "We'll need a lot of space to see these properly. That was another reason I wanted to meet with you down here."

Sparten, plainly intrigued, followed. Marquez trailed along behind, having the distinct impression that he had been forgotten.

There was a highly sophisticated holographic projector sitting in the exact center of a large open space, right in the middle of the cargo center. Judging by how much hardware was shoved up along the walls of the compartment, and the fresh-looking tracks and scratches on the floor, a lot of gear had been cleared away quite recently in order to make room.

DeSilvo went to the projector's controls and set to work. "This is what you brought to show me," he said. A view panel appeared over their heads, a holographic projection of two-dee images—a virtual viewscreen, floating in midair.

DeSilvo brought up playback of a few moments of the images Sparten had recorded—jerky, sometimes blurry two-dimensional video images of the windmills, the solar arrays, and the three figures pointing up into the sky toward the camera, moving toward it. The video ended, looped back to the beginning, and started again.

The quality shifted back and forth between marginally acceptable and dreadful. The best that could be said of the images was that they existed. But they did the job; they proved that Last Chance was there and that people still lived there. It was plain to see on Sparten's face that he was pleased and proud of what he had accomplished.

"And here," DeSilvo said, "is what I can show you— part of it, at any event." Sparten's video froze on a blurred two-dimensional image of the solar power array, the central structure behind it, and the three figures pointing toward the camera.

Then the virtual view panel started to grow translucent.

A three-dimensional projection of the same spot, adjusted to match the perspective of Sparten's video, bloomed up all around it. The two images remained there for a moment, overlaid with each other, and then Sparten's images faded away, quite literally a pale shadow of what appeared in their place.

A full three-dimensional schematic of the underground facilities appeared, the point of view pulling back to expose the vast expanse of the place. Level upon level of underground tunnels, chambers, compartments, and workshops came into view. Plumbing, wiring, ventilation diagrams appeared, overlaying themselves on the displays. Statistics popped up: current population: 567. Trend line: declining approx 2 percent per decade. Average age: 34.2 standard years. Life expectancy: 58.3, trend line flat. Power grid output: 42.3 percent rated capacity, trend line projecting down average 1 percent per Solacian year, rate accelerating. Food production per capita: marginal-sustainable, trend line down. Life support: air/heat/light/water: good; trend line flat.

DeSilvo smiled, and gestured upward. "The people of Last Chance Canyon—Canyon City, as they usually call it. If you had merely waited a day or two longer, you would have learned all about them, in greater detail, and at far less risk, than was the case."

A list of names, along with images of faces, appeared off to one side, and started to scroll past. James Ruthan Verlant IV, age 47 and looking fifteen years older. James Ruthan Verlant V, age 24, a thick scar across the right cheek marring his youthful appearance. James Ruthan Verlant VI (deceased, age 4), with a picture of a smiling boy who would smile no more. And, heartbreakingly, James Ruthan Verlant VII, brother to the dead child, age 2, health reported as frail. Other names trailed past, over and over again—Helen Gahan Derglas V, VI, VII, and VIII, a run of Yuri Tamarovs, a sequence of Boland Xavier Sheltes.

"They stick with it, whatever it is," DeSilvo said quietly. "Look at the records. The names tell you that. If a child dies, the next child of that gender takes the same name, and if that one dies, the next, and the next, until one survives. They do that with everything—fighting on and on until they succeed, no matter what."

"How the hell did you get all this?" Marquez demanded. "You must have tapped in to all their records."

"Yes, obviously. You did one flyover," DeSilvo said. "I sent in a whole fleet of nanoscouts, the same day you landed on Glister." He reached into his cloak and pulled out an object. It was the size and shape of a large egg. He tossed it into the air. It promptly sprouted a levitator and hovered in midair. "That's the delivery system. It gets inside and drops a hundred nanoscouts. They do visual recon, scan the data systems, and transmit back. The units I sent to Canyon City have all stopped sending. Probably our friends found a few of them, realized outsiders were taking an interest, then tracked down and destroyed the rest. In other words, they were warned. That's why they were ready to take a potshot at you. That I didn't anticipate, of course, or I would have warned you off. But no harm done, fortunately, and otherwise all to the good."

"Why is their shooting at us good?" Sparten asked.

"It's not the shooting," DeSilvo said. "It's the knowing that we're there to be shot at. *We* want them to know we're around."

"Why?" Marquez asked, in as pointed a tone of voice as he could manage. "Why do we want to scare these people? Whatever they do about it is going to use up resources and effort they just plain can't afford."

"They will gain a great deal more than they lose, I promise you," said DeSilvo. "We will gain as well."

"How?" Marquez asked.

"That is what I brought you both here to explain," DeSilvo said. "We need them almost as much they need us. I was most glad to find them."

"You went *looking* for them?"

DeSilvo nodded. "As soon as the *Dom Pedro IV* arrived and I emerged from temporal confinement."

"But that's seven hundred kilometers from here!" Marquez protested. "How the hell did you find them?"

"Before I entered temporal confinement over a hundred years ago, I searched the terrain and identified about twenty good potential sites for diehard colonies. My probes checked them all again when I emerged from temporal confinement—and there was Last Chance."

"Hold it," Marquez objected. "Why do *you* need *them*?"

DeSilvo gestured back toward the viewport and the earthmoving machinery at work beyond. "My machines are burying this base. Other robots are at work on a concealment plan that goes much further than burying the station. There is also a deception operation, and, Mr. Sparten, your friends at Last Chance Canyon are very much a part of it—as is the *Dom Pedro IV*. That is why you are here, Captain."

Marquez struggled to hold on to his temper. "Please stop talking in riddles and just tell us what's going on."

"I was about to. It goes back to the fact that I had to draw you all here. To do so required that I leave clues that pointed this way. It seemed almost inevitable that, somewhere along the line, your group's activities would draw the attention of the authorities, or that the authorities would find some way to monitor you."

Marquez just barely resisted the temptation to glare at Sparten. *For example, by planting a spy on your ship.* But best to leave that be for the time being. "Go on," he said.

"It seemed—and seems—very likely to me that the authorities, in one form or another, would be able to follow the same clues as you did and come here as well."

Marquez nodded. "Yeah. The admiral even wondered if they'd get here first."

"Fortunately, they did not. I had contingency plans for that circumstance as well, but I must confess that even I had little confidence in them. Based on what you all have told me about your adventures, and what I know of how the Chronologic Patrol works, I would venture a guess that we have a few weeks, possibly longer—but there is no point taking chances. Burying this station, concealing it, is only part of the plan. The main idea is to let them find what they are looking for—somewhere else. They will find the Last Chancers picking through the rubble of this station—or what appears to be this station—about a thousand kilometers from here, well to the south of Last Chance Canyon.

"The Last Chancers will tell them they detected a large explosion, investigated, and found a large facility full of odd equipment, much of which was wrecked or buried by the explosion. The Last Chancers will also find a large store of supplies that survived the explosion. In the process of salvaging them, the Last Chancers will so muddle the evidence of the explosion that it will be all but impossible to do a full forensic examination of the site—if and when the Last Chancers allow the investigators to get near their treasure trove.

"That is what they will find on the surface. In space, Captain Marquez, I regret to say they will find the shattered wreckage of the *Dom Pedro IV*."

"What!" Marquez was standing three or four meters in front of DeSilvo, still looking up and ahead at the simulation. He spun around and took a step or two toward DeSilvo, reached out to grab him. "You wrecked my ship! You miserable—"

DeSilvo held up his hand for silence. "That is what *they* will find," he said. "What *you* will find, Captain Marquez, is that the newly refurbished *Dom Pedro IV* has become the fastest ship in Settled Space." He pressed a key on his control panel, and the view of Last Chance Canyon vanished. Marquez looked up and saw—his ship reborn. The image of the *Dom Pedro* took up half the interior of the cargo center, ten meters long at least. The image was brilliant, gleaming, razor-sharp, real enough that it took an act of conscious will to know that the ship itself wasn't there, floating a few hundred meters away in the darkness.

He swore under his breath. The *Dom Pedro IV* had undergone a full refit before departing Solace—but that was no more than a new paint job compared to the transformation DeSilvo's robots had wrought.

"It is the used, worn, and obsolete parts stripped

from the *Dom Pedro IV,* complete with identifiable serial numbers and so on, that will provide the wreckage for them to find. So, as you can see, if—or I should say *when*—your pursuers show up, Last Chance Canyon and the *Dom Pedro IV* will play a big part in convincing them that they have found what they were looking for, without any need for their disturbing us.

"Unless we are very unlucky indeed, your pursuers will see that ship wreckage in orbit, find the destroyed base on the planet, and hear the probably vague, unclear, and contradictory testimony of the Last Chancers. They will conclude that an aircar from the *Dom Pedro IV* overflew Last Chance while looking for my base of operations. Shortly thereafter, the ship found my base, and blew it up, but I managed to revenge myself on the *Dom Pedro IV,* destroying it with a missile launched just before the explosion. I will of course launch that missile from my decoy site, on a trajectory that overflies Last Chance, and there will of course be a suitable explosion in space that will in fact leave blast damage on the old bits of the *Dom Pedro IV* we will leave behind."

" 'Leave behind?' " Marquez echoed. "We're going somewhere?" But his mind was not on the question. He was too busy staring at the ship, *his* ship, seeing what had been done to her, for her.

DeSilvo answered the questions that his eyes were asking and not the one he spoke out loud. Each system lit up as he mentioned it, portions of the ship's hull fading to translucency to reveal each subsystem in turn.

"Virtually all of the outer hull was replaced with a lighter and stronger composite. Two new auxiliary craft replace the pair destroyed as you departed Mars. The aux ships are three or four design generations ahead of what you had. Improved navigation system, better power management, a rebuilt temporal confinement system that will draw less power, various improvements to the life-support systems. And the cryogenic canisters, and all the plumbing for them—gone. Completely removed."

"But the cryocans were the backup in case the temporal confinement system failed."

"Ah, but it's the temporal confinement that's the backup now," DeSilvo replied. "There just in case you do need to make a timeshaft run—just in case the main system fails. The FTL system."

Marquez nodded absently, scarcely aware of anything but the ship that hung in the gleaming darkness. "The toroids?" he asked. The *Dom Pedro* was a long, lean cylinder—but now three rings encircled the hull, perpendicular to her long axis. There was one ring at each end and one amidships. A dozen slender spokes held each ring in place. The *Dom Pedro IV* was the axle, and the three rings were three wheels centered on that axle.

"Exactly. The toroids are the external foci for the FTL field generators. In fact, the FTL generators are in the same deck space that once held the cryocans."

"They'd never make it through a timeshaft," Marquez objected. "Tidal stresses would tear them to shreds."

"True. You'd have to jettison them before making a run through a timeshaft. I'd suggest doing it well before the run, or else the Chrono Patrol ships on station might be tempted to ask some questions. But I doubt that will ever come up. Barring disaster, the *Dom Pedro IV* will never traverse another timeshaft. She won't need to. Why should she, when now she can make the crossing from Glister to Solace in eight days? From Solace to Earth in something between a month and five weeks. That's direct, no timeshafts, no eighty years in temporal confinement for the hull. Just a few weeks of straight-line travel, at an aggregate power cost per light-year of about a tenth what it would be via timeshaft."

To Marquez, who had spent uncounted decades in cold storage or temporal confinement, the offer was downright irresistible. He would have paid any price for such a gift, and here it was not merely being offered to him, but *forced* upon him.

So what's the catch? some cynical, subterranean bit

of his mind wanted to know. *Whatever it is, who cares? I'll take it. I'll do it.* But even as he was being used, led, manipulated—even as he *knew* he was being manipulated—Marquez could see, even admire, how carefully DeSilvo had planned the thing, down to the tiniest detail, even down to DeSilvo's aiming the holoprojections so that the viewer's natural inclination would be to stand in front of DeSilvo and look up—putting Marquez's back to DeSilvo and the control panel between Marquez and DeSilvo. That right there had been enough to slow Marquez down, just long enough for DeSilvo to do some fast talking and keep Marquez from tearing his head off.

And then there was the bait itself—the fastest ship in Settled Space! Hell's bells, the fastest ship in the galaxy! "But I'll never get to fly it," he objected. "The first port of call I come to, the Chrono Patrol will seize the ship, lock me up, and throw away the key."

"They'd have to catch you first," said DeSilvo. "And the Chronologic Patrol is a cat who has spent so long watching mouseholes that she's forgotten how to hunt. They stand guard over the timeshafts—the one place you'll never have to go. Arrive in a system, keep the *Dom Pedro IV* out of sight, send in the aux craft to ferry cargo and supplies back and forth, and then be on your way. That is, if you're still a freighter captain. Are you? *Can* you go back to such a quiet life after all you've seen and done?"

Marquez stared up at the wondrous ship and did not answer for a moment. DeSilvo had a point, damn him. Things had changed for him, had changed *him*. He was moving on a larger stage, dealing in far larger questions than how much cargo he could haul. And yet—and yet—if his power costs were *that* much lower, and he was moving *that* much faster—there was no telling the profits he could make! He could be rich. *If you have the sense to quit before you get caught,* he reminded himself. He, Marquez, could tell at a glance that the *DP-IV* could no longer traverse a timeshaft. So too could others. It would take little thought to realize that a ship that could not use the timeshafts, and yet still arrived after only a few days or weeks of transit, must have some fairly interesting means of propulsion.

He would have to keep her out of sight, far away from inhabited worlds and stations. The need for security would make arranging for maintenance tricky as well. He would have to trust his crew absolutely—and carrying passengers would be right out.

He would be forced to take on every high-risk, no-questions-asked deal that came his way. And sooner or later, either he would have to quit while his luck still held, or else he would get caught. And Marquez knew enough about his own character, about what would tempt him and what would not, to know that the odds were against his quitting while he was ahead.

No, he could not go back to being a trader, a freighter captain. Not if he was piloting the only FTL starship in Settled Space. But if he knew that, DeSilvo must know it too, must know that his offer was impossible. And besides, there was another thing. When—not if, when—Marquez did get caught, the authorities would examine the ship, the ship's log, the ship's crew—and the ship's captain. They were not likely to be gentle about it. One way or another—probably a very unpleasant way—they would learn what they wanted to know. It was highly likely, close to a certainty, that they would be able to trace the ship back to its source, to Glister—to DeSilvo. If DeSilvo set the *Dom Pedro IV* loose on the trade lanes, he would be pointing an arrow back at himself, back to his hidden base. DeSilvo wasn't likely to do that—and therefore his offer wasn't realistic.

But the *ship*. Fastest in the galaxy. Faster than light. Marquez stood looking up at the image of the *DP-IV,* and longed to get his hands on the controls, to see how they worked, to see what it could do, to spend days and weeks studying the manuals, learning all about it.

With a sudden flash of insight, he saw why Norla Chandray was not with them. DeSilvo had no bribe for her, nothing that she would want as much as he wanted that ship, or Sparten wanted help for Last Chance.

Or did DeSilvo have temptations for them all? Was he meeting with each of them, in groups of two or three, or one-on-one when he thought that would best suit his purposes?

But still, none of that mattered. He still wanted that *ship*. His ship. He wanted her back, and he wanted to see what she could do. He almost—almost—didn't care what jobs she would be doing.

All right then. DeSilvo had him. There wasn't any point in pretending otherwise. The only question left was: How high the price?

"Okay," he said. "You know we want what you're offering. So what's the deal? What do you want in return?"

DeSilvo, to give the man credit, did not play any of the games Marquez had expected. He didn't turn coy, or pretend not to understand.

Instead, DeSilvo nodded and shut down the holographic projector. The shining image of the reborn *Dom Pedro IV* faded away to nothing. "In a sense—but only in a sense—I want nothing at all from either of you. If I am allowed to do precisely what I want to do, I will, as a direct result, give you both what you very much want. I brought you here to warn you that you *won't* get what you want if I am thwarted." DeSilvo held up his hand to stop their protests before they could begin. "That is not a threat, or a demand. But it is a fact. You have seen my resources—they are vast. But they are limited, and they are vulnerable to detection and attack. I will use both the Last Chancers and the removed sections of the *Dom Pedro IV* as part of the deception plan I have described—once my larger plan goes into operation. I will need the *Dom Pedro IV,* or a ship with her new capabilities, to make that larger plan happen. I might add that equipping a ship the size of the *Dom Pedro IV* for FTL required the use of nearly every FTL generator I have available. I had to strip gear from just about every other FTL-equipped craft I had. I have no regrets on that score. The *Dom Pedro IV* is by far the best choice from the available spacecraft, for many reasons. She will need a captain, and a crew—and I of course turn to you.

"But I cannot afford to expend my resources, or risk them, unless I advance my own plans by so doing. If I aid the Last Chancers, there is a chance they will track me back and take everything I have—and wreck plans that will save far more lives than we could save by aiding them. Their law is—and for their sake, must be—survival first and above all. If their leader judged the best way to keep his people alive was to kill us all and take over this base, rest assured, Mr. Sparten, he would do it. They are a noble people, a courageous people—and a desperate people. They are wolves, hungry wolves—and there is great danger in throwing meat to starving predators. I will not take that risk unless it advances my cause.

"Nor can I afford to give away the ship that would best serve my purposes. And, forgive me, Captain Marquez, but I think you saw through my rather insincere suggestion that you return to your former work as commander of a freighter. I think you can see why it could not work—and why I could not permit it."

"I do see," Marquez said. "But it's all right. I don't think I'd be suited for that line of work anymore anyway."

"No. No, you would not be suited. Your horizons have been widened too far. You wouldn't do much of a job buying or selling—your mind would be on much larger matters."

"I agree," said Marquez. "But where does that leave us?"

"Right where we were, with the facts in front of us," DeSilvo said. "That is all I had to say. I offer no deal, suggest no quid pro quo, and ask nothing of you. If my plan is accepted, you will get what you want, as part and parcel of my plan. If it is rejected, if your people will not help, then I cannot afford, cannot risk, to do any of it. I will have to husband my resources, conserve everything, and search harder for a way forward, a way that I can act without help—though I frankly admit that right now I can't imagine how."

"What—what will happen to us?" Yuri Sparten asked, speaking for the first time in a long while. "If we don't do what you ask, if we don't help with, with whatever it is— what happens to us? You just said you wouldn't, couldn't, let Captain Marquez take the *Dom Pedro IV* back. And you couldn't afford the risk of our talking, voluntarily— or ah, otherwise."

Marquez frowned. That angle he had not considered.

"All true," said DeSilvo. "I won't kill you. I promise that. Perhaps the simplest answer, for those who would be willing, would be to put you in temporal confinement here until such time as it wouldn't really matter if you talked. Or perhaps put you aboard a slowboat bound for Earth on a long enough trajectory that it wouldn't matter. It would have to be Earth, of course. By the time it would be safe for you to emerge, I doubt many other worlds would be worth visiting. Or, of course, you could stay here."

"Here in DeSilvo City?" Sparten asked.

"So long as you did not interfere with the work you refused to assist. Certainly. Why not? I would appreciate the human contact, even without the help. But if you did not wish to stay, or it became clear you could not be trusted to stay—I don't know. But, if it came to that . . ."

DeSilvo pointed to the airlock, and the frozen hell beyond, and the big machines out in that hell, working to shovel dirt and gravel up over the station. "If it comes to that, Mr. Sparten, it's as I said before. You'll always have a way out."

Chapter Eighteen

A MATTER OF TIME

Dr. Oskar DeSilvo tried to calm himself. It was time to go. The meeting was scheduled to start in just a few minutes. More than a century after he had put his plan into motion, after the endless days waiting out the news from Greenhouse, after all and everything, it was time.

His nerves were not what they should have been. He stared into the mirror, and smoothed down his yellow scholar's robe, checking fretfully for any untoward wrinkle or stain. Not that there was any need to worry, of course. His ArtInts had cleaned it just that morning, and they never missed a thing. Even in his present state of mind, that brought a smile to DeSilvo's face. *My ArtInts might fail to report the theft of an aircar or the unauthorized departure of two people, but at least my laundry comes back looking good.*

He was nervous. No, no sense fooling himself. He was *scared,* downright frightened. This was the moment it all came down to. As much as it galled him at times to realize it, he *needed* these people.

He had gotten as far as he could by himself, and perhaps a bit farther than he should have, riding on the backs of ArtInts and robots and fabricators and autofacs. He knew it was something of a wonder he had accomplished as much as he had. He needed skills and abilities—and judgments—that machines couldn't give him, that only human beings could provide. He needed intuition, political advice, social skills. He would need an army of people, with every skill imaginable—if things went according to plan.

His long-dormant instinct for the political aspect of things was coming back to him, and it confirmed what he already knew: He needed *these* people in order to get all the *other* people he would need later on. They would be the lever that pried the door open. They would give the plan credibility that only they could bring to bear— Koffield especially. Outsiders would listen to Koffield.

But DeSilvo needed more. He would need facilities, facilities far larger, far more capable, and far more accessible than this remote and tiny base.

But before any of that could happen, he would have to convince his guests, convince them of what must seem a mad scheme—and do so after he had done everything in his power to demonstrate to them that he was a madman. And he would have to do it by himself, alone.

Alone. He had been alone so long, in so many ways. He had forgotten the ways of people, how to deal with them, how to talk with them, how to be one of them. He had made several near-fatal mistakes already. Yuri Sparten had tried his best to kill Dr. Oskar DeSilvo—after DeSilvo had pointlessly and needlessly provoked him. Waving Last Chance Canyon in front of Sparten had neutralized that danger, at least, but DeSilvo knew he had made any number of lesser such errors.

He *had* to make them see. He *had* to succeed.

Two hours later, they were all assembled in the main conference room. DeSilvo half listened to Koffield's brief and polite opening remarks, then stood, nodded to Koffield, and began to speak. "Thank you, Admiral. Before I begin my main remarks, I would like to report that the results of the Greenhouse NovaSpot Ignition attempt are in. The Ignition attempt was successful, though it seems there were more than a few anxious moments. As I believe you will see later, this news greatly simplifies planning for the project I am about to propose."

Oskar DeSilvo paused for a moment and looked about the room.

"Two plus two," he said, "equals four."

That drew the reaction he had expected. They shifted in their seats, gave each other odd looks, and were plainly not much convinced of his sanity. Good. He would move from the odd to the sane and bring them with him.

"Two plus two equals four. With a little thought, all of arithmetic, and a good deal of mathematics and geometry, can be inferred from that one statement, by trying inversions and reversals, by testing alternate cases. Having added them together, you might be tempted to remove two from two, thus inventing subtraction, and discovering zero, all at the same time. Subtract once again, and you will invent negative numbers. Two plus two can be restated as two twos—two times two. You have invented multiplication. Multiply the result by two again, and you have invented geometric expansion. Another brief intuitive leap, and you will invent division, the reverse of multiplication. Take a piece of graph paper, set one box equal to each unit of what you are multiplying, and see it as geometry.

"More and greater leaps of intuition would be required to discover or invent irrational numbers, imaginary numbers, calculus, and so on, but plainly those leaps were made.

"Two plus two equals four. Think of Ulan Baskaw's first book as the terraforming equivalent of that simple formula. Just as our first simple equation opens the door that leads to all of mathematics, her book opened the door to a real science of terraforming. All that was new and important in her later works was there, in latent form, implied and inferable, in that first work. And yet those intuitive leaps, those connections, were not made for a thousand years.

"It was Anton Koffield who brought her work to the scientists on Greenhouse who could make the best use of it. But they were not exposed to Baskaw's last and greatest known work, simply called *Contraction*.

It is the knowledge in that work that makes the doom of all the living planets, including Earth, utterly predictable.

"Two plus two equals four. In the field of interstellar transportation, the timeshaft wormhole might be thought of as that same equation, with a similar wealth of possibilities implicit and inferable from it. And yet it would seem *none* of the logical connections were ever made in the last thousand years or more, that *no one* in all that time ever made the intuitive leaps that would have revealed so much more. We use a crude form of time travel to traverse the stars. Consult the sources, far back in the middle near-ancient period, and you will find that the idea of a wormhole between two points in space *predates* the idea of a wormhole link between two points in time. Yet there have been no explorations of that concept for uncounted generations. Timeshaft wormholes use time travel to facilitate travel through space, but it would seem there has been no exploration of what *that* implies. We know how intimate the relation is between time and space. To transit one is to transit the other. Then why have none of the connections been made?

"The answer, of course, is that they *have* been made, over and over again—but the discoveries have been suppressed just as often. *That* is the true secret of the Dark Museum. Any invention that would slightly improve conventional interstellar travel, for example by making timeshaft dropships faster or more efficient, is suppressed as long as possible. Sooner or later, there is an 'outbreak,' and a given improvement reaches the general public before it can be suppressed. A good example of that is temporal confinement systems. Compared to the plumber's nightmare that is a cryogenic canister system, the new temporal confinements are vastly cheaper, safer, less costly, and require less space and mass aboard ship. They have significantly reduced the barriers to interstellar travel, even in just the past few decades.

"But still, the powers that be have managed to slow the rate of improvement. Nor are their motives dark and sinister. They seek to prevent otherwise inevitable chaos and suffering. By my admittedly rough and uncertain calculations, they have significantly delayed or permanently suppressed enough minor improvements to prevent at least three additional worlds from being terraformed. Three worlds that will never experience the sort of collapse and upheaval that killed Glister—and is about to kill Solace.

"But follow this logic to its extreme, and you'll find that the best way to prevent death is to see to it that no babies are born. Furthermore, this policy of delay and suppression merely puts off the inevitable. Earth and all the other worlds will die just the same—just not as quickly."

"What—what about going the other way?"

DeSilvo frowned at the interruption, but managed to keep his temper. It was *essential* that he keep his temper. It was Jerand Bolt who had spoken up, of course. The man never was shy about barging in on a presentation. For once, however, he seemed to be asking a serious question rather than making a snide joke.

"What do you mean, Mr. Bolt?"

"Suppose instead they—we, humanity—pushed technological advancement so far and so fast that we *expanded* from world to world, terraforming so many worlds so fast that we were expanding faster than the collapses could keep up with? There are always new worlds ahead, and we don't fall back on Earth."

DeSilvo frowned. "I'm not sure I followed that."

Koffield spoke up. "I think I did," he said. "In other words, we collapse *outward*, if you will. We terraform one world, and before it collapses, we terraform two worlds farther out, beyond the worlds we've already used—and used up—in Settled Space—to hold the eventual refugees, and while those worlds are being settled, we terraform four more still farther out, and so on."

Bolt nodded. "Yeah, like that."

DeSilvo scowled harder, but held on to his composure. The idea had never even occurred to him, and he had no ready answer. But Koffield and the others came to his rescue.

"The galaxy's big, but it's not infinite," he said. "And we couldn't use all of it anyway. All of Settled Space is one tiny little spherical volume, centered on the Sun, in the midregions of the galaxy. The studies I've seen project that large swatches of the inner and outer zones of the galaxy would have virtually no terraformable planets. Too much hard radiation and other nasty stuff in close and in the spiral arms, plus there are problems with the relative abundance of various elements in large volumes of the outer galaxy. That still leaves a lot of possible planets for expansion—but a geometric rate of expansion would take much less time than you might think to use them all up. And then what? We've talked about the Collapse Wars that will come toward the end, as the last worlds still surviving struggle to keep from being overwhelmed by refugees and so on. Imagine the Collapse Wars multiplied by a thousand."

"Even if it could be done, I'd be against it," said Norla. "It makes humanity into some sort of plague expanding out from a central point, devouring all in its path, and then moving on after it has wrecked everything. How many worlds like Glister do you want? How many worlds like Mars?"

"I'd even suggest it's immoral," Ashdin said. "Life is obviously rare in the galaxy, but it's plainly not impossible—*we're* here. It might have arisen elsewhere—or might arise elsewhere in the future. Suppose we terraformed every available world to suit us? We'd leave a whole galaxy full of contaminated, used-up, dead worlds of no use to anyone for the rest of time. We'd wreck all those potential living worlds forever, just so we could terraform them to suit us for a very brief span of time."

"All right, all right," Bolt said. "I promise not to rape the galaxy. It was just a question." He turned to De-Silvo. "Sorry, Doctor," he said. "I didn't mean to sidetrack things. You were talking about contraction and suppressing technology."

"Um, ah—yes." Oddly enough, the interruption seemed

to have gained him some points. Bolt's apology for the interruption was by far the most courteous and respectful DeSilvo had ever seen Bolt. "Yes. Technological suppression. But that type of suppression is merely part of the story. Any and all efforts to invent faster-than-light transportation or communication have been ruthlessly put down—but not just for the obvious reasons. While it is true enough that FTL transport would massively destabilize the whole of Settled Space, drastically increase the rate of interstellar settlement and expansion—and probably bankrupt the Chronologic Patrol, which would no longer collect revenue from the timeshaft wormholes it would still have to guard—those are almost trivial considerations up against what I believe is the main issue."

He paused, took a sip of water from the glass in front of him, and looked around the conference table. He had them. At least for the moment, he had them. All of them, even Yuri Sparten, were listening to him. All of what he had said had been sane, at least so far. But would he still have them when he crossed the next line? That was where it would start to sound lunatic.

"Two plus two equals four. That simple equation points the way forward, if only we have the wit to see it. Timeshafts are wormholes that move us through time. But inside the math, the engineering, the computational modeling required to build and control a timeshaft hide the tools and the knowledge needed to build an FTL spacecraft. They are hidden as deeply as calculus is hidden inside two plus two equals four.

"I can offer no proof of it, but I believe that this fact is a major reason that the Chronologic Patrol has always maintained a strict monopoly on timeshaft wormholes.

"But I digress, if only slightly. Two plus two equals four, and space and time are intimately linked, different sides of the same coin. The timeshaft, a crude and limited device for traveling through time, taught hu mankind how to travel faster than light. What was there that FTL could teach?

"There is an ancient joke about a physicist explaining relativity. The physicist tells his friend it is easy to envision the basic principles. Imagine, he tells him, a spinning toroid—a doughnut-shape—being fired out of a cannon. Then you just take away the cannon, and the doughnut, and the spin, and there you are. We rely so fully on the timeshafts that it is about that hard for us to envision true faster-than-light travel. But we must go a step further.

"FTL lets us travel between the stars without time-shafts. But knowledge implicit and inferable from the tools used to invent FTL, combined with information that can be derived from the study of large and powerful temporal confinements, points us forward to a way to *travel in time without a timeshaft.*"

The room was silent, his audience plainly shocked. Time travel was the great evil, the great danger, against which all the precautions, all the defenses of the time-shaft wormholes and the whole power of the Chrono-logic Patrol were directed—and space travelers, above all other groups, were endlessly indoctrinated on the subject. He had spoken blasphemy, sacrilege, to a con-gregation full of true believers.

He pushed it further. He had to go on, say what he had come here to say.

"The crowning mistake of my career," he said, "was in following Baskaw's ideas in the wrong direction. Her work made it plain that the faster a world was ter-raformed, the sooner it would fail. I cannot now say for certain why I refused—willfully refused—to see and un-derstand that, when it was plainly there before me." Confession was good for more than the soul. Let them see that he was sorry, that his past behavior was hard for even *him* to comprehend, and perhaps they would better believe in his present sanity.

"The best explanation I can offer—and I know it is only a partial explanation—is that I believed too much in myself. My ideas, my organization, my plans and de-signs, were so brilliant and polished that I was certain they could overcome the immutable laws of nature en-shrined in Baskaw's equations. I was more than wrong—I was blind. Not only were the proofs that two plus two equals four in front of me, but so were the keys that would unlock the future. Because the future is made in the past."

The room was dead silent. Some of them could already see where he was going. But even those who could not were alert, sensing that answers were at hand.

"Take a hundred years to terraform a world, and it will last a hundred before collapse. Take five hundred years, and it will survive five hundred years. *So what will happen if we take a million years?*"

There it was. Out in front of them. Now for the rest of it. "We shall expand outward, as you suggested, Mr. Bolt. Deep into unknown space. Out to a planet as yet undetected. But also deep into time. We shall find our planet, but be careful to determine no more than its mass and its orbit. We shall detect no information that we might change, for fear of skewing causality. We shall move from our time to the distant, deep past, and initiate the terraforming process. Then we shall visit that world in different times, always moving forward in time relative to our initial visit. We will let a thousand, ten thousand, even a hundred thousand years pass between one visit and the next. We shall spend more time allowing a single wave of species to establish themselves, one small phase of the operation, than was ever spent on the longest-term terraforming project to date.

"This is not a project for one man, or eight or ten people, or even hundreds. We will need thousands of workers and technicians. We will need facilities, supplies, spacecraft, technology. I believe that Greenhouse would, for many reasons, best suit us as a base of operations—especially now that NovaSpot is operational."

"Where are you going to get all that?" Norla Chandray demanded. "How are you going to recruit that many people? How are you going to convince Neshobe Kalzant to hand over that sort of hardware?"

"I'm not going to," said DeSilvo. "You are. That is a major reason you are here. You are the people to whom Kalzant and the rest of the Solacian leadership will listen. They certainly will not listen to me. But they will know what you have seen, what you have learned. They will hear and believe what you tell them."

"But this is madness!" Koffield cut in. "I can't even begin to list all the reasons it's insane. Go back in time *a million years*? That would create endless threats and dangers to causality."

"And we shall guard against those threats and dangers," DeSilvo said. "For example, we will have strict restrictions on who and what can go into the deep past. No vehicle that could reach Earth, no device that could generate any sort of signal or static that might be detectable from long range."

Strong, unreadable emotions played over Anton Koffield's face. "It *can* work," DeSilvo said. "We can make it work." He took a datapad from the hidden pocket in the sleeve of his robe and held it up. "All the plans and projections and engineering estimates are here. Full information on the plan so far."

"The plan doesn't matter," Koffield said. "I can't believe for a moment that it could possibly work, but even if it could—*if* it could—I have sworn an oath to protect the past from the future, to protect casuality. That is the sworn duty of *every* officer and enlisted person of the Chronologic Patrol."

"You *aren't* a CP officer," Yuri Sparten said. "Not anymore. I finally thought to check in the copy of the Grand Library data we took from the Solar System. It includes detailed service records of CP personnel. You're listed as dead for more than a century, Admiral. Off the rolls. No pay accumulating, all survivor benefits long since paid off to your sister's descendants. I checked the law sections too, and the CP regulations. There have been a few other cases of time-stranding and mistakes where people were kept in cryogenic storage for too long, that sort of thing. They've got regs that cover your situation. The way I read them, they're supposed to let you off the hook and get on with your life. It also protects the CP from having to pay you full benefits forever, and it keeps the accountant ArtInts from having to keep an active file on you for the rest of time."

"What do the regulations say, Mr. Sparten?" DeSilvo asked.

"I've, ah, got it right here. It's ah, CP Regulations Part Three, Section Two, Paragraph 23.4 subparagraph B." He cleared his throat and began to read from a datapad in front of him. " 'Should any officer or enlisted person be reported as presumed dead for a period of ten or more standard years, such officer or enlisted person in fact surviving but prevented from communicating with any or all commands or offices of the CP, by reason of physical incapacity, chronologic displacement, malfunction or failure of equipment, or similar unforeseen and nonpreventable circumstances, said circumstances not resulting from any dishonorable act or dereliction of duty on the part of said officer or enlisted person, or from the incarceration of the officer or enlisted person as a *de facto* or *de jure* prisoner of war or by incarceration by nonmilitary organizations, then that officer or enlisted person shall be considered as honorably discharged and/or retired effective as ten standard years from the date listed on the certificate of presumed death'—and it goes on from there to cover lots of other contingencies."

"I think I followed *most* of that," said Jerand Bolt. "If you're listed as dead for ten years, but it turns out you're not, you get ten years' pay and benefits and a discharge. But what's the deal about being incarcerated? Why should it matter whether or not you're locked up if you're listed as dead?"

It was Koffield who answered. "If not for that clause, then a criminal gang or an enemy military could fake your death and keep you locked away, and have all that time to work on you, convince you to help them. After ten years and one day, they could show you the regulation, and your own death certificate, and say—'You're discharged. You're released from your oath. Now it's okay to help us with a clear conscience—and you're still entitled to back pay from the CP.' "

DeSilvo could not help it. He stared hard at Anton Koffield in astonishment. When, precisely, had he worked up the nerve, or the curiosity, to check the regulations? How long had he been *pretending* to be an admiral? How long had he let them all assume it? Or did it matter to this group? A glance around the room made it clear it did not.

It was a subtle concession to him, to DeSilvo, that Koffield considered himself free to act guided by nothing but his own conscience. Why else would Koffield have specifically mentioned being released from oaths?

"Thank you for clarifying that point, Admiral," DeSilvo said, careful to use the title that Koffield had just admitted had long ago become merely a courtesy. It was a delicate moment, and one that he would have to handle carefully. He looked around the room, to all of them. "I understand your concerns. I have studied the potential flaws in this plan—technical objections, scientific objections, ethical objections, even the very basic question as to whether it is physically possible in the first place. I believe I have answers to all those objections, and we can discuss them when we review the plan in more detail."

DeSilvo turned back to Koffield. "But your objection, Admiral, I regard as the most serious. That is why I wanted *you,* more than anyone else, to come here, to Glister, and hear me out." *Because if I can convince you, you can convince everyone else,* DeSilvo added silently to himself. *And if I can convince you, I can convince anybody.*

"I think that Mr. Sparten has made a good case that you are no longer legally bound by your oath. Whether or not you are still morally or ethically bound is, of course, a matter that you alone can decide.

"But I would suggest to you that, whatever its wording, the *intent* of that oath was not to protect causality—but *history.* To prevent the future from attacking, invading, the *human* past. To prevent someone from going back a hundred, a thousand years and altering the outcome of a battle, or an election, or an assassination attempt. But should the temporal laws and the CP oaths be extended to infinity, through all of time and space?

There are any number of precautions we can and will take to prevent interference with history."

"You can take all the precautions you want," Koffield said. "None of them will make damage to causality—to history, if you must—absolutely impossible. There will always be a risk."

"Yes," DeSilvo said, thrilled to spot an opening, a gap in Koffield's shield of honor and absolutes. He had granted the difference between *history* and *causality*. That *had* to mean something. "There will be a risk, I believe, an extremely small one. But perhaps I am wrong. Perhaps it will be a very large risk. Perhaps we will discover later, after the fact, that it was a virtual certainty that our plan would result in massive damage to causality. If so, then I say to you it would still be worth the risk.

"Why? Because if we do not act, *our history, our chain of causality, is going to die.* All our projections show that not just our interstellar civilization, but the human race itself, will die out. Barring a miracle, we'll be extinct somewhere between eight hundred and three thousand years from now. And not just the human race, but *all* complex life-forms. Earth will be blanketed, choked, and killed by a symbiote-mold thicker than the one on Mars, unless the planet is infested by something worse.

"Maybe—*maybe*—something will be dragged from the wreckage someday. Life of some sort will still survive on at least some of the ruined worlds. Some, perhaps even many, of the failed worlds will reevolve complex life in a few tens or hundreds of millions of years. Earth is probably the most likely world for life to reemerge. Perhaps some forms of complex life will even survive the collapse. Cockroaches, or rats, perhaps. But that is the best—the *best*—we can hope for. If you remain absolutely faithful to the letter of your oath, and not to its spirit, that will be the best possible result of your choice.

"You have seen Solace dying, and Glister dead, and Mars, a corpse of a world tormented after death by the parasites that killed it. That is our future, if we leave the past alone. You know that. You have seen it."

Koffield nodded, most reluctantly.

"It comes down to this, Admiral Koffield: I offer you a choice between absolutely rigid, literal-minded adherence to an oath that I doubt still binds you—and the survival of the human race, of life itself. Which shall it be?"

The silence hung heavy in the room, but the longer it lasted, the surer DeSilvo was of Koffield's answer. He felt his heart singing, his soul shouting in triumph, as he read the face of his adversary, his ally, his mirror image.

At last, Admiral Anton Koffield, Chronologic Patrol (ret), nodded once again, paused a moment, then came to his feet. He looked around the room, at all the faces there—and seemed to see beyond them as well, to far-distant horizons, of past and future. Finally, he looked directly at Oskar DeSilvo.

"You are sure of your plans," Koffield said. It was not a question, but it required an answer.

"I am," said Oskar DeSilvo. "I am sure we are doomed without them, sure that there is a least a chance they will work, and sure that we must try them."

"Very well," he said. "I believe there is no hope if we go on as we are. Therefore, we have no choice but to change things. We must take great care, and great precautions. But it would seem our only hope of a future lies in visiting the past. Even if I personally believe that my oath still binds me, the law releases me from that oath, and in any event here we are beyond the reach or bounds of any law. Under the circumstances, my own opinion of myself must weigh very lightly in the balance."

He paused one final time, very briefly, then plunged on to the end. "The past calls to us," he said at last. "Let us go there."

Part Four
LOWDOWNS AND DIEHARDS

Chapter Nineteen

CAPTIVE AUDIENCE

"That's it, Kalani," said Burl Chalmers. "Not much else to see for the next few light-years."

Kalani Temblar reluctantly pushed back from the viewport. Truth to tell, she had long since lost sight of the Five Goddess Delta Wormhole Station. No doubt the long-range cameras could pull it in with ease, but it hadn't been that dazzling a sight, even at short range— just a collection of tubes and struts and hab modules stuck together in whatever way would cost the least money. Reluctantly, she pushed the button that swung the external shield back up and over the viewport.

Five Goddess Delta Station wasn't much to look at, but it had been the *only* thing to look at, besides Burl Chalmers—and she was, once again, about to be doing plenty of that in the temporal-confinement chamber. She had *already* done plenty of it on the first leg of their journey. The *Belle Boyd XI* had just spent three and a half decades traveling from the Solar System to the Five Goddess Wormhole Farm. Kalani and Burl had spent that time in the TC chamber. The chamber had done its job and made those thirty-five years pass in a mere thirty-five hours. But that was a day and a half cooped up in a very small space with a very large man.

The run through the timeshaft had sent them seventy years back into their own past, thirty-five years before their departure date. The ship would spend another thirty-five years ambling along through interstellar space, so as to bring them to their destination about a month after the calendar date of their departure from the Solar System—though the ship would have aged seven decades in that time, while Burl and Kalani would have experienced only about a total of ten days of personal subjective time.

But those ten days would include two thirty-five-hour sessions in the TC chamber. Considering that it was supposed to make time pass more quickly, it was astonishing how slowly time passed in the TC chamber. What was even more astonishing was how long Burl could sleep at one time—and how loudly he snored. The TC chamber was in zero gee, and you weren't supposed to be able to snore in weightless conditions—even so, Burl found a way.

And now came the time for her to experience it all over again. With a weary sigh, Kalani started to follow Burl aft from the command center down to the temporal-confinement compartment.

The *Belle Boyd XI* might be a comparatively small ship, by Chronologic Patrol standards, but she was still a formidable vessel. Like all ships designed for transit through timeshaft wormholes, she was a long, all-but-featureless cylinder, with all external protuberances stowed for transit through the wormhole.

Her rigging for the long journey through interstellar space wasn't much different. Only a few sensor booms were deployed, and the basic optical navigator viewports left open. Everything else was kept sealed shut. Interstellar vacuum was a whole lot of nothing, but they would be traveling through much of that nothing at very high velocities. Impact with one tiny dust mote—or even a somewhat thicker patch of vacuum, with a few more molecules per cubic meter—could do damage. There was no sense in exposing any more equipment than they had to.

She looked like most other ships in transit. But the volume and mass other ships would use for cargo or passenger appointments, the *Belle Boyd XI* gave over to weapons and sensors. When she arrived at her destination and started sprouting her external systems, she would look nothing at all like a peaceful freighter or passenger ship. Kalani had spent most of her time aboard learning the ship's systems—and what she learned was enough to make Kalani's blood run cold. Strange that a ship with such a pretty name could do such ugly things.

She had wondered about the name, in fact, and had taken the time to research it. Tradition held that the Chronologic Patrol Intelligence Service's overt ship be named for celebrated intelligence agents of years and centuries and millennia gone by. Unfortunately, almost by definition, a good intelligence agent wasn't ever detected, let alone celebrated. It was usually the failures that got famous—when they got caught.

If one searched all of history for generally admired, or even generally tolerated espionage agents, the resulting list would be surprisingly short. Perhaps that was the reason Belle Boyd's name had been used on eleven ships—so far. Boyd was an agent for the losing side during a major insurrection in North America, in the early near-ancient period. She was captured more than once, and the last time she was, she wound up seducing—and marrying—her captor. Kalani was not entirely sure she approved of either Belle Boyd—the person or the ship.

But then, it had been a long time since anyone had much worried about how *she* felt about things. With another long weary sigh, she followed Burl into the TC chamber.

WILHELMTON
WILHELMTON DISTRICT
THE PLANET SOLACE

When at last it came, the point of a knife at Elber's throat was almost a relief.

He had certainly spent enough time waiting around for it. There had never been all that much to the village of Wilhemton, and after all the hard luck of the past few years, there wasn't much left. Empty stores, empty houses, empty streets.

Elber learned a lot, and learned it fast, about just what hard times could do to a town. And discovered just how much easier life in hard times could be—for those with money. Back in Solace City, his daily stipend as authorized by Sotales would have allowed him to live in reasonable comfort—if he shopped carefully. But in Mistvale, prices had fallen so low that he had an effectively unlimited expense account. He could not eat or drink enough in a day to use it up.

Food was scarce, water was scarce, fresh linens were scarce, even heating and lighting were too expensive—for everyone but him. It shamed him to wave so much money around—but it seemed as though, within a day or so, that the whole town was absolutely dependent on his spending as much as possible. Money also made people much more willing to talk, about anything or everything. Elber asked a lot, and listened a lot, and the money smoothed the way.

Besides, flashing the cash helped make him visible, caused talk, and that was what he was trying to accomplish. It wasn't long at all before everyone for kilometers in all directions knew that Bush Lord Destan's old friend Elber Malloon was in town, and sure would like to get together with him.

Once that was accomplished, it only remained to wait and see if Zak Destan would take the bait. There was something nerve-wracking about waiting around to be kidnapped.

But it would appear that the days and nights of spending big and talking to everyone about everything had just met their reward. The feel of the blade against his skin was sharp and cool as the darkness just beyond the cottage porch where he had sat, night after night, offering himself as a victim, positioning his chair to make it easy to come up behind him. He never saw or heard the approach of the person who now stood behind him, reaching around to balance the knife point on his Adam's apple.

"Take it easy, friend," said the voice from the darkness at his back. "Nice, and slow, and quiet. Hands on the table, and don't turn around."

Elber set down his drink and put his hands flat on the table. "Okay," he said. The knife blade dug in just a trifle as he spoke.

"Good. Real good." The knife point shifted to the side of his neck, then was gone. "There's a friend of ours that wants to talk with you. We're going to go meet with him. Right now."

Elber was about to reply, but then a black cloth bag was pulled down over his head. After one breath of whatever the cloth was saturated with, Elber passed out cold.

It was hard to tell for sure that he was awake. The banging, clattering, jouncing ride he was getting in the real world seemed all too similar to the nightmare ride he had just been on while unconscious. Nor could his senses tell him for sure that he was finally awake. The black bag was still over his head, and though the knockout chemical had obviously dissipated enough for him to wake up, there was still enough of it to make him woozy and make his eyes sting. Sound was reaching him, but it was oddly distorted, echoing and booming from all directions, the way it did sometimes during a high fever. He was lying on his back, strapped down at the chest and thigh on some sort of padded surface, his hands tied together in front of him, and his ankles bound together as well.

It was impossible to judge how long he rode like that, or how much of the ride he made awake, or asleep, or unconscious. Later on, he would have no way of telling how far he had traveled, or in what direction. He would even be hard-pressed to say what sort of vehicle he had been in. Some sort of clapped-out wheeled motorized transport, as best he could judge from the sound and the way it moved. He was probably in the cargo compartment of some sort of delivery van, but that was just a guess.

Elber had been born a lowdown, a peasant, and had found himself suddenly back in the lowdown world—though, as a visitor from the outside, flashing upper cash and wearing upper clothes. But for all of that, he was back in his old world—and the old reflexes came to the surface. If there was one thing a lowdown peasant learned, it was fatalism. Some things could not be changed, and there was no sense trying. It was best instead to wait it out, to endure, to preserve yourself and survive.

Elber Malloon closed his stinging eyes, shifted his position slightly to get as comfortable as he could, and willed himself to sleep.

He woke again to find the vehicle stopped. He heard the sound of slamming doors and loud voices and felt the movement of people climbing out. He heard a metallic door swing open from somewhere off beyond his head, then people climbing into the compartment that held him. Unseen hands undid the straps holding him down and the bonds around his ankles. They left his hands tied and the black hood over his head. No one spoke.

The invisible hands guided him, firmly but gently, to his feet, then led him out of the vehicle. A hand pushed his head down just as he stepped from the vehicle, presumably to duck him under a low doorway. The surface under his feet felt like grit-covered concrete, and something about the background noise, and the timbre of sound, made him think that they were at some sort of loading dock.

The hands led him through a set of doors and down an echoing corridor. At last they halted in front of a door. He heard the rattle of keys in a lock, and he was hustled forward and guided to sit in a chair set with its back to the door. Then the door slammed shut behind him, and the room was silent. After a moment, he discovered that the bonds around his wrists had been undone. He pulled them off, reached up, and pulled the hood off.

He was in a clean, plainly furnished room. Concrete walls, ceiling, and floor. The floor painted the sort of cold gloss brown used in factory floors, the walls and ceiling white. A bed, the armchair he was sitting in, a wooden table and wooden chair beside it. A set of shelves, with all the possessions he had traveled with neatly arranged on them, his luggage sitting on the top shelf. A curtained doorway to the left, the steel door behind him, and a large double-hung glass window in the wall opposite—with bars on the inside of the glass. He could reach through the bars to slide the window open, but he could not possibly get out. It looked to be early morning. He must have spent all night in the truck. The window looked out onto a small field, backing onto a browning forest.

It was almost precisely the equal in comfort to the cottage he had been renting. He would have considered it the lap of luxury before he wound up on SCO Station. And it really wasn't all that much smaller, or plainer, than the quarters he shared with his wife and child, back on SCO.

He did not bother trying the steel door—he had heard the keys in the lock and the bolt sliding to when his unseen guides had left. He stood and pushed aside the curtain in a doorway off to the left. As he expected, it led to a tiny kitchen area, stocked with some basic foodstuffs, and an even smaller bathroom. All spotlessly clean. All quiet. And that was all there was.

Elber was born a lowdown peasant, and peasants knew more than fatalism. They knew to use what was given to them. He headed to the bathroom and got himself cleaned up.

He spent the day lying on the bed, sitting in the armchair, staring out the window. Peasants were good at waiting. Twice he prepared simple meals for himself using the food left in the kitchen for him.

Mainly he reflected on everything he had heard and seen since his arrival from Solace City Spaceport. Back in the insurance office on SCO Station he had learned it was important to weigh the evidence, to consider each fact not only by itself but also in relation to all the others. What fit, what didn't? What preconceptions were helping him to see? What assumptions led him in the wrong direction and should be abandoned? What had Sotales really intended when he sent Elber Malloon, once and maybe future lowdown peasant, to see Zak Destan?

He found himself starting at the beginning, over and over again, checking off all the evidence, one item at a time—then, over and over again, reaching a point where it was impossible to reach further conclusions without further information. But he could only get so far with such lines of thought before they turned into sterile, fretful guesswork. He needed more—and he needed it from Destan.

They waited until twilight, and then the door swung open. The lights were low and the two guards were wearing hoods over their heads—though theirs were equipped with eyeholes and mouth holes. Each wore a sidearm, but neither had his weapon drawn.

They did not speak, but led him with gestures out of the room and along the corridor, one of the guards dropping back two or three steps to cover him in case he tried anything. But Elber had no death wish, and besides, he was already going where he wanted to go.

They led him outside, down a short flight of steps, and onto a dirt path that led off under the dying trees. He didn't get a chance for more than a quick glance backward, but what he saw confirmed his earlier guess. They were keeping him in one of the old agriculture transfer stations. Once, they'd been where the farmers brought the crops for transport to the cities. Now there weren't many farmers, and even fewer crops.

After about a five-minute walk, they arrived at a campsite, seven or eight large tents pitched in under the trees.

That puzzled Elber for a minute. Why put him in a permanent structure while they lived in tents? Then he understood. The agtran station was secure. They could lock down a prisoner. But it was also a fixed target. Tomorrow, this campsite would be empty. Movement was their best defense.

Whoever, exactly, "they" were. Elber was fairly certain he was about to find out.

His two silent guides brought him to the largest tent and took up positions on either side of the entrance. One of them pulled open the tent flap and gestured for him to step inside.

He did, into a warm, brightly lit interior, comfortably furnished with the very best portable gear. And there, working at a camp desk in the center of the room, was Zak Destan himself. His black hair was cut short, in an almost military style, and his beard was trimmed short and neat, a darting, dapper triangle of salt and pepper that gave his chin a bit of dignity and style. But the eyes were the same. Dark, deep-set, expressive eyes, jet-black eyebrows that set off his pale skin. Eyes that could smile, or threaten, or warn, or laugh, or hate with astonishing eloquence. Eyes that warned of the dangerous mind behind them.

As Elber walked into the room, Zak stood up and smiled broadly. He was dressed in what looked at first to be a fieldhand's coveralls—but no fieldhand ever wore coveralls that well cut, or well made. There was some sort of insignia sewn on the shoulder of the coverall, and the name DESTAN was stenciled below it. "Elber! Good. Very good. They said it was you—but I couldn't quite believe it. But come and sit down."

Zak led him to a dining table off to one side of the tent. A bottle of red wine was waiting there, along with two glasses. Zak gestured for Elber to take a seat, poured two glasses of wine, handed one to Elber, and sat down himself.

Elber accepted the glass and took a polite sip of wine. Did Zak remember? Was he trying to make a point? Or was it sheer chance? The last time Elber had seen Zak was on the night of the Long Boulevard riot—a riot touched off when Zak brought a wine bottle down on a security guard's head. Elber might have wanted to know, but didn't see any way to ask. Instead, he let it go at, "Hello, Zak."

"Hello, Elber," Zak said with a wolfish smile. "What the hell are you doing here?"

"*Doing* here?" Elber echoed. "I'm being kidnapped."

"Before that. Waiting around to *be* kidnapped, by the look of it. Drawing attention to yourself, dropping my name all over the place, choosing a place to stay on the outskirts of town where no one would be watching. That wasn't all chance."

"No," Elber said. "I *was* hoping you'd—ah—come get me. I didn't think I'd have much luck if I went out looking for you myself."

"No, that's for sure. That would have put you in a nailed-shut box for sure. But the way you worked it instead was pretty dicey too, my friend."

"It worked," Elber said. "That says something for it."

"Well, it worked so well it almost didn't work at all," said Zak. "You were so damned obvious that it got my boys nervous. They had to check back with me, clear it, make sure it was all right to take you."

Elber shrugged and covered his uncertainty with another sip of wine. "I'm new at this sort of thing," he said.

"That's what I figured. You'll learn."

I'm going to get more practice? How many times do you expect to kidnap me? But no, that wasn't was Zak meant. He was talking about intrigue in general, plotting, games in the dark. "I guess I will," he said.

"You will if you want to live," said Zak, his voice suddenly earnest, the playfulness gone. "Whoever sent you won't leave you alone after this, no matter what they promised. They can't. Just by doing this job, you've already gotten to know things they don't like people knowing."

"I know," said Elber. "I figured that much out a while ago."

"So who did send you?" Zak asked. "Who sent you, and why?"

Elber looked Zak straight in the eye and wished desperately for time to freeze in that moment, the way it had in that temporal confinement up on Greenhouse when they did the Ignition.

He knew—he *knew*—that he had exactly one chance to answer the question, one chance to get it right. And it wouldn't be enough just to give the *correct* answer. He would be judged by the way he spoke as well. Hesitate, seem unsure—and his daughter would be short one father. *That* thought cleared his mind, focused things sharp.

"Sotales sent me," he said, his voice calm and collected. "He wanted to establish some sort of contact with you."

Zak stared at him, hard, for a handful of seconds, and Elber had time to get scared all over again. "All right," he said, and Elber knew he had passed a test, perhaps the first of many. He was going to be allowed to live, at least a while longer.

"So Sotales wants contact with me," Zak repeated. "Why?"

Elber shrugged. "He *said* he was doing it as some sort of favor for the groundcops, but I'm not sure. I think *Sotales* himself wanted a contact with you. Everyone has always said Sotales likes to play a lot of games at once."

"You're being awfully honest with me," Zak said, eyeing him thoughtfully.

"You want me to lie some?" Elber asked.

"I want to know whose side you're on. You say Sotales sent you, then you start telling me what you think of Sotales. Turning on him already?"

"He didn't hire loyalty," Elber said. "He set me up—fake arrest that made sure I lost my job. He just promised he'd take care of me if I did what he asked—made sure I knew things would get bad for me and my family if I didn't. I'm just a messenger boy. Why pretend while I'm here, with you?"

Zak studied Elber thoughtfully for a moment and emptied his wineglass. He set the glass down and reached for the bottle to refill it. "You've changed a lot since I saw you last," he said.

"I've changed a lot in the last few *weeks*," Elber replied. Changed enough to amaze himself. Where *had* he found the wit and the nerve that it had taken to get him to Zak Destan's headquarters? But he knew the answer—it was the answer to just about every question he asked of himself. *Zari and Jassa.* They were motive enough to make any man do what he had to do.

"Well, here we are, having a nice chat, sipping wine. So what were you supposed to *do* once you'd established contact, for Sotales, or whoever?"

"I'm supposed to find out what you want," Elber said.

"*That* shouldn't be too hard," said Zak. "I'll take you around to one of my caches, and you can make a list of what's there. I take what I want, and I want what I take."

"That's not what they think," said Elber. "They think it's something more. And I think so too."

Zak snorted derisively. "*You* think so? Farm-boy Elber Malloon, master spy—*and* he knows how to think? When did *you* ever think a thought in your life?"

"Not until just a little while ago," he said, calm and quiet, not even tempted to rise to the bait. "Not until Sotales set me up. But you said yourself I'd changed, Zak. And I've had a lot of time to think—and to see, and to hear, since I came back to Solace."

Zak laughed, a little longer and harder than he should have. Maybe the wine was doing it. "Okay, Mr. Thinker. Let's see how you do as a mind reader. What do *I* want?"

Out, Elber told himself. *You want out, even if you don't know it yet.* He didn't feel quite bold enough to say that out loud. Not just yet. "I'll tell you," he said. "But first you tell me a few things." He hooked his thumb up, toward the sky beyond the tent. "Sotales and the others up there said you were just a plain old robber, a crook. They allowed as how some might think of you as a reiver. Even *the* reiver in these parts. Folks back in town called you Reiver Boss Destan—even Reiver *Lord* Destan. Some called you Bush Lord. What do you call yourself?"

"So they call me different names," Destan replied, plainly dodging the question.

"Names mean things. 'Reiver' is just a fancy name for a big-time robber. Reivers can be folk heroes—but they're not respectable. No one wants his daughter *marrying* a reiver. A Lord is lord *of* something—a place, or an armed force, usually. And a Bush Lord might be a real leader for the people. Ask someone what they call you, and you'll know what they think of you. So what do you call yourself?"

"What do *you* call me, Elber?" Destan asked.

"I haven't decided yet," Elber said, astonished at his own daring. But Zak had always been the sort to push harder when he sensed weakness. Acting meek and mild could do Elber no good. "I've asked you twice, and you still haven't answered. What do you call yourself?"

Zak looked hard at him, sighed, and slouched back in his chair. "I haven't decided yet, either," he admitted. "It was a big deal for me when I heard them call me reiver, then *the* reiver—and then the Lord stuff started. But, okay, you hit the target there, Elber. Lord of *what*? Buy this town's loyalty, give that mayor a new car, bribe those cops, pay for those weddings—and you've got a bunch of peasants who will love you until they notice the money's run out. I oughta be able to do more'n *that* with what I got."

Zak stood up, paced back and forth across the tent. "And then, then—" He stopped, turned around, and glared at Elber. "Hell. You know what? Sotales was damned smart to send *you*. You knew me back then. I can't pretend in front of *you*. I'm no mystery man to you. I'm the drunken thug who started a riot with a wine bottle because he got bored." Both men looked toward the bottle on the table, and both of them smiled. "All right, you caught me. I *thought* you'd remember." Destan shook his head. "Anyway, they think I'm the big man because I know how to rob the convoys and steal from the uppers and get away clean.

"I'm a real big powerful man—until some farmer

comes cap in hand to one of my boys and says his farm is dried to dust—or washed away like yours was, Elber. Farm gone, and can I help? What am I supposed to *do*? Buy him a new one? Steal one from a convoy and give it to him? I can't give *all* of 'em food enough to see 'em all through. If I steal *all* the high goods from *all* the upper convoys and hand 'em all out, it *still* won't be enough to fix it all."

"No," Elber said. "It won't. But I'll answer my own question now, and then yours. I'm guessing *Bush Captain* is about right. More than just a reiving man, but not a lord of all. Close?"

"Close as can be," Destan admitted. "I like it when they call me that. But what about the other one? What do *I* want?"

"To buy that farmer a new farm," Elber said. "You near as much tried it, a few times, from what the villagers say. To get the medicine for the sick children—but you've told your troops to steal no food, no medicine, because that's just saving here by killing there. Makes it harder to do good."

Destan laughed hard and sat down again behind his camp desk, a little bit away from Elber. " 'To do good.' The joke is that it's no joke. I wake up in the morning, and I'm not thinking about the next hit on a convoy— I'm thinking about food for starving farm kids."

He looked over at Elber. "Don't get me wrong—I'm still a son of a bitch no-good reiving thug. When this blows over—I'll look out for me again. But—but hell, Elber, you ain't the only one who's changed. Look at a kid, a kid from a family you know all your life, and that kid's got a swelled belly and ribs stickin' out and can't run, can't play, and the uppers won't stir, and you've got a warehouse full of stolen upper booze and goodies that won't do her a damn bit of good—ah, hell—*you* try not wanting to do something." He reached out a hand, swept the papers from his desk. "Hell, I even got a village teacher to show me how to *read,* just so I could study the problem better."

"I know. I know," said Elber. "But study all you

want—you can't do anything, Zak. Nothing that will do any good. Not down here."

"What are you talking about? I'm going to do plenty. New plan, different plan."

"Let me do some more guessing," Elber said. "No more just stealing from the uppers. You're going to chase the uppers out, do what they're supposed to do—take care of the lowdowns. 'Cause the uppers—they've broken their side of the deal. We do the hard work, they keep us safe. That's the way it's supposed to be. But now it's not happening that way."

Destan glared at Elber. "Your guessing is a little too good," he said. "You working for friends who've been listening in?"

"I don't need to," Elber said. "And I don't think they needed to listen. They just needed to *look*—at you, at all the other reiver bands popping up. My guess is Sotales is contacting all of them, as best he can, using people like me, when he can, other ways when they have to. He's the chess player, and I'm one of his pieces. He's putting his pieces where he needs them for the next part of the game."

"And what is the next part? To buy the reivers off?" Destan growled. "Is that why you're here? A big bag of cash for me, and I won't care so much if Farmer Muglehorner's daughter dies of starvation?"

"No, Zak," Elber said gently. "That's why it's me they sent." He patted himself on the chest. "That's why Sotales chose *this* chess piece instead of some other one. You know my little boy's buried out there, in a grave that got flooded over when the waters came. Buy you off for trying to help, and I'd be dancing on little Belrad's grave."

Destan grunted. "Maybe so. Then why are you here?"

Elber shook his head. "I *think* I'm here to have you tell me you're going to start a revolt if the uppers don't do what they should, and make things right. Then I'm supposed to go back and tell them that and have you see I'm a good little messenger boy. Maybe then, maybe later, the grown-ups will push me aside and take over. Then, maybe, you'll hold off your revolt for a while, while everyone negotiates, and you cut a deal everyone can live with—for a while. You get to see they stick to the bargain, whatever it turns out to be.

"Then—then when things turn *really* bad, maybe you'll trust them enough to believe the truth about the real bad news." Elber looked hard at Destan. "You and the other reivers are getting stronger—groundcops and all the uppers are getting weaker. Start a relationship with you, now, they figure, and it'll save time and lives later on, when the crunch hits and you really need to talk and act fast."

"What crunch? What are you talking about?"

"The news they figure no one down here is ready for yet," said Elber. "But I think I've got it figured out, now, and maybe you'll believe it coming from me, now. If I tell you now, and make you believe—maybe, maybe, I can save time, and lives. So here goes."

If. If he could make Zak see that, now, today, then how many lives would be saved? "It's not just this valley, or bad weather the last couple of years, Zak. It's the *planet*. You can't see it from here, but I can from up there. Look out the window from SCO Station every day and you'd see it too. The *planet* is dying. The uppers can't fix it. No one can."

"What are you talking about?" Destan objected. "How can a whole planet die?"

"Ask anyone from Glister," Elber replied. "I'll bet there were a lot of protests and revolts there, too, before the end came. 'Fix it or we'll take over and fix it ourselves!' Is that pretty much what you want to tell the uppers?"

Destan picked up a pen, doodled aimlessly on a scratch pad, then dropped the pen and crumpled up the paper. "Yeah," he admitted. "Pretty much. The uppers sure aren't doing the job."

"How you going to fix it, Zak? *How?* What aren't they doing that you will? Relief supplies only last as long as there's a place in decent shape to send the relief from. Look around you. Remember what this land *used* to be like. Hell, remember what it was like *last year*. The house is on fire, halfway burned down, and you want to kick out the firefighters and put your own people in charge of putting it out. Makes sense if the firefighters *are* slacking off—but suppose they're doing their best, but there's no water for the hoses? And even if the uppers don't fight you at all, what about the time and effort lost in the handover? Besides, they will fight. You know it."

" 'Only fools fight in a burning house,' " Destan said. "Once they see that they can't stop us—"

"It'll be too late. The house will be burned down. It's already too late, Zak."

"You ought to be more careful, Elber. It's not too smart to get your kidnapper angry at you."

"I'll risk it," Elber said. "Kicking out the uppers won't do any good. All your plans won't help. Fixes to the rules won't fix anything, food buy-ups will just drive prices up, and it's fool's work to repair buildings and machines that will have to be abandoned in an evac anyway. The sooner you realize I'm right, the sooner you can start thinking fresh, the better a deal you can get for your people. *Your* people, Zak."

"What do you mean, *mine*?" Destan demanded.

"You wouldn't be planning to take them from the uppers if you didn't feel they were yours to begin with. They started being yours the second you wanted to do something about that starving farmer's baby."

"Damn you!"

"Tell me it's not true," Elber said.

The room was silent for a time, and the night outside seemed to grow darker, though the lights in the room stayed as bright as ever. Destan glared at Elber, but Elber returned that gaze, steady and calm, though his heart was pounding.

At last Destan called out, "Halbern!"

One of the troopers reappeared at the tent flap. "Sir?"

"Escort our friend back to his box," he said. "Stick him in there and keep him there until I say so."

"Yes, sir."

Elber stood up and crossed the tent, wondering if he was going to pay for his pretty speeches with his life.

As his captors led him back, stumbling through the darkness to the agtran station, he tried to tell himself it didn't matter. He had delivered his warning—a louder, clearer warning than Sotales had intended. If they killed him, the warning would still have been delivered. But maybe it did matter—a lot.

Sotales had plainly felt Destan wasn't ready to hear the whole story—otherwise he would have arranged for Elber, or some other courier, to tell it. Instead he had felt it wiser to start with a slow, cautious approach, establishing contact, getting the lines of communication open, so they'd be ready for use later on. *And you decided to be the big smart guy and slice through all that,* Elber told himself. *Suppose Sotales was right, and Destan not only wasn't ready to listen—suppose thanks to my pushing him too hard now he never believes? Kills me, kills the next guy to try, tells himself it's all a plot—and all the people he could have saved, should have saved, wind up dead?*

Elber tripped over a tree root and went sprawling, facefirst, into the ground, barely getting his hands in front of him in time. His guards waited impassively as he stood up, brushed himself off, and resumed the walk. *Or suppose you've just plain guessed wrong—about the planet dying, about what Sotales has in mind, about where they're supposed to go? Then what?*

He kept moving, one foot in front of the other, on through the dead woods. He had meant well.

But Elber Malloon was learning the hard way that just meaning well could be a hell of a good way to make the problem twice as big.

He moved on through the darkness, straining to see his way ahead.

Zak Destan paced angrily back and forth across the interior of his tent. *Damn the little twerp! Damn the little hayseed, better-than-you, do-the-right-thing, lowdown, know-it-all little* twerp! *Come in here with a story like that—especially when it's true.*

He stopped pacing for a minute and poured himself another glass of wine from the bottle. *True.* It *was* true, and, in his gut, he knew it. *That* wasn't the part that bothered him. What bothered him was that he saw it, saw it clearly, the second it was in front of his face. Things had been getting worse for so long it was hard to see how they could ever get better. There was one other thing that got him mad—damned angry in fact—at himself. Maybe without really intending it, Elber had rubbed Zak's nose in something, something he hadn't even been aware of before.

He, Zak Destan, Bush Lord—well, Bush Captain of Wilhemton District, would-be leader of a lowdown rebellion, had still had in his head the idea that the uppers *could* fix it all—but simply refused. His plan for rebellion had been simply to take over and force them to make it all better.

It was part of the culture he'd been raised in, the culture that had molded Solace, and been molded by Solace, since the first days of the terraforming effort. He'd been bred and trained for so long to believe that the uppers could dole out whatever rewards they liked, he had, quite unconsciously, clung to that instinct, that hope.

He snarled at nothing at all, finished his glass of wine at one gulp, then took a long pull of the bottle. He'd made himself a big noise, a big man. Reiver Lord! Bush Lord! And then along came Elber know-it-all Malloon.

And all of a sudden Zak was forced to ask himself if he was truly leading a rebellion—or if he had merely been stirring up enough trouble so they'd pay attention when he went, yelling loudly, waving a gun, but even so, cap in hand, to the Big Manor, to plead with Mr. Lord High Upper to wave his magic money-and-power wand and make it all better, please, and bow politely when you ask.

He frowned and set down the empty bottle. He was tempted to call for another, but thought better of it. He was blurry enough for a night when he needed to do some real clearheaded thinking. All right, then. *Think.*

Think it through. It wasn't just Wilhemton, not the district, not the country or the continent. The whole planet.

If so, what was the point in raising a warning? The Big Run had shown there just wasn't room in the habitats for everyone on Solace. Zak had no idea of the numbers, but he knew that only a relative handful of those who had tried had made it as far as a ship heading for orbit—and even that handful had come damned near wrecking the habitats through overcrowding.

But if there was nowhere to go, what purpose could be served by "establishing contact" with the likes of Bush Captain Zak Destan? To buy him off? Keep things quiet, keep them calm long enough for the uppers to evacuate back to Earth and Blue Haven and the other high-class planets?

Much as the idea appealed to Zak's streak of paranoia, it was far too risky a policy for a chess player like Sotales. Sotales always looked five or six moves ahead before he did anything, and it was almost inevitable that someone would talk—Elber just *had* talked.

Then what? What *was* the plan? Zak reached over, cut off the lights, and stared into the darkness, trying to think.

Elber woke up to find a knife at his throat again. The room was pitch-dark, dead silent, but he didn't need to hear or see—he remembered what the point of a blade felt like against his skin. He would remember that for the rest of his life.

"I'm—I'm awake," he said in a half whisper, not wishing to speak louder for fear of causing the knife to move.

"What's the plan, Elber?" Destan asked, his voice a throaty growl next to Elber's ear. Elber could smell the wine on Destan's breath, the whiff of dried sweat from his clothes, a mix of other, fainter smells—coffee, machine oil, sulfur and smoke and burned gunpowder, vying with each other to tell the story of how Destan lived.

"What—who—what plan?" he asked, still muddled by sleep and disoriented.

"We can't live here if the planet's going to put four feet in the air. Sotales wouldn't warn us if there wasn't something we could do. So there must be somewhere else. Where are we going?"

Elber tried to shake off his fear, his confusion, his exhaustion. "Zak, Sotales didn't tell me. Didn't tell me anything, hardly. I did some digging, some guessing, on my own."

"So do some more guessing," Destan said, and the pressure behind the knife blade's point increased by just a hair.

Give him an answer he doesn't like, and you die, Elber told himself. *Will he like the truth?* "I'm guessing, I'm guessing, Zak. But I think—I think that's what Greenhouse is really for."

"Greenhouse?" Destan demanded. His voice was still hoarse and angry, but at least the blade point didn't dig any deeper.

"Think on it," Elber said, trying to talk fast and talk calm, in pitch-dark, with a knife resting on the big vein in his neck. "All that time and money for the NovaSpot job. They say it's all so they can fix up domes, and build new domes, start up the bio projects to grow new breeding stock, revive Solace, fix things up again. But if I'm right, and Solace is too far gone for a fix-up, Kalzant and the uppers know that better'n anyone. *They've* got all the info. So why spend on NovaSpot unless they're going to use Greenhouse for something *else* big enough to make the job worth it—a job that'll need all the domes and gear they're talking about?"

"Greenhouse can't hold everybody," Destan protested— but still the knife didn't go deeper.

"I don't know all the numbers," Elber said. "I'm just guessing from the info I could get. They could work it lots of ways. Maybe they're going to build a lot more domes than we think. And there are a lot of abandoned domes that they can start using again, now that NovaSpot is throwing light everywhere. Maybe Greenhouse will be a way station where they can hold people before evac to someplace else. They could just evac the worst-off—or best-off—from Solace and stretch how long Solace will last that way. Probably some of all that. Anyway they do it, they buy time."

"Buy time for what? To fix the planet proper?"

Elber shrugged, and instantly regretted the movement, as it jogged Destan's hand and caused the knife point to scrape back and forth against his throat. "Maybe. I don't know. Maybe just so more people can get away when they evacuate to other planets."

Destan grunted, and remained silent for a moment. Finally, the knife point vanished from Elber's throat. He heard motion across the room, then the light bloomed on, blinding-bright for a moment before his eyes adjusted. He levered himself up on his arm, then swung his feet out of bed. He watched as Destan pulled a set of infrared goggles down off his face, so they hung by a strap around his neck. Destan grabbed a chair from by the table, and dropped into it heavily. "Okay," he said. "Your guessing gets you about where mine gets me."

So I get to live, Elber thought. "Good," he said. "So what next?"

"You got ways to contact Sotales," Destan said.

It wasn't a question, but Elber answered it. "Yeah, sure."

"So use one of them. Tell him whatever it'll take to get me a meeting with someone who can deal. Someone who can make things—big things—happen. I want you to stay around here too. You're a direct line to Sotales, and I might need that. But when the big upper comes, I want to hear a deal, an offer—and I want to hear about Greenhouse in the offer, and something about getting my people there. I'll listen to whatever offer they make, and I'm reasonable. I know Greenhouse ain't ready yet—they're still putting the place back together, now that the NovaSpot is done. So I'll be calm about times, schedules, and so on—but I won't accept less than I need.

"And if I *don't* hear something I can agree to, or if they don't keep their side of the deal—well, Wilhemton District isn't going to be a very nice place to be a cop—

or an upper. If they won't take us someplace we can live safe—we're going to have to take, and take, and take, just to live at all—and *no one* around here is going to live safe. Make me a good offer, keep up to the deal we make, and things will be nice and safe and quiet here for everyone. You got all that?"

Elber, barely daring to move, still feeling the bite of that knife in his throat, forced himself to nod, to speak. "I've got it."

"Good," Destan said, and stood up. He headed for the door. "My people brought all the gear you had with you. Contact Sotales. You have what you need."

Another not-question. Elber glanced over his possessions, neatly arrayed on the open shelves. His eyes lit on a fold-frame flat-photo of Jassa and Zari that he had brought along. One of Destan's people had carefully set it right where he could see it from anywhere in the room. "Yeah," he said. *Everything I need except them.*

"Good. Then you'll stay here for the time being. We'll keep you safe, but you'll get exercise and time outside and so on. Tell your guards if you have problems, or need something."

Destan walked to the steel door, knocked on it, and an unseen someone outside unbolted it. He left without another word, and the steel door boomed shut behind him and the lock bolt slammed home.

Elber nodded faintly at the empty room, trying to tell himself that it was good news, that Zak Destan had done exactly what he had hoped he would do.

But they were, all of them, a long way from being safe. Sotales might or might not wheel out a big enough shot to make Zak happy. But even if he did, that was not to say Zak would agree to the deal that was offered—or that Zak would keep his side of the bargain. Bush Captain Destan would—but suppose it turned out Zak was just a no-account reiver after all?

Between time zones, message queues, and his other duties, it was nearly a full day later when Olar Sotales received the message from Elber. Despite the elaborate bugging system built into Elber Malloon's body and possessions, Sotales didn't even know Elber had indeed made contact until Elber himself reported in.

Olar Sotales didn't like being surprised, and he did not like machines that didn't work. But when he checked, he found that the bugging system was working perfectly. It was simply that various technical limitations, and the security situation, meant that it took a while for the data dumps to find their way to Sotales, then more time for his ArtInts to process them and edit them down into something marginally coherent.

He elected to delay his reply to Malloon until he had at least viewed the portions of the playback that the ArtInt had flagged as of most interest. But the contents of those sections—the two conversations between Elber and Destan—were so startling that he viewed them several times and checked several other passages, just to see if he had missed something. Malloon had made so many accurate guesses that Sotales half wondered if some mysterious someone *was* somehow feeding him information.

He left Malloon hanging awhile longer even after that, as he took time to reflect on what he had learned. It was plain to see that he had badly—even grotesquely—underestimated Malloon. Still and all, the results of that underestimation were more than he could have dared hoped for. Destan was demanding, with threats, to get exactly what Sotales had hoped to get him to take reluctantly, after long and weary negotiations.

Malloon had done remarkably well, but that did not necessarily mean he should be rewarded just yet. It might well be best to let the fellow go on thinking he had gone too far, presumed too much.

And, of course, there was always the awkwardness, and even the danger, inherent in having a superb source of information. Sotales dared not do or say anything that would even hint at the existence of the body-bug system. He knew he would likely have to forgo a number of otherwise useful moves in the future, so as to preserve the continuation of the bugging system—and its wearer. After all, if Destan discovered the bugs, it was almost certain that it would be not just the minitransmitters, but Malloon himself, that would be deactivated. Sotales was not willing to risk that. Not yet, anyway. Malloon was likely to be very useful indeed in the times to come.

In fact—that gave him an idea. Sotales had plenty of sources and contacts and so forth in the spaceside operations on Greenhouse and among the upper ranks. But he didn't know enough about the situation on Greenhouse itself, on the ground, where they were actually working on the habitats. And the habitats were going to be the key. They'd need them, sooner than just about anyone realized.

He could arrange for Malloon to be permanently assigned to—what was his name? The young fellow that had saved Groundside Power. Benzen! That was it. He could put Malloon on Benzen's habitat-building team—doing liaison work for Destan, or some such. That would position Malloon to provide Sotales with information, not only on Destan, but on the habitat operation as well. It might be wise to start putting things in position to make that possible.

But there were other issues for Sotales to contend with beforehand. Malloon had said some rather unkind—and perfectly accurate—things about him. But he was quite willing to accept as a compliment the comparison to a chess player. This was indeed a game of position—and Greenhouse was where it would be won, or lost. He needed to get his pieces on that part of the board.

He would have to consider his next move most carefully before he responded to Elber Malloon. Sotales shook his head. The farm-boy had made a lot of things happen, no question.

Not that it mattered, really, but Sotales was starting to wonder which of them was the pawn—and which the player.

Chapter Twenty

THE TALE OF THE
GENEROUS TRAVELER

DeSilvo City
The Planet Glister

"Everything is harder and takes longer," Captain Marquez growled as he walked into the dining room with Koffield and Norla Chandray. Everyone else was there except DeSilvo, who tended to dine alone in the evening. The others were just finishing up their evening meal as the trio entered.

"And usually costs more money," Koffield replied with a smile, sitting down beside him. "That was a long simulator run."

"Yeah," Marquez said, eloquent in his brevity. They had just completed their dozenth simulated run through a simulated FTL transition field in a simulated version of the *Dom Pedro IV*'s newly rebuilt control system. Marquez felt certain that he, for one, could now do the whole procedure in his sleep—and the sleep would by no means be simulated. He was *tired*.

Norla Chandray, who had been a step or two behind them on the short walk from the simulator to the dining room, laughed out loud as she sat down next to Koffield. "Thank the stars we're not the ones paying for *this*." She gestured to indicate not only the dining room, but the whole of DeSilvo City.

Bolt, seated on the farside of the large circular table,

looked up from his meal and frowned. "Who *did* pay for it, do you suppose? I mean, DeSilvo stole it all, fair and square—but who, exactly, did he steal it *from*? And how much was it? I mean, if you did the accounting, how much did he take from whom?"

"I doubt it would even be possible to come up with a meaningful answer," Koffield said, accepting the plate that the serving robot offered him. "How do you put a price tag on the plans for that FTL drive? Or on a whole fleet of surplus transports that probably were ready to be put out for scrap? Or all the earthmoving gear salvaged from a dead city on a dead planet? That part isn't theft—unless you argue that the diehards had first claim on it, because they were here first and had greater need."

"At least the diehards are going to get some of it back," said Yuri Sparten. Sparten and Norla Chandray were now off report and had more or less settled back into their old routines. Still, Yuri had quite unconsciously seated himself so as to be as far as possible from everyone else. He seemed quite comfortable there.

"*Some* of the diehards will," Bolt replied. "Your friends at Last Chance Canyon, anyway."

Sparten looked confused. "What are you talking about?"

"Think it through. Ah, sir." Bolt clearly wasn't quite sure about the etiquette of addressing Sparten. Was he still, technically, an officer? How much informality—let alone insolence—was acceptable under the current very unusual circumstances? He glanced at Captain Marquez, but Marquez was plainly too busy eating his dinner to provide any sort of guidance. He shrugged and moved on. "DeSilvo said he started searching for them the moment he came out of temporal confinement. He didn't mean Last Chance Canyon in particular. He meant a diehard colony—and one that would suit his purposes. Probably it had to be close enough, and the right size, and maybe he had some other criteria."

"So? He found them."

"So why assume they were the only ones he found? A planet is a big place. What are the odds on his finding exactly the right sort of diehard group, exactly where he needed them, *and no other groups at all*? It's got to be that he shopped around."

"What do you mean?" Sparten asked.

"He means that DeSilvo probably found a number of such groups," said Wandella Ashdin. "It's sad to say, but there has been enough experience with collapsed planets that studies have been made. From what I know of the subject, there are probably somewhere between a hundred and five hundred such groups surviving here on Glister, though the low end of that range is the most likely. Nearly all of them at least as difficult to find as Last Chance Canyon, with most of them far better hidden. They hide from each other, not from outsiders. Probably failing at the rate of five or ten a year, if the statistics are anything to go by—and it's wars between the ones that find each other that do in most of them."

"*Hundreds* of colonies?" Sparten asked in astonishment.

Norla cocked her head at him. "I thought you'd read up on the subject. You didn't think Last Chance was the only colony, did you?"

"Well, I, ah, well—I didn't really think about it," Sparten admitted. "But—but if there are all those other diehards—how—what can we—"

"How do we help them?" Wandella Ashdin asked. "Is that it?"

"Well, ah,—well, yes," Sparten said.

"Pretty easy," said Sindra Chon as she worked on her dessert. "We don't. We can't."

"But—but—" Sparten protested. "There has to be *some* way."

"*Why* does there have to be? Because there isn't. Sir. There really isn't," said Sindra Chon, exhibiting some of the same uncertainty about Sparten's status that Bolt had. "The diehards would be the first to tell you that. Even if this was our place and our stuff, instead of DeSilvo's—"

"And we just got done saying he stole it fair and square," Dixon Phelby reminded her cheerfully. "It's his, and he'll make sure it stays that way."

"Right," Chon agreed. "But even if we *could* offer it all up, share it all out—what good would it do?"

"The food and equipment and supplies that'll still be here after the decoy operation?" said Sparten. "It could keep a lot of people alive, that's what!"

"How many, sir?" Chon asked. "And for how long? And then what? And will they share nicely? And what would it do to the big plans that DeSilvo has worked up?"

"I can't answer all that," Sparten protested. "Okay, it might cost us if we tried to help. It might not solve everything. But all you've given me so far are a lot of good reasons for doing nothing. There are always good reasons for doing nothing. Why not try?"

"You sound like the Generous Traveler," said Dr. Ashdin.

"Who?" Sparten asked.

"It's an old story," she replied. "The Generous Traveler was a reasonably well-to-do young man who went to a far-off land to see what things were like there. He found the people were very poor, and the streets full of beggars. He gave a coin to the first beggar who approached him, and the next, and the next and the next. When he had no more money, he gave away all his possessions, one by one.

"Sometime later, when the Traveler failed to return, his friend went in search of him. His friend retraced the Traveler's steps and found all the same beggars. All had long since spent the coins the Traveler gave and gone back to begging. Each of them pointed the way that the Traveler had gone. But when the friend got to the last beggar who had been helped by the Traveler, all that beggar had to do in order to direct the friend was to point to the beggar standing next to him—who was, of course, the Traveler."

"The version of that I heard was about a teacher," said Dixon Phelby. "On his way to teach farmers how to grow more food, or something. And because he gave away everything and got himself stranded, the farmers didn't learn, and the people there starved."

"We heard it about a doctor who never got to where the sick people were," said Sindra Chon.

"Great, fine, so there are lots of different versions. So what's the point of that story?" Sparten demanded.

"To relate a very cruel truth," said Dr. Ashdin. "Wealth can be spread so thin that it does no good, and in fact increases poverty, by impoverishing the wealthy. The Traveler sets out to help everyone, and winds up helping no one—and needing help himself. In the teacher and doctor versions, and others like them, about an engineer or a builder, or even a simple repairman, he winds up making things far worse than they would have been because he never gets to where he could do some good. And you are quite right—that story can stand as a specious and selfish argument for not trying. The tale, or some version of it, becomes popular among the well-off, or at least the better-off, in a society that is growing poorer—such as Solace."

"Even if we *could* find the other diehard settlements, we could easily do more harm than good," Koffield said in a gentle voice. "As Dr. Ashdin said, it's the wars between the diehard colonies that kill most of them off. We might well set off such a war—and be among its first victims. But there's something else I'd like to remind you of, Mr. Sparten. The day you first met Officer Chandray and me, on SCO Station. Right at the height of what came to be called the Big Run, with the whole satellite overrun with refugees. I trust you remember that day."

"Yes, sir. As clear as I remember anything."

"Something you said on that day struck me. You pointed out the endless refugees, and said something like 'The worst of it isn't that they took everything we had. The worst part was that they took it and made less than nothing out of it. They're no better off than when they got here. It's as if we had done nothing at all for them—and we did so much that it nearly killed the station.' That's very close to your words. Do you remember?"

Yuri Sparten shifted uncomfortably in his seat. "So, all right, I said that. Does that mean I was right then and wrong now?"

"You were, and are, wrong and right, then and now," said Koffield. "That's the hell of it. But the hope of it, the answer to it, is there, too. All of what's been said can be boiled down to one thing: If you slice up the pie, the wealth, thin enough for everyone to get a slice, you can wind up with each person getting a slice so thin that everyone starves to death."

"So that's your hopeful answer?"

"No," said Chandray. "The answer is to make another pie. Make a new world."

"Write it larger, and that's the whole show, the whole story," said Koffield. "Ulan Baskaw saw that the way humanity was making new worlds was fundamentally flawed. The Chronologic Patrol and Earth's government saw that, and could see nothing better to do than to slow expansion, make sure humanity made as few worlds as possible, retreated gracefully, and then, as best it could, shared out what remained for as long as it lasted. Earth—humanity—would be the Generous Traveler—but with no friend to come looking for him. We're looking to do something mad and desperate—perhaps even something very wrong—to show the way out, to make that new world."

Sparten frowned and nodded. He spoke, staring down at the table, looking at no one. "And we can't do it if we stay here looking for diehards that don't want to be found, handing out food that isn't ours to people who might kill each other and us to get a bigger share than we want to give them. I guess I knew all that already—but stars above, it's grim."

"It's called poverty," Wandella Ashdin said. "Humanity as a whole is getting poorer and poorer. The scale is so grand, the process so gradual, and masked by so many other events, that no one notices—but it's happening, all the same. Our population is stable, or even declining a little. But the resources available to us are declining much faster. The solution, obviously, is not to share out the poverty more fairly—but to make new wealth by working harder and better."

"And that work isn't getting done right now," Marquez observed, having demolished his meal while everyone else was talking. "Phelby, Chon, you're supposed to be tracking status on everything. Where are we?"

The two were seated next to each other, and exchanged slightly worried looks. Phelby shrugged. "Well, sir, the key word in what you said is *supposed*. We're doing our best to track everything, and DeSilvo's agreed to work with us, of course—but we're not getting a great deal of information from him. As best we can tell, the cargo-loading on the *Dom Pedro IV* is going fine, and the checks we can do via telemetry are all good—but none of us has even *been* on the ship yet. There's no way of knowing anything for sure, and it's not much use asking DeSilvo. I don't think it's that he's deliberately keeping us out—it's just that he's so used to working alone."

"And he *knows* this stuff," said Chon. "Knows it backward and forward and inside out. If we try to help him with something—well, in the time it would take to explain something, he could have done it himself twice over." She closed both her hands into fists and punched them both forward a little to emphasize her words. "He's *eager*. *Hungry* for it."

She gestured toward the lower levels of DeSilvo City. "He's at it, day and night, checking and rechecking everything, running new simulators, checking on our training, monitoring events in the Solace system, doing another tweak on his deception plan. I don't know why he hasn't collapsed from exhaustion—but he's still going at full speed."

"And he'll keep at it until we peel him away from it," said Dixon. "He wants it all perfect, perfect, perfect."

Marquez grunted. "Wonderful. Better is the enemy of good enough, and perfect is the enemy of getting done. All right, so you can't say all that much about what *he's* doing. How are *we* doing?"

Phelby shrugged. "We're ready. Except we'll never be ready in a million years—pardon the expression. We've all gotten the briefings and training on Harmonic Gate Theory and long-range terraforming. We can probably all talk fast enough and wave our hands hard enough to be convincing. Ship handling—Chon, Bolt, and I have run the simulators on the new auxiliary craft." The next aux ships were replacements for the two that had been destroyed near Mars. "We can manage the basic maneuvers in emergencies. I can't speak for how far along your group is in training—but I think our group is at or near or maybe beyond the point of diminishing returns. And I think we've gotten about as far as we can in simulators."

Marquez nodded. "Agreed. We're in about the same place—though we might be a bit shakier on the new aux craft. Less sim time. But I don't see how we could get much farther ahead than we are without getting in the real ships."

Dixon Phelby smiled. "So you're waiting for us to get ready, and we're waiting for you?"

"And we're both waiting for DeSilvo. That's the real story."

Sindra Chon frowned. "He's had a hundred years to get ready. What's *he* waiting for?"

More than once, in the rare moments when he allowed himself a chance to rest, Oskar DeSilvo asked himself the same question. He had run large projects before, projects with high stakes and long time lines. Those issues shouldn't have bothered him—and in truth, he didn't think they did. But something was.

He was in his workroom, the one place, above all others, where DeSilvo the architect had labored to be sure that DeSilvo the workingman would be most comfortable, most at ease, most efficient. He had changed the room, adapted it, modified it, scrapped it and started over endless times as his tastes, his moods, had changed. What once had been an elegant, austere, gentlemanly scholar's retreat had, over time, turned into something that resembled a one-man Mission Control Center, with display screens and datapads of all sorts on every wall and desktop.

The lights were dimmed to make it easier to see the displays, turning the rest of the room into warm dark shadows, cut here and there by lurid displays and bright, tight-focused task lights.

There were a half dozen service robots of various types in the room, two fetching and carrying datapads, fresh food and coffee, reference materials, and so on, two trying to keep the place organized as DeSilvo shifted from station to station, and two simply trying to guess which object or bit of information DeSilvo would want next. He was the queen bee, with all the worker bees clustered about, dancing attendance as he moved about the hive.

He took another swallow of coffee—though his system was so awash in caffeine that another whole cup, or another whole pot, wouldn't have had much additional effect—and tried once again to concentrate on the cargo manifest in front of him. There was one and only one ship in the universe that he could call upon to do his freight-hauling. There was no other ship that he could lay hands on that had both sufficient hauling capacity and the physical robustness to stand up to FTL conditions. The *Dom Pedro IV* was the only game in town— and he was well aware that, sooner or later, the game would be up—if not on the first round-trip, then the second, or the third, or the twentieth.

He had to prioritize the cargoes, make sure that only the most vital equipment was on the first run, that there were no items scheduled for the second run that would be useless without some gadget scheduled for the fifth—

Suddenly he shoved his datapad away from him and walked out of the room, ignoring the crowd of robots that scuttled out of his way as he moved. He stepped out into the corridor, walked purposefully to the far end, and stepped into the waiting elevator. "Topside Access," he said, and the elevator car doors slid shut.

The car came to a halt, the door opened, and he stepped out into the unheated, windowless chamber that was Topside Access. The main feature of the place was the airlock, big enough for a small ground vehicle, though there was none such parked there. There was a rack of pressure suits in various bright colors off to one side of the lock door, but he did not bother with them.

There was also, incongruously enough, a very ordinary old-fashioned wooden coatrack, with a bright orange insulated coverall hanging from it, and a bright red parka hanging next to it. A pair of bright blue insulated boots stood next to them. Glister still retained a reasonably thick atmosphere: One did not, strictly speaking, need a pressure suit at all on the surface. The basic hazards were the absence of sufficient breathable oxygen and the cold. As long as one dressed warmly enough, and used a breathing mask, one could function perfectly well on the surface—for a short time, at any rate.

DeSilvo moved immediately to the coatrack and started putting on the outerwear. Coverall first, then boots, then the hooded parka. Finally, he put on a compact breathing mask, with a tank of compressed air hanging from the rack by a strap. He slung the strap over his shoulder, put on the mask, and adjusted the airflow. He pulled the hood of the parka snugly up around his head, put on a pair of bright orange mittens from the pocket of the parka, then moved toward the airlock.

There wasn't much of a pressure difference between inside and outside, and the lock cycled quickly. A few seconds later, he was outside, standing on the frozen hell of Glister's surface. He hadn't done this in a long time, and he might well never get the chance again.

He *needed* to get to the surface, to come out, to be under a *sky*, instead of in a tunnel or a compartment or spacecraft or a confinement chamber or a habitat dome. He could barely remember the last time he had been out in weather, out in the world, instead of sealed off away from it in one way or another. So much of humanity lived that way. They had even grown to prefer such a molelike existence, to fear wide horizons and open air as strange, unnatural.

The main facilities of Base Glister were built into the side of a hill. Topside Access stood in a hollow near the summit. The cargo transfer center was at the bottom, far below. From where he stood, DeSilvo could see the rubble pile the earthmovers had built over the cargo center airlocks and the end of the tunnel they had built to allow continued access. Soon the camouflage would go over the entrance, and over Topside Access, and over the landing field's dome. Base Glister would vanish.

Vanish, and not be seen again.

He stared out at the steel grey landscape, cold enough to freeze a man solid if he stayed outside for very long at all. The wind howled and screamed overhead, and the cold bit into his skin, stabbed at his face. He looked up, at the blue-black sky, so dark it seemed as if he ought to be able to see stars in it, even at midday.

This might be the last time you are ever outdoors, he told himself. A terrifying thought, but not at all an unrealistic one. When was the most recent time before this that he had been outdoors?

The last time. Perhaps that was what frightened him so. It was getting to be close to the last time for lots of things in his life. *And more than the last time,* he thought. *It's your last chance, just like your friends in that canyon south of here.* The last chance he had to redeem himself, to make good all the harm he had done, to rescue his reputation from the biographers and historians who would, sooner or later, surely learn the truth. *And the last chance for everyone,* he reminded himself. He had not the slightest doubt any longer—if this effort failed, and no other answer was found, then humanity would die. History itself would end.

No wonder I wanted to get out, he thought. *Out and away from all that.* He walked away from the airlocks of Topside Access and moved carefully downslope over the loose rock and hard-frozen ice, with no particular goal in mind beyond out, away. The wind shifted, and he could hear the earthmovers at work, just over the next rise. He walked over to where he could see them. They were nearly done with their work. Soon the rest of his grand base would be hidden under rock and ice, carefully arranged to resemble the "natural" appearance of this most unnatural landscape.

Buried alive. He almost slipped and fell on his face as he walked over a loose pile of scree. He overbalanced and sat down suddenly. The cold hard stone jabbed at him, distinctly cold and uncomfortable even through his superinsulated clothing. He was starting to feel cold, feel his years. Perhaps, even, feel his own mortality. He stood up, slowly, carefully, painfully.

Ashdin's words had cut to the bone. Cryocans, temporal confinement, empty tombs, all the rest of it—he had spent half his long life pretending to be dead. And even now, his grand plan was to entomb himself again, and to leave his treasure hoard buried beneath the frozen desert, with elaborate plans to fool the grave robbers from finding the place after he ascended, godlike, into the sky. All that was missing was the construction of a pyramid over the site; then the resemblance to the Pharaohs' ambitions would be complete.

Cold. The cold was reaching into his bones, pulling the life from him, pulling him into the cold, cold ground. He turned back toward Topside Access, moving slowly uphill. Time to go back inside—perhaps forever. Time to be entombed for good and all inside one set or another of steel-and-concrete walls.

He looked up, toward the low concrete building—and saw to his astonishment that he was not alone. A figure, wearing a bright blue pressure suit with the swivel visor open, was standing by the entrance. It looked as if the person was calling to him, but the wind made it impossible to hear. DeSilvo lost his footing, and almost fell again. He recovered just barely in time and moved forward more carefully over the loose rock and ice.

The wind was picking up speed, cutting at his face. The breathing mask felt as if it had frozen to his face. He hurried toward the suited figure, peered into the helmet—and saw that it was, of course, Koffield. Who else could it have been? Koffield raised his hand and waved, and shouted something that was drowned out by the howling wind. DeSilvo could hear a loud roaring hiss—Koffield apparently had the suit's oxygen line wide open. That let most of the oxy escape unused into the atmosphere, but left enough for Koffield to breathe.

DeSilvo got up close to him, and grabbed him by the arm to steady himself and draw Koffield closer.

He pulled his breathing mask off his face. "You found me again!" he shouted.

Koffield grinned and shouted back, "It was a lot easier this time!"

DeSilvo smiled, but made no further effort to talk. He was not in the mood for shouting. He put his breathing mask back on and pointed toward the airlock. Koffield nodded in return, and closed his helmet visor.

The two of them trudged back toward Topside Access, leaning hard into the cruel wind that pushed against them. DeSilvo slipped once again, and Koffield caught him, holding him up by one shoulder and the opposite arm, half-supporting him, guiding him forward. DeSilvo let it happen, let the younger man be the stronger one. He submitted to Koffield's aid, gave in to it. For the brief moments of the walk back inside, DeSilvo had intimations of his own decrepitude, his own incipient frailty, long forestalled. How much longer could he hold it off, force his ancient body to play at being young and vigorous? What would it be like to rely on others for his care, to be needy, to be weak and *old*?

They entered the airlock together. Koffield sealed the door and started the lock cycling. The two men stood without trying to speak as the air pumps worked. The airlock matched pressure with the interior, and DeSilvo opened the inner door.

The room that had seemed a cold and grey place just minutes before seemed a warm and welcoming riot of color after being out on the surface. The bright-colored pressure suits seemed to light up the interior. DeSilvo found he was shivering, in spite of his heavy clothing. He pulled off his mittens, stuffed them back in the parka's pockets, removed the parka, and started to take off the breathing mask. Somehow the relative warmth of the place seemed to drive out whatever weakness the cold exterior had revealed in him. He felt suddenly revived, invigorated—indeed, he felt far better than he had in a long time.

Koffield watched him for a moment, then proceeded to get his own suit off, moving with the careful practiced speed and efficiency of a man who had entrusted his life to pressure suits many times.

"How *did* you find me?" DeSilvo asked.

"It wasn't hard," said Koffield, setting the suit's helmet on the rack. "I was coming to see you. I was walking toward your study when you came out and went bowling down the corridor in the opposite direction. I called to you, but you didn't seem to hear me. When I got to the elevator, I could tell by the indicator where you had gone."

"But why did you follow me out there?" DeSilvo asked.

Koffield made a gesture that took in all of Topside Access's one dismal room. "No windows up here. I was worried about you."

Worried about what might happen accidentally, or what I might choose to have happen? DeSilvo didn't ask, and Koffield gave no clue. *Leave the ambiguity alone.* "I see," he said.

"Just out of curiosity, why *did* you go out?" Koffield asked, his casual tone not altogether convincing. *Just out of curiosity, did I just stop a suicide attempt?*

DeSilvo shrugged. It crossed his mind that, perhaps, Koffield had. "I wanted to get out." It was not until the words were out of his mouth that he realized that he had committed his own ambiguity. Out for a walk, or out of the situation? Or, just—out?

"I see," Koffield said again, in a careful tone of voice.

And suddenly DeSilvo found himself talking, explaining himself. He had been ready to fend off the challenge if Koffield poked or prodded—but somehow, the failure to challenge him was a pressure he could not resist. "I'm not sure I can say it any better than that," he said. "I wanted—I want—to get out *both* ways. A breath of fresh air, maybe my last ever. And yes—out. Out of this life, out of this secret war of mine, of ours, against—against my own failed achievements, my own failures."

He paused and gathered his thoughts again. "Dr. Ashdin's analysis was harsh, even brutal, but, I must confess, reasonably accurate, if not wholly so. But you were not the only ones judging me. Dr. Ashdin's words forced me to judge myself. I haven't thought of myself in a long time." *Another bit of ambiguity.* "A strange thing for a man as self-absorbed as I am to say, but you know what I mean."

DeSilvo gestured toward the floor, toward the workshops and simulators below. "All of that was for me, me, me. A place to build wonderful machines that I could play with, and take the credit for, so all of Settled Space would admire me. But give me the credit for abandoning all that and adapting this base to our present purposes when I saw it would be necessary. I could have gone forward with my original plan and let others worry over the fate of worlds. The inventions that would have come out of this place would have been of great benefit to many people, whether or not I created them, or merely rediscovered them."

"Assuming you could have a found a way to prevent the Chronologic Patrol from 'suppressing' you and your inventions quite permanently."

DeSilvo smiled. "Oh, I had plans to deal with that. I had plans for everything."

"But what benefit would it all have really brought?" Koffield asked. "Your rediscovered inventions were suppressed for a reason—perhaps even a good reason. The people would praise your name, but *you'd* know that you'd just made eventual collapse come sooner and harder."

"That was what brought my plans crashing down—that understanding," DeSilvo said. "But that understanding came so *late*. All my plans were close to complete. This place was ready. I was ready. I was at the end of endless planning and effort and scheming—and then, at that moment, I realized the truth about the coming collapse and my part in the collapse of Solace. But if I were to make amends, then I was merely at the *beginning* of my labors. I had climbed the mountain to its peak, and discovered it was merely a foothill. And now, the same again. All of my efforts were to bring me to this point—where the *real* work, far greater than what I have done, can begin. The political job, the engineering job, of organizing a new terraforming operation, a new kind of terraforming operation—while constructing the time-travel system at the same time."

"And all that, just to prepare for the *real* real work— a million-year terraforming operation," said Koffield. "More mountains that turn into foothills. I don't blame you for wanting out. *I* want out, for that matter."

"Yes. Yes." DeSilvo's mood had crashed again. The way ahead seemed so hard, so long. "Out," he said once more, his voice wistful and low.

But that was as much as he allowed himself. They had to keep going. They had to. "Still, that's all to one side," he said, failing to make his cheerful tone sound anything but forced. "We have work to do. A lot of it."

He got his boots off, stood up, and stepped out of his overalls. He checked the purge and clean valves on the breathing mask, wiped it down, and hung it up exactly where he had found it. He hung the coveralls and parka carefully, and set the boots out by the coatrack, making sure all was neat and orderly, placing each item where it belonged. *As if I'll be back to use this gear tomorrow. The odds are good that that parka will still be hanging right there a hundred years from now, or a thousand. Once I'm gone, it won't be used again. I might as well wad it up in a ball and throw it on the floor.* But no. There was something in his soul, a need for order, a hunger to finish things properly, that would not let that happen. He put his things away carefully, as he spoke to Koffield over his shoulder. "What was it you were coming to see me about?" *What was going to make you enter my most private place, and made you follow me up here?*

"It's time to go," Koffield said.

Time to go back inside, down below, where it's warm? Or time to quit making plans and act, time to close this place for good and all, leave Glister, and get on with the job? More ambiguity. He looked Koffield in the face, studied the calm, gentle, tired face for a moment. *No, not ambiguity. Duality. Not one or the other. Both.* "Yes," he said. "Yes." He moved toward the elevator and took Koffield by the arm, leading him along as gently, but as firmly, as Koffield had led him, out on the surface. "Come," he said. "Let us be on our way."

Chapter Twenty-one

SIGNS AND PORTENTS

CANYON CITY
LAST CHANCE CANYON
THE PLANET GLISTER

By wild chance, James Ruthan Verlant V—known to all as Jay—was out on the surface when it happened, trying to see if the most recent solar array failure might be repairable. When the first missile, or whatever the hell it was, went up, he was there to witness it.

The radar caught it first, of course. They'd felt obliged to dust off at least the low-power radar system since the flyovers had started, since the detection of the nanoprobes, buried deep in the info-systems. No one liked wasting the power, but it was plain to see *something* was out there, looking for something else. Since no one came for Last Chance, even after it had been located, some at least speculated that whoever was doing the flyovers wasn't interested in Canyon City.

Even so, the radar was running, more or less. No one quite knew how far to trust it, after generations of disuse. The operators had to be trained out of the instruction manuals.

And so Bol—Boland Xavier Shelte VI—was watching the scopes, and all of a sudden he saw something big and fast, climbing from the east. Jay heard his voice, loud and excited, on the general work comm loop. "Target! Target!" he called out.

Jay had the array's access panel open and his head stuck halfway into it when the call came. He pulled himself clear as fast as he could and tried to hunker down under the array, which, by a bit of good luck, had jammed at the full horizontal position, making for ease of access and good overhead concealment. *If you could call a jammed array good luck, considering how starved for power we are,* Jay reminded himself, even as he ducked down. Everyone had agreed it would be best to stay out of view of the flyover craft if at all possible.

"Where is it, Bol?" he asked.

"Ah, out of the south, moving fast, a bit north and east but mostly *up*—ah, Jay, it's not like the others," Bol replied in a calmer voice. "Not an aircar. Moving too fast, and nearly straight up. Some kind of rocket or missile. I'm showing it at ten kilometers high already, and accelerating."

"A *rocket*?" Jay only knew about the outside world from what he read in the histories; but from all he ever saw, you didn't use a rocket except if you had to boost off the surface of a planet with atmosphere, and even then only if you couldn't possibly avoid it. Otherwise, you used reactionless systems. Less power per second but massively more efficient.

"Yeah, still heading up. It's gonna get out of our range real soon. I'm gonna try and flip to visual tracking. Stand by."

Ten kilometers up, well to the south and headed for space. It wasn't looking his way. Jay straightened up and stepped out from under the array. He looked to the south, and spotted it almost at once—a flame-bright dot of ruby light, climbing up into the black-purple sky, reaching for the zenith.

It was only because he was looking that way in the first place that he saw the other one—the one headed the other way.

It was no mere dot of light, but a fiery yellow streak, blazing out of the sky, diving for the south.

It flashed below the southern horizon, and, mere seconds later, there was a sudden bloom of light from the same direction. Jay stood there, transfixed and astonished, unable to understand what he was seeing. A life spent almost entirely underground had left him with little practice in interpreting the appearance of things far off, but it was more than that. These things were not just strange, they were unheard-of.

The ground trembled, ever so gently, under his feet, and, long seconds afterward, a low, faint *boom* echoed its way into the helmet of his heater suit.

"Jay—Jay—are you there? Please respond!"

He suddenly realized that Bol had been hailing him, over and over. "Yeah, yeah, I'm here. Did you track the southbound one?"

"I did, more or less, but it was moving too fast for my gear to get good readings. And you should *see* the seismograph readings. It's going nuts. What the hell just *happened*?"

"I don't know," said Jay, "but I *think* that something came out of the sky and hit, real hard, somewhere near where that northbound object came from."

"But *why*? What's going on? What can you see?"

"I don't know. There's still a sort of glow on the southern horizon, but it's dying down."

"What about the other one?"

Jay looked up into the sky. "Can't see a thing," he said, still straining his eyes. "Lost to view. Did the optical tracker pick it up?"

"For a wonder, yes. Still has it, too, headed almost exactly straight for the zenith. It doesn't look like it's trying for orbit at all. It's just going—"

There was a sudden blast of light, high in the sky. "What the hell!" Jay shouted, and instinctively raised his right hand to shield his face.

"Jay! The optical tracker's flipped out! What happ—" Bol's voice suddenly cut out, died altogether, just before a roar of static came over the heater suit's headphones. Then that cut out as well—along with the hum of the suit's ventilator fan. Jay spun around, looking toward the main access structure, just as every light in the place died. He checked the status display on his suit's left forearm—and found himself staring at blank displays. His suit was dead. The radio was dead. And it looked as if Canyon City had just died as well.

Fear swept over him—but then he forced it back. Only clear thinking could keep him—keep all of them—alive. Jay forced himself to calmness.

He had spent his whole life convincing machinery and computers and ArtInts to keep themselves going. He'd never seen a failure this *massive* before. But maybe that was a good thing. If there was one big problem causing all of it, maybe—maybe—there was one big answer as well.

Or else this was, at last, the inevitable day when Last Chance Canyon would write the final chapter of its history. Every Last Chancer knew that there would be such a day, sooner or later. "Not today, there won't be," Jay told himself.

First things first—get inside and get the hell out of the heater suit, and meet up with Bol and Yur and the others. They would be working the problem already. Jay's suit was of course well insulated. He had plenty of time to get back inside before he would start to lose appreciable amounts of heat. Probably bad air would be a problem sooner. But there was no sense wasting time. He moved a little faster.

Not today. Last Chancers had been promising that to themselves for generations. So far, Jay reminded himself, they had always been right.

Then, the lights bloomed on in Main Access just as he reached the door, and he allowed himself a sigh of relief. They had fixed as least part of it. Maybe it *wouldn't* be today.

The miniflyer was getting close to its target. All was going well. But that only left Jay to wonder what other surprises might be out there. There had certainly been enough of them already—even if, two days later, they understood them better.

Jay had always been the history buff of his generation,

the one who read the old stories about the outside world, and, occasionally, found something in them that might conceivably be of use in Canyon City. It was for that reason that he couldn't stop kicking himself. He should have recognized the cause of the massive power cutoff.

He had read about it more than once: an electromagnetic pulse, a side effect of some high-altitude nuclear explosions. Gamma rays from the nuclear weapon produced an electrically charged field in the atmosphere that in turn sent an electrical power surge through virtually every electric circuit under the blast point. The pulse had tripped virtually every circuit breaker in Canyon City—and in Jay's heater suit. For the most part, all they had to do was to reset the breakers. Some components had gotten fried, but nothing crucial seemed to have been damaged.

But it still remained to find out what the hell had happened—and whether it would happen again, and if so, what it might do to Canyon City the next time.

They weren't going to have much luck studying the explosion itself. Between the pulse's scrambling their power supplies, the severe limitations of their optical systems—as Bol put it, a pack of mole people didn't have much need for telescopes—and the intricacies of orbital mechanics, there was almost no hope at all of locating the blast point in space, let alone doing a good examination of it. Besides, that had been a nuclear explosion. How much was going to be left?

The ground strike was another story. The seismograph data was good enough to allow a close triangulation of the blast epicenter. They could find it. They could get to it. And they were doing just that—carefully.

Their maps showed an abandoned domed-over habitat exactly where the seismic data said the impact had been. Bol's admittedly rough and inaccurate backtrack of the outbound missile's trajectory indicated a launch from the same place, or very near it. What records they had had told Bol and Jay that their ancestors—not some figurative and vague ancestors, but their great-grandfathers, the men they had been named for—had done a gleaning survey of the site decades before and found it stripped clean, like everything else within easy reach of a surviving diehard city.

The miniflyer they sent in was one of Bol's improvisations, cobbled together from the scavenger heap. Three other miniflyers had gone out already. They were all flying in circles at maximum altitude so as to provide line-of-sight over-the-horizon relay linkages with the sensor-equipped flyer.

Bol was controlling all four vehicles. The relays weren't hard to handle. He just had them set to fly tight circles over given points on the map. But the spyflyer was another question. He was flying it by remote control, using the forward camera view being transmitted back to guide him.

"Be gentle with her, Bol," Jay reminded him. He stood behind Bol, watching the view from two hundred kilometers away. "We can't afford to lose her."

"I know, I know," Bol muttered. "But name one thing we *can* afford to lose."

Jay smiled at that. Last Chancers were pack rats, and they knew it. They had to be. They needed everything because they had so little of anything, and needed all of it to fix something else. All that they owned had been built up out of whatever scraps they had scavenged and saved, just in case.

And they didn't have much in reserve. Even putting four miniflyers in the air had represented a major expenditure of resources—but for once, there was no debate as to whether it was necessary. Whatever it was had just come close to killing them all. A larger electromagnetic pulse would have done more than trip circuit breakers. It would have fried half the wiring in Canyon City. If it happened again . . . Well, there was just no two ways about it. They had to know more.

And they were about to find out.

"Coming up on it," Bol announced, quite needlessly. Jay could see the display as well as he could. And, therefore, could see the still-smoking wreckage as viewed by the miniflyer's cameras. And they could see what had been scattered by the blast.

"Devils in hell," Jay said, half in a whisper. "Look at all that. Just *look* at it."

"I don't believe it," Bol said.

"I do," said Jay. "I believe in every scrap of it." He *had* to. He knew, far better than Bol, or most of the others of his generation, just how close to the edge Canyon City was. He had known ever since the last windmill failure that it would take a miracle to keep them going much longer. But there, spread out below the miniflyer, he saw their miracle.

To any other eyes but those of a diehard, the scene would have been one of complete devastation. But Jay and Bol saw manna from heaven, raw materials and finished articles of all sorts strewn about the surface.

It looked as if the incoming missile had smashed into a dome, a big one, and explosive decompression had done the rest. The dome's outer shell had been blown to bits; whatever had been inside the dome was strewn across the landscape.

What it had scattered were jewels beyond price to a diehard's eyes. What looked to be high-end long-store ration packs, the sort normally only broken open at feast days—were strewn about the landscape. Jay's mouth watered at the thought of eating something, anything, besides what the processors put out. There were enough packs just scattered about down there to feed the whole colony for a month. And clothing—coveralls and work suits and warmgear of all sorts, in all sorts of colors—some still clean, some caught in a bit of mud or debris, some with burn damage but still good. Even the worst of the clothes made what he was wearing look like rags. Other goods, other things he could not readily identify, had been thrown about as well.

Some more massive items hadn't been scattered by the blast. A stockpile of construction supplies—girders, cables, sheet metal, welding gear—would be enough to repair all the windmills, with spares left over. Vehicles— not spare parts or broken-down wrecks, but what appeared to be *functional* ground transports and earth-movers. He spotted what looked like an industrial-size power generator.

And all that was just the beginning. Access ways to lower levels suggested that this dome was like most—a smaller surface facility, with far more storage and living space below ground. There would be more down there, and most of it in far better condition than the stuff caught in the dome when the missile hit.

It seemed obvious that people had been living there, and very recently. But neither Bol or Jay gave the least thought to survivors. No one could have survived that impact. Besides, diehards couldn't afford to worry about outsiders. The Canyon City saying that meant something like "Leave well enough alone" was "Save one stranger, and you'll kill five cousins."

It was pretty obvious that these strangers had been the ones who had launched the missile that had caused the electromagnetic pulse effects at Canyon City—and the overflights and nanoprobes made it pretty clear that they must have known Canyon City was there. The missile launchers plainly hadn't been worrying too much about Canyon City's welfare. If anyone down there *was* still alive, they weren't going to get much help at the hands of Canyon City folk.

"We've *got* to get in there, Jay," Bol said. "Full gleaner team."

"Gleaner team, hell. We need a full expedition. We need everyone we can spare over there full-time, setting up camp there, figuring transport routes, standing guard on that place. We have to get to it before some other city does."

The odds were good that other nearby diehard outposts—if there were any that still survived—would investigate the explosion as well. If Canyon City got in there first, and showed that it was able to defend what it had found—and, perhaps, hide or remove the best stuff fast, before anyone else could see it, that might dissuade others from making a try.

But the devil himself forbid if two or three diehard

cities tried to stake their claims simultaneously. That was what set off diehard wars. The thing most likely to kill off a well-established diehard city was a resource war, a bread war, with another group. Such wars often killed off both sides.

If someone else got there first, even with just a small contingent, the wisest course would be to abandon all claim to even so tempting a prize—but who could be that wise? They had to get in there *fast* before that danger arose. They couldn't risk war or the conditions that might lead to war. A fight could rapidly escalate, until both sides had consumed resources—and lives—worth far more than what they were fighting over.

But what diehard could see what Jay was seeing, and not want to fight for it, no matter who was in possession? There was a saying for that, as well, that meant something along the lines of "Better safe than sorry" or "Don't risk what you can't afford to lose." It went: "Wealth starts wars, but poverty ends them."

Well, there was wealth enough down there, just scattered about on the surface, to start a dozen diehard wars. *Get in there first,* Jay told himself, *and all our troubles will be over.*

But if they got there second, he knew, then their troubles would have just begun.

Chapter Twenty-two

ALL THE SKILLS OF TREASON

Berana Drayax had felt she was due for, and quite entitled to, a long vacation—maybe even one that would merge seamlessly into retirement—after first pulling Ignition Day off against the odds, then dealing with the endless small-bore bureaucratic work of closing out the project and handing NovaSpot off to the engineers who would actually operate and control it.

Her idea of a vacation did not include sitting down, in the dead of night, at a secret meeting, across the table from a bandit chief with delusions of grandeur in a semiabandoned agricultural transfer station.

But then, things didn't always turn out the way one planned them.

Villjae Benzen, duly praised and promoted after rescuing Groundside Power—and thus the whole Ignition Project—was seated alongside her at the table, and plainly as uncertain of his role as she was unhappy with hers. He had just been settling into his new job managing habitat dome construction and repair when he'd been pulled out of it for this assignment. But that was part of the way things worked, and, Drayax believed, it was time he learned it. Crises and politics were and always would be part of large-scale engineering. Selling the project to the powers that be—and the would-be users of the project—was part of the game he would have to learn if he were to advance much farther in the field. The job would be part of his education.

To her left, on the short side of the long table, as if to moderate—or serve as interpreter—was Elber Malloon. Sotales had warned her that he had underestimated Malloon, and that she should not do the same. He certainly did not seem very impressive. It was plain he did not want to be where he was. Malloon looked as unhappy as Drayax and as uncertain as Benzen.

The only person at the table who was plainly pleased to be there was the quite lupine, even sinister-looking, Zak Destan, who looked downright smug. Berana Drayax regarded it as her first mission to put a stop to that, at any rate. The pleasantries, such as they were, had been gotten out of the way in short order, and it was now time to get down to business.

"All right, Mr. Destan"—not Reiver, not Bush Captain, certainly not Bush Lord—"you've got your big upper who can make big things happen. Here I am, and I made NovaSpot happen. So what is it you want? It won't be what you get, but what do you want?"

Her opening remark had the desired effect—the smirk on his face went away. "Wait a second," he protested. "That's no way to open a negotiation."

"It isn't? It is where I come from—unless we're just supposed to hand you the keys and the deeds and leave. So—what do you want, and, while you're at it—what will you give in return that *we'll* actually want and that *you* can actually give?"

Her rudeness was sincere—she did not want to be there, and she did not like this man—but it was nonetheless calculated. There were people who viewed courtesy as being weakness, a reasonable attitude as being halfway to surrender. That he had demanded that someone of high status pay this covert call on him, and that she had come, were concessions enough. The mere fact that she was there meant her side knew he had some chips on the table. He had to know her side had some too.

"I thought you were here to make me an offer."

"I am. At my own discretion. But your demand for an offer 'I can agree to' was remarkably broad. I can think of a lot of things I'd agree to—but no one in his right might would offer them to me. So be specific. What do you want? What will you give?"

He stared at her, unmoving, unblinking, for a solid twenty seconds before he spoke. "Greenhouse," he said at last. "And in exchange, we promise to be good. Mostly."

Drayax resisted the temptation to laugh out loud, but then wondered if she should have bothered to resist. "I hope that's a joke," she said.

"Ah, Zak," said Malloon, "maybe you ought to clarify that a little."

"Nah," Destan said, still staring straight at Drayax, not turning to look at Malloon. "She asked what I *want*. And she promised I wasn't going to get it."

Drayax returned his steady gaze—and found herself caught in an old-fashioned, completely childish staring contest. Destan was just the sort to *practice* his staring, so he could play just this sort of domination game. Well, turn that against him too. "Fine, Mr. Destan," she said. "You can stare at me until your eyes burn twin holes in my head. For my part, I feel there are other things more worth looking at than you. You win. You're the very best starer in the whole room." She glanced down at her datapad and looked up again. "If you're done, then, is it our turn now?"

Destan glared at her. "Yeah. Sure thing."

"Very well. Mr. Benzen. If you will offer a quick summing up of the offer?" Drayax was none too pleased with the offer she had been instructed to make. That was part of the reason she wanted Villjae to describe it. And it was also a demonstration of authority. Villjae Benzen did what she said.

"Ah, yeah. Yes," Benzen began. "It's simple enough—and generous." *Good,* thought Drayax. *He listens and obeys*. He had been specifically instructed to emphasize how "generous" the offer was.

Benzen went on. "The planetary government will withdraw from the area your people already more or less control—basically Wilhemton District, with a few details to be negotiated. It will become an autonomous region—still part of the overall planetary nation, and ultimately under planetary government control—but all local authority will be ceded to your organization, and all district-level government operations—courts, hospitals, road maintenance, and so on—will be discontinued, in conjunction with an orderly handover to your people. The government will deed over most of the public property in the area to you—with some exceptions to be discussed. The government will provide a one-time-only delivery of food aid, and a one-time financial package. Those who wish to depart the area ceded to you will be allowed safe passage out, carrying any and all of their property with them. Very generous," he finished up.

"There you have it, Mr. Destan," Drayax went on. "We name a date, sort out the handover details, and you can declare the autonomous region of Destania, or whatever you want to call it. All yours. You win."

Zak was silent for a moment. At last he spoke, not to Benzen, but to Drayax. "Last month, I would have jumped at that. Last month, that would be my dream come true, what I would hope to pry loose after five or ten years of fighting and bushwhacking and killing. But it's not last month anymore. And he"—he stabbed a finger in Elber's direction without actually looking at him—"has been putting some ideas in my head. Ideas about how the planet's falling apart. Can't get fixed, either. That's right, pretty much, isn't it?"

The conventional move at such a time would, of course, be to lie, even if her opposite number knew she was lying. Drayax considered the option. But this wasn't about old politics anymore, about who was up and who was down, about keeping the lid on and keeping the machinery working. And the new politics was going to be about saving lives, as many as possible, controlling the situation to avoid panic and chaos, as they evacuated the planet. Like it or not, Zak Destan and his kind were going to be their partners in that job. They were going to have to trust each other, and someone had to go first.

"Yes," she said, a long heartbeat after he asked the question.

"So why not sell a house cheap—or give it away—once it's already caught fire? Is that the idea? But you have to make the offer fast, before the customer can notice the flames." Zak Destan shook his head. "It's not last month anymore," he said again. "What good would it do me to rule a patch of land, or half of Solace, or even the whole planet, if the planet dies? I don't want to look up ten years from now and realize I'm running a diehard colony. No. I want more—and I'm willing to offer more to get it."

Drayax cocked her head a bit to one side and shifted a bit closer to Destan. They were movements that indicated gentle, pleasant surprise, and a willingness to listen. Once again, the reaction was sincere—but once again, it was calculated as well. Let the body language send the message. "Go on," she said.

Destan responded. He leaned forward in his seat, leaned his elbows on the table, and clasped his hands together, his expression suddenly eager. "Elber here talked about your pal Sotales being a chess player. Well, I've been staring at the chessboard myself, and I've thought a few moves ahead. I think I've seen what he's seen—what you have too: Surrender is the only road to victory."

A strange way to put it, but Drayax nodded. She understood, even before he explained. "Go on," she said again, letting her face reveal her careful interest.

"We fight each other, we both lose," Destan said. "Time is the enemy. Wasted effort is the enemy. Your side sees that too, or else they would have sent a flunky, and then a bigger flunky, then maybe a medium-big hotshot, and *then* someone like you—just to show they were bigger than I was."

Drayax nodded. In normal times they would have

played it that way, for that reason—and had chosen not to, precisely for the reasons Destan had suggested. "I'm listening," she said.

"So if you know that—why offer me, whaddya call it—the autonomous region of Destania?" He looked at her for a moment and answered his own question. "To keep me quiet," he said. "Let me have the headaches of patching potholes and collecting taxes. Let me find out I can't fix all the stuff I've been complaining that the uppers can't fix. Let me spend my energy running the place, instead of giving the cops headaches. And why do that? To ease the pressure on the cops and the government, yeah, sure. Give away what they've already lost and what's gonna be worthless real soon. But more'n that, I figure. Wear me down, let me see that there's no future here—and when the time comes when you've gotta—*I've* gotta—evacuate 'Destania' "—he managed to get sarcasm into his speaking of the word—"I'll go along quietly and be glad for what I get. How am I doing so far?"

"Not bad at all." Sotales should have warned her not to underestimate Destan, either. "Please continue."

"So let's pretend all that's happened already," he said. "I surrender now, instead of ten years from now. But why would I do that? What would I get?"

"A spot at the front of the evac line." It was Malloon who spoke. "Instead of one toward the back."

Destan grinned and nodded at Malloon. "Got it in one, Elber. That's the deal. If my people are granted early space in the evac operation, and relocation to a high-end habitat on Greenhouse, I'll place my militia under the covert—and I mean *covert*—authority of the Planetary Executive. No one on my end is going to know about it, 'cause if they do, the way I'll find out is when I wake up and notice my throat's been cut. I'll call off my reiver troops, and cooperate actively in policing the area—but *without* any public support. Give us what we want, and we promise to be good from now on, even if we don't admit it."

"We haven't even said that there *is* an evac plan," Villjae Benzen protested.

Destan chuckled. "Yeah, you have, Benzen—just then."

Benzen reddened, embarrassed to be caught.

Drayax let it go. They were far enough along that Villjae's gaffe was right up there with admitting the sun rose in the east. Besides, the locals were looking at Benzen for the moment, taking their attention off her and giving her time to think. "What makes us trust you?" she asked.

"The gun to his head," Malloon answered. "Real life, not what people see or think, this won't be a sellout. But if the deal comes to light, it will *seem* enough of a sellout that it gets him overthrown—or killed."

Destan nodded energetically. "What he said. The secret—that I'm cooperating with you—will have to come out at *some* point. But that won't be until later, until you've started evacuating us to Greenhouse. Till then, you've got a whip hand over me. All you'd have to do is leak news of this meet, here tonight, and I'd be a dead man politically. Maybe a real dead man." He leaned back in his chair, grinning. "Now. You tell me. What make me trust *you?*"

"The gun you have to *our* head," Benzen said. "It works the same way. It would cost the government a lot of credibility to admit to having met with you. It'll hurt them even more to admit that they had cut a deal for something as big and juicy as an early place in line for the evacuation. The government would lose face— maybe enough to drive it from office. And if the deal came to light, it would set a fatal precedent: Rebel, and the government will give you preferred treatment."

Drayax allowed herself no external reaction, but she winced, just a little, deep inside, to hear Benzen list all their weaknesses. Still, the answer could do no real harm. It was plain to see Destan was more than smart enough to have worked all that out for himself anyway.

"Let's see if I have this straight," Drayax said. "We agree we can destroy each other—and agree not to do it. In exchange for covert cooperation on your part and a cessation of illegal activity and violent attacks, we start the evacuation of Solace to Greenhouse by moving your people. We keep it quiet as long as possible, or until the evac is far enough along, and going well enough that the propaganda effect for both of us would be positive, not negative. About like that?"

"About like that," Destan agreed.

It was Drayax's turn to stare at Destan, study his face for signs of what he was thinking, how much he meant of what he said. She didn't rush her answer. No one would regard thinking this one over as weakness. "Very well," she finally said. "We might—might—have the start of something here. There are lots of details to sort out. Schedules, follow-up meetings, protocols. But I think— maybe—we might now understand each other. But we have to get some sort of idea of what's practical. Do you have any worthwhile population statistics?" she asked. "How many in bad enough shape we should evac them soonest but well enough to survive the trip? We need to know how many people we're talking about moving, and how fast."

"I've got some pretty solid figures," Destan said. "But it's not just how many we move and how fast. It's where do we put them?"

Drayax turned to Villjae Benzen, to call upon his real area of expertise. "Domes, Mr. Benzen. Habitats. Population capacity. What's the status and schedule?"

It was toward dawn before Drayax and Benzen climbed aboard their stealthed aircar and made a very quiet departure. Drayax let Benzen do the flying. Rank hath its privileges, and reclining her seat back all the way, closing her eyes, and relaxing was just such a privilege. The real blessing was that they had gotten away when they had.

Dawn had been their departure deadline; stealthing system or no, neither side wanted to risk a daylight run and perhaps have the aircar be seen. Drayax's sincere desire not to spend a day cooped up in a decrepit agtran center, not daring to venture out for fear of being seen and having her well-known face recognized, was a great impetus to making the negotiations go rapidly.

The aircar lifted silently and moved out at treetop level. It had been a long night, but a most useful one. They had hammered out most of the major points of the deal, but it was clear more would need to be done—and also plain that Drayax was going to have to talk things over with Planetary Executive Kalzant.

Drayax had exceeded her authority—but the risk was worth the potential reward. Kalzant might fire her, or even arrest her—but if they could get Destan under control and buy some quiet, that would ease a lot of pressure on the local authorities. More important, it would create a model for other agreements, other restive areas. Once they could go public, and all of Solace could see that even such a man as Zak Destan was getting a square deal from the government, then all the rest would follow, and follow willingly. She would risk her career for that, given the odds.

A lot had been done, but there was much to do. Both sides agreed it would be safer all around if the principal figures met as rarely as possible. Benzen and Malloon would have to meet again soon—and, no doubt, frequently, to sort out various technical details. *Good,* she thought. *Let someone else do the work. There's even the excuse of saying it's more good training for him.* She snuggled down a bit deeper into her seat and started giving serious thought to taking a nap.

"Is it really going to work, ma'am?" Benzen asked. "Do you think so?"

Her eyes came open. So much for her nap. But, this, too, was training for the lad. "It might," she said. "I'd say it probably has the best odds of working, out of all the choices before us. It's got a very clear, direct trust mechanism built in, or perhaps mutual threat mechanism might be closer. Each side has a gun pointed at the other's head. If either side goes public in an effort to hurt the other—well, the usual term is *blowback*. The gun shoots both ways at once."

"But why deal with him at all?" Benzen asked. "Why didn't Sotales have a couple of goons hidden in the trunk of this aircar, or something like that? Destan's on all the wanted lists, for who knows what crimes."

"These are cruel times, and Sotales wouldn't hesitate to use cruel methods if need be. If he had decided to go that way, Sotales would have been more likely to kill him than arrest him. He could have even dropped a warhead in while we were still there, left nothing but a crater, and accepted killing us as a fair price to pay for taking out Destan."

Benzen looked at her in alarm. "You thought he might do that, and you went in anyway?"

"It seemed very unlikely," Drayax said calmly. "He would have had to do a lot of explaining to PlanEx Kalzant. Safer to make a try once we've served to pinpoint Destan but are out of the way—right about now, say. My guess is that Destan is taking *that* possibility seriously and hightailing it out of the area right now, and taking precautions against being tracked. But suppose Sotales did arrest him, or kill him—or vaporize him. Then what?"

Drayax answered her own question. "The mob Destan leads would still be there and would be angrier and less controllable than ever. The mob as an uncontrolled force would be far worse than a mob chivvied into some sort of disciplined group by Destan.

"He might be a criminal leader, but he is a *leader*—and Sotales argues pretty convincingly that he was already evolving into a revolutionary leader, a political leader—and we've just given him a powerful shove in that direction. Yes, he's no angel—but you know better than most how much time is working against us. We don't have the luxury of shopping around for someone we like better, or waiting and hoping for Destan to be overthrown."

"But it can't last," Benzen protested. "It can't last. Something will go wrong, and one side or the other will break the agreement. It *can't* hold together long. And the precedent it sets is too dangerous."

"All true—but it misses the point," Drayax said sadly. "The point is it's already too late. On Solace, *nothing* can hold together for much longer. We have to move fast, and not worry too much about the long term. Precedent won't matter when the planet—and its political and social system—all collapse. We're *all* going to Greenhouse, and sooner than most people might think. *Everything* will be different. It's absolutely inevitable that the rules of the game—and the game itself—will be different as well."

A brand-new game, she told herself. *Who'll cheat first?*

Olar Sotales stood up from behind his desk, stretched, and yawned mightily. He had, of course, been watching the tap on Malloon. It was remarkable how bad the video and audio were when he watched in real time. The ArtInts did an impressive job cleaning up the sounds and images they stored and edited for later playback.

Surprising results. Surprising all around—but not necessarily unwelcome. It moved things forward, a good deal faster than he had expected. And it had another advantage—one that he very much hoped that Destan had not yet thought through. One that would be greatly to Sotales' advantage, if push came to shove. Destan was thinking of Greenhouse as a world of refuge, a world where his people would be safe. All true, if all went as planned. But Greenhouse was domes and buried habitats, confined and walled in against the cold and the vacuum. It was also a world where people could be confined, very easily.

And, if push came to shove, it was also a world where Zak Destan could be controlled, if need be, simply by cutting off his air supply.

But it won't come to that, Sotales thought as he powered down his secure systems. *At least,* he corrected himself, *it probably won't.*

Chapter Twenty-three

MEANS AND MOTIVES

The *Belle Boyd XI* cut her engines and settled down into a standard polar search orbit that sent her arcing high over the ice fields of Glister. Kalani Temblar stared eagerly out the command center's starboard-side viewport, down onto the first extrasolar world she had ever seen.

A new world. *This* was why she had joined the Chronologic Patrol in the first place. It made all those endless days spent in her bullpen cubicle, and the endless hours spent in the *Belle Boyd XI*'s cramped temporal confinement chamber with Burl, seem worthwhile. Almost. She glanced over at Burl, who was craning his neck to see out her viewport. There was nothing but stars to see from the viewport on his side—and they had both seen plenty of those on approach. A planet, though—even a dead ice planet—was something else.

Even from this high up, Glister seemed a cold and hard place. Glaciers, ice floes, bare rock and frozen rivers, shattered and forgotten cities, all painted the colors of cold and death. There was beauty in it, but nothing warm, or welcoming, or human. It was nature showing her most cruel and unforgiving aspect, shaking off humanity's efforts to control her, setting her own course and her own way, away from the frantic pace of a living world, and back toward the slow, cold ways of rock and ice and wind. *Glister is a warning,* Kalani told herself. And yet she could not tear her eyes away. She had studied the case files. Koffield had studied Baskaw's books on terraforming, so Kalani had done the same. And if Baskaw had it right, there, before her, was the future. All the worlds of humanity would look like that, or like Mars, or like something even worse. And there was nothing that could be done to stop it. The best they could hope for was to slow it down.

"All right," said Kalani, turning away the mesmerizing view. "Let's go after that debris."

"Let's do it," Burl said agreeably, and reached for the controls.

The *Belle Boyd XI* immediately ejected a remote-operations pod. The op-pod scooted away from the ship, boosting for another orbit, unfolding its four work arms as it traveled.

They had spotted a couple of interesting things on her run in toward the planet, the most interesting being what looked to the long-range sensor system like the debris cloud left by a near-miss nuclear attack on a large spacecraft. The op-pod had been sent off to examine the debris. The other item was an area with a remarkably high level of activity for a dead world. The *Belle Boyd XI* carried the Chronologic Patrol's best sensor systems, and the CP's best were very good indeed. Those sensors were showing lots of infrared, lots of artificial light in use during local night, lots of air travel between two points about two hundred kilometers away from each other. It had to be DeSilvo—except it *couldn't* be DeSilvo, because he would have sensors good enough to spot the *Belle Boyd XI*'s arrival and the sense to hide out from such a ship.

Therefore, it had to be some sort of diehard colony activity—except it couldn't be, because no diehard colony would be able to afford the simple expenditure of that much sheer *energy.*

Therefore, what the sensors were picking up could not exist. But it did.

Therefore, it was worth taking a very cautious look. Cautious, because the debris field in orbit made it seem likely that someone on the surface was touchy about visitors.

Kalani turned her attention back toward the planet—but in a more clinical and technical frame of mind.

Burl Chalmers cursed and pulled his hands away from the manipulator controls. He had never been much good at remote handling, and chasing ship debris that had been slapped around by a nuke didn't seem to be doing much to improve his skill. He was still aboard the *Belle Boyd XI,* of course, but his mind was thousands of kilometers away, concentrating on what the op-pod's cameras and sensors were showing him.

And what they were showing him, one widely separated piece at a time, was spinning junk. Not surprisingly, every bit of scrap was tumbling on three axes—Burl was just about ready to swear some of them were tumbling on *four* axes.

Every fragment had, of course, assumed its own highly eccentric—in every sense of the term—orbit. The op-pod had had a hell of a time catching up with any of them—and most of them weren't worth catching in the first place.

What they were after was identifiable debris. Something with a serial number, a batch number, a bulkhead stencil, or an embedded microcrystal pattern—something they could check in the *Belle Boyd XI*'s ship registry database.

So far all he had found were bits and pieces of hull plating. But up ahead, tumbling like mad, was a real prize. It was a main engine, or at least a big piece of one. It would have any number of identifiable parts—if he could catch it.

The op-pod carried exactly one capture net in its tiny cargo hold. The net was in essence a weighted fishnet with rocket engines and a fast-thinking ArtInt. Capture nets were tricky as hell to use, but in theory one would do the job. It was a painstaking job to use the op-pod's remote manipulator to unpack the net, unfold it, power it up, and aim it at the target. Burl nearly got the thing tangled up in itself a few times before he had it properly deployed, stretched flat in space, with the net's sensor head positioned where it could see the engine. Then it was time to back the op-pod itself off to a respectful distance.

That accomplished, Burl stabbed a nervous finger down on the op-pod command panel. Several thousand kilometers away, the pod relayed the command to the capture net. The net fired its corner jets to put itself in a slow, stately spin, using the centripetal effect to hold itself flat. Then it fired its forward jets and started moving straight toward the wrecked and tumbling engine. The burn was very tidy, very accurate, but even so it set the fabric of the net rippling, the cables moving in a wave-like pattern. It looked like a giant spinning jellyfish, moving with unlikely purpose, right for the prey it intended to envelop.

Things moved very slowly after that, at least for a while, the net closing in at something like a half meter a second. If it went in any faster, there was a risk that the net would simply bounce off when it hit. There was something dreamlike about watching the slowly spinning, slowly moving net, its loose-knit cables still undulating very slightly as it edged closer and closer to the wildly tumbling engine.

Then, in the blink of an eye, the net touched the engine, and the action shifted from almost imperceptibly slow to fast, violent, hard. Suddenly the net was wrapped completely around the engine, and its thrusters were firing madly, so hard and so long Burl started to think that there had been some sort of major malfunction. But then the tumble rates started to slow, and the jets started to fire shorter, less frequent bursts. Sooner than Burl had thought possible, the engine, with the net wrapped around it, was floating motionless in space, all tumble rates at zero.

Now came the next step, and the next, and the next. Capture the engine with the op-pod, haul it back to the

Belle Boyd XI's orbit, bring it aboard, disassemble it, analyze it, run any ID numbers or other identifying marks through the database. *It's a good thing they sent Intell people on this job,* Burl told himself. The next zillion steps after examining the engine were going to be at least as painstaking as catching it. *Regular combat types wouldn't have the patience for it.*

But then, just at the moment, he wasn't sure he would, either.

Midday a few days later found them both in the wardroom of the *Belle Boyd XI.* "So," Burl said as he shoveled in another forkful of lunch, "what have we got? Run it all down for me."

"Well," said Kalani, who had finished eating ten minutes before and been waiting since then for Burl to shift from small talk to business, "we launched our latest unmessage probe about two hours ago."

"My goodness, that's the most exciting thing I've ever heard," Burl said in a flat, emotionless monotone. He sighed and shook his head. "Seems like such a damned waste of time sending back message pods with no messages in them."

"No argument from me," said Kalani. "If we're not at the point of doing ourselves more harm then good with security features, we're teetering right on the edge. Of course it doesn't really matter yet. We don't exactly have anything awe-inspiring to report—everything *else* is taking longer than it should."

"Like hauling that engine here, for example."

"I was coming to that. It took four days to do it, but the op-pod got that engine aboard. Metallurgic tests and radiation checks confirm it was caught by a near miss of a fusion weapon. Judging by damage to the engine, and how much it was thrown around, the best fit is a clean, low-yield weapon detonating about a kilometer from the ship. We backtracked the trajectories of the engine and the other debris to where and when they all intersect. It looks as if the strike took place about forty-five days ago. But."

Burl looked up from his food. "But? There's something you don't like?"

"Lots of somethings—about the ship, and the groundside evidence too. But I'll come to that. We had every document pertaining to the *DP-IV* in the Chrono Patrol archives lasergrammed to us while we were boosting out of the Solar System. The best we can say from the ship registry database is an engine with those markings was purchased by Felipe Marquez for use aboard the *Dom Pedro IV*. There's no documentation we have with us that says that engine was ever installed—and there's no way to be sure the markings weren't forged anyway."

"You're saying you think someone's gone to the trouble of planting evidence out *here* on the off chance we'd come looking for it?"

"That 'someone' would be Oskar DeSilvo. We're still working on the assumption that he's alive and well—and if so, he *had* to know it was better than an off chance that we'd come looking, once Koffield pointed the way for us. And who else would have a better motive for deceiving us, or better resources for giving it a try?"

"You *are* slightly paranoid."

"Well, they're out to get *somebody*. I might as well assume it's me. But all I'm really saying is that we can't get too far ahead of the evidence. We have records—which come from public documents that anyone could get—saying a starship engine with such-and-such numbers on it was purchased for the *Dom Pedro IV*. We have an engine that matches that description, that has wear and use patterns that would be more or less consistent with what we know about the *Dom Pedro IV*. We *don't* have sufficient evidence to let us say for sure that the engine we've taken aboard was installed in the *Dom Pedro IV* a month and a half ago when that ship was destroyed by a nuclear weapon."

"And I suppose if we retrieved every bit of that debris, you'd still say more or less the same thing, right?"

"Probably. But there's other problems. There's not *enough* debris. Granted, it was a nuke. Maybe it went off a lot closer and a lot of the ship just got vaporized. Maybe a lot of the debris reentered and burned up. Maybe some of it we haven't spotted. But even taking all that into consideration, my gut—and my ArtInt's analysis—say there's just not enough junk in orbit. It bothers me."

"Groundside?"

"That's more straightforward," Kalani said. "For starters, we can eavesdrop on the diehards chitchatting over the radio. Their conversation dates the impact there from just about the same time as we have for the in-space nuke, which apparently caused an EMP event down there. From the chatter, it seems the two events happened within minutes of each other—and the diehards have been scavenging the impact site ever since. From what they're telling each other, *gloating* to each other about, they found enough gear to feed, clothe, and equip an army."

"You're not saying that DeSilvo has been planning a *military* strike, are you?"

"What? Oh, no. Not at all. Just a bad choice of words. They found enough stuff 'for a lot of people.' "

"Okay. Just *me* being careful." He shoved his plate away, and leaned back in his chair. "So. Paint me a picture. What does it all tell us?"

"What it *seems* to tell us is that the *Dom Pedro IV* came blasting in here about a month and a half ago, bent on revenge, and fired some sort of kinetic-impact or conventional explosive weapon at Oskar DeSilvo's fiendish secret headquarters. But, just before he was destroyed, the evil Dr. DeSilvo fired a nuclear missile at his attackers, and, even in death, had his last bloody revenge. The end. A nice, neat little melodrama. It might even be true. But it's *very* neat, and it gives us exactly what we'd most like to find: proof that what we were looking for was here, and proof that it's been destroyed, so we don't have to worry anymore, or search anymore. Too neat, too pretty."

"So we gotta check it out," Burl said, nodding. "Okay. Though maybe I'm not so cynical. You'd have to go to a lot of trouble to fake something like this."

"That's almost the point. This is *DeSilvo*. It's exactly what he would do. He *loves* making things complicated, inventing puzzles. And we're working on the assumption that he's stolen half the Dark Museum, plus the forensic-accounting study showed that he must have diverted a hell of a lot of material from the Solace terraforming job. He's got amazing resources."

"Point taken—but it still seems like a lot of work just to fool little old you and me. Two other wrinkles, though. One: We have *no* other clues as to where he might have gone if it *is* all a fake. Two: Even if it *is* all a fake, and it turns out it *doesn't* fool us, maybe that doesn't matter."

"Why wouldn't it matter?" Kalani asked.

"If we're reading this right, DeSilvo led Koffield here and had to know the odds were good that we'd follow. He wanted Koffield for a reason, some reason. To do *something*. Probably something we *won't* want done. And maybe he doesn't need to fool us in order to make it happen. Maybe all he needs to do is slow us down."

Kalani looked at him long and hard, thinking about how long the odds were, how high the stakes. "I think I'll stick with slightly paranoid," she said at last. "It's a lot less scary than downright devious."

"Maybe so. I can't tell the difference anymore. Let's get to work," he said. "Let's get down on the ground and check it all out."

Kalani spent most of the next day trying to think it all through, make sure they didn't miss anything.

The diehards were profiting tremendously from the incident, and there was no reason to assume they hadn't been the ones who had launched the attacks in the first place. Besides, even if the diehards *hadn't* done the attacking, that by no means meant they could be assumed to be peaceful or trustworthy. After all, diehards were not known for being kind and welcoming to strangers.

That being said, they had to make contact. The trick

would be in doing so in a way that might lead to their getting some answers—if possible, without anyone getting killed.

She didn't want to think about what she'd have to do if that *wasn't* possible.

Chapter Twenty-four

RULES OF EVIDENCE

Jay Verlant stepped carefully through the shattered doorframe of what he'd been using for an office and out into the sublevel one main corridor of the ruined habitat. As he headed for topside, he had to sidestep Clan and Lenay Fortlan, who were hauling some oversize pieces of gear into the one working freight elevator.

Jay took the emergency stairs up to the surface, climbing over the last few pieces of uncleared rubble. Things looked vastly different than they had when he and Bol had first peered through the miniflyer's camera view. The surface had been picked absolutely clean of smaller debris. Bol and his team had repaired all but two of the vehicles, and the two beyond repair had been hauled away as well, to be stripped for parts in future. Nearly all the other large gear was gone and the topside area cleaned up and put to rights, both for reasons of safety, and to make sure they didn't miss anything of valve.

There were still a few pieces of lower-priority wreckage topside, neatly stacked to one side, but for the most part topside didn't even look like a wreckage field anymore. Nor did it look to be heavily defended, although it was. They were now ready to hold off any uninvited guests. Up until that day, the site had been bristling with weapons set in plain sight. Now they were carefully hidden, as only a diehard could hide things. They had an invited guest due, and Jay did not want her to see all of their defenses. She might be invited, but that didn't mean they trusted her.

Their visitor was, so far, merely a voice on the radio, a loud, clear signal cutting in on the command circuit. Exactly once before in his life, he had seen and spoken to outsiders—but he had been a little boy, and they had just been representatives of another diehard settlement, coming to talk with Jay's father. This was different. A person from off-planet, a person from outside the Glister system altogether—this was an outsider in the truest sense of the word. It got him nervous.

Jay checked the status of the clear-out operation on his brand-new (only about a hundred years old, and only a few scratches on the display) datapad, and nodded in satisfaction. Things were going well. So well he wondered if he had been wise in dealing with that voice on the radio that had claimed to be Chrono Patrol. Canyon City was richer than it had been in generations—possibly richer than it had ever been. It could well be they didn't even need what that voice had to offer.

But she was, after all, offering a power supply, a portable unit with more output than their whole solar array even when it was working, and—or so she claimed—a source they could switch on and off at will, and which could provide that level of power without refueling for fifty years. They could take the solar power system off-line and rebuild it, top to bottom, at their leisure.

Bol was standing at the top of a nearby hillock, running his newly improved miniflyer from a newly improved portable control pack. Jay went over to him. Bol was wearing his heater suit with the helmet open and a breathing mask on, just wearing the helmet liner to keep his head warm.

"What have you got?" Jay asked as he reached the top of the hill.

Bol looked around to acknowledge Jay, then returned his attention to the control pack. "Well," he began, his voice muffled by the breathing mask, "a lander brought her in about an hour ago, dropped her off, and left."

Their visitor had taken the precaution of keeping the lander out of reach. In other words, she wasn't taking any chances that a salvage crew would jump on it the moment she was away from the ship. Not that diehards wouldn't do just that, if things were desperate enough to risk taking on the Chronologic Patrol. "Go on," Jay said.

"She's where she said she would be, and she's alone, and she's standing next to something that's the right size and shape for the power supply."

Bol handed him the control pack, and Jay looked at the screen. It showed a view from the miniflyer, twenty kilometers due west of their present location. The flyer's belly camera was tracking on a point on the ground in the center of a half-kilometer-wide circle, the camera swiveling constantly to keep that spot in view.

And there, in the center of the camera's view, was a figure in a pressure suit and a white packing crate about two meters long, a meter high, and a meter wide. The figure was standing by the crate, arms at its side, all but motionless. The helmeted head looked up toward the flyer now and then, but that was all. She wasn't leaning on the crate to seem casual, or pacing to seem anxious, or constantly checking a comm device to let them know she was still in contact with her ship. *Neutrality*. That sent a message all by itself. She was who she was. She didn't need to prove anything, or ask anyone's permission, or act in any particular way.

"We could really use that power supply, Jay," Bol said.

"Yeah, Bol, I know." He hadn't wanted the job, but the council had given Jay the final go/no-go on dealing with their visitor. If he didn't like the look of things, he could walk away. And he was tempted to, sorely so. Diehards rarely did well for themselves by dealing with outsiders.

But, on the other hand, their visitor didn't want much in exchange. And, after all, she probably *was* just what she said she was—a Chrono Patrol investigator. *Something* strange and violent had happened here, and in space. Jay didn't have any problem believing that someone would want to investigate.

Furthermore, if she was CP, that meant a CP ship in orbit—and Jay knew just what sort of frightfulness such a ship could rain down. If they didn't give her what she wanted, she could take it—quite literally over all their dead bodies.

No. They were safer now than they had been in Jay's whole life. It wasn't time to take risks they didn't need. No one knew better than diehards that staying alive was much harder than dying.

Jay handed the control pack back to Bol. "That power supply is heavy. Send transporter three," he said. "But you don't drive it, or get anywhere near her. Just in case."

"But what could she—"

"She could kill you, or kidnap you—and we need your training and talent to get all this new gear up and running. Send someone else. Two someones—one to drive, and one to watch her. Tell 'em not to answer any questions she might ask." He thought a moment longer. "Tell them to pick her and the power supply up, but don't drive both back here." He pointed toward a nearby rise. "Park the transporter on the other side of that hill, say a kilometer from here, and leave it there with the power supply on it. Bring her here in a terrain car. Leave the power supply right there until she's gone—and until you can check it out very carefully and we know it's not a bomb."

"A *bomb*?"

"Think it through. She gets the information she needs from us, leaves, we take the shiny new present she gave us back to Canyon City, and boom! Suddenly she doesn't have any loose ends. There were two sides to this fight. If someone from the *other* side comes asking questions, we won't be here to answer. And after she's gone, we still play it safe. The power supply stays out of the city. We can build a structure for it on the surface, on the other side of North Slope Ridge. Run cable from there back to the city."

"We'll lose power efficiency," Bol said doubtfully.

"And the city won't be vaporized. That's the way we do it. She doesn't get near anyone but me, the transport driver, and the watcher, and the power supply doesn't get near here or the city. And I'm going to order everyone here to stop work and leave. Clear the site and keep it clear while she's around."

"Clear it? We'll lose half a day's work, at least. Why?"

Jay laughed grimly. "You start thinking differently when you draw a job like the one the council handed me today. We give her the information she's paying for—but not one bit more if we can help it. If she can't see us, she can't count us and know how many people we have. If she can't talk to our people, there's no chance one of our people will talk to her and tell her something she shouldn't know."

"But she already knows all about us, from the nano-probes that got into our system."

"Why do you assume *she's* the one who sent them? Why not the folks who ran this place instead? Besides, it's not just information I want to protect. If we're not all here, she can't wipe us all out with a suicide bomb," he said.

"But where will we send all the workers?"

Jay shrugged. "Back to the city. For once, we actually have enough transport."

Enough. A strange word for a diehard to use. What was more, they had enough of practically *everything*. And Jay was nervous about losing it all.

Two hours later, Kalani Temblar found herself bouncing along in an impressively decrepit terrain car, wedged into the cabin between the driver—a closemouthed young man in a grungy heater suit—and his companion, who found ways to say even less.

As last, the car came to a halt near the half-disassembled

ruins of a habitat dome, plainly the one they had spotted from orbit. The driver and his companion both got out and simply walked away from her, the car, and the dome, leaving her alone in the car. Kalani climbed down out of the cab and looked around. She started walking toward the wreckage of the dome. Even from a hundred meters away, she could see that she wasn't going to be able to gather much direct evidence.

The place was deserted. Or at least, so it seemed. Somehow, a suited figure materialized behind her and came up beside her. Being careful not to betray her surprise, she turned to face the newcomer—a man with a young-old face and the pasty white skin of a life lived mostly underground, his right cheek cut by a slashing scar.

"Hello," she said. "I'm Lieutenant Kalani Temblar, Chronologic Patrol."

"I know," said her host. "The site is ready for you to examine." He walked toward the dome, leaving her with no choice but to follow.

"Nice to meet you too," she muttered at his back.

It took very little time for her to establish that while the impact crater itself was still there, dominating the landscape, everything else that might have told her something was gone. She could not even be sure if the crater had been caused by an explosive device or by force of impact.

"What happened to the wreckage of the attacking missile?" she asked, though she already knew the answer.

"Salvaged," her host said.

"Some of it must have been buried by the impact. What about those parts?"

"Dug up. Salvaged."

"Right," she said. "Fine. Look, you'll let me know if giving me such long detailed answers is wearing you out, okay?"

"I will," he said, and kept walking.

All right. If they wanted to try pushing her around, the hell with them. She'd let them know she could push right back. She stopped and called to her host. "Hey, you!"

He stopped and turned around.

"You have a name?" she asked.

"Yes," he replied.

"Very clever. I think I learned that one when I was twelve. I'll ask another question. Did you know that my ship could drop a kinetic kill vehicle on that nice new power supply on five minutes' notice? It would take out that nice transporter truck, too, of course," she went on. "I don't like to pay for something and then not get it. The deal was access, information, *and cooperation* in exchange for the power supply. So tell me your name, and start helping me out—or else you might as well start figuring out how you're going to explain losing a fifty-year reserve power supply just because you were rude to the nice lady who came to visit."

Silence for a moment longer, then he spoke. "Verlant," he said at last. "James Verlant. Mostly they call me Jay."

"Good," she said. "Very good. Now help me out, cut me some slack, and I'll be out of your way before you know it."

She examined the surface facilities just well enough to confirm her suspicion that there was nothing left there that would tell her anything. She concluded almost as quickly that the underground levels were just as much of a dead loss.

What she was looking for was evidence—more than evidence, *proof*—that Oskar DeSilvo had been there and been killed there. What she found was at best ambiguous. There were papers, datapads, designs scattered everywhere, tossed aside by Canyon City scavengers in search of more useful loot. Quick glances through them made it plain they came from DeSilvo.

Kalani pulled copies of the text of every datapad she could and filled her suit's carry pockets with whatever paper texts looked to be of the most interest. Of the documents she examined quickly, then and there, there wasn't a one of them that couldn't have been forged and planted there. The same would be true of whatever documents she missed.

Nor did she see the hardware she should have. She had walked the aisles of the Dark Museum. She had seen what DeSilvo had taken away, gotten some idea of what he was after. None of it was there. *Might as well not have come here,* she told herself as she came up out of the underground levels. But even that absence was ambiguous. The impact had collapsed tunnels, sealing off sections that might hold anything.

She glared at the surface wreckage in annoyance, as if it had been deliberately arranged as it was to make her job harder—as perhaps it had been.

That was the nub of the thing. Everything she had seen was either solid proof of what would be most convenient for her to believe—or it was all tricks and forgeries. It didn't even have to fool her to work. As Burl had said, maybe all DeSilvo needed to do in order to win was make them unsure, make them have to check, make them move slowly.

"Bodies," she said, turning to Verlant. "There weren't any survivors here when your people arrived, right?"

"No, none," Verlant agreed. "Everyone was dead."

"So there were bodies, right?" she asked.

"Yes, of course. I saw several corpses myself."

"Where are they now?" she asked. "Buried somewhere? On ice?"

"Salvaged," Verlant replied, and his face turned hard and expressionless.

"Ah. Of course," she said, looking him straight in the eye. Her stomach went cold and tied itself in knots. "Of course." If they didn't hesitate to convert Aunt Minnie into nutrients for the hydroponic tanks, why would they be squeamish about total strangers? Diehards didn't waste *anything.*

Right at the moment, Kalani felt as if she had wasted everything—especially the one thing she had least of. Time.

Jay could tell his visitor was disappointed. It was plain to see that she hadn't gotten what she came for. Jay walked her back to the terrain car and even carried a second bag full of datapads and papers for her. Jay Verlant had not expected himself to feel bad about his behavior in front of an outsider. Outsiders didn't count. And this Kalani Temblar person was a *real* outsider, from off the planet. Her reactions, her behavior, should have mattered not at all to him.

And yet, they did. "I'm sorry it didn't work out," he said as they approached the car.

"What? Oh." Plainly distracted by her own worries, it took a moment for her to look over at him. She smiled sadly. "It's that easy to tell, huh?"

"I'm afraid so," he said. He opened the rear hatch of the terrain car and dropped in the bag of documents. He hesitated a minute, then turned and waved off their two silent companions, still trailing along behind. "I'll drive you to the pickup point," he said.

"Thanks," she said as she dumped her bag in next to his. "I'd appreciate that."

They got into the vehicle. Jay got behind the controls and started driving. They bounced along in silence for a time. It occurred to Jay that he'd never see this stranger again, ever. Somehow that was a more disconcerting idea than the notion of *meeting* a complete stranger. *So anything you have to say, anything you could tell her or ask her, has to happen right now,* he told himself. Another strange idea.

"Look," he said. "I don't know the first thing about what all this is about. Maybe if you told me something about it, I'd know something that would help."

She turned her hands palms up and shrugged, exaggerating the gestures a bit to make them noticeable through her pressure suit. "It's a very long, very complicated story," she said. "What it boils down to is that there was a man named DeSilvo who stole a lot of very powerful and dangerous equipment. We tracked him as far as Glister. It seems very likely that he caused the explosion that knocked out your power. It's also clear that he used that abandoned habitat we just left for *something*. I *think* he set it up and staged the attacks here and in space just to attract your attention and get you to take a look at the site. You'd go in and, ah, salvage everything, and in the process you'd disrupt all the evidence that might tell me for sure whether or not DeSilvo was there."

"Was there anything you saw that *proves* he wasn't there? Any evidence that it was a fake?"

"No," Kalani conceded. "And the only way I can think to prove he was there, was killed there, would be to identify the body. I have lots of images of him—"

"I saw most of the human remains," Jay said sharply. "The bodies—and body parts—weren't recognizable. Photos of what they looked like before wouldn't help."

"Then I guess I'm out of luck. The unidentifiable bodies could have been planted. Plenty of frozen corpses on Glister."

The terrain car creaked to a halt back at the site where her lander had dropped her off, well away from the actual touchdown point. "Do you call in now? When will they come and get you?"

"I've already signaled. The lander will be here in thirty-five minutes."

"Might as well wait here in the car, then, and stay out of the wind."

"Right. Look, as long as we're here. There's one kind of evidence I haven't really dug into yet. Eyewitness accounts."

"I told you before you got here, when we talked on the radio, about what happened on the day of the attacks."

"Well, maybe we should go through it again. But there's something else. It might be a rude or awkward question—that's why I haven't asked it before."

Jay chuckled. "But now that the visit's almost over, you'll take the chance of insulting me?"

She smiled back. "Something like that. And I was hoping I might get the answer some other way, from seeing or hearing something that would tell me."

"All right," he said. "Go on. Insult me."

Another smile, a lovely one. "All right, then, I will. It's this. The wrecked habitat was only a bit more than two hundred kilometers from Canyon City. How could it be that you didn't know about it before?"

"Not much of an insult there. Well, we had maps and so on that showed an abandoned habitat there, and we have records of gleaner parties doing sweeps through there—but it was picked clean long ago. We don't have any record of anyone from Canyon City being there in the last fifty years."

"All right—now we come to the insulting part. As I understand diehard culture, one of the most common patterns is for you to, well, *hide* from each other?"

Jay shifted in his seat and drummed his fingers on the control panel. "Yes," he said. "We do. It's best for everyone."

"But you must try and keep an eye on each other as well."

"We have detector systems of one sort or another, and sometimes gleaner parties spot settlements, or clues that point to settlements."

"But each group settles in one spot, and those spots are usually existing facilities you take over. So mostly, you *can't* hide from the other diehards, because they have maps and records too. What really goes on is that you know where the other groups are and you stay out of each other's way."

He shifted again, very uncomfortably. "We, ah, *check* on each other every so often. If, ah, something has happened to a nearby settlement, then you send in gleaner teams. Before someone else does."

"So if there had been a lot of activity at this wrecked habitat over an extended period of time, wouldn't you have spotted it?"

"Probably. Maybe." He hesitated. "You're right. We know *who* our neighbors are, and *where* they are. We watch each other—some. Not a lot. We never have resources enough that we can waste them on patrol flights or expeditions. If there had been a lot going on at that site for months on end, well, yes, we should have spotted it. But this site is just outside our usual two-hundred-kilometer sensor perimeter. And there's no other settlement in this direction for a thousand kilometers."

"So—you should have noticed something going on, but you could have missed it."

"Yeah. Easily. The first we knew about anyone being around was the nanoprobes."

She looked startled. "*Nanoprobes?* What *nanoprobes?*"

He laughed. "That's just about the first thing *you've* told *me,*" he said. "We thought your people might have been the ones who sent them. But you weren't, were you?"

"No. We're trying to work fast. No time for anything subtle or sneaky. When was this?"

"We found them just about three months ago, and Bol doesn't think they were there long. Relaying historical data, and engineering data, mostly. Then we started getting flyovers—that first one from the northwest, that made us get our detection systems back on full power. Then the ones coming from over in this direction."

"Why do something as hidden as nanoprobes, then something as obvious as flyovers?"

It was Jay's turn to shrug. "Ask this fellow DeSilvo when you catch him, if he isn't dead. Maybe the first flyover was part of a crisscross search pattern that happened to spot us on a southbound leg."

"But the nanoprobes got there first," Kalani objected. "Those would have pinpointed your location."

"Two sides got killed in the fight. Maybe the ship in orbit dropped the nanos on every active settlement, to have them sniff for DeSilvo. DeSilvo detects the nanoprobe's transmissions and sends flights out to search for the source."

"Could be," Kalani conceded. "It seems thin, but it could be." She leaned back in her seat and stared straight ahead, at where her lander was going to put down. Jay couldn't read her expression all that clearly through the helmet, but it looked as if she were thinking.

And thinking hard.

She kept thinking on the flight back to the *Belle Boyd XI,* as she gave Burl a somewhat distracted debriefing, as she ate a dinner she didn't taste, as she laid her head on her pillow.

The same sequence of thoughts kept cycling through her mind, over and over, though she never quite seemed to reach a conclusion. It was like a dream where she had to go through some long involved job she never quite understood, only to have it all come apart on her just as she was finishing, so she was forced to start over. She hated the restless, fretful mood of those dreams. Lying awake in bed, staring at the overhead bulkhead, only made the feeling ten times worse.

Some endless time later she gave it up, swung her feet out of the bunk, and switched on the lights. She was so wide-awake she might as well be working. She moved over to her worktable and started to reach for the data-pad that held all the data she had copied. But no. It would be a waste of time. The documents were just part of the diversion, the misinformation. Studying them would just tell her how good a forgery DeSilvo could manufacture. She shoved the datapad to one side.

She no longer had the slightest doubt that it was all a fake. The very absence of proof was, in a sense, proof all by itself. The ambiguities were all so elaborate and complete that it was impossible to believe they had not been deliberately manufactured.

She sat there, staring at nothing for a moment. There was something Verlant had said. *The sight and sound recording from my pressure suit camera and mike,* she reminded herself. *All that data should have been copied out of my suit's memory store into the ship's log as soon as I came aboard.*

She reached for the datapad again, linked into the ship's comm system, and brought up her suit's sight and sound. Kalani skipped ahead in the playback, almost to the end, and stopped it on an image of Verlant sitting in the cab of the terrain car. She ran playback at normal speed for a moment, as Verlant said. *". . . just outside our usual two-hundred-kilometer sensor perimeter . . ."*

She stopped it, skipped ahead a little bit, and ran it

again. Verlant spoke again. "*. . . we started getting fly-overs—that first one from the northwest—*"

The plan never works perfectly, Kalani told herself. *There's always a hitch, a flaw, a breakdown, a surprise. Someone doesn't do what they're supposed to—or someone does something unexpected.* If you were smart, if you were experienced, if you had been through this sort of thing before, you took that into account. You made the plan flexible. You watched events carefully. You came up with ways to work around. You improvised. You found ways to hide the mistakes.

All right. Good. Assume all that was true. Assume there was a mistake. It would be what *didn't* fit in with the rest, the thing that broke the pattern.

So let's say that someone off the Dom Pedro IV *causes some trouble, or a machine breaks down. Something breaks the pattern, and makes enough of a mess that DeSilvo needs to patch it over.*

Everything was secret, hidden, out of sight or over the horizon—until the first flyover of Canyon City. The only flyover that *didn't* come from the direction of the wrecked habitat she had just visited. All the later fly-overs had come from almost *exactly* the opposite direction. Like a magician gesturing wildly with his left arm to make you forget the card you had spotted, tucked up the sleeve of his right arm. And then, the flash in the sky to get them looking, the blast down to the south to tell them where—and the EMP burst to make sure they felt threatened enough to act. All of it designed to get the diehards—and, ultimately, one Kalani Temblar—looking at DeSilvo's left hand.

But what about his *right* hand? She brought up a map of the surface on the datapad. "From the northwest," she muttered. "And outside their sensor perimeter, so more than two hundred kilometers away."

She stared at the map, willing the answers to spring forth.

Part Five
THE HARMONIES OF TIME

Chapter Twenty-five

PRODIGAL RETURNS

FOUNDER'S DOME
GREENHOUSE

"Can't resist another look?" Villjae asked with a smile as he looked up from his desk.

"You've seen it all before a thousand times," said El-ber, staring out the third-story window of the tallest building in the dome—just about the only habitable building in the dome, at the moment. "It's all new to me."

He looked down at the tree-lined park, complete with chuckling fountain. The newly planted saplings had taken root and looked to be thriving. So did the new grass in the park's neat green lawns.

The green turned to brown not so far off—but it was the rich, healthy black-brown of well-tilled soil, already sown with new life. Here and there, he could see a faint green haze over the good earth. He knew that if he looked closer, much closer, he would see the thin tender shoots of the seedlings, just sprouting up. Elsewhere were the new-built, nearly finished, not-yet-occupied dormitories, the commons hall, and all the rest of the structures that seemed to have sprouted out of the ground even faster than the plant life.

Farther off was the solid anchor wall of the dome structure and, mounted atop it, the transparent dome itself, a gleaming soap bubble seen from the inside. Beyond that, the cold hard-vacuum landscape of rocks and dust and craters that was Greenhouse. Near the zenith of the jet-black sky, the looming gas giant planet Comfort hung overheard, showing itself in waxing half phase, its surface still not fully recovered from the shock of NovaSpot Ignition.

There were no fewer than three "suns" visible at the moment. Lodestar, the true sun of the Solacian star system, was closest to the horizon, too bright to look at, but only providing a small fraction of the light and heat that it gave to closer-in Solace. A bit higher up in the sky, almost ready to set, was NovaSpot, a painfully bright dot of glory, barely large enough to show a disk, and yet illuminating a world. Just barely visible in the glare of the NovaSpot was a dim dot of light, all left of the old SunSpot, guttering down to the very dregs of its remaining nuclear fuel.

Between the dome and the sky was a strange and wonderful landscape—and one that held warning of all that could go wrong. Scattered about on the exposed surface of Greenhouse were smashed-up bits of dome material, the torn-up limbs of trees, blackened by heat and vacuum, mats of fire-damaged algae, and other wreckage that was impossible to identify. All of it had been blasted out of the habitat, back when they deliberately blew the dome, not so very long ago.

The environment inside Founder's Dome had become so infested with mold and algae and other unpleasantnesses that it had become impossible to clean it or repair it. It was easier to destroy everything, kill everything, and start over.

Elber frowned. The message was clear. *Habitat domes failed.* He had checked the actuarial tables himself and been surprised by the rate of failure. He had the sense that he could almost write a predictive algorithm, the way they did with risk assessment back in the insurance office, that would tell how soon the next one would go and how often they would fail. All of which was cold hard proof that a dome was not a sealed and balanced ecology, but merely a first approximation of one. A domed hab was too simple, not deep or robust enough to last forever—or even for all that long.

Sooner or later, for every dome, would come the day when the balance would fail. This newly refurbished dome already held not only the seeds of new life but of its own death.

But then, every birth was, in the end, balanced with a death. This was the beginning of things. Later would be soon enough to worry about endings.

Beginnings. The first load of refugees had already been flown to SCO Station, transferred to a long-range transport, and launched toward Greenhouse. Jassa and Zari would be here soon. That was enough of a new beginning to keep him from worrying about anything else.

The two young men left the admin building and walked along the pathway that led toward the nearly finished dormitories. The dorms were currently home to only ten or fifteen final-prep technicians, tweaking and tuning the habitat's systems, making them ready for full use. Villjae and Elber were part of the handoff team who would make sure the new occupants knew how to run the place. Elber had emphasized repeatedly that he had reason to know that teaching dirt-farming peasants the ways of life in a habitat dome was going to be a big job.

Still, the resettlement would serve as a splendid bit of propaganda. All of Solace would see that, out of nowhere and nothing, the government had built new places for the Wilhemtonians to live, domes that would provide refuge from the current climate problem. They would see low-downs, peasants, relocated to a big, new, modern up-to-date habitat dome.

The key to it all was to keep the operation *quiet* until the refugees were safely in place. The thing Villjae really dreaded was some muddleheaded official wandering out in front of the cameras and telling the good people of Solace that there was no need for alarm. Nothing would be surer to start a panic than that.

"What's that over there?" Elber asked, pointing to a

low, six-sided stone building visible down a side path. "I've noticed it a few times, and wondered, but I've never managed to ask when I had the chance."

"It's *supposed* to be Oskar DeSilvo's tomb," Villjae said. "There are a lot of funny stories about it, though. Probably just rumors."

"DeSilvo's tomb?" Elber was impressed. "I ought to go look at it some time. What are the stories about—and what do you mean 'supposed' to be his tomb?"

"Mostly, the stories are that he's not in there—maybe never was. Back when they blew the dome, supposedly some group went into the tomb and grabbed the cylinder that had his ashes in it. When the survey crews came back into the dome to look things over after it was blown, the cylinder was gone. But then the cylinder got put back later. There are all sorts of stories about what happened. Probably none of them true.

"A lot of fragile objects were removed when they blew the dome. My guess is that the cylinder with his ashes just got added to the list at the last minute. They had to rush in and grab them in a hurry, and maybe they damaged the cylinder so it had to be repaired."

"Oh, well," Elber said.

"What? What's wrong? You sound disappointed."

"I guess I was just hoping there would be more to the story, that's all. To give the tomb more history, sort of."

Villjae chuckled and patted Elber on the back. "Who knows?" he said. "For all we know, there's a lot more to the story than anyone ever heard."

THE *NOVA SOL*
OUTER SOLACIAN SYSTEM
INBOUND FOR GREENHOUSE

The rumors and legends had had lots of time to age, but even so, the *Dom Pedro IV* had earned enough of a reputation that it was best she stay out of sight whilst in the Solacian system. Even if she had not been well-known, she might draw attention by approaching the Solacian star system, not from the direction of a timeshaft worm-hole but on the straight-line bearing from Glister. And the three large toroids that now adorned her were bound to attract notice. So the *Dom Pedro IV* did what she had done on her previous journey to Solace: She would hide, in the fringes of the outer system. One of her auxiliary craft would carry a party in to make contact.

By all rights, so far as Norla Chandray was concerned, the *Cruzeiro do Sul* should have made the run. Norla was very much of the opinion that a strong case could be made that the old *Cruzeiro* could claim as much right to fame as the *DP-IV*. She should have been in on the finish.

But it was the very fact that she might be known, remembered, and recognized that kept her in her service bay aboard the *Dom Pedro IV*. The contact party traveled, therefore, aboard the newly named *Nova Sol*, one of the two new auxiliary craft provided by DeSilvo.

The *Nova Sol* was designed for a complement of three. Koffield had to go to prove that he had come back. DeSilvo had to go to prove he wasn't dead and to present his plan. Norla Chandray took the third seat, and was proud to know that she was the unanimous choice of DeSilvo, Marquez, and Koffield.

But, the honor of the thing to one side, by the end of the journey to Greenhouse, Norla Chandray had come to the conclusion she was not all that glad to be along for the ride.

The flight to Greenhouse was as quiet as a tomb at midnight—and every bit as comfortable and relaxing, so far as Norla was concerned.

The *Nova Sol* was a small conical three-deck lander of conventional design. The flight deck on top, living quarters mid-deck, and a lower deck divided between engineering spaces and a cargo compartment. The engineering spaces were far from comfortable, but the lower cargo deck was a fair size and serviceable enough to use as living space for a few days. It had been Norla's suggestion that they divvy up the decks, treating each as a private cabin as much as possible. The two men both agreed at once, with Koffield

382 / Roger MacBride Allen

opting for the cargo deck as most private and DeSilvo taking the mid-deck as the most comfortable. That left her with the flight deck, and the best view.

That was practically the last she saw of either of them. DeSilvo would summon Koffield and Norla at mealtimes. As he was in possession of the lander's pocket galley and sanitary facilities, he played the gracious host at mealtime, preparing tasty meals out of the dull food available aboard the lander and keeping the conversation light and pleasant at all times. Anton Koffield likewise demonstrated that he could be charming when he wanted to be. Norla almost enjoyed herself at table. Almost. It was hard not to notice that the smiles were forced, the courtesy determined and deliberate rather than easy and natural.

The moment mealtime was over, Koffield would make a polite farewell and instantly vanish back into the cargo bay. DeSilvo would then make it politely but abundantly clear that he desired Norla to retreat back up to the flight deck as well. She was always eager to take the hint.

There was no great mystery about what the two men were doing. They were studying, cramming for the most important final exams of their lives—perhaps of anyone's lives. Political questions, technical issues, finances—there were endless details to deal with, endless possible questions to prepare for.

And endless new information coming in. That was what kept Norla busy. The main comm center was on the flight deck, and she was pulling in massive amounts of information from Solace and Greenhouse, mostly in the form of public broadcast transmissions, but from other sources as well—ship-to-ship transmissions, for example. Indeed, the number of ships transmitting was a datapoint in and of itself. There was a hell of a lot of traffic between Solace and Greenhouse.

Even so, once she had the ArtInt more or less trained to watch for what interested her, the collection process was largely automated and she had a great deal of time to think.

Few of her thoughts were comfortable.

Five days into their journey, with one day left to go, the pattern of their days ended. Apparently without any discussion or prearrangement, Koffield and DeSilvo not only stayed together after breakfast, but even ventured up into the flight deck.

There were other reasons for it, but the main thing was that it was time—and perhaps past time—for all of them to get a look at where they were going. After all the mountains both the men had climbed, for good and ill, it was time to face the start of the last and greatest challenge.

"Things have changed down there," Koffield said as he stared out the main viewport. "More than I would have believed possible in the time we've been gone."

Norla could only nod her head. She had been staring at Greenhouse, and at Comfort and NovaSpot, for the last three days. She had been there too, back when Koffield had been on the world they were approaching. That was in the days when the SunSpot was dying, its waning light focused down into an elliptical beam that could only illuminate a narrow band around the equator.

As a result, virtually every habitat dome outside the equatorial region had died. Even many of the habs near the equator had failed. Some were simply abandoned. Others, badly infested by one or more unpleasant organisms, had been deliberately blown after the interiors were set afire, using heat and explosive decompression—followed by a stiff dose of vacuum—to kill everything inside. Others had been killed more gently, simply by venting the air and cutting the power, letting the vacuum in to kill but preserving the integrity of the habitat and dome structure.

The habs had died almost in order, moving from the poles toward the equators. Little by little, the small world of Greenhouse had grown dark and dreary.

Now the NovaSpot was ablaze, lighting Greenhouse from pole to pole—and it seemed that every abandoned habitat had already been restored. That was impossible, of course—but certainly many of them had been brought back to life already, and it was plain from the radio traffic Norla had intercepted that more were being revived almost every day.

The Greenhouse they saw was a grey stone flecked with glittering jewels, the domes of the habitats on the daylight side catching the light of the NovaSpot, and those on the nightside shining by their own light, cast from streetlights, office lights, and the lights of new-found homes.

"It's not so different from the last time I saw it with my own eyes," said DeSilvo. "But even back then, the SunSpot was starting to dim. It was a dying place. Now it's come alive again. The difference is almost something you can see."

"A difference you can't see at this range is the amount of traffic, inbound and outbound," said Norla. "Enough that they've established much more sophisticated landing control than they used to have. I was sort of envisioning us just setting down outside some semi-abandoned dome without anyone noticing, then just sneaking into town to place our call. That's not going to happen."

"Leave that to me," Koffield said. "It's part of what I've been working on these last few days. I'm pretty sure I can send the proper requests and queries to get us cleared for landing wherever we want."

DeSilvo chuckled. "I wouldn't worry too much about getting down safely, Officer Chandray. That ought to be the least of our troubles."

They were only a kilometer off the ground, descending smoothly under automatic control, in the most normal manner possible, when it occurred to Norla just how *unusual* a normal approach or takeoff had become for her. The set-down on Glister, the Mars landing and take-off, even that long ago—or was it that long ago?—docking with SCO Station. . . . It had been a long time since she had flown any maneuvers as boring as these, without being forced to make split-second choices every few seconds, without the stakes being life-and-death—or higher. She found herself enjoying the ride.

It was automatics and ArtInts all the way to the ground. The *Nova Sol* set down neatly, smoothly, without any trouble—and without Norla so much as touching the controls. She wouldn't want that as a steady diet—but it certainly did make for a refreshing change of pace from all the endless emergencies.

They landed at the spacefield for Research Dome, the main center for terraforming work on Greenhouse. Their entry into the dome was every bit as nondramatic as their landing. An automated personnel carrier mated with the *Nova Sol*'s airlock, they entered the carrier's pressurized cabin, and rode in comfort to Research Dome's airlock center.

Then the airlock opened. With a hat pulled low over his eyes, and wearing a big, bulky coat, Dr. Oskar DeSilvo set foot on Greenhouse for the first time since his supposed death, roughly 115 years before. With him, Admiral Anton Koffield, who had gone out from this place sworn to track him down, sworn to seek justice and vengeance—and who now walked alongside him, as a partner and ally.

And Norla Chandray was the only one there to take notice. She paused, just inside the airlock entrance, and took a moment to witness the event, see the two men walking ahead of her. Even the two principals seemed unaware of the moment's significance, more concerned with whether either of them would be inconveniently recognized and which exit tunnel to use to get them where they were going.

It should have been a moment of grand historical drama. Norla could almost see the great mural that would be painted of the moment *The Arrival of DeSilvo and Koffield,* full of dramatic color, rendered from some impressive angle, with both figures striding purposefully forward, eyes lifted on high, each pointing to the way to the future. She could almost see the plaque that would be placed in the wall. *Dr. Oskar DeSilvo and Admiral*

Anton Koffield first entered Research Dome together through this airlock.

"There! Up ahead!" Koffield cried out eagerly.

She laughed at herself and at the two worried-looking men up ahead of her. She hurried to catch up. She was looking forward, into history. They were looking for a comm booth.

The Diamond Room
Planetary Executive's Mansion
Solace City
The Planet Solace

Planetary Executive Neshobe Kalzant bustled about, straightening her desk, checking her carry case, and generally fussing about as some people do before a journey.

Olar Sotales, who had arrived shortly before, summoned from SCO Station by the PlanEx, still didn't have the whole story straight in his head, despite his wiretaps and Kalzant's explanations. It had, apparently, been a tumultuous twenty-seven hours. It had all been set in motion by the initial coded comm call from Koffield—nothing more than a prearranged signal that he had arrived.

"So you're actually going?" Sotales asked again.

She looked up at him in surprise. "Yes, Captain Sotales, I am. We confirmed the contact with Admiral Koffield four hours ago—and I'll be aboard the *Lodestar VII* in another four. I want you to be aboard as well."

Sotales frowned, and chose his words carefully. He still was not sure what she assumed he already knew. "If you want me along to offer security advice, I'll start off by saying it is not only dangerous, but even improper for the head of government to go roaring off halfway across the Solace system, just to meet with—with some adventurer. It could be dangerous—and if it gets out, it won't look good."

"Well, as far as security goes, given the danger of his

being spotted, and the mess things are in now, I don't think it would be advisable to bring him *here*. Besides, we have an excellent cover story."

"And that would be?"

"One of your pet projects. Renewal of the habitat domes on Greenhouse."

Sotales reddened a bit. Apparently the PlanEx knew more about his activities than he had thought. "Oh," he said. "That."

"Yes," she said dryly. "That. The formal reopening of Founder's Dome is next week, and I have let the powers that be know that Planetary Executive Neshobe Kalzant would gladly accept an invitation to attend. I was toying with the idea of going there, anyway. It's an excellent cover story, don't you think? And it has the advantage of being completely legitimate."

"I see," Sotales replied. "That eliminates my objections insofar as appearances go, but there is still the security angle. It's a long journey, and you'd be away from Solace for a critical period of time. And I still don't see what your friend Admiral Koffield could have brought back that would be valuable enough to merit all this effort." But, of course, Sotales reminded himself, even he had never been briefed on the whole Koffield file— hardly anyone had.

"I don't know, either, exactly," Kalzant admitted. "All that Koffield's told me is that he has returned, and that he has gathered a lot of useful information. In fact, he said he had brought back everything—*everything,* he emphasized that—he had gone in search of, but that all of it was trivial compared to other things he had found. He promised me that the trip to Greenhouse would be well worth my while."

"What, exactly, was 'everything'?" Sotales asked.

" 'Everything' consisted of two main items," Kalzant replied. "One—a faster-than-light drive."

Sotales snorted derisively. "A fairy story."

"If so, it's one that Koffield believes in. And I got the impression that they had used one to get back here."

"I didn't believe that rumor when it was floating

around a couple of years back, and I don't believe it now," he said, shaking his head. But then he looked at Kalzant quizzically. " 'They'? Who is 'they?' "

Kalzant grinned. "The other item on the list he promised to bring back. Dr. Oskar DeSilvo."

Sotales looked up sharply. "But—but he's been dead for, what? A hundred and fifteen years or more!" Officially, at least, he wasn't supposed to know otherwise. Better to play it that way.

"Apparently," Kalzant replied, "he's feeling better now." She closed her case and looked up at Sotales. "So," she said. "I'll leave it up to you. Are you coming, or not?"

Olar Sotales found himself impressed with the Planetary Executive's skill as a speaker. She had managed to make it sound as if there were more than one possible answer to that question.

But there wasn't, of course.

Chapter Twenty-six

COUNCILS OF
WAR AND TIME

FOUNDER'S DOME
GREENHOUSE

"There you are!" Berana Drayax announced as she poked her head around the door.

Villjae and Elber looked up from their main planning chart. The first contingents of refugees—correction, *settlers* was the officially preferred term—from Wilhemton District on Solace had landed two days before, and they'd been busy ever since.

Zak Destan had been aboard, which was the bad news. So had Zari and Jassa, and that was the good news. Elber had enjoyed a brief, almost frantic, reunion with his family—then been forced to return to work, precisely because his family, and several hundred of their companions, had arrived.

"Good morning, Madam Drayax," said Elber.

"Morning, ah, ma'am," Villjae echoed.

"As if either of you had slept enough to call what came before night," Drayax said. "I hope you weren't planning to get any rest today."

The two of them had been up half the night trying to deal with cargo gone astray, a power system that had gone dead in two of the dormitories, and the discovery that the standardized personal effect boxes issued on Solace were, somehow, exactly eight centimeters wider than the officially designated lockers intended to hold them on Greenhouse.

"What is it, Madam Drayax?" Elber asked politely. He was always respectful, always courteous—but still he got a secret thrill at being allowed to address, and deal with, as important a person as Berana Drayax.

"I'm not sure myself," she admitted. "We just got a call that there's some sort of big meeting that's going to happen, over in Research Dome, rush-rush, this minute. They won't say why, but they think they might want to allocate some domes away from settlement for some big new project."

Villjae groaned. "Not more poaching," he said. "We've just got our dome space allocation rejiggered from the last time."

"It gets better," Drayax said. "Sounds like maybe they want to grab some of our people for the project. Who knows? Maybe an hour from now, you won't have to worry about dome space allocation. Come on."

Villjae glanced at Elber. "Ah, both of us?"

Drayax shrugged. "They didn't say. Might as well. You two are joined at the hip anyway. Why not? You both might learn something. And besides, it's going to be a meeting. Maybe you can sleep through it."

Twenty minutes later they were aboard a runcar, moving through the newly restored tunnel system that once again connected Founder's to the other domes in the area. A quick transit through the airlocks—normally kept open, but sealed for some reason at the moment—a ride up a lift, a brisk walk across part of Research Dome, then the three of them found themselves at the doors of the Terraformation Research Center.

Elber's peasant reflex for trouble came to the alert the moment he saw the armed guards on either side of the entrance. Drayax herself frowned, for half a second, but then her face became a mask of calm, noncommittal cheerfulness.

Elber and Villjae exchanged worried, surprised glances. The sight of the guards had surprised Drayax.

That was something that just didn't happen. But the guards knew her, of course, and they waved her party through the front door of the building, and it was too late to worry about it.

Inside, another guard carefully checked all of their IDs, held a brief and whispered discussion with Drayax, then over a comm handset, and personally escorted them to a large, well-equipped conference room.

There was a big, elegant, oval polished-stone table in the center of the room, with extremely comfortable-looking padded work chairs for about twenty set around it. The walls were lined with about thirty or so severe-looking high-backed chairs for assistants and fetchers and carriers of one sort or another.

They were the first to arrive. Drayax took a seat at the far end of the table from the door and signaled for Villjae and Elber to sit behind her, against the wall.

Elber sat down nervously, not at all sure he was glad to be where he was. He had just barely been keeping up with things as they were. This room, and all its quiet elegance and power, fairly shouted out loud that he was way out of his depth.

Then the doors opened, and the others started to arrive. They came in by ones and twos, some with assistants trailing behind. They seemed to be scientists for the most part, and it was plain they knew as little as Elber did about what was going on. The room gradually filled, with the higher-rankers like Drayax at the table, and the smaller fry seated around the sides of the room, where Villjae and Elber were seated.

Then, suddenly Drayax stood up, very briskly, just as a well-dressed, worried-looking, extremely upper-class lady strode into the room, surrounded by a whole cloud of aides and assistants. About half of the room's occupants shot to their feet as fast as Drayax, with the rest a bit slower on the uptake. Villjae gasped and got to his feet himself. Elber scrambled to stand up, without knowing why. It was only after he was standing that he realized that the upper lady was the highest upper there was—Planetary Executive Neshobe Kalzant.

But his eyes didn't bug out of his head altogether until he noticed one of the "assistants" she had brought along was someone he had met before—Captain Olar Sotales. Elber felt frozen in place, as incapable of motion as a deer caught in a carry van's headlights late at night. Then Sotales saw *him,* and nodded absently, the way one might with a colleague seen across the room.

Elber was still standing there when Villjae gave a tug at his arm and guided him back into his seat. Somehow, Elber had missed the moment where PlanEx Kalzant had taken her seat, and everyone else had sat down as well.

He looked to Villjae and saw that his friend was as shocked and bewildered as he was. Plain to see there had been a big mistake. They shouldn't have been allowed into this meeting. But it was also plain that it was already far too late. There were secrets in this room, that was clear, and Elber and Villjae knew there were secrets—which was almost as bad as knowing what they were. Elber could already see there was no possible way they could be let out.

Kalzant was explaining something, no, announcing someone, but the roaring in Elber's ears, and the shock and mortification in his head, made it impossible for him to follow it. Besides, what he *thought* he heard couldn't be right.

But then everyone in the room—including PlanEx Kalzant—was standing, *applauding,* as three new arrivals entered the room. The first was an average-looking woman somewhere in her thirties. He had the feeling he had seen her before, long ago and far away. The man behind her likewise looked familiar. Then it came to him. He *had* seen them, or their twins, years before, when he was a refugee on SCO Station. They had been riding on a runcar that paused close by where his family was camped. He remembered, vividly, the expressions on their face—shock, loss, astonishment. That was why they stuck in his mind. They were uppers, but with the look of refugees in their faces. They looked found now, and grim, and worried. The man's face—it seemed to Elber that he had seen that face elsewhere, as well, perhaps in a book or a history presentation.

But when he looked at the third person he knew at once precisely who it was—and who it could not possibly be. *That* face looked down from the wall in every schoolroom on Solace. That face belonged to Oskar DeSilvo.

He was so taken aback by it all that he didn't think to listen to what Oskar DeSilvo was saying. But it wouldn't have mattered. Even after all that had gone before, he *still* wouldn't have believed what the man had to say.

Oskar DeSilvo risked a split-second glance away from his presentation to look over the audience, and confirmed his hopes: Almost a half hour in, coming close to the end, and things were going well. They were listening, thinking, allowing the ideas in. They might not yet be saying yes—not by a long shot—but at least they were not screaming NO! and running for the exit.

The airspace over the center of the table was alive with charts and diagrams and holographic images. He cleared away two or three that were no longer needed and expanded the image of the Harmonic Gate.

"To emphasize once again—the Harmonic Gate is, in some ways, a close relation to the timeshaft wormholes we are familiar with. In theory, paired Harmonic Gates could in fact be used in place of wormholes, and would be far cheaper and easier to create and operate."

"So why don't we?" Sotales asked.

"Several reasons," DeSilvo replied. "First, theory and practical reality don't always coincide. In this case, gates that are too close together in time interfere with each other—they jam each other, if you will. Harmonic Gates get their name from the fact that they interact with each other through a phenomenon closely analogous to the behavior of sound waves. When both are properly tuned, and the two gates are in the same relative energy position to a continuously present anchor mass, one gate will fall into temporal resonance with another, and a timeshaft will form spontaneously between the two gates."

"What—what was that about anchor masses?"Drayax asked.

"My apologies," DeSilvo said. "I tend to get too glib with jargon at times. For our purposes, what it means is that both gates must be in roughly the same orbit about a large body, such as a star, that doesn't change mass all that much or that rapidly during the time period separating the two gates. If one gate was placed in a radically different orbit, or moved to another star system—or if the star went nova, or somehow added or ejected a large fraction of its mass all at once, then the timeshaft simply wouldn't form."

Drayax nodded. "All right. I'd want to see the math, but all right."

"Very good. To continue: The main reason we can't build timeshafts using Harmonic Gates instead of wormholes is that the frequencies required to tune one gate to another increase as the time period grows *shorter*. The increase is very gradual for longer periods, but it piles up dramatically as the interval decreases. In round figures, to tune in on a gate one year away would require a frequency a million times higher than what would be required to tune in on a gate that was one thousand years distant. At the same time, producing those higher tuning frequencies induces all sorts of other resonances at other frequencies. You get massive interference—static—that jams the tuning signal. It would require truly horrifying amounts of power to overcome it.

"The long and the short of it is that it is far easier to induce a Harmonic Gate pair to form a timeshaft when the two gates are distant in time from each other."

"What's the shortest practical interval?" Drayax asked. "And is there any upper limit on how far back or forward you can go?"

"So far as I am aware, the shortest time interval practical would be about twenty thousand years. The longest possible interval is somewhere in the range of two to three million years."

There were sharp intakes of breath, some quiet exclamations, and a few curses in reaction to that news.

"Obviously, that is another reason this technology is not practical for use in a timeshaft transportation system," DeSilvo went on. "There are others. For example, a gate draws power, a lot of it, while running. Therefore, it is not suited to continuous use. A wormhole, once established, remains after the power source used to form it is cut, though of course the nexuses and other equipment need to be powered up and maintained. Harmonic Gate timeshafts need to be turned on and off, at both ends—obviously, that requires coordination and timing."

DeSilvo paused and looked around the room. They were all watching, listening, considering. Good. Good.

"There is one thing a Harmonic Gate can do that no wormhole ever could. It can establish a link with the past *without another gate at the other end*. It requires vastly more power than a link anchored by gates at both ends, and it is massively inaccurate. Aim for a million years in the past on the first try, and you might hit 1.2 million, or 750,000. However, it should be possible to calibrate the gate to within about a 5 percent variance either way—which ought to be good enough for our purposes.

"There are a few other main points," he said, "though the first is so general that I would almost be tempted to say it is philosophical rather than technical.

"Let me start with what is something of a shopping list." He used his right hand to count on the fingers of his left, ticking off each item as he mentioned it. "Temporal confinement. Timeshaft wormholes. The artificial gravity generators that are so commonplace nowadays that we never think of them. The faster-than-light transportation and communications systems we have discussed already. And now, Harmonic Gate time travel. These wondrous technologies—and *all* of them are wondrous, it is just that we are more used to some than others—these technologies are not each off by itself, isolated one from the other. They are, instead, different aspects of the same thing, different facets of the same jewel, if you wish to be poetic.

"And it is not just the long-hidden wonders that have been distorted by the CP's policy of technology suppression. The development of even the old familiar ones have likewise been crippled. Temporal confinement was held back for centuries, made much more expensive and difficult to operate and manipulate than it really had to be.

"You are, all of you, I am sure, justly proud of what you accomplished with the Ignition Project. But I tell you the planet-sized temporal confinement that made it possible need not have been a new and untried technique. I can show you evidence from the archives of the Dark Museum that demonstrates that procedures and technologies similar to what you used were known at least seven hundred years ago."

"Just a moment, please," said Captain Sotales. "Are you suggesting that the Chronologic Patrol, of all institutions, has been deliberately harming all of humanity by withholding and suppressing technology?"

"If I might answer that, Dr. DeSilvo?" asked Koffield.

"Please, yes, Admiral." The answer would go down better coming from him.

Koffield turned to Sotales. "I dedicated decades of my life to the Chronologic Patrol, and I do not regret a moment of it," he said. "The Patrol has done great good—and continues to do great good—for all of humanity. But that is a long way from saying the CP is incapable of doing harm, or of making mistakes. Tech suppression made sense, for a while. It still makes sense—if you assume there is no way out, no hope, and only failure and withdrawal to come—or if you believe the coming collapse will spare Earth. *If* they believe that Earth will survive, but no other world will, then a policy of managing the contraction of interstellar civilization—slowing the rate of expansion, reducing the overall population and thus reducing the eventual number of refugees—is a humane and civilized choice.

"But all *our* studies show that Earth, too, will die. We will *all* die. Then all we are balancing is life or death for some, now, against how soon death, extinction, will come for all. How you can make a moral or humane choice, how you can strike that balance, I have no idea.

"All the evidence points to universal death in about a thousand years if we go on as we are. Either the leaders of the Chronologic Patrol do not know that, or they cannot allow themselves to believe it, or they are hoping for some sort of miracle to solve the problem—or perhaps they do things as they do them because that is what they have always done. The Chronologic Patrol has survived longer than many civilizations. Perhaps that is simply too long."

DeSilvo moved on. "Thank you, Admiral. There is another point concerning the relatedness of all this technology," he said. "The project we have described today will require the skill and effort of many people. And, of course, it will require expertise in terraforming. Greenhouse has the expertise—and is importing the people, even as we speak.

"It will require expertise in large-scale generators similar to those used in temporal confinement. It will require the ability to manage a massive power source and experience in large-scale engineering. You have all of those things here, thanks to the Ignition Project, and in large part, those resources, built at great expense and used but once, are now simply gathering dust.

"You here, now, have all the tools you need to make this plan work. Much of what it would cost you, you have already spent. Most of what you need, you already have, and do not otherwise need. *You* can do this. I doubt very much whether anyone else can. Please, *do this job*. The future is in your hands—if only you will reach deep into space, and far into the past, and create the hope that all of humankind needs."

The room was silent, and the faces around the table were blank. DeSilvo understood. *This is no time for applause, for enthusiasm, for praise,* he thought. *Fair enough. But what does this silence mean?*

"All right," said Neshobe Kalzant, her voice striking that silence so hard it seemed to bounce off it and come back again, echoed and amplified. "Enough," she said.

She stood up, so suddenly that the rest of the gathering was caught off guard, everyone scrambling to get to their feet as she rose. "We'll all meet again later."

She turned to Sotales. "No one is to leave or enter this building until further notice. Confiscate or secure every comm device. There are to be no communications in or out, of any kind, except with my prior approval. I can think of about sixteen problems you'll have in obeying that order, and I don't care about any of them. Make it happen."

"Yes, ma'am."

"Right," she said, and turned toward the door. "Admiral Koffield, you're with me." She walked out of the room without bothering to confirm that he was following.

She led him to an office down the hall—the director's office, judging by the look of it. Koffield had a feeling that the director wouldn't be seeing it for a while. Kalzant wouldn't ease the lockdown she had just ordered until she felt very much in control of the situation, and that wasn't going to happen anytime soon.

Off to the left there was a big, fancy desk, with a very comfortable-looking chair behind it. A separate conversation area, with equally comfortable-looking armchairs, side tables, and a fully automated service system was off to the right. There were large windows in the wall behind the desk. They looked out into a small park. The lights came on and adjusted themselves as soon as they were in the room, and soft music began to play.

At the moment, the most noticeable features of the view from the windows were the security personnel who had been stationed at the entrances to the park and, no doubt, all around the perimeter of the research center.

How wide a cordon will Sotales throw around us? Koffield wondered. *The research center? A surrounding two-block radius? The whole dome? All of Greenhouse?* It occurred to him that he had once again more or less volunteered to become a prisoner.

He looked out the window behind the desk. He had

walked in that park, with Norla—how long ago? Only a couple of years or so, judging by the calendar. A lifetime or more, judging by how much they had all been through. He remembered thinking then that his work was over, that he had done all he could, and could hand off the tasks in hand to those best able to deal with them. It hadn't quite worked out that way.

Kalzant didn't pay any of the room's comforts the slightest attention. She walked to the far side of the room and slapped her hand down on the window opacifiers. All the windows turned a dull, solid silver. The room lights adjusted themselves. Kalzant turned around, but stayed standing where she was, back to the wall.

"So," Kalzant began, "all you're asking me for is a declaration of war against all the laws of our civilization, against causality, against our universal doom, against history, against the Chronologic Patrol and Earth if they find out. Is there anything or anyone *else* you want me to take on?"

There seemed no way to answer that, and Koffield did not try.

Kalzant was quiet for a time. "He's not crazy," she said, crossing her arms. "DeSilvo. At least you don't think so, or you wouldn't have brought him here. So I won't bother asking your opinions on that score."

"Agreed," Koffield said. "You'll just have to judge his sanity, and mine, for yourself."

"Oh, good," Kalzant said. "And don't forget I'll have to judge my own. It's in question, you know, on the face of it. After all, I listened to all of that in there." She leaned the back of her head against the wall and shut her eyes. "So we'll skip ahead to the next question. Can it be done? Even if you and DeSilvo are both sane, you could simply be wrong—or the victims of some sort of huge fraud, or hoax. Maybe even part of some huge Chronologic Patrol front operation, a setup to test whether we would dare violate causality. Or some damn thing like that."

"The best answer I can give is to say that I arrived

here aboard a spacecraft, a starship, that traveled faster than light. The transit from the outer system, where our ship is, took nearly as long as the journey from Glister to the Solace system. I cannot imagine the Chronologic Patrol willingly setting an FTL ship loose just to entrap us, or you. The risks would be far too great."

"Risks!" She laughed. "I've got nothing but risk all around me. In fact, I don't have *risks,* I have a certainty. No matter what I do, or don't do, my planet is going to die, and my people will have no place to live. We can keep them here on Greenhouse, at least for a while, at least most of them. But not forever."

"If your planet is going to die," Koffield said, "perhaps it is time to find your people a new one. Or make one."

Kalzant nodded toward the conference room, and DeSilvo. "Can it work?" she asked. "Is it even *possible* to build a habitable planet this way?"

"I've studied that question as carefully as I could, and yes, I believe it is. Of course, saying it can work is a vastly different thing from saying it *will* work."

"All right. *Will* it work?"

"I think the odds of producing a new Eden on the first try are, shall we say, limited. If we are not discouraged by failure, if we study our mistakes and profit from them—then, yes. I believe it will work—eventually. But—if we persevere, at the end of the day, we will have a living world. That, I suggest, is a prize worth a high price—and it is only part of the prize we will win."

"I know," Kalzant said wearily. "Hope. We will win for all of humanity, by showing that it can be done, and so on and so forth." Kalzant started pacing the center of the room. Koffield sidled over to the desk and leaned against one corner of it, giving her room. "So we fail two or three times," Kalzant said, "and then, maybe, we succeed. Then it's a mere question of transporting our entire population—if they haven't all died by then—across who knows how many light-years, to their new home."

"The transport is doable," Koffield said. "We know

how to move a lot of people over long distances. Big transports, shuttling back and forth. If we put the passengers into temporal confinement, and use the FTL drive, we won't have much in the way of life-support needs."

"That's a comfort, I suppose," Kalzant muttered. "Next question: Can we get away with it? Can we keep the project secret long enough to terraform the world?"

"I don't know," Koffield admitted. "DeSilvo did a pretty fair job of making it look like we fought each other and killed each other at Glister—and let's just say that it wouldn't be too hard to believe that I might want to kill DeSilvo. I assume the Chrono Patrol will track us that far, sooner or later. How much farther they will get, I don't know."

"But if they *do* catch us, and we're lucky, it's a one-way trip to a domed penal colony on a very unpleasant world for anyone who knows anything, or even *might* know something."

"Yes."

"Next question. The Chrono Patrol would want to stop us because we'd be going into the past to take action, and they equate that with doing harm, with endangering causality," she said. "Are they right? *Can* we take adequate precautions? Can we be sure that we won't accidentally set up some horrible paradox? Can we be absolutely certain that, for example, a deranged person couldn't steal an FTL starship, go into the past, fly to the Solar System, and drop an asteroid on East Africa before *Homo sapiens* has evolved? Can we be sure we won't make humanity extinct?"

Koffield shook his head. "No. We can set up layer after layer after layer of precaution, but nothing is ever foolproof. Any tool can be abused. But—we *can* be sure humanity will be extinct. All we have to do is nothing, and the job will get done, in a thousand years or so."

"Damn you!" Kalzant said, but her voice was cold, controlled. "Why the *hell* did you bring this to me?" She paced back and forth, back and forth, a time or two, then spoke again. "It's like the balance you were talking about before. What the CP is doing—allowing this piece of technology, suppressing that insurrection, slowing down or speeding up those refugee flows is merely balancing present comfort against the time remaining until extinction. But for us to act might be the death of us all—might even prevent us, prevent all of us, from ever existing in the first place."

Koffield let her pace, let her think, a moment longer before he replied. "You're right, Madam Executive. The danger in acting, is that we *might,* despite all precautions, go back and kill our grandparents. The certain result if we do *not* act is that we will be leaving all our grandchildren to die."

She stopped pacing and looked at him sadly. She walked around behind the desk and turned off the opacifiers. Sunlight flooded the room, and the room lights dimmed down to nothing. She stood there, staring out at the lovely garden, one of thousands humanity had placed on the cold and barren world of Greenhouse. "That garden deserves a chance to live," she said. "So did the people who made it."

She turned, pulled out the director's seat, and dropped heavily down into it. She pulled the chair into the desk and set her hands down flat on top of it. "People like to tell me that leadership is about choices. And yes, sometimes it *is* about choosing one action over the other. But you know what I know. Sometimes it's in having the courage to see that you have no choice and pressing on, moving forward, no matter what. Gods and stars for my witness, I don't know if I *have* that courage." She looked up at him, and she was scared. Terrified. "But I'm going to try to find it," she said, her voice close to breaking. "I'm sure as hell going to try."

Anton Koffield felt almost ashamed to see her so exposed, with all defenses down, humbly accepting the nightmare he had thrust upon her. But he, too, had led. He, too, had been taking paths he had no choice but to take.

"Yes, Madam Executive," he said at last. "We're all of us going to try."

Chapter Twenty-seven

THE LONG WAY AROUND

All of them did try.

Zak Destan tried, without even knowing what it was about. There was a lot of work for his people to do, not so far different from what they had done before—planting and plowing and sowing for the new plants in the new-made domes, fertilizing and composting for next season's plant life, reclaiming and recycling all the debris and biomass from the wreckage of past dome failures.

But there were other jobs, too, that weren't anything like farming. One of the biggest jobs was the disassembly of the Ignition Day Power Reception Array panels, followed by the reinstallation of the individual receptors themselves on new panels.

There was a strong prejudice against hand labor in the highly automated, upper-heavy culture of Greenhouse. Even their agriculture had been largely automated, and perhaps would be again, someday. But Zak knew he had a winning hand. "You need warm bodies," he told the Greenhousers, over and over, "because there's not enough cold machines. And that means you need *us*."

He said it loud enough, and often enough, to be heard. Soon his peasants were busily cannibalizing Groundside Power, working by hand, stripping the receptors off the Array panels as fast as the service robots could remove them from their stanchions and bring them inside.

Villjae Benzen tried, constantly pressed forward, not only by what DeSilvo and Koffield had said but also by all that he had learned from the near disaster of Ignition Day. But more than either, he was endlessly haunted by what Beseda Mahrlin had said, in her strange, clipped cadence, once Ignition Day was all over. She'd warned him then of the pattern that seemed burned into the Solacian culture. *"Always the same. Big delays, then the quick fix, the rush job. That's how we started. DeSilvo spent forever telling everyone he'd found a way to terraform fast, lost time getting ready—then cut enough corners to say he got done on time."* Now they were all in another crash program, to build a time machine—a time machine!—and dive a million years into the past.

Even so, the words she had said next were the words that echoed loudest for him. *"We can't go on this way,"* she'd said. *"Have to change. But I don't know. Might be too late. Maybe the way things are, the way we are— maybe we find out that we just plain can't go on at all."*

And yet, what choice did they have? There was so little time. Solace was dying, failing, even as they worked. Greenhouse could be a lifeboat, but it could not support the whole population of Solace forever. They needed a new world, as fast as possible. They had to find a suitable candidate world. And just to begin work on the hardware they would need to use instruments, power systems, generators that did not yet exist.

That was part of DeSilvo's plan for securing the massive power supplies that would be required. His solution was typically audacious: They would refuel, refurbish, and restart the old SunSpot, reorienting it so that its light beam shone outward. No one had ever considered restarting it before, or even thought of it as possible. Once the NovaSpot project was under way, there had been no reason for restarting the SunSpot. But now there would be, and DeSilvo was making it happen.

The cannibalized receptors were part of that plan. They would be boosted into orbit and put to use there, channeling power from the SunSpot to the Harmonic

Rings, beginning with the Test Articles they were already starting to build.

Elber Malloon tried, because he knew far more than he wanted. After the massive security lapse that had resulted in Elber and Villjae being present at that first big meeting, it was a near thing indeed that Elber wasn't slapped into detention for the duration, just on general principles. It was, ironically enough, Olar Sotales who vouched for him, saying flatly that Elber could be trusted. Sotales, in fact, went farther out on a limb than anyone could quite understand. Elber, however, was not going to argue.

Nor was he going to tempt fate by not living up to Sotales' assurances of his loyalty and honesty. He was instrumental in making the deals that got Zak Destan's people to work replanting the domes. He endlessly pestered Beseda Mahrlin, who had taken over for Villjae, to get more work, more responsibility, not only for "his" people, but all of the lowdowns and peasants who were starting to pour in.

Elber also simply tried to *understand*, studying the problems, the history, the physics as best he could. He tried out what he had learned on Villjae, late one night, back in the common room by the dormitory. Villjae had fished out a couple of beers from somewhere, and the two of them were doing their diligent best to relax. "So," said Elber, "the core problem is, the *faster* you terraform a planet, the faster it dies, right?"

"It's a lot more complicated than that, but yeah, close enough."

"So they figure they have to take a long time—a *real* long time—to terraform a planet, so it'll last? Work a million years, and it'll last another million?"

"Or even longer. After a while, the terraformed planet will develop a lot of the self-correcting features of a natural ecosystem—it'll be able to fix itself, more or less. If something throws it out of balance, the natural feedback systems will respond and correct. It ought to last a lot *longer* than a million years."

"But how can they keep at the job that long?"

"They can't, of course. That's the beauty of it. The problem with all the previous terraforming techniques was there wasn't enough *time* for each process. Instead of, say, giving algae ten thousand years to convert an atmosphere to a nitrogen-oxygen mix, they'd give the algae fifty, doing everything possible to force it along—and they'd be doing ten other jobs at once. This way, they drop the algae, and leave it alone for ten thousand years—maybe twenty thousand, just to be on the safe side. Let it really dig in, take over the place." Villjae thought for a moment. "Like Mars, sort of. You've seen pictures. Basically one life-form took over the whole place. It's had time to establish itself."

"But they don't want to end up with something like Mars!" Elber protested.

"No, of course not. We don't want to end *up* like Mars—but an interim step might look that way. What the symbiote-molds on Mars have done is mostly stuff you'd *want* to have happen, in the early stages of terraforming. The molds have processed the soil, broken up the surface, generated a lot of dead organic matter. And, sooner or later, that mold will have eaten up all there is to eat on the planet. It'll die, or go dormant, or something. That's when you drop in something—maybe five or six somethings—that really like to eat dormant mold. Then you wait another ten thousand years, and drop in twenty species that like to eat those five or six somethings. And so on, and so on."

"I guess I get it. Go on."

"So, anyway, they wait a long time. Then they come back, see what's worked, what's gone wrong—taking as much time as they like to study things, make corrections, get everything just right before they take the next step. And there are other things where it's good to take more time—like comet drops."

"*Comet* drops?"

"I'm no expert, but that's the usual way to get water to a planet that doesn't have enough of its own. Go out to the outer system and redirect comets to drop on the planet. Trouble is, it takes a *lot* of comets to do it, and they beat the hell out of the planet. Big impacts, that can kill off everything you've been trying to grow. On a regular terraforming job, where you've only got a few centuries for the job, you *have* to drop them in as fast as you can. But if you have a million years—hell, just set some robots loose. Program them to find comets, slice them up into little pieces—snowballs, say a meter across—and throw them at the planet, over and over and over again. Instead of maybe a couple of dozen, or even a few hundred major impact events, you get a few million snowballs that all get vaporized when they hit the atmosphere. Much gentler. You do everything that way—slowly, carefully, finishing one step before going on to the next. Leave the planet alone in between, and just keep coming back every few thousand years, until you've reached the present."

"All right. I guess I've got all that. But what's the bit about having to use an undiscovered planet?"

"Well, strictly speaking, an *unsurveyed* one—one that no one knows anything about, aside from its mass, orbit, and what star it's orbiting. But my guess is that they'd like to find their own completely undiscovered planet, just to be sure. See, right now, before we've done the job, the planet we're going to do is just dead rock. But once we start messing around in its past, its *current* appearance is gonna change. Even from a few light-years off, you'll be able to detect water, oxygen, temperature changes, and so on. But, if we know that, in our future, we're going to go back into that planet's *past* and change the planet—well, if we check its spectrum and temperature *right now*—what will we find?"

Elber frowned. "Wait a minute—if we haven't already changed it, but we're going to change it, then right now if we look at it—" He shook his head. "I don't know."

"Neither does anyone else. They figure the safest thing is not to look at all—pick someplace no one has ever looked at, so there's no prior record that could produce a paradox. The plan is that they never even *look* at the present-day planet until the job is done. They'll do all their time traveling from as far away from it as possible, so they won't be close enough to see it from now. They'll drop into the past light-years from the target, and go to and from it on slowboat ships using cryonics. They sure as hell don't want to risk taking FTL drives or timeshafts or temporal confinements a million years into the past."

"But that's crazy!"

"Yeah, but the math works. So we pick a planet, but don't peek at it, then go back in time and terraform it."

"Suppose it turns out that something's wrong with the planet—something they couldn't tell because they didn't look?"

"Then they move on to the next planet on the list." Villjae shook his head. "A hell of a way to do business, if you ask me. There ought to be a better way."

Elber Malloon nodded thoughtfully, finished the last of his beer, and frowned down at the table, trying to understand.

Olar Sotales, ordered to provide security and keep the project secret, tried, and succeeded quite well, at least in his own area of expertise. The number of persons in the inner circle increased only a little as time went by. His office concocted plausible cover stories, prevented any number of potential leaks, conducted a most efficient rumor control service, performed regular inspections of facilities, and also conducted weekly security interviews with those in the know. It was during his second such interview with Malloon, about three weeks after DeSilvo and Koffield had dropped their bombshells, that Sotales noticed something about Malloon that no one else had—not even Elber himself.

Elber had developed four small, almost undetectable red blemishes—one at the outside corner of each eye, and one on each earlobe. Sotales found excuses to wander into Malloon's office several times over the next few days so that he could check on the blemishes. As best he could tell, they only lasted a day or so, and didn't ever cause Elber any particular distress.

The blemishes were, of course, the only outside indication that the microcameras and microphones were breaking down, dissolving away. Presumably, there were larger, and perhaps more tender, blemishes on Elber's upper arms as well.

So much for what had been a most productive intelligence source. There was no practical way he could see to arrange installing a new set of microbugs in Elber. It was over. Sotales took the matter philosophically enough. He had gotten a great deal of use from the bugs.

At least, he thought he had. His own actions had in large part been guided by what the bugs told him on the one hand and by the necessity of protecting their secret on the other. One could almost make the case that Elber had been running *him,* instead of the other way around.

He wasn't the first spymaster to get tangled up inside the web he himself had spun. Besides, it was due to him that Elber got to Destan, and thus set in motion the chain of events that led to the smooth and orderly journey to Greenhouse of all the Wilhemton refugees. The propaganda surrounding *that* accomplishment had allowed the movement of refugees to Greenhouse to be generally smooth and orderly as well. Result: no major panics, just a few minor riots, hardly any mob violence. That was no small accomplishment.

No one would ever know the role he had played, but still he had his rewards. Founder's Dome was a small place, and he met little Zari Malloon a time or two. The knowledge that he had contributed, however tangentially, however secretly, to making that little baby girl happy and safe, and that he had done the same for quite a number of others, was compensation enough.

It wasn't easy, being a secret policeman with a heart and a conscience. Sotales had always tried to keep the fact that he had both strictly secret.

But even he knew, deep in his heart, that if anyone ever spotted him watching Zari on the playground, his cover was going to be blown wide open.

Marquez, and the remaining crew of the *Dom Pedro IV,* tried. Sotales had been most insistent that they keep the ship herself concealed, simply to prevent the sight of her from exciting gossip. He was even more emphatic in saying that under no circumstances could she use the FTL drive.

For all they knew, the *Dom Pedro IV*'s FTL drive would light up the right sort of detector like a nova bomb from twenty light-years away. If there were such detectors, it was a sure bet the Chrono Patrol had them. And if they had them, then it was a virtual certainty that those detectors were powered up and operating.

Therefore, until they had the time to bring in some physicists and theorists and engineers who could study the drive, and its potential field effects, in detail, or unless some dire emergency required it, the *Dom Pedro IV* would stay out of sight and powered down.

That, of course, left the crew at loose ends, but not for long. The *Dom Pedro IV* had been designed to take care of herself for fifty or a hundred years at a time, self-navigating the transit between stars. She could easily be left in standby mode for a month or two, even a year or two. The two auxiliary craft still with the *DP-IV*—the *Nova Sol*'s sister ship *Terra Nova* and the *Cruzeiro do Sul*—could certainly be put to use—there was a systemwide shortage of spacecraft of all types. The whole ship's complement came on in—but not before following, to the letter, DeSilvo's infuriatingly detailed instructions on what cargo should be brought along and what should be left behind. There were parts, tools, equipment, training manuals, and any number of other things they would absolutely have to have to build the first Harmonic Gates.

Once they arrived, Marquez and the members of his crew were immediately put to work on any number of transport jobs—anything where it might be necessary for someone in the know to do the work. By using the *Dom Pedro* people to the fullest, Sotales was able to hold to an absolute minimum the number of people who had to be informed.

On the same principle, Wandella Ashdin was made administrative director. Her scholarship had always been focused and organized—but nothing else in her life ever had been. But Sotales judged that a marginally competent, but utterly trustworthy, head of admin who was already fully briefed was preferable to a briskly efficient and experienced bureaucrat who would immediately start asking some very awkward questions.

Norla and Koffield tried—tried to be everywhere at once, meeting with everyone who needed a meeting, coordinating a thousand different details, helping Ashdin unsnarl her paperwork when it got too far out of control, troubleshooting—and frequently helping DeSilvo in his work.

For DeSilvo was trying, too. Perhaps trying harder than anyone else.

They had gotten away with his wearing an improvised disguise and risking movement through the public areas of Research Dome on first arrival, but no one wanted to take any more chances than necessary on his being recognized. Rumors had started to circulate, despite Sotales' best efforts. One or two of the wilder stories floating around actually mentioned DeSilvo by name. That put his face and image in people's minds, and so vastly increased the odds that he would be spotted if he did go out.

If DeSilvo were to appear publicly, it would cause the sensation of the century. The founder of Solace, returning from the dead—there would have been no hope of suppressing the story.

Sotales absolutely forbade him to go out in public, and even DeSilvo was forced to see the logic of that. So he was a prisoner, of sorts—but he was also the managing director of a massive engineering operation, working closely with Berana Drayax. He also served as a sort of one-man faculty, running training sessions on a half dozen subjects, from Harmonic Gate operations to FTL navigation. It was a strange situation. The teacher knew only the basics of the subjects, but he knew more than any other person alive. It was a question of telling his students as much as he understood, then getting out of the way and letting them at the source materials he had brought along from Glister.

Terraforming of any sort was a nearly forgotten discipline, a topic generally regarded as being for historians to study. What the researchers at the Terraformation Research Center called terraforming might more accurately be called climate repair, or ecology maintenance. Here too, DeSilvo—the Founder of Solace, the grand old man of terraforming, rediscoverer of the works of Ulan Baskaw, who knew the subject backward and forward—was the teacher.

It was perfectly reasonable for him to present his lectures on the subject, but it was also deeply ironic. After all, he was, of course, also Oskar DeSilvo, the wrecker of Solace, the grand old fraud of terraforming, and the plagiarizer and bowdlerizer of Baskaw's work, who didn't know the subject well enough to have kept Solace from its present crisis.

There was further irony in that he had spent his career seeking ways to make terraforming faster—and now he proposed to do it a thousand times more slowly than it had ever been done. All of them did try.

The wonder of it all was how close they came to success.

They did let DeSilvo out, occasionally, under controlled circumstances, and by prearrangement. One evening Sotales set things up for him to stroll about in Founder's Dome, and he asked to be accompanied by Koffield, Wandella Ashdin, and Norla Chandray. All of them agreed at once.

Norla understood what the walk was for and felt quite sure the other two had guessed as well. DeSilvo's crimes might have been unspeakable, beyond any possibility of suitable punishment—but the man was clearly doing penance, along with making heroic efforts to make amends. He had no right to require their presence, but they were willing to give it to him if he asked.

It was hard not to think of the last time the three of them had made the same journey. They had traveled on the surface, in pressure suits, because Founder's was about to be destroyed, and all the tunnels had been sealed.

He was waiting for them just outside the airlock entrance of the tunnel that led back to Research Dome. "Good evening to you all," he said, his courtesy much more practiced, and at the same time far more real, more natural, than it had been when first they had seen him on Glister. It was clear to Norla that he was relearning the skills of living among people and making good use of the lessons. "Thank you for coming," he said. "Captain Sotales' people have cordoned off a large portion of the dome for our use, but they've made it clear it can only be for an hour or so. Shall we be on our way?"

There was no false, coy, coming-upon-it-by-chance games about their walk. Perhaps the old DeSilvo would have led them around in circles for a half hour before arriving, by startling coincidence, at his own tomb. They would have been left to wonder if he was counting on their good manners not to point out he wasn't fooling anybody, or if, instead, he was determinedly fooling himself, forcing some part of his mind at least to believe, most sincerely, that it was all chance.

That would have been his way in days gone by, Norla reflected. Now he led them straight to the place.

The tomb was, at first glance, much as they had left it. Their journey, in a very real sense, had begun there, on that very spot. It had led them to Asgard Five, to the Grand Library, to the Permanent Physical Collection, to Earth, to Mars, to Glister—and back again.

A low, six-sided marble building, one side open to the elements—or at least, to the interior of the dome—the open side aligned with the west. The whole affair was seated on a set of six stacked hexagonal platforms, each smaller than the one below and centered on it, thus forming low, broad stairs to the upper platform. The five exterior walls were decorated with somewhat overworked allegories and symbols.

But on second glance, Norla could see the changes time had wrought—the marble showed scars and scratches where the violence of the dome explosion had thrown shrapnel hard enough to mark it. Norla could see two or three places where the stone had been repaired, leaving a cemented-in patch of stone that did not quite match the original. There were still faint scorch marks noticeable on the lowest step, where some burning brand had fallen and remained there, roasting the stone, until the dome itself blew open, and all the air roared out.

"Around in a circle," Norla said. "Here we all are again."

"Not *quite* true," said DeSilvo with a smile. "You three have been here before. I have not." He laughed, but there was little of humor in the sound. "I wasn't really those ashes in the urn. I was only pretending to be dead," he said. "Again."

He walked up the low steps, and into the structure, the others following. Norla stepped inside, then turned and looked out from the entrance. The last time they had been there, she had looked out through the same doorway and seen the fires of hell, the belching smoke of doom. Now the sun—no, NovaSpot—was setting over a cool green lawn, dotted with vigorous young saplings. Things had changed.

She turned back to the interior. There was more damage there, and less effort at repair, as if the inside of the tomb didn't matter so much. And in a sense, it didn't. After all, the man it had been meant for was right in front of her, gazing at the memorial he had designed for himself. A marble sphere in front of the wall of the tomb opposite the entrance, and a gold cylinder of understatedly simple design, sat upon the sphere. The single word DESILVO was etched into the urn, and the legend THE FOUNDER was carved into the floor beneath the sphere.

DeSilvo looked up at the urn that still purported to hold his ashes, for he was still dead so far as the outside world was aware. "When at last I *do* die, truly die," he said, "bury me anyplace but here. Stick me in the ground, cremate me, donate me to science, or to a medical school—or to a museum of prosthetics, or a carnival show, if you think it more appropriate—but do not put me here. This place is a lie. Let us not dignify the falsehood by making it true.

When people know the truth about me, let them vandalize the place if they like, or turn this place into a storage shed, or a puppet theater for the children. That might even be a fitting indignity, somehow. I treated enough people like puppets, with me to pull the strings. You three perhaps most of all." He was silent for a time, staring up at his own false tomb. "My apologies, to all of you."

"We cut the strings a while back," Koffield said, and gently put his hand on the older man's shoulder. "And somehow, I don't think they will vandalize the place when they learn the truth—because they'll learn the *whole* truth. I promise you that. The good, the bad, and all that's in between." He looked around himself, considering the tomb's interior. "Perhaps a monument to Ulan Baskaw," he said. "Or perhaps a small museum, just a few small exhibits about her, about you—"

"And about *you*," said DeSilvo. "You had something to do with what happened."

Koffield smiled. "All right, something about me as well. But *not* a storage shed. And, with all due respect to a noted architect, I don't think it would make a very good puppet theater."

DeSilvo, in their presence, was saying good-bye—not to them, but to himself, to DeSilvo the myth, the hero, the De-Silvo who could be no more. Farewell to all of the things he had been, for they all required illusions and deceptions and concealments that simply weren't there anymore.

He could never again play the part of the lord of all he surveyed. No more could he be the revered and spotless hero of the founding of Solace, his portrait hung everywhere. The acts he had set in motion made it inevitable: Sooner or later, the universe would know that he was far less—and far more—than the Founder.

They did not remain inside long, and DeSilvo was unusually silent as they came outside. He turned and considered the structure for a long time. "Dr. Ashdin—back on Glister, you noted at some length my habit of repeatedly finding ways to simulate death, to pretend that I am dead—and this place proves your point. But I think there is another side to the story.

"I have spent most of my adult life being afraid of life itself—of human life, of real contact, real events, of emotion and passion. I know that is why I was attracted to architecture. Clean, straight lines, solid, permanent shapes, right angles and the ideal shapes of geometry brought as close as possible to being real.

"Being dead was one way to hide, to keep my distance. I think perhaps that being revered, lionized, was another. Who would dare come near me? Perhaps building my own world was just a way to let me escape from the universe of humanity and be turned into a nice, safe, sterile icon."

"You can paint a lot of pretty pictures with psychology," said Wandella Ashdin. "But it doesn't mean they are true. And a lot of people deal with a fear of life's disorder without terraforming planets. You are what you are, and you did what you did."

"All granted," he said calmly. "I seek an explanation for my actions—not an excuse."

Norla decided it might be wise to change the subject.

"They'll be ready soon," she said, gesturing upward toward the sky. No one had to be told she meant the first tests of a Harmonic Gate Ring. "It's all gone amazingly fast. Another week or two, and they'll be ready to do the first engineering runs."

"Yes," said DeSilvo. "They've done very well, and they're learning quickly. Soon, they won't need me at all." There was something halfway between pride and wistfulness in his voice.

"They're using the *Lodestar VII* as the command center for the first tests," DeSilvo said. "I hope you'll all be aboard."

Wandella Ashdin smiled. "Of course," she said. "I wouldn't miss it for the world."

As Captain Marquez remarked several times as the day of the first test approached, everything was harder and took longer. There were inevitable delays, waiting for this component to arrive, for that ArtInt to be properly programmed, for those two or three construction mistakes to be repaired—and for the correction of one design flaw that would have caused the gate to fail within nanoseconds, if a junior engineer hadn't had the nerve to question an obvious mistake that had been approved four times already. The delays were almost comforting, the sorts of headaches that attended any technical construction job.

Every department that didn't *cause* a given delay was grateful for the gift of time each delay supplied. When Department A caused a delay, Departments B, C, and D used the time to upgrade, improve, and make right whatever had been done on the rush—with the result that Department B wasn't *quite ready* once A had sorted things out. And, inevitably, A, C, and D also thought of things that needed doing while they were waiting . . .

Koffield didn't envy Drayax her duties as test director, and especially didn't envy Villjae Benzen the even worse job of assistant test director. Still, somehow, they managed to ride herd on all of the problems, allowing the absolutely needed repairs while keeping the endless fiddling and tweaking to a minimum. Somehow or another, only a month or so later than expected, they were ready—or nearly ready.

They were using the same shipboard command center as had been set up for Ignition Day. However, the first Harmonic Gate test was a secret, and a closely held one at that. There were seats for twenty-five controllers on the main level, but only eight were in use. And though the observation platform was large enough for a hundred or more, even after Koffield's party came aboard there were usually only about half a dozen or so people actually there. There were ten or fifteen observers aboard the ship, but there was precious little to observe until one or two last glitches were ironed out, and the test itself could take place.

Koffield guessed that most of his companions were in the *Lodestar VII*'s legendary Executive Bar, reputed to be the best-stocked ship's lounge in all the Solacian system. He planned to investigate the truth of that for himself presently, but for the moment he was content to lean over the railing and watch the test crew at work and to look upon the object of their attention.

The large display was showing a medium close-up of the most unromantically named Harmonic Gate Test Article, with inset images of different views set in the four corners, and blank bits of the screen filled up with the sorts of charts and diagrams that seemed to make people feel better.

The Test Article was in a distant orbit of Comfort, with *Lodestar VII* station-keeping, a few kilometers ahead in the same orbit, close enough for telescopic lenses to provide an excellent view. The main structure of the Test Article consisted of three rings, each nested inside the other. There was no physical connection between the rings, but they were held rigidly in position relative to each other by induced gravity fields.

The whole affair was twenty-five meters across. The rings had been painted white, with location numbers to aid in later image-analysis of their interactions. The inner ring was numbered in red, the center in green, and the outer in blue. The camera had the center ring face on and it was easy to read the labels: 2A, 2B, 2C, 2D. One wag had suggested labeling one location 2B and all the others Not2B.

The opposite side of the rings were studded with some of the power receptors scavenged from Ground-side Power Reception. The SunSpot wasn't going to be anywhere near refurbished or ready for use in time for the first tests, but then, the Test Article wouldn't require anywhere near as much power as the SunSpot could provide. A much smaller, off-the-shelf conventional power-sender beam would be sufficient to charge the Test Article's power accumulators.

Each of the three rings would generate its own distinct field, and the fields would interact with each other. Once they achieved a certain precise pattern of interference, their harmonic resonances would interact as well, cutting a three-dimensional hole in time. In theory, once the gate was activated, anything within the volume of space defined by the spinning inner ring would be projected into the past.

For the first runs, at least, the plan was to leave that volume empty and to expend terrifying amounts of energy merely to send a sphere of high-grade vacuum back in time. Later they would send calibrators back to give them at least some idea of temporal range. The calibrators were barely off the drawing board, but in essence they were to be extremely durable cameras attached to thrusters that would boost them away from Comfort and into highly stable orbits. From there, they would photograph the apparent positions of the stars, and the planets in the Solacian system.

After the calibrators had been launched into the past, special teams would go search for them in their predicted orbits. If any of them were found, the images they had preserved would, with a little luck, provide the needed dating information.

Koffield could not help but wonder. Would this latest last-ditch, all-out effort be enough to save them, or would this effort, coming on top of the Ignition Project and the renewal of Greenhouse, be enough to bankrupt them, defeat them, once and for all? Wandella Ashdin had warned them, long ago, that it was one all-out effort, and then another, and another, that had finally left Glister too exhausted to survive. And yet what choice did they have? It was either take the chance of later failure, or give up and die now.

The key thing was to get past this initial phase. They had to be close to the workshops and resources of Greenhouse and Solace, but that proximity made them easy to spot and vulnerable to attack. Koffield did not speak much of his fears on that point, as there was very little that could be done about them in any event.

But once they got their initial engineering done and were able to transport the Harmonic Gate equipment well away from Solace, to some secret location out between the stars—then they would be much harder to find, far harder to interfere with. Not completely safe, perhaps, but far better-off than they would be here. For the moment, they were months away from any chance of cutting loose from the machine shops and the expertise and equipment available at Greenhouse.

Koffield glanced away from the giant images of the Test Article, and over to the other people lingering on the observation platform. He noticed Elber Malloon, who was looking intently down at the control center itself, as if trying to read its secrets from on high.

He walked over to where the young man was leaning over the railing. "Hello," he said.

Elber looked up, startled. "Oh. Hello, ah, Admiral. Ah, sir. Is there, ah, something—something wrong?"

"No, no, it's all right," Koffield said, well used to people feeling too nervous to talk with him. "It's just that I like to know the people I'm working with, and we've never really had a chance to talk."

"We—we nearly did, once," Elber said. "From what I heard about later, it was your first day on SCO Station. You—you and Officer Chandray were on a runcar, going through Ring Park. My family was, ah, *staying* there. Your car stopped for a minute, right in front of us." Koffield thought Malloon was blushing, but it was hard to tell in the dim light. "I was, ah, thinking of that, just now, when you were looking at the Test Article. I was just thinking we both took the long way around to get next to each other again."

Koffield chuckled. "So we did—both of us. The long way around. All of us. Sometimes I feel as if I can't remember the last time I went straight for what I wanted to get. And now we're going to go a million years into the past to build the world we want for the future."

Elber nodded solemnly. "Yes, sir. I've thought about that a lot. Seems like such a big, complicated, *risky* thing to do, going back in time to make a living world."

Koffield nodded at the spot where he had just been. "I was just standing there, thinking pretty much the same thing. But I keep coming back to the question: What choice do we have?"

Malloon didn't seem to have any answer for that. The two of them stood there in silence, watching the test crew, each console in a pool of warm yellow light, each set about with the calm glowing colors of its display screens and their operations panels, islands of light that seemed to float in the dim-lit expanses of the command center. The image of the Test Article looked down from the main display, three neatly lettered concentric rings of purest white, hanging in the still darkness of space.

The first intimation that something was wrong came from the Test Article itself. The bright green lettering on ring two was suddenly blazing, glowing, while the letters on the other rings started to blacken and bubble. The whole ring took on a distinct greenish glow, and then the Test Article seemed to lurch to one side.

Down below, the test controllers, moments earlier calm and collected, were suddenly moving frantically. Red lights and warning buzzers went off on every panel. Suddenly people were calling to each other, shouting out alerts that no one could hear in the sudden pandemonium. Koffield heard one voice clearly through the welter of voices. "Temps off scale high!"

That was enough for him. He turned and ran to the comm panel on the back wall of the observation platform and punched in an emergency code.

"This is Koffield to ship's bridge. This is an emergency! No drill, emergency. Get away from the Test Article, as fast and far as you can. Now, now, now!"

"This is the duty officer," a puzzled voice answered. "Say again."

"This is Admiral Koffield," he said again, hoping his name and title would for once do some good and get the fool to listen. "Look at your views of the Test Article! It's going to go up! Get us away from it, now!"

Acceleration Klaxons sounded, and there was a massive jolt that knocked Koffield off his feet before the acceleration compensators corrected. In fact, they corrected so well, it was impossible to know if the ship was accelerating at all. He looked behind him, at the big screen, and saw that the view had not changed. Then he realized the imagery must have been coming from a remote camera platform in the first place. There was a small display on the comm panel, and he managed to use it to pull up a tactical display. Good. Good. The *Lodestar VII* was boosting away at high acceleration.

He turned his attention back to the view of the Test Article. Even in the few seconds his attention had been elsewhere, things had plainly gotten worse. The lettering on rings one and three had burned off completely, the surface of ring two was turning black, and the paint was bubbling up on ring two's lettering as well. A white-green plume suddenly sprouted from the edge of ring three, the outermost ring. Something was venting violently. The Test Article's drunken tumble grew worse, more violent. Then whatever had been venting gave way all at once, a bright flash-puff of gas that dissipated at once, revealing an ugly black hole torn in the ring's outer hull.

Any second now, Koffield thought. *Any second.*

It happened far too fast to see. One moment the Test Article was still there, badly damaged, but still recognizable. In the blink of an eye later it was gone, replaced by a flash of light, a flaring green-white cloud, and a sky full of cartwheeling debris.

After it was far too late, people started to rush in. De-Silvo, Norla, Sparten ran out onto the observation platform. Down below, Berana Drayax was rushing to her console and starting a hurried—and now pointless—conference with Benzen.

"What happened?" Norla demanded of no one in particular, and suddenly everyone was talking at once. "What was it?" "Did you see it?" "Did it go off by itself?" "What happened?"

Elber Malloon just shook his head, still in shock. "I don't know. I don't know. *No one* knows what happened!"

"No," Koffield said. He stared out at the expanding cloud of debris that had been all their hopes. "*I* know what happened," he said.

He had seen it with the eyes of the captain of a fighting ship, the perceptions of a practiced tactician. A long tracking burn shot from a gigawatt laser meant to disable, to pin the target and keep it from escaping. A green laser, which was why the green lettering reflected the light best, and held out the longest. Then, a volley of iron shot launched from a railgun at near-relativistic speed, the kill shot, intended to destroy. A very carefully timed and targeted attack, for the railgun shot must have been fired before the laser in order for the time-on-target to work out. At a guess, the attacking ship would be about fifteen thousand kilometers out, just coming up from behind Comfort's disk.

A ship that would smash more than just the Test Article. A ship that would turn all their effort, all their hopeful new beginnings, into nothing more than so much smoking wreckage.

"What happened," he said quietly, "is the end."

Chapter Twenty-eight

THE DEPTHS OF TIME

The debris cloud bloomed out as Burl and Kalani watched.

Kalani Temblar had often wished that she could have had it in her to give up, to decide to stop, to turn around and walk away. Other people seemed to manage it. She never had.

It had taken a solid month, and then some, before she and Burl had found DeSilvo's *real* Glister headquarters, roughly nine hundred kilometers northeast of the decoy.

By the time she found it, Burl Chalmers had been within a day or so of doing what he never did—issuing a direct order—so as to force her to give up. But Burl didn't issue that order, and Kalani had kept up her search, working from old maps and visual scans from orbit. When those failed to turn up anything in the area she suspected of containing DeSilvo's HQ, she powered up other sensor systems. And still Burl had kept his patience—barely.

The best she had been able to do was establish that one small settlement shown on the maps had disappeared—not exactly remarkable, given conditions on Glister. Still, all the other sites were still visible from orbit, and the site of the missing settlement was in about the right spot. It wasn't much to go on, but it was all she had.

Once the radar scans from orbit made it clear that there was something *big* buried at the 900NW site, as they came to call it, Burl eased off, at least a bit. On the other hand, as he pointed out more than once, there were a *lot* of buried installations on Glister. They had buried practically everything just before the final collapse of the planet.

Once on the surface, all she had to go on at first was an impression that some of the rock looked to have been moved recently—but neither she nor Burl was a forensic geologist, or whatever the expert on that sort of thing might be called—and neither of them knew remotely enough about the weather on Glister and how long it would take to wipe that "newness" off a shifted pile of rock.

But once she had indisputable readings that showed what could only be large, active, shielded power sources on standby, there beneath the surface, then at last Burl conceded defeat. In a sense, the difficulty in finding the base was part of the proof. The Chronologic Patrol's sensor systems were the best available, bar none—and even they had failed to find anything until they were right on top of the target.

The sensors told them there were machines and electronics still operating down there, all most carefully hidden. Unless someone *else* had been wandering about Glister, planting supersecret installations thither and yon, it had to be DeSilvo.

Which left them with the non-trivial task of getting into 900NW, somehow, and the further task of getting past DeSilvo's security. After plenty of false starts, they got in—after spending another month-plus on the job. Then, once they were in, they were for a time all but defeated by the simple immensity of what they had found.

They lost even more time searching the place for leads, until Burl found an unencrypted datapad that someone named Wandella Ashdin had left behind.

The datapad that told them the whole plan—and the reasons for it, in tremendous detail. They lost more time in the effort required simply to believe it could possibly all be true.

But too much effort had gone into preparing the information, and into hiding it, for it to be a lie. Too much of it rang true with all that Kalani had seen and learned before she ever got to Glister.

They had made copies of as much information as their own datastores could hold, then prepared to leave, making sure to leave Base Glister as well concealed as before they had found it.

It was a sore temptation to destroy what was near to being a second Dark Museum—but the place was a treasure trove of knowledge and equipment. It would be criminal to destroy it all. What decided Burl at last was the realization that DeSilvo had all the information already. He would not have traveled to Solace without taking full copies of the data with him.

Besides, the very existence of the Dark Museum demonstrated that Chronologic Patrol policy was to retain, conceal, and suppress dangerous technical knowledge, not to destroy it. Some or even most of the suppressed technology stored in Base Glister had been altogether lost to the Chronologic Patrol when the Dark Museum was destroyed, then looted by DeSilvo. The CP would have to know all about that hardware, if DeSilvo had the use of it. They left Base Glister intact.

All that accomplished, they began the long and weary journey to the Solace system, transiting the Starshine Station Wormhole en route. With so much material to study, they bought time by the simple expedient of cutting back on their stays in temporal confinement, staying in objective time for several months longer than they otherwise would have.

They had learned a lot in those months of study—enough to know what DeSilvo and company would be up to upon their arrival. Enough to understand what he was doing and to be scared to death by it.

Enough to stop him.

And enough to wonder, just a little, if they should.

But they had, anyway.

Kalani stared sadly at the expanding cloud of dust and debris that had been a small-scale Harmonic Gate a few minutes before. She did not feel proud, or even relieved. *Mission accomplished,* she thought. *Now Earth will die in a thousand years.*

"Hey, Burl?" she asked.

Burl glanced over at her from the pilot's console. "What?" he asked.

"I was wondering. Did we just score a stirring victory for death, defeatism, retreat, and extinction?"

He shook his head. "I dunno," he said. "I was asking myself the same question." He was silent for a time, watching the expanding cloud blooming outward into the nothingness that seemed to be the fate of all. "Come on," he said at last. "Let's head in and sweep up the pieces."

Admiral Koffield had warned them what might happen, long before. As usual, he was right. Koffield, naturally enough, handled the initial negotiations over the radio. It was agreed to hold the face-to-face negotiation—or perhaps surrender would be a better word—in the *Lodestar VII*'s main hangar deck. Not the most comfortable place to meet—but it would hold everyone and keep the issue of contact under some sort of control.

Koffield spoke to the group just before they went into the hangar deck. "There isn't much time," he said, "so please listen carefully and take what I tell you seriously. You were all briefed on this contingency as a hypothetical possibility. Now it's all real. We have lost everything we were working toward. All we can do now is make sure the people of Greenhouse and Solace do not pay for it—with their lives.

"I have spoken with the commanding officer of the Chronologic Patrol ship. They found DeSilvo City, entered it, and know everything. They have spent months en route, studying the material. So it's no good trying to fool them, or trying to be clever—and you shouldn't try

it in any event. The only way—the *only* way—the planet
Solace can survive this is by our confessing to everything
we have done, by our cooperating completely, and by
making sure they're confident they've swept us all up.
Work on the assumption that they'd burn the planet if
they felt it necessary and think they were saving all the
other worlds by so doing. Don't hold back. Don't play
games. Don't try to outsmart them. If you do, *everyone
dies*. Is all that clear?"

He got the nods and muttered yesses that he was looking for. "All right," he said. "Let's go welcome our
guests."

As per arrangement, what was already being called
the "core group" assembled on the hangar deck as soon
as the gig from the *Belle Boyd XI* docked with the big
ship's external lock. Koffield had instructed all of them
to pack a bag, bring it with them, and be ready to travel.
The CP might want to take them into custody at once,
and Koffield didn't want to give them any problems that
he could avoid. Elber had taken the chance to change
into the best clothes he had along. He was glad to have
done so, for just about everyone else in the group had
done the same.

He was gladder still when the airlock hatch swung
open and the two CP officers came aboard. The two of
them were in full dress uniform: handsomely cut silver-
grey tunics and jet-black trousers. An older, heavyset
man, sad and calm, and a younger woman, plainly much
more on edge than her companion. It wouldn't be hard
to imagine that she had been crying, not so long ago.
Well, Elber had shed his own tears already, and would
likely do it again soon, and often. Jassa and Zari. He
would never see them again. They would likely never
even know why he had vanished.

The two CP officers came a step or two into the airlock and stopped. The group from the *Lodestar VII*
formed into a semicircle in front of them.

The older man spoke. "I am Lieutenant Commander
Burl Chalmers, commanding the Chronologic Patrol Intelligence Ship *Belle Boyd XI*. This is Lieutenant Kalani

Temblar. First, before all, I must speak of our security arrangements."

"Excuse me, Commander," said Admiral Koffield. "My name is Koffield. I served in the Chronologic Patrol, and know your procedures." He gestured toward the others. "I have briefed them already about such matters."

"Yes, Mr. Koffield. I recognized you." It was impossible to miss the failure to call him "Admiral." Perhaps Chalmers felt a man caught in the act of betraying the Patrol was not entitled to full military courtesy—though he was otherwise quite polite. "I am sure you have told them all that you know about such matters—but you have been away a long time, and things might have changed. In any event, the consequences of mistakes could be—*would* be—so high that I do not want it on my conscience that there could be any chance of confusion or misunderstanding. And in any event, I am required by standing orders to follow the procedure I am about to describe—and I am also required by the same orders to describe the procedure. I have no discretion at all under the applicable standing orders."

He turned his gaze away from Koffield and addressed them as a group. "Lieutenant Temblar and I are wearing biomonitors, and are carrying certain other devices, all of which are in constant communication with our ship. In the event that either of us, or both of us, should be harmed, or if we are simply cut off from contact with the ship for any significant length of time—then the *Belle Boyd XI* will shift over into marauder mode. She will attack and destroy this ship. You will not be able to stop her. She will attack and destroy any ship that attempts to challenge her. She will move on to Greenhouse and attack and destroy all of its orbiting installations— including, and indeed starting with, the NovaSpot. I am fully aware what the destruction of the NovaSpot would mean, and I trust you are as well.

"The *Belle Boyd XI* will continue her attacks on Greenhouse, then on Solace, until her weapons are exhausted, or until she is damaged or destroyed. I doubt she would survive the detonation of the NovaSpot—but I doubt that would matter.

"We have left an automated message unit at the downtime end of Starshine Station. If we fail to return there, and fail to send the proper stand-down code, a message that we failed to return will be carried on the next ship to depart Starshine, and the next, and the next, and the next, until the stand-down code is sent. Once that message arrives at Earth, a fleet of Chronologic Patrol Ships, each of them far larger and more powerful than the *Belle Boyd XI,* will launch for the Solace system—and they will not treat you gently."

He looked around the group again, at the ring of silent, shell-shocked faces. "Is all of this clear? Do all of you understand that Lieutenant Temblar and I must not, *must not,* come to any harm?"

There was a stunned chorus of assent, and Chalmers went on. "Very well, then. I need only mention that the consequences of anything short of full cooperation with the Chronologic Patrol will be met with similar reprisal, adjusted for the circumstance. You *must* cooperate with us, if there is to be any hope of Solace or Greenhouse surviving. Is *that* clear?"

Another chorus of consent, scarcely more audible. "Thank you," he said. "For what it is worth, which is perhaps very little, neither Lieutenant Temblar nor I are happy about this—quite the contrary. You will understand that the scale of the—ah—*violations* being attempted here left us no choice or discretion whatsoever." He turned to Dr. DeSilvo. "Sir. I recognize you from photographs, of course. Can you confirm that this is the core group, those with substantive knowledge of your plan to go back in time to terraform a world?"

DeSilvo blinked, swallowed a time or two, and then found his voice, his self-control. "Of those aboard this ship, yes. Obviously, the rest of those aboard knew we were doing *something* secret—and they saw the Test Article destroyed, and saw you arrive. But these are all of those who knew what it is—what it was—all about."

Temblar looked them over and spoke for the first time. "Doesn't seem like very many."

"There are others on Greenhouse, and a few on Solace," said Koffield.

"Including your head of government and head of state—your, ah, Planetary Executive?"

The room was silent.

"Is your Planetary Executive aware of this project or not?" Chalmers repeated.

"You can't take the sovereign leader of a *planet* into custody!" Drayax protested.

"We can, we have in the past—and we will, in this case," said Chalmers. "Otherwise, the planet will suffer the consequences."

"Planetary Executive Kalzant will cooperate with you," said Koffield.

"That does not directly answer my question, but, very well," said Chalmers. "I will not press the issue further—just yet. But you *must* provide me with a complete list of persons with knowledge of the time-travel plan, and technical knowledge of the equipment."

"You'll get it," DeSilvo said tersely.

"Good. There is more we'll want—much more—but that will do for now." Chalmers gestured toward the docking-port hatch, and the CP auxiliary ship beyond. "Let's get going," he said.

Elber gasped. "You—you mean, that's it?"

"That's it," said Lieutenant Temblar. "What were you expecting? Speeches and a funeral march?"

"But—but what happens now?"

She pointed to the hatch. "We go aboard the aux ship. It'll be crowded, but we can all fit for this short a trip. We fly over to the *Belle Boyd XI,* and all of you, except DeSilvo and Koffield, get shoved into our temporal confinement. While you're in there, we'll interrogate DeSilvo and Koffield, and probably we'll pull several of you out of confinement to get your statements—to check on what Koffield and DeSilvo have told us. That'll be a real tight fit in the TC chamber, but you'll only be in there for a few seconds of subjective time, maybe a minute or two tops, while we make more permanent arrangements. Probably we'll build a larger confinement on some unpopulated moon somewhere in the outer system and plant you all there until arrangements can be made for a transport to collect you and move you to a penal colony.

"But you all know too much to be put into any general prisoner population. More than likely, your group will be isolated. Permanently."

Elber looked to Admiral Koffield in mute appeal, but Koffield could offer no way out of this disaster. "I'm sorry," he said. "But there it is. We ran the risks—and lost the game. Now we have to pay. Or risk letting all of Solace and all of Greenhouse die."

The aux ship wasn't much more than a short, squat cylinder with a docking hatch on the nose and thrusters on the bottom. Its interior was one large compartment, with a pilot's station to one side and the rest of the space left open.

It was going to be a very tight fit indeed to get everyone aboard while still leaving room for Chalmers to strap in at the pilot's station and fly the ship. It would be altogether impractical to power up and tune the acceleration compensators so as to allow for the extra mass of the passengers for such a short trip. That meant everyone was going to have to be able to hang on, or else get knocked around every time a thruster fired. But the CP officers had planned ahead, and had wrapped stretchnet panels around the interior of the compartment, leaving a gap in the net so that Chalmers could make his way into the pilot's station.

Temblar had as many as could fit lean their backs against the netting and hold on to it, while the rest crowded in, standing up, in the middle of the deck.

The CP officers had strung a few vertical hang-on ropes as well, stretching them between the deck and the overhead bulkhead through the center of the compartment. That gave everyone who got shoved into the center a place to hold on.

They stowed the prisoners' pathetically small amount of luggage in the space between the netting and the inner hull, and then they were ready to go.

Elber was one of those caught in the middle, hanging on to one of the vertically strung ropes. It was impossible to look around at his companions, all hanging on to the netting and the ropes, and not see them all as trapped in a net, snared in a giant web.

Lieutenant Temblar stood where she could watch them all, in the center of the deck, hanging on to one of the vertically strung ropes—looking just as caught and trapped as all the rest of them. Elber found himself standing in front of her, holding on to his own rope. He was almost nose to nose with her. In her face he read anger, fear, sorrow, guilt, utter exhaustion, resignation. All of it, none of it, was there, moment by moment.

The overhead docking port slid shut, and they heard the *bang-bang-bang* of the docking latches letting go. Chalmers worked the ship's controls. The forward thrusters fired, all but lifting everyone off their feet. The little ship came about and fired its rear jets, dropping everyone back into the deck.

The overcrowded little ship began its brief journey back to the *Belle Boyd XI*.

Elber looked at Temblar. Admiral Koffield had warned them all not to play games with the CP officers, but he hadn't said anything about not *talking* to them.

"You were at Glister, right? At Dr. DeSilvo's base?"

Temblar had been staring over his shoulder at nothing at all. She blinked and took a moment to focus on him. "Hmm? Yes. I was there."

"I wasn't. I've never been out of Solace system. But I heard about it. Everything there. You saw the simulators? The ones that show what's going to happen with all the planets?"

"Yes," she said, plainly somewhat puzzled and distracted. "We even ran some simulations ourselves."

"So you know," he said. "You know what this does here."

She frowned. "What do you mean?"

"Earth dies," he said. "Everything dies. *Everything*."

"I know! I know," she said. Everyone was listening now, and she looked around the compartment. "I saw it all. But not for a long time. A thousand years—"

"Maybe less time than that."

"And maybe more," she snapped. "I was going to say, a thousand years is a long time. Lots of time to find an answer."

"Do you think someone thought 'we have lots of time' five hundred years ago? Do you think they'll think it in five hundred more?"

"Maybe. How should I know?"

"Will they even still remember that there *is* a problem?" Koffield asked, very gently. He was holding on to the netting, off to the left of Elber. "I doubt anyone in Chronologic Patrol Central Command knows anything at all about it anymore."

"We'll remind them when we get back," Temblar said stubbornly. "They'll work on it. They'll find an answer. *The* answer."

"Do you think so?" Elber asked. "Really?"

"I hope so," she said.

"You better hope pretty hard," said Norla Chandray. "You're betting the future of the human race on it."

"They'll find an answer," she said again, but even Elber could see she couldn't really believe it.

"We have found an answer," he said. "*We* have."

"You've found a fancy way for the human race to commit suicide," Chalmers said, climbing out of the pilot's seat. He looked to Temblar. "Controls are locked, autopilot on," he said. "We've got a twenty-minute ride until we need to maneuver." He turned himself to face Elber. "You're saying a thousand years isn't enough future for people to find an answer—but a million years of past isn't long enough for someone to find a way to screw things up?"

"They'd do the time traveling away from any star system that was going to be inhabited."

"Yeah, but they'll *do time travel*. And they'll have ships. And if you make it happen on this first planet, don't you think there will be others? Don't you *want* there to be others? Maybe dozens, hundreds, of deep-time terraformed planets? And do you think every one of those operations will have perfect control, absolute security, over their Harmonic Gates, or whatever the hell you call them? Do you think no gate will *ever* be misused?

"And tell me what happens if some ship is in the past, maybe on the very first mission to go back, and the time-travel gate breaks down, and the one hope for survival is to put everyone in cold storage and point the ship at the one world in all the universe they *know* has air to breathe and food to eat? Or suppose some clown figures out he can get rich if only he can get to Earth and scoop up a few fancy species that have gone extinct? Or suppose someone gets homesick? No problem—except if someone coughs after they land, and the germs get blown to the right spot in Africa—and poof! humanity is wiped out before it can get started. Or suppose someone, somewhere in all the thousands of years the job will take, decides to do the job on purpose? The voices in his head tell him humanity is evil, and God has sent him into the past for the explicit purpose of wiping out the blot on the universe? What's your answer then?"

No one answered. Chalmers looked around the compartment. "You can't dive that far back into the depths of time and assume you won't make waves! That far back, all it would take was one tiny, tiny change—and everything is dead a million years ago, instead of a thousand years from now."

Elber looked at him, hard, and whatever it was in him that had made him able to face Sotales, face Zak Destan, face vanishing forever in order to save his family, showed that it was still there. "You don't believe there is any hope," he said. "You don't think they'll find an answer in time."

Again, the compartment was silent. All eyes were on Chalmers. "You're right," he said at last. "I don't think they will." He gestured to DeSilvo, hanging on the netting between Koffield and Chandray. "Your models and projections were pretty convincing," he said. "Lieutenant Temblar and I spent half our waking hours on the trip here trying to find a hole in them. We couldn't. And they match up with too many things we already knew. Things we haven't had the courage to admit to ourselves for a long time." He looked back at Elber. "A thousand years is all the future we have left," he said. "But that gives us no right to risk a million years of our past."

Chalmers looked around at all the faces turned toward him. "You want an answer? You'll have all the time in the world to find one, after we've locked you all away. Find a way to do it without time travel, and then we'll talk," he said. "Take a million years to terraform your planet if you like. Just don't do it in *my* past."

He turned to Temblar, and spoke again, but in a different tone, one that signaled that the topic was closed, nothing more to discuss. "Kalani, crank up the cooling system," he said. "It's getting kind of toasty in here with all these warm bodies." Then he turned his back completely on Elber and started to climb back into his pilot's chair. Discussion over.

But Elber barely noticed. Something had come to him.

"Wait a minute," Elber said. "Wait just a minute."

Chalmers turned back to him, the annoyance plain on his face. "Enough," he said. "It's over."

"No," said Elber. "No. Wait just a minute." He *had* to get this idea clear and straight in his head. The future . . .

"No time travel, you said, right?" he asked.

"Yeah, fella, that's right."

"Is that what you mean? Or do you mean time travel *into the past*?"

"What the hell are you talking about?"

"I'm—I'm no expert. But the timeshaft wormholes are really only good for going into the *past,* right? I mean, you have to build them before you can use them, so you can't use them to travel forward from—what do you call it? The uptime end. Right?"

"Yeah, right. Of course you can't. So what?"

But Elber wasn't listening. He was talking to himself, thinking out loud. "A timeshaft wormhole is, is, like a *tube* with two ends. You can go from one end to the other and back, uptime and downtime, but that's all. You can't travel any other time distance, or travel to before or after the period when both ends of it existed. *But Harmonic Gates aren't like that.*"

Elber turned toward DeSilvo. "That's right, isn't it? You *can* use two Harmonic Gates to create a timeshaft, but you don't have to, right? It can be open-ended?"

DeSilvo was just as mystified as anyone else, but it was plain he could sense Elber's excitement. "Well, yes, of course," he said. "We were preparing to do just that when, ah, we were interrupted. But yes, in theory, you ought to be able to create a link to any moment in the past."

"The past! It's always the *past*!" Elber looked around and saw that they still didn't see it. "You've all been trained by the timeshafts," he said. "Time travel is what you do *to go into the past*." He gestured at Chalmers. "The—the whole Chronologic Patrol is based on that. From the stories I heard, the only reason those Intruder ships were able to attack at Circum Central is that no one ever thought of anyone trying to go *from past to future*."

He could see by DeSilvo's expression that he had gotten it. So had Koffield. He turned to Chalmers again. "The future. If we went into the future and made our world—would that be all right?" It seemed insane, even to Elber, to ask permission that way, but how else was he to phrase it? "Would it?"

Chalmers was starting to look a little alarmed. He backed away from Elber a bit. "Well, yeah, fella, I suppose. Sure. But what would be the point? What good is a terraformed world a million years in the future going to do for you?"

"I know, I know. But would it be all right if we *brought it back*?" Elber looked at him eagerly. "The Chronologic Patrol is supposed to keep the present from interfering with the past. Would it be all right if we interfered with the *future*?"

Again, silence. Elber wanted to say more, but he didn't dare. He could *see* the future balanced on knife edge, trembling there. The slightest jolt could send it tumbling, falling down into the depths of time forever. He had done his part. Let the others do theirs.

Chandray spoke first. "Stars in the sky," she said. "Would it *work*?"

Koffield looked at DeSilvo. "Is it even *remotely* possible? Could you scale things up that much?"

DeSilvo looked stunned as well. "The engineering challenges would be enormous, of course—but the odd thing about the gates is that it was always a question of scaling them *down*. I don't know how to put it more elegantly than to say the process *wants* to be big. Most of the challenge has been in forcing the chronoharmonic effects to work on smaller masses and volumes over shorter periods." He looked to Elber. "Tell me again," he said. "Tell me what you have in mind."

Elber stabbed a finger at Villjae Benzen. "Just like what he told me about the first terraform-in-time plan, only backward. We were going to go back a million years, come back to now, then, I dunno, what?—get to 990,000 years, then 970, and so on, back to now. Instead we go, say, 20,000 years into the future and come back to here. I mean now. Then, 30,000, 100,000—until we get the planet how we like it. Then—then when it's done, we bring it back to here and now."

"Bring the planet back? Why not just send the people forward? The masses involved . . ." DeSilvo asked. His lips starting working silently as he worked the problem through.

"No, not if you want to keep paradoxes from happening," Koffield said. "A lot of people wouldn't want to be cut off from the rest of the human race forever. A lot of people who'd be willing at first might not be after a while. They'd try to come back anyway. Mr. Malloon is right. The planet comes back to the present."

"And if we were going into the future," Villjae said, "we wouldn't have to worry at all about screwing up causality. Especially if it's a dead planet. All we'd have to do is have a really strong setup to make sure that no one leaves the star system while they're in the future. Plus we make sure anyone who gets information about anything about the future outside that system is stranded in the future, with no way back—and we make sure they can't have kids, of course. Not easy, but that part would be a lot easier than the precautions you'd need in the past."

"In fact," said Koffield, "probably the safest thing you could do, from a causality point of view, would be to ban interstellar flight altogether for the terraformers. Make them remain in their home system, working with a planet that's already dead—or is going to be dead soon." He looked at DeSilvo. "We'd have to stay here," he said. "We could—we'd *have* to—reterraform Solace."

DeSilvo looked up sharply at Koffield.

Koffield kept talking. "Mr. Benzen's right, you'd have to have other safeguards as well. But the *safest* thing to do, from a causality viewpoint, would be to quarantine the project by banning all forms of interstellar flight during the time period you were doing the terraforming. That way, any possible causality breach would stay isolated to that one system—and there wouldn't be any starships floating around the time-travel portals to tempt anyone. Quarantine the system where you're doing the terraforming."

"This is nuts!" Chalmers protested. "We can't listen to this."

But Lieutenant Temblar grabbed him by the arm. "Burl! Burl—yes, we can," she said. "We have to."

"*What?*" Chalmers whirled about to face her. "This is all insane."

"Yeah, I know," she said. "But it's *less* insane than going a million years into the past—and a *hell* of a lot less insane than letting the whole human race go extinct because we can't afford to take any risks!"

"Pulling a *planet* out of the future?" Chalmers protested.

"Yes," said DeSilvo, coming out of his half reverie.

"Yes. I need time to work it through, I need to talk the idea over with the right people—but *yes*. It ought to be possible—and feasible. A distinctly possible piece of large-scale engineering. I'd put it roughly on the same scale of effort and expense as building a timeshaft wormhole."

"Burl, you've got to turn this tub around," said Lieutenant Temblar.

Chalmers's eyes looked as if they were about to bug out of his head. "Turn it *around*?"

"And get us docked back to the *Lodestar VII*," Temblar went on. "We won't take chances. We'll lock this group up on the hangar deck, seal them in. We'll have the ship's crew haul in worktables, datapads, sleeping cots, field meals, and so on. Keep them locked up. We can order the locals to deliver anyone they say they need to help with the work. We can cut off all their outgoing communications, just to feel safe. They'll cooperate. You know they will. But we've *got* to let 'em have time to work the idea through."

Elber looked from one CP officer to the other. He found himself wondering which one of them was *really* in command. The expression on Chalmers's face made it plain he was wondering the same thing.

"We've *got* to," she said again. "You said it yourself. We don't have much future left. Maybe—*maybe* they can go get us some more future, a *lot* more. What have we got to lose if we spend a week watching them find out they're wrong? But suppose we say no, and it turns out later it *could* have been done? We did damned good work scooping them all up—but are we going to spend the rest of our lives getting medals pinned to our chests, even though we know it's for not letting them try to save us all?"

"We can't just let these lunatics loose in the universe!" Chalmers protested. "They've got half the technology from the Dark Museum!"

"Then lock us in," Koffield said. "Blow the wormholes that lead to Solace." He glanced at DeSilvo. "We have people who could tell you how. Put *us* in quarantine, so the crazy ideas won't spread—unless they work."

"What if you fail?" Chalmers asked. "You won't be able to evacuate your refugees."

"No, we won't," Koffield agreed. "We'd have made ourselves into a whole planet, a whole planetary system, full of diehards, stuck where we were. Think of it as giving us an impetus to try harder. Besides, what would it matter, really? Do it your way, and you know as well as I do that the race will be extinct in a thousand years. If *that's* true, then the whole human race is just one huge diehard colony with nothing left to do but try and hold off the end as long as possible."

"You have the FTL drive," Chalmers objected. "The quarantine wouldn't hold. You could get out."

"Not if the Chronologic Patrol could detect an FTL drive—and I *know* you can at least detect one as it comes out of FTL. I saw what an FTL arrival signature looked like way back at Circum Central. Believe me, it's hard to miss. Pass around orders to shoot to kill FTL ships, and that ought to discourage most people from trying it."

DeSilvo spoke up. "Besides, the reason the Dark Museum technology was suppressed was because terraformed planets fail, and that makes refugees, and that speeds the collapse. If we create a world that does *not* fail, and we show the universe it *can* be done, then there will be no reason for the suppression. Success would mean *everything* changes."

And it was in that moment that it happened. Elber could see it, see it plainly in the expressions on all of their faces. It was as if the clouds had finally broken open, and the sun was shining through at last. A look of hope, of possibility, that had not been so even moments before. It was even in Lieutenant Temblar's eyes. Chalmers was the only holdout—but he could see what Elber saw.

Chalmers shook his head in bewildered resignation. "All right," he said. "You're nuts, all of you. But all right."

Norla Chandray stepped away from the netting she had been holding, that had been holding her, and stood on her own two feet in the middle of the deck. She looked around at all of them, her eyes shining, her face flushed with excitement.

"Let us begin," she said.

Chapter Twenty-nine

THE OCEAN OF YEARS

The *Belle Boyd XI* was a good half billion kilometers from the Starshine Station timeshaft, but even from that distance, the explosion was clearly visible—and both of those aboard the *BB-XI* were in the command center, at their posts, watching for it, waiting for it.

"Well," said Burl, "I think we can look forward to a very interesting joint court-martial. Or do you think my odds would be better if I requested separate trials?"

"I have no idea," Kalani said calmly. "I can give you fair warning, though. I'm planning to mount a most unusual defense strategy."

"Yeah? Such as?"

"The truth. The full, unadorned, everything-we-did-and-found truth."

Burl looked over at her and shook his head as theatrically as possible. "Oh, boy," he said. "*Definitely* separate trials. *I'm* going to split hairs and hide behind technicalities as much as I can. For starters, I'm gonna make sure they know *we* didn't blow all the timeshaft wormholes leading to Solace." He pointed back at the timeshaft and the Solacians. "*They* did it."

"Yeah. All we did was know all about it ahead of

time and not shoot down the sabot drone that followed us to the wormhole, waited until we got through, and did the job for us."

"Technicalities," said Burl. "Mere technicalities."

They sat there, in silence, watching the blast front expand outward, fading away into darkness as it bloomed.

"How many ships are you showing?" Burl asked.

Kalani checked her displays. "Two, count 'em two, Chrono Patrol ships. It looks like the phony recall of the uptime ship did the trick."

Koffield had worked out that part—managing to program the robotic sabot ship to beam a crash-alert emergency recall signal into the message traffic transmitted to the uptime ship.

Obviously, the uptime guard ship had acted on the alert and gone through the wormhole just before it was blown. Koffield, of all people, would not have been party to deliberately stranding a CP ship on the uptime side of a timeshaft. "Good," said Burl. "Let's hope they can pull the same stunt on the other two timeshafts."

"They will," Kalani said. They sat there, watching the last of the blast cloud fade away. They remained there some time after, looking at the stars. There was a lot to think about.

"Speaking just a bit more seriously," Kalani said, "*are* they going to court-martial us?"

"I don't know," Burl said. "I think we could make a pretty good case that we were sent on this mission without a whole lot of guidance. The brass back home will have to decide if we established new and wise policies— or committed twelve kinds of treason."

"That's really going to be up to our new friends in the Solace system, isn't it?" Kalani said. "*If* they manage to build a new world, and we saved humanity from extinction when we decided not to arrest them—who knows? Maybe the court will go easy on us."

"The trouble is the court won't know, one way or another, for quite a while. No one will."

"Maybe they should just throw us into temporal confinement until they know, one way or another—then decide whether or not to hold the court-martial."

"That's not such a crazy idea," Burl said. He stabbed a finger toward the ruined timeshaft. "Collusion in the unwarranted destruction of timeshafts. That's going to be the charge they *really* care about. The Chrono Patrol loves its timeshafts."

"A lot of good that'll do them if FTL travel gets loose," said Kalani. "I think you're right, though. Let's hope they take a good hard look at that word *unwarranted*. With a little luck, they'll realize they can't afford to let the chance go by for Solace to try its little experiment—and maybe they'll even realize they don't want Solace too close while it's happening. They might *like* the quarantine." She stared out at the stars a while longer. "I wonder when—or if—we'll find out if they pulled it off," she said.

"I don't know," he said. "Ask me in twenty years."

"I'll do that," she said.

"Won't be hard to find me," he said. "I'll be in the next cell down from yours."

Kalani laughed, stood up, and stretched. "I'm headed aft," she said. "You coming?"

"In a bit. I'm gonna get something to eat first."

She smiled. "I should have known," she said.

Kalani took one last long look at the timeshaft that wasn't there anymore. She thought of all the wonders lost in the Dark Museum of Mars and how some small handful of them had been found once more, only to be hidden away again on Glister—to protect them from the Chrono Patrol, because the Chrono Patrol knew progress would only get more people killed faster and bring the final collapse sooner.

But if the Solacians managed to change all the rules, out there in the darkness—would all those wonders be free at last? And what would be happen to the Chronologic Patrol in a universe where FTL travel was allowed to happen?

The Chronologic Patrol had started out, long ago, with the laudable goal of defending causality, of protecting the past from the future. From there it was not such a long journey to protecting the present, the status quo, from hazardous change. Later, in effect, the CP had determined to *prevent* the future, to hold back change and innovation, to drag history itself to a halt, to do nothing more than let the end come with as little pain as possible.

But even that had not been the last phase. The end of all was forgetfulness. The Chronologic Patrol did not even remember why it had to prevent the future. The CP just did it, because that was what it had always done. Every day, every year, must be like the one before it.

The Chrono Patrol was a senile giant, without the slightest hope of adapting to new days and new ways. Change would kill it. Kalani felt damned bad and guilty about that.

But if things *didn't* change, that would kill all of them. It wasn't so hard a choice, even if she had regrets.

"Good luck to you out there," she said, and headed aft, to the temporal-confinement chamber, to home, and to whatever fate awaited her.

SOLACE CITY SPACEPORT
SOLACE CITY
THE PLANET SOLACE

Five Years On

Norla Chandray cut power to the *Terra Nova*'s thrusters, and let the little ship drop gently down on the landing pad.

That was the last of it. The touchdown of the *Terra Nova* marked the absolute dead end of interstellar travel to and from the Solace system for the duration. The last of the last of the last. No more delays, no more extensions or exceptions.

She glanced over at Marquez in the pilot's seat, and

saw that he felt it as well. For all that he knew it was necessary, he didn't have to like it. It was a sign of his mood that he had let her land the *Terra Nova.*

On the other hand, Marquez must have been thoroughly tired of the run back and forth to Glister. He plainly had not been happy when they had asked him to do it again.

"Powering down nav and propulsion," she announced. As of this moment, the *Terra Nova* was no longer an auxiliary ship, for the *Dom Pedro IV* was no longer in service. There would be plenty of work for her in the years to come, and for the *Nova Sol,* and the *Cruzeiro do Sul,* and for every other ship they could lay their hands on. But they weren't going to need starships for a while.

At least part of her was glad the trip was over. Solace was home, now, and would be, for at least a little while longer, before they all moved on to Greenhouse, along with everyone else. She sat there a minute, shut her eyes, and let the tiredness flow over her. At times she felt as if she couldn't remember when she *didn't* feel tired. But these days, the exhaustion seemed worthwhile, a fair exchange for work accomplished. They were getting there.

"Cross-check," Marquez said, examining his own displays. "Confirming power-down. Switch all systems to groundside standby status."

"Switching to groundside standby." Time for the *Terra Nova* to go to sleep too even if she would only get a quick nap of a few hours or so. No doubt three other crews were scheduled to fly her on as many missions in the next few days.

They had gotten the last of the high-priority gear from Glister four years before, but then other things had come up, and kept coming up. Whenever it seemed they were just about to go out and get the last of the gear, some new crisis would boil up.

But, at long last, there had been enough of a break in the schedule to allow them to finish the job, make one last run. Norla had half expected to discover that Jay

Verlant and his friends at Canyon City had finally gotten there, or that the Chronologic Patrol had finally converted DeSilvo City into a smoking crater, but instead they had found the base intact—and begun the tedious job of shuttling the last of the gear from the surface to the *Dom Pedro,* loading it, hauling it back to the Solace system—and going back for more, run after run.

But now it was done. The last of the cargo had been removed from DeSilvo City, and the *Dom Pedro IV*'s labors were at an end, at least for the present. They had left her asleep, out in the comforting cold and dark. The big ship was in free orbit of Lodestar, out beyond Comfort, all major systems powered down, the FTL drive deliberately disabled, just to keep any would-be pirates from getting ideas. She would stay that way until the job was over.

Quite often, these days, Norla thought back to her last-ever flight on a timeshaft ship years before. Trawling, ever so slowly, back and forth across the sky, sliding down the timeshafts, and in and out of years—a hundred-year journey just to get anywhere at all.

Somehow, you came out of a timeshaft ship *knowing* how long the trip had truly taken. You knew, even if you never spoke about it, that every flight was a heroic, dangerous voyage across the vastness of space, across the storm-tossed ocean of years.

Direct interstellar passage via FTL just seemed too *easy.* It really *did* take only a week between Glister and Solace. No tricks, no illusion. You didn't step out of a ship, having aged only a month or two, while the ship had endured a hundred years between the stars. FTL almost seemed *disrespectful* of interstellar distances, as if it trivialized the effort, the untold saga, that had once been required to traverse between the stars.

Maybe it was a good thing they were stopping FTL flights altogether, closing the last way out of the quarantine. When they started again, FTL flights would seem special, exciting to those who had never traveled the hard way, and to those who had had time enough to forget the old ways.

She set the last of her switches, confirmed the entry in the autolog, and undid her seat restraints. "So much for that," she muttered.

"What?" Marquez asked.

"That's the end of that for the Glister run," she said, choosing to put a positive spin on things.

"Amen to that," he said. "Let's go do something else."

They climbed down out of the flight deck and onto the cargo deck. Marquez punched the buttons on the airlock controls to match pressure with the outside world, the hatches came open, and they stepped out onto the waiting mobile stairs and into the strangely blue-sky world of Solace City.

The locals still used the phrase "Sure as rain in Solace City" to mean something was utterly reliable and definite—but the phrase was not entirely accurate anymore. The seemingly permanent rain shield over the city had been becoming less and less reliable over the past few years—a pleasant side effect of the more unpleasant effects of the climate collapse. It only rained about every other day or so now—positively drought conditions, compared to what it used to be.

Norla paused at the top of the stairs for a moment and looked up into the sky, to the south and east. There it was, already plainly visible even in daylight. A bright white streak, like a chalk line drawn across the sky. The first sections of the Grand Harmonic Gate, seen nearly edge on, from the inside. The start of Grand Gate construction had been the last nail in the coffin of secrecy surrounding the project. It just wasn't possible to keep a ring around the planet secret.

PlanEx Kalzant, in a series of carefully planned addresses to the public, had come clean and told them that the planet could not be saved by conventional means, and that the "temporary" and "partial" evacuations to Greenhouse and the orbiting habitats would in fact be permanent and complete. But the plain fact was that people already knew it, in large part because of a series of leaks masterfully orchestrated by Olar Sotales, who thus demonstrated that intelligence work and propaganda were not so far different from each other.

But the real factors that kept panic and disorder from spreading was the demonstrable fact that the government was managing to settle the evacuees, and the knowledge that the government had a long-range plan. That a large majority of the population thought the plan was, to put it mildly, far-fetched, almost didn't matter.

"It gets me nervous," Marquez said, "seeing that thing up there already when they haven't even cleared the satellites yet."

"They can't, until the evacuations are a lot further along." Another one of the thousand tasks made necessary by the Grand Gate Project, one of many jobs that would have been considered a major effort, all by itself, in any other age. Every habitat and facility orbiting the planet was going to have to be towed completely out of planetary orbit and placed in free orbit around Lodestar, well away from the planet itself. But those habitats—most especially SCO Station—were urgently needed as way stations for the constant stream of evacuees headed for Greenhouse. They couldn't be moved just yet.

"I know, I know," Marquez growled. "But it still gets me nervous. Suppose SCO Station crashes into it when the time comes to boost it into free orbit?"

"They've got the vectors worked out," she said.

"Right," he said. "Nothing can go wrong."

Norla laughed and shook her head. Everything else might change, but Marquez stayed the same.

They went down the mobile stairs, hooked a ride on a passing runcar, and were in the main terminal five minutes later. They detoured around the jostling crowds in the departures area—and got a surprise in the arrivals hall—two surprises, in fact.

Yuri Sparten was there, just down from orbit, and still wearing his SCO Station Service uniform. Norla hadn't seen him in years. But she got a greater shock when she recognized his companion. She let out a low whistle and nudged Marquez in the ribs. "Talk about strange bedfellows," she said, nodding toward Yuri.

Marquez looked, spotted Yuri—and then realized who he was with. "Well I'll be damned," he said.

"Probably," Norla said smoothly, and called out, "Yuri! Yuri, over here!"

Sparten turned at the sound of his name, then grinned and waved. Norla and Marquez walked over to him. "Norla! Captain Marquez. Good to see you both." The three of them greeted each other and Sparten introduced his companion—though he no doubt knew full well no introduction was needed.

Dapper, well coiffed, elegantly dressed, Zak Destan grinned and offered Norla his well-manicured hand. The rabble-rouser turned reiver turned bush captain had transformed himself once again, into a smooth and polished politician. He read the surprise in both their eyes and tugged at the lapel of his tunic. "I know, I know," he said. "I've heard it all before. But you've got to give the people what they need to see. I gotta look sharp, these days." Norla couldn't help but think it wasn't all that much of a burden for him.

"What are the two of you doing here, of all places?" Norla asked.

"And what are you doing *together*?" Marquez asked, far more bluntly.

Sparten blushed, but Destan just laughed out loud. "We've just come in for another propaganda tour. Fourth or fifth one we've done. People see a station man and a transplanted lowdown who's done well, traveling together, talking up evacuation, answering questions. It helps. But most of the message gets across the moment we show up, side by side. Proves you can do all right, and that the orbit-side uppers will treat you all right."

Not exactly, Norla thought. *It just proves one particular transplanted lowdown did all right.* But it wasn't the time or place to make such observations. "I see," she said.

"We go around from town to town in the areas scheduled next for evacuation," Sparten said. "It helps," he added, echoing Destan. Norla had the feeling he did that a lot.

"I'll bet it does," Marquez said.

They all had enough time for a quick drink together at the spaceport tavern—just enough time to remember a few of the good old days without dredging up all the old fights and disagreements and personality clashes.

Almost inevitably, Marquez and Destan got off onto the subject of politics, and how the Grand Gate Project *ought* to be run. Their conversation became so animated that she found herself effectively alone with Sparten, for the first time since Glister.

"You know," she said, "there's something I've always meant to ask you, Yuri. But I never had the chance, somehow. What's it *feel* like to have changed the course of human history?"

"Huh? What are you talking about?"

"Back on Glister," she said. "Temblar told us she had gotten damned close to giving up on finding us. Chalmers was pressuring her to accept the evidence they had—the evidence DeSilvo planted—and head for home. But they didn't, because you had to go look for Canyon City."

"I still don't follow."

"Think it through," she said. "She was near to giving up. All the evidence pointed toward the decoy cache being real. But there was one, just one, bit of evidence that didn't fit. Our overflight gave her *just* enough reason to look in the direction of the real DeSilvo City—in the long run, just enough to find it, break in, read the files, find out what we were planning, get to Solace system in time to blow up the Test Article, shut down the project, and get us all arrested.

"If all *that* hadn't happened, we'd probably still all be working on terraforming a planet we hadn't found yet a million years in the past. I don't know for sure if that would work better, but it sure as hell would be *different*. Everything would change. Who lives and who dies? What sort of world their descendants will have?

And maybe the fate of the human race, of all Earth-based life, depends on our making this work. It could be you saved us all when you insisted on looking for the diehards—or maybe thanks to you, humanity will go extinct."

Yuri Sparten could do nothing but open and shut his mouth and stare at her, goggle-eyed. Marquez and Destan both checked the time and started making preparations to leave, but Sparten just sat there.

Norla stood, gathered up her own belongings, and made ready to go. But having plunged the knife in that deep, she couldn't resist giving it one last, almost-deserved twist. "The hell of it is," she said, "if the Grand Gate works, you'll never know for sure if you *really* made a difference. But if it fails—well, I'll know how we got to that point. And *you'll* know. Our little secret," she said as she adjusted her jacket. "Bye now!"

He didn't reply, which did not surprise Norla. Yuri was not going to be much for conversation for a while.

"Glad Sparten's doing all right as a station man—or playing the part of one," Marquez muttered as he walked off with Norla. "He never was much as a ship's officer."

"No argument from me, on either point," said Norla, already feeling guilty about having tweaked Sparten that hard. Well, she could have done worse. She *could* have asked Yuri while Marquez was listening.

Not long after, Norla said her good-byes to Marquez, hailed an aircab, climbed in, and told it to take her home. She shut her eyes, happy to let the aircab's ArtInt do the work. *Tired,* she thought, then she thought again about Yuri and Destan. Oddly enough, the sight of the two of them together offered the proof of another point the propagandists were forever pounding away at. The Grand Gate Project was huge—and everyone had a part to play. Maybe having Zak Destan wandering the landscape looking prosperous—and being friendly and co-operative with an SCO Station Service official—wasn't such a bad idea at that. Anton had told her, not so long ago, that half the reason the evacuation was going so well was that they could afford to keep opening domes and habitats quickly, because they weren't even pretending to repair the Solacian climate anymore. The low-downs still out on the farms must be in pretty poor shape. Seeing a sleek, stylish, well-fed Zak Destan just down from Greenhouse would be a powerful argument in a lot of ways.

She smiled to herself, eyes still shut, and snuggled back deeper into the cab's very comfortable seat.

She was actually starting to get the feeling they were going to pull this thing off.

FREEORBIT TRANSIT GATE STATION Y1

Ten Years On

Dr. Oskar DeSilvo sealed the hatch of the transit pod behind him, strapped himself into the travel chair, and set to work at the task of waiting impatiently.

He had already been bumped twice by rush loads of revised soil bacteria that were behind schedule for deployment and had just come in from Greenhouse. The last time DeSilvo had been on Greenhouse, he had concluded it was a wonder there was still room to do any terraforming-support biology at all. The domes, all of them, seemed filled to bursting. Still, only two domes had failed in the last year, and disturbances were surprisingly rare. There hadn't been a riot for eighteen months. Considering the austere conditions in the domes, that was a major accomplishment.

The transit pod boosted itself away from the station proper and across the five kilometers of empty space that separated it from the Transit Gate itself, then braked itself to a smooth and perfect stop in the precise center of the gate, leaving DeSilvo to fret and fume through another extremely brief delay.

At long last, so far as he was concerned, the concen-

tric rings of the gate began to spin up to transition velocity. Almost fast enough to satisfy even DeSilvo, the rings
got up to speed, and the gate's angular momentum rota-
tor field generator activated, instantly forcing the inner
and outer rings to convert their rotational energy by
ninety degrees, which in turn forced a harmonic temporal field to form. A femtosecond later, DeSilvo and the
transit pod were gone—

—and one hundred thousand years into the future,
they appeared again, as DeSilvo watched the rings of
the receiving gate spin themselves down to standby
mode.

The transit pod boosted itself away from the Harmonic Gate, and toward the Y100K Station. Y100K
was the fourth station so far, and the prefab parts for its
eventual replacements were already in place, back at
what everyone still called Y1 Station, even if it was already in Year 10. DeSilvo didn't care what they called it.
Such points seemed like hairsplitting from the lofty vantage point of Year 100,000.

At long last the transit pod docked with the station,
and DeSilvo hurried aboard as soon as the hatch was
open, as blasé as any commuter who rode the same
overtram route back and forth every day.

Twenty minutes—plus a hundred thousand years—
after his departure, he was in the control center. Berana
Drayax greeted him with a cheerful smile.

"How's the patient?" he asked.

She nodded toward the main displays. "Better and
better," she said. "But see for yourself."

The Solace of his dreams hung in the display—but
this was no simulation, no projection. It was the real
world, seventy-five thousand years into a *real* job of terraforming.

Solace was lovely, cool, a blue-green jewel set in the
darkness of space. "The patient is responding—magnifi-
cently," DeSilvo said.

Given the inability of Harmonic Gates to bridge short
spans of time, and also given the need to allow for a
margin of error, they had only really made a start at

terraforming in Y25K—twenty-five thousand years after the first death of Solace. Even allowing for the loss of twenty-five thousand years, that was still seventy-five thousand years of carefully controlled species introduction, regulated comet-ice delivery, intensive soil generation, and all the rest of it.

Those twenty-five thousand years also allowed for margin of error on the forward transition of Solace planned for Year 20 of the project. They would have to do that transition with no calibration, in effect shooting blind. But that was a worry to face years later. DeSilvo was no longer in the least taken aback by the fact that the Year 20 was in the effective future as seen from Year 100,000 Station.

"All well and good," Drayax agreed, standing up from her console to stand beside him. "But at this point, we can barely take credit for her recovery."

"The less we fix things, the less they break," DeSilvo said, his eyes flitting from one status screen to the next. Oxygen levels, water temperatures, air pressure gradient, gross biomass, diversity index—all of them were strong, far stronger than even the best ever achieved on the best-terraformed worlds.

DeSilvo gloried in the images of the planet, in the sensor readings, in the *hope* that seemed to be shining down from the display screens "I know what you'll say, of course, but I must admit I'm tempted to go early. We could transit this Solace back now and be ahead of the game."

" 'No rush jobs, no crash programs,' " Drayax said. "You should never have written that memo. I can only imagine how many times it's been quoted back at you."

"Point taken," he said. "But even so. Look at that planet. How much better can it get?"

Drayax laughed. "Why not wait and find out?" she asked.

THE DIAMOND ROOM
PLANETARY EXECUTIVE MANSION
SOLACE CITY
THE PLANET SOLACE

Fifteen Years On

Neshobe Kalzant checked the time and sighed. It was really time to go. She stopped work on her speech. She could finish it on the trip to SCO Station for the farewell ceremonies. The station had been gradually raising and shifting its orbit for the last two years, until now it rode in a highly elongated polar elliptical orbit. Tomorrow, after the ceremonies were done, and Neshobe's ship had safely departed—Olar Sotales had insisted on that point—SCO Station would reach its apopoint and make the final high-power burn that would break it free of the planet.

That it was the station itself bidding farewell to the planet made the occasion somewhat unusual, but the journey itself was one she had made many times—though this would be the last time, at least for a long while.

The last time . . . nearly everything one did these days was the last, or almost the last time. The whole planet was getting its affairs in order. She stood up, stretched, and walked over to the south-facing windows and their spectacular view of Solace City.

Ever since the rains had stopped, for good and all, a few years back, you could actually *see* the city from here—what there still was of it. The dust blown in by the wind was definitely starting to accumulate, but there was not much point in clearing it away from most sections of the half-depopulated city. There was no one left to be inconvenienced by it. "Will the last person to leave the planet please turn out the lights," Neshobe muttered to herself. The joke had gotten old so long ago that it had turned into a catchphrase.

She looked up. The spectacular dark blue skies of the past few years were likewise at an end. The airborne dust saw to that—and also reflected away enough sunlight to reduce the average temperature significantly. The same dust that was burying the city and masking the sky had turned the waters off the shores of Landing Bay a murky brown.

Neshobe turned away from the desk, packed up her work, put on her air mask, bundled into a warm old overcoat that would have been considered far too worn and shabby for the Planetary Executive back in the old days, and headed out of her office.

Moments later she stepped out of the pressure-sealed confines of the Executive Mansion, across a few meters of bitterly cold exterior courtyard, and to her waiting aircar.

But even as cold as it was, she could not resist the temptations to look up again, high in the southern sky, for another look at the Grand Gate. They had finished the basic structure only about a year ago. There was still a great deal of work to do, of course—but no one could look at the sky and doubt that progress had been made. The three pure white arcs of the inner, center, and outer rings would have reached from horizon to horizon, but for the dust that turned all the edges of the sky a muddy, murky brown. But never mind the dusty horizons. She looked straight up and gloried in the view.

Her solitary pilot-guard waited patiently for her to finish—and even sneaked a peek himself. Every human being in the Solace system had a stake in the Grand Gate—and nearly every one of them had played some part, however small or remotely connected, in building it.

At last she got in. The pilot-guard checked her safety restraints and the door locks, then climbed into the forward compartment to tell the ArtInt that did most of the actual piloting to get moving.

One guard, where once there had been a small army. In its way, that was another pleasant side effect of hard times. The threat had diminished, both as the on-planet population had dropped and as the general sense of frustration and despair had given way to a sense that something was being *done*. On the other side of the ledger, the government was frantically trying to cut costs wherever possible—and trained personnel of any sort were in permanently short supply. If the trend continued much further, she'd have to start flying her own car.

Neshobe liked the sound of that. It was something a regular person would do. But she was not going to be a regular person again—not for a while, yet. The Grand Council had more or less insisted on extending her term. She had agreed, most reluctantly, to continue in office until thirty days after Reception. She sighed. That translated into another five years or so of making decisions and delivering speeches.

Which reminded her. It was time to get back to work on what she would say at SCO Station. She pulled a datapad out and returned to the task of writing.

THE *LODESTAR VII*

Twenty Years On

Before the new world could arrive, it was necessary for the old world to depart. It ought to be quite a show—and Villjae Benzen was going to have a front-row seat.

The twenty years since the Ignition Project had been kind to Villjae Benzen. They had given him a lot: interesting work, challenging assignments, a sense of truly contributing. He had not so much aged gracefully as matured well. Berana Drayax had given him a good start, way back when—and he had made good use of it.

Was there some other director of operations out there, right now, calming down some other scared-to-death second assistant in charge-of-nothing-much who just got the whole job dropped in *his* lap? Who was out there, right now, battling to fight back exhaustion, sweat, hunger, hysteria, and the voices on the headphone, all while trying to refrebulate a disconkelized uberlewhatzit with a worn-out trammis that barely frebbed at all anymore? There *had* to be. There always was. "Good luck to you, wherever you are," Villjae muttered, and lifted his glass in salute to his imaginary comrade in arms.

All the fixtures from the Ignition Project days—the overblown observation platform, the needlessly elegant control consoles—had been stripped out long ago. Dents and dings and paint scrapes and well-used hold-down clamps were ample evidence that the cargo hold had been put to endless uses ever since. No one had let the fact that the *Lodestar VII* was officially the Planetary Executive's personal long-range spacecraft stand in the way of getting use out of a big, powerful vehicle with a capacious cargo bay—and a fair-sized hangar deck, as well.

He looked toward the hatch that led to the hangar deck and thought back to the frantic days and nights he and the others had spent locked up in there, working around the clock to come up with the basic plan that was, at long last, about to be put into operation.

He strolled about, enjoying his drink and the thrill of rubbing elbows with the greats and near greats. DeSilvo, Koffield, and their crowd were going to watch the show from someplace else—but Kalzant was here, and Drayax, and quite a few others.

A tone sounded. Villjae half expected to hear someone announce "This is the voice of Departure Control" or some such in dramatic tones, but, thankfully, they weren't inflicting *that* particular torture on the guests here today. Instead, a gentle voice said, "We are approaching the final countdown. Please take your assigned seats."

The hum of conversation in the room grew louder, and the tension grew almost palpable. From here on in, everything had to go right. The stakes could not possibly be higher. Villjae felt his stomach tighten, his pulse quicken as he moved toward his seat. He apologized to the owlish-looking woman already sitting in the seat next to his. He passed in front of her, and sat down. "Villjae," a voice beside him said. "You made it. Good."

He turned to the woman next to him—and was astonished to recognize Beseda Mahrlin. "Hello, Beseda," he said faintly. Well, why *shouldn't* she be invited here? He was, after all. Come to think of it, the last he had heard, she had been doing some of the theoretical work for the Grand Gate Project. "Nice to see you," he said, not quite sure if it was.

"Sure," she said, and left it at that. She glanced at the time display at the top of the big screen. "Not long now," she said.

"No," he agreed. He had forgotten what talking with her could be like.

The old, tired, dead world of Solace floated in the darkness, the three rings of the Grand Gate encircling it, three gleaming white bands set around a terribly flawed ruin, a parody of Saturn and his rings. Or, perhaps, more accurately, a parody of Uranus and *his* rings, for the Gate Rings were at right angles to the equator of Solace, face on to Lodestar, the local sun. The sunward sides of the rings were covered in accumulator panels, far more advanced than the old Groundside Power receptors. The three rings exposed a surface area almost as great as that of Solace itself to Lodestar.

Between the high efficiency of the panels, and the massive surface area devoted to them, the Grand Harmonic Gate could, given time, easily absorb enough power to perform the Dispatch operation. Reception would be another matter altogether—but there were plans in hand to deal with that.

The sun-opposite, or spaceward, side of all three rings of the gate sported geometric patterns, set at regular intervals around their circumference, placed there to allow easier visual confirmation of their spin. The varied checkerboard patterns let the people who had paid for the gate, who had sacrificed all to build it, truly see for themselves that something was happening.

The rings were spinning at standby speed already, the inner and outer rotating clockwise, and the center ring in the opposite direction.

Villjae had read the popular accounts of what was

going to happen next, and had the training and expertise to understand them, and even go at least a bit beyond. They needed to make room for Solace-R. "R" for Solace Reborn or Renewed, or Reterraformed, as it had come to be called. Officially, the "R" stood for Reception, to indicate it was the instance of Solace that was to arrive. Villjae, for one, was glad the name Solace Y1000K had never caught on.

But if Solace-R was to arrive, that meant Solace-D—and no matter how often people were told it stood for Dispatch, or Departure, everyone knew "D" stood for nothing but Dead—first had to go someplace. Or rather, somewhen.

At the same time, they needed to ensure that Solace-R and Solace-D were never *in* the same time *at* the same time. The solution to both problems was to knock Solace-D into the future, at the Grand Gate's minimum range, nineteen thousand to twenty-four thousand years ahead.

They would be sending Solace-D forward without benefit of a receiving gate on the other end. The physicists all said they couldn't predict with any great accuracy when in time the planet would arrive—and they strongly advised that no one try to find out. There was no point in leaning harder on the Uncertainty Principle than they had to.

When—rather if—Solace-R was pulled in from the future, she would be received directly into the gate that had propelled Solace-D forward. Solace-R would thus arrive at the start of a stretch of twenty thousand years, more or less, in which they could be quite certain there was no other instance of Solace to be found.

Which begged the next and obvious question. Villjae had heard the answer—or rather, the various answers—many times. It occurred to him that Beseda, of all people, might be better equipped than most to set him straight.

"Make me feel better," he said to her. "Tell me what happens in twenty thousand years when Solace-D pops into existence, right in Solace-R's lap?"

"It won't," she said, never once taking her eyes off the display as she spoke. "It can't. *Hasn't*. We've modeled it, *tested* it with smaller masses, hundreds, thousands of times—every time we've used the Transit Gates to send people or equipment forward or back."

That hadn't occurred to Villjae. "That tells you enough?" he asked. "Doesn't it matter that the masses are bigger, or something?"

"Course not," Beseda said. "One atom, one planet— the mass is irrelevant so far as immediate temporal effects go. Every time you do a time-gate jump, you are forming or collapsing a world line. You're spawning a new universe, identical to the one you were in, except for the effect you've imposed."

"But what's to keep us from accidentally producing a universe where Solace-D *does* pop up right next to a future Solace-R in twenty thousand years?"

"It can't," Beseda said. "Except of course, for universes where it does—but we won't be in those. By deleting Solace-D from the current time line, we are imposing a major effect, and that spawns a new universe—lots of new universes, in fact. When we activate the gate and launch Solace-D, we're not producing *two* choices, but trillions of them. *Every* possible variance in the conditions causes a slightly alternate outcome. If a particular component is a microdegree cooler or warmer, so that more or fewer electrons flow through it, that's enough. A difference of one electron more or less moving through a circuit is enough to spawn a universe, just as much as a planet's being there or not.

"Then, in each of *those* trillions of new universes, each one will have very slightly different initial conditions for the reentry of Solace-D. Mostly those will cause it to arrive a bit earlier, a bit later. Trivial. In some universes, it won't arrive at all, or it will appear very late, or in the wrong place—inside Lodestar, or something. In *those* universes, of course, when the terraformers go to look for Solace-D, it isn't there, so they can't reterraform it."

"Go on," he said.

"It's a cascade effect, more and more universes forming with each event. Every action in every universe with more than one possible outcome spawns a new universe. What we want to have happen is for Solace-D to be kicked twenty thousand years ahead, spend just under a million years being terraformed into Solace-R, then get kicked back to about now, about a week after Solace-D left. Then Solace-R proceeds forward in time. *Every* one of those major events, and all of the minor ones, spawns a new world line. By the time Solace-R gets to the twenty-thousand-year mark, it is on a time line that's diverged completely from the one in which Solace-D first appeared in that era."

"And nothing goes wrong in any of those universes?"

"Of course things go wrong. In all those trillions of trillions of spawned universes, all of which *will* happen—yes, there will be world lines where everything goes utterly wrong and, somehow, Solace-D drops into a line with a Solace-R. Such events will make all such universes evaporate spontaneously. Solace-D and -R don't have to strike each other, or even be physically near each other. Two instances of the same body—again, electron or planet or galaxy, size and complexity don't enter into it—two instances from the same root body from the same root world line *cannot* exist simultaneously. That's fundamental. It's what makes time travel possible. It *has* to be that way. I could show you the math."

"No, no, that's all right," he said hurriedly, for fear she'd pull a datapad out then and there. "But wait a second," Villjae objected. "What about the timeshaft wormholes? They throw—what did you call them—instances—of the same object back and forth all the time. There are timeshaft ships that have crossed through the same set of years dozens and dozens of times."

"Apples and oranges," Beseda said dismissively. "Yes, that's time travel, but it's a totally different *type* of time travel. Nuclear fission and nuclear fusion are both nuclear power reactions, but they're still completely different from each other. Those repeated timeshaft ships *aren't* different instances, as the word is defined in chronophysics. They are continuous and contiguous portions of *one* instance of the same object moving forward and backward through time. Passage through a timeshaft wormhole doesn't span universes, outside of the normal actions of probability—it merely moves you through a fold in space-time, from one point to a contiguous point, with the connection through the singularity. Completely different process."

"I thought wormholes were singularities, outside our universe," Villjae objected.

"Better to think of them as singularities, outside the universe as we perceive it, but enclosed *within* the chronouniverse that also contains our perceptible universe," she said.

"All right, I'll take your word for it. Both ways seem to work. But, getting back to the way *this* thing works"—he gestured toward the image of the Grand Gate—"it seems so *extravagant*. How could there *be* that many universes? And do we have the moral right to create them, when it seems inevitable that some of them will turn out very badly, if not for us, then for analogues of us?"

"We can't help but do it. Watch this," said Beseda. She lifted one hand up in front of her face, wiggled her fingers, then dropped her hand back in her lap. "I just created a few thousand universes distinguishable from each other above the quantum level. Some universes where I wiggled faster, some universes where I wiggled slower, or with the other hand, and some where I didn't do it at all. That's the action of normal probability I was talking about a second ago. *But* most of those universes are already remerging with each other, as the differences between them are worn down by the passage of time. Whatever air molecules I moved would have been moved by something else by now.

"That's harmonics. Once a difference doesn't make a difference anymore, the universes produced by the creation of those differences coalesce back together. Universes aren't merely being created and split off constantly—they're being destroyed and merging together as well. A difference creates dissonance, which produces a universe to split off. Once the difference fades away, later in the world line, harmony is reestablished, and the split between the two is healed. It's not universes spawning endlessly out of control, more and more and more every femtosecond. It's occasional eruptions of significantly different universes against a background of continuous spontaneous splitting *and* merging, along with self-destruction of any universes that generate effects that render the universe in question impossible.

"In the present case, *not* to act will leave undisturbed a world line where humanity is extinct in a thousand years. How is *not* acting a morally superior choice? In any event," she concluded, nodding toward the big display, with just the barest hint of a smile on her face, "it's a little late to worry about it *now*."

He looked up and was startled to see that the countdown had only a few seconds left to run. Only Beseda could have calmly delivered a lecture on chronophysics at such a time without being flustered. It was almost as remarkable as Beseda making an effort, however feeble, at humor. Villjae was willing to bet there were a great many universes where *that* hadn't just happened. But there were greater wonders yet to behold than Beseda making a joke.

The clock reached zero, and the Grand Harmonic Gate began its work. The three rings began to spin themselves up, gaining rotational velocity with remarkable rapidity. The rings were *big,* and it simply took time to get them up to speed. Furthermore, they couldn't take any risks of damaging the rings. After all, they would need them again—to pull in Solace-R. So they did the power-up, and the spin-up, as gently as possible.

There had been no possible way to conduct a complete test of the Grand Gate. It had, out of necessity, been built *around* the planet and could not be activated without sending the planet somewhere—or rather, some*when*. It had to work the first time.

There was something hypnotic in watching the rings spinning faster and faster, moment by moment, until the checkerboard patterns began to blur and smear, then become lost to sight altogether.

The room was silent, all conversation at an end, as the moment, *the* moment, grew closer. It wasn't hard to imagine all the people of the Solace system silent, watching, holding their breath.

The activation sequence moved on, everything happening as it should, all according to plan. Time seemed to slow down, drag to a halt altogether, yet seemed to rocket forward at blinding speed as they all drew closer to the precipice, gathering speed for the jump across, already moving too fast to stop, with no choice but to press on, move forward, go faster, and pray.

"One minute," Beseda whispered. "Momentum translation in one minute."

Come on, Villjae told the ring, the universe, the laws of physics. *Hang on just a little while longer. Just a few more impossible things. Hang on.*

Thirty seconds, and they'd find out if the engineers were as good as they thought they were, if they could truly build materials strong enough for what was needed. *But it's not the grand plan that fails,* Villjae reminded himself. *It's the stuck switch, the plus sign that should have been a minus, the spilled drink shorting out a control panel.* He knew that, better than anyone. *If it fails, it won't be big, or structural. It'll be that someone spilled lunch sauce onto a momentum damper six years ago.* Whatever the cause, failure would almost inevitably be catastrophic. The Solace system simply did not have the resources to try again. All, or nothing.

Ten seconds.

Villjae found himself wanting to shout, wanting to scream, but somehow he could not. He was as frozen as the moment, unable to do anything but let it all crash into him.

Suddenly the inner and outer rings were gone, leaving only the center ring, spinning by itself. For one gut-freezing moment, Villjae thought the other two had simply disintegrated—but then he realized they were there, and doing exactly what was intended. In a process no less miraculous than inertial damping, the angular momentum of both rings had been instantaneously rotated through ninety degrees, sending both rings revolving about, end over end, their axes of rotation perpendicular to each other and to the unchanged center ring.

Now that he looked harder, Villjae could see the inner and outer rings, or rather a pair of translucent spheres that marked their spinning paths, one inside the other, the center ring between them, and Solace-D in the center of all. The temporal field strengths started to climb as steadily as the spinning masses, and the field generators built into them, began to interact. Suddenly there were flashes of light, massive lightning discharges arcing between the rings—but even those massively powerful energy surges were inconsequential compared to what came next. For it was not when the temporal fields formed that mattered so much—it was when they collapsed.

The process was beyond any control now, human or ArtInt, and only the laws of physics could govern what happened next. The fields moved toward the intended temporal phase harmonic state, but without a gate on the other side of the temporal jump to modulate and stabilize the fields, there was no way to govern that movement, to retard it or speed it up. The energies had been loosed, and the Grand Harmonic Gate was, for a brief time at least, its own master.

Suddenly, all the telemetry screens went blank, and the lightning discharges resumed with a thousand times their previous ferocity. Solace-D was all but lost to view inside that violent, seething cauldron, unspeakable powers unleashed and out of control—

And then it was over. The fields collapsed and the rings discharged their angular momentum, there was a flash of strange blue light—and suddenly there were simply three rings floating motionless, lined up neatly in one plane—and an empty space inside, where once the planet Solace-D had been. The telemetry screens came back to life, showing all peaceful, all quiet, all systems green and at standby.

The room was silent with shock for a moment. Then

it erupted in cheers, shouts, screams, backslapping, people surging into the aisles—and there was Villjae, standing next to Beseda Mahrlin, who had been calm as could be throughout the whole affair—but was plainly now scared to death by the tumult all around her.

Villjae felt he ought to do something for Beseda, but couldn't for the life of him think what—until he thought of the hangar deck. It ought to be quiet down there. He waited until things settled down a bit, then led her away, threading her along through the shouting and the dancing.

It was not until long after that it occurred to Villjae that he should have been annoyed with her for forcing him into the role of nursemaid and handholder at such a moment. He had earned his chance to celebrate as well. But then he thought he understood why. After all, Beseda Mahrlin had watched *his* back, on that long-ago day back in Groundside Power. *She* had kept him going, back then, and gotten him what he needed when he needed it. If she had not done that, he had not the slightest doubt that Ignition would have failed. No NovaSpot. No Greenhouse as lifeboat. No place for the refugees of Solace. No experience in running vast projects. Without her help that day, *this* day—the new cloud of universes they had, according to Beseda, just created—would never have come to pass.

All in all, repaying a bit of *that* debt seemed a fair exchange for missing the rest of the party.

Sure enough, the hangar deck was cool, and quiet—if not anywhere near empty. Villjae should have thought of that. With the number of big shots on board, of course the hangar deck would be filled to capacity with shuttle pods.

But even so, it was room enough to move around and quiet enough for Beseda to recover her wits. Better still, from her point of view, she managed to pull up repeater screens, showing the telemetry results. The numbers meant nothing to Villjae, and he took another swallow from the bottle of wine he had liberated on the way down while waiting for her to look them over.

"Good," she said at last, and shut off the display, looking and sounding very pleased—and more animated than he had ever seen her. "Short of actually jumping forward and looking at Solace-D, that's the best data we'll get. And it's good. It worked. Phase One worked like a charm."

Beseda gave Villjae another surprise when she reached for the bottle herself, took a healthy-sized gulp herself, and did so with obvious pleasure.

She held on to the bottle for a moment, and took another swig from it. " 'Course," she said, "we won't do it *that* way that many more times," she said. "Glister, maybe. That's the next one. After that, we'll know enough about temporal confinement to reverse the effect, large-scale. *That's* the way to go."

"What are you talking about?"

She gave Villjae a puzzled look, plainly surprised that he hadn't understood what she had thought was a perfectly clear explanation. "So far we've only used temporal confinements to slow *down* time inside a confinement. Theory says there's no reason we couldn't flip the sign from neg to pos, and use tempo confinement to *speed up* time flow inside the confinement. Make the inside of the confinement experience a million years while the universe ages by a decade or two."

"So, what, we do what we did with Greenhouse? Throw a confinement around a whole planet?"

"Nah. That's small-time," she said, and it seemed to Villjae her voice was a little blurry. "Wouldn't work, anyway. Planet needs sunlight, for one thing. And remember, TC power has to come from the *inside*. We couldn't store the power to run the thing for more than a few minutes of objective time, unless we melted the planet."

"Okay, so what instead?" Villjae asked.

"Throw the confinement around the whole *star* system. Planet and star inside it together, aging together. Inner system, anyway. Gravity would still work—the outer planets wouldn't go flying off—just get way cold and dark when the confinement shut off their sunlight. Configure the temporal confinement to double as radiation shielding, heat dump. Hang collectors around the star, and use *it* for the power source. Suck up every watt that's not going to the planets and dump it into the confinement. Set up your first phase of terraforming, switch it on. Wait a few minutes, switch it off. Bam! Five thousand years gone by inside. Set up the next phase, and do it again. Bam! Big. Powerful. Elegant. No chance for time-travel headaches. Pain in the neck, time travel. Best thing is to avoid it whenever you can."

Villjae had the distinct sensation that his head was spinning. How many leaps of faith, of imagination, would it require before such a technique was even remotely possible? And yet, there was Beseda Mahrlin, of all people, describing it almost as an accomplished fact, a foregone conclusion.

Maybe success does that, he thought. *Maybe it lets you consider what comes next, not just what to do when things go wrong. It makes you look forward.* "I like it," he said. "I like it very much."

But, he reminded himself, success was not yet assured. Just as Beseda had so happily confirmed, there was still the small matter of a planet to be retrieved from the future.

They were, all of them, in the position of a lunatic thrill seeker who had jumped from an aircar without a parachute, in the hopes of finding one on the way down.

And the ground was coming up fast.

Chapter Thirty

THE SHORES OF TOMORROW

LODESTAR VII

Neshobe Kalzant waited, alone in her cabin. It couldn't take much longer. Except, as Captain Marquez was fond of saying, *everything* was harder and took longer.

It had been a solid week since the departure of Solace-D. Apart from various physicists and astrogeologists who were eagerly making use of the rare chance to study firsthand the effects on other bodies of removing a large mass from a planetary system, that was one week too long. The Grand Gate *seemed* to have come through the transport of Solace-D in good shape, but everyone had seen just how violent an event that was. And while the power beam from the rebuilt SunSpot was working fine, there was never a gate engineer who didn't want as much power as possible stored in the rings' accumulators.

Nor was it far from anyone's mind that it didn't matter so much if Solace-D got a little bit roughed up during transit—but Solace-R was another matter altogether. No. Let the engineers take their time, and get it right.

At last, they had declared themselves satisfied, and the SunSpot's power beam was brought to bear, one more time, aimed at a huge mirror orbiting just a few thousand kilometers sunward from the Grand Gate. The power beam reflected off the mirror and struck the sunward-side power receptors of the Grand Gate, more than quadrupling the rate of power being delivered to the gate.

That had been thirty-six hours ago. No one could say for certain how long, or at what level, the gate would reach maximum power storage capacity. When the engineers decided they had reached that point—then it would be time to go.

That was fine with Neshobe. She could wait as long as they wanted. Alone, in her cabin. This time, *really* alone, with no security detail at all. Alone, to contemplate the most welcome notion that she would not be Planetary Executive much longer.

In a very real sense, she was already out of power. If they succeeded, and she did step down on schedule, the next PlanEx would have almost nothing to do, no decisions to make—for the job ahead would be so clear, so obvious, that the demands of the times would be enough to make the job happen.

And if they failed, if Solace-R did not appear, or was somehow destroyed in the process of arrival—well, the habitat domes on Greenhouse could hold out another year, or two, before they started failing in large numbers. There was nothing else she or anyone else could do about it. Long before the final blackout, the planetary system of Solace would cease to have a government at all, let alone a PlanEx.

She could not help but think back to the time she had spent in this cabin during the long wait for NovaSpot Ignition. Then they had been involved in a last-ditch effort that they knew could do very little more than keep the patient alive a little bit longer. The only hope they had had that day was to keep things going long enough for a miracle to come and save them. Today, it was the miracle itself they waited on, and hope was all around them.

The door annunciator chimed. There were precious few people she would want to see—but it might be someone with news.

She stood, checked the security camera view of the hallway, and opened the door at once.

"I was just thinking about you," she said. "The trouble-maker. Please, come in."

Admiral Anton Koffield smiled and walked into her cabin. He glanced at the display screens on the wall, saw that they were dark and blank, and nodded. "I thought you might have your displays off," he said, "and your intercom was set to private. I just wanted to come and give you the news that they're ready to go. The final six-hour countdown to the start of the Reception Sequence should begin any minute. That's all," he said. "I won't disturb you any further." He bowed to her, very slightly, and turned back to the door.

"No, please, sit down," she said, directing him to an armchair. Suddenly she found herself hungry for company—at least, Koffield's company.

He hesitated briefly, then took a seat and smiled at her, plainly unsure of what, exactly, to say.

She was at a bit of a loss for words herself—but then she found the way to begin. "That was most unkind of me, just now, calling you a troublemaker. You saved us all, you know. Thank you."

He gestured awkwardly. "I don't know what to say to that," he replied. "Sometimes, these last few years, when I've thought about it, I'm not so sure I should get the credit for very much, especially if motive counts for anything. I think that all I was trying to do was redeem myself for the loss of Circum Central and the harm that did. Later, all I was really doing was saving my reputation."

"I don't believe that for a moment," said Neshobe. "And deep in your heart, I don't think you do either. I don't know why, but it's not at all uncommon for a good man to try to avoid taking—or accepting—credit for what he's done." She thought for a moment, then shook her head. "No, strike that—perhaps I *do* know why."

"Do you? I'd be very interested to hear," Koffield said.

"You've accomplished things far larger than yourself," she said. "Things you know are worthy of respect, in and of themselves, regardless of who did them. They don't *belong* to you anymore, for you've given them to all of us.

To claim too much credit would be to say that your accomplishments are, after all, small enough for one man to own, that they don't really belong to all of Solace system. Accepting credit would come close to diminishing your own estimation of all that you have done."

Koffield thought it over first. "There's something in what you say," he admitted. "But even so—*especially* if it's so—I'm not going to feel too comfortable talking about it for quite a while."

"We'll leave it there, then," she said, and they were both quiet for a time.

"Have you heard about the message pods?" Koffield asked.

"No. What message pods?"

"It was Captain Marquez's idea. He's got some engineers who were done with their part of the Grand Gate—which is nearly everyone, by now—working on it. They're digging up every surplus long-durability component they can, and putting together pods that will carry complete records of everything we've done. Most of the data is aboard the pods already. They're just waiting to find out what happens in, ah, six hours or so."

"But, why? If we succeed—"

"They're not in case we succeed," Koffield said quietly. "They're in case we fail. In case some tiny, trivial error turns around and bites us hard enough to kill. Then they'll send the pods out, at sublight-speeds, multiple copies to every inhabited star system, adjusting their boost schedules and their velocities so they'll all arrive at just about the same time, in every system. That way the CP won't be warned by their arrival one place to be watching out for them other places.

"Marquez is going to time them to get to their destinations a hundred standard years from today, or as close as he can manage it. Once they get where they're going, the pods will start broadcasting a basic report of what we've done and how we did it. The locals will home in, make pickup—and find the complete record on board. Everything. What we did, what we learned, what we got from the Dark Museum—everything from Harmonic

Gates and FTL, right on down to improved power storage in temporal confinements. And, if we can figure it out, we'll include a report on what went wrong, as well."

"Marquez would think of something like that," Neshobe muttered. "Still, it's a good idea. But why build the pods now? Why not wait until we see if they're needed?"

"Marquez told the team it was just something to do, something to keep them busy while they were waiting out Dispatch and Reception. But the real reason for doing it now—well, maybe if we *do* fail, maybe no one is going to be in the mood for stuffing messages in bottles and throwing them into the ocean."

Neshobe nodded. *Or maybe the inevitable disturbances will be so violent it won't even be possible.* "Tell Marquez to send them out even if we succeed," she said. "*Especially* if we succeed."

"Aren't we supposed to stay in quarantine from the rest of Settled Space longer than that?" Koffield asked.

"If I felt like splitting hairs, and the CP complains a hundred years from now, I'll say we agreed not to use wormholes or FTL," Neshobe said. "Besides, what are they going to do if we do announce early? Sue us?" She gestured at the Grand Gate. "Make us build a new one, and send Solace-R *back*? Tell him to send the pods no matter what happens. It'll be good for morale." *And enough publicity might keep the CP from moving against us, if they do turn totally reactionary by then, instead of just falling apart they way they should.*

"All right," Koffield said with a smile. He stood up. "But I should be getting back."

"You're more than welcome to watch the show from here, with me," she said, standing up herself. "I've just decided to give myself the gift of *not* watching it in public. After all, what can they do to *me* for not showing up? Throw me out of office?"

He laughed. "You don't seem much worried about the consequences of your actions today. But no, thank you, Madam Executive. There are two ladies who would be very cross with me if I wasn't with them for this."

Neshobe nodded. "Of course. Give my regards to both of them." She shook her head. "Perhaps *I* will come along myself, after a little bit, to one of the smaller receptions. I don't care to be out in the public galleries, but this won't be something to watch all alone."

"I quite agree. I'll see you down there, then, Madam Kalzant."

She saw him out and shut the door. It was only after he was gone that she realized with a sudden thrill that "down there" could mean more than one thing. She turned on her display and brought up a view of the Grand Harmonic Gate, and the emptiness at its center. There was not yet any "there" there.

But it was starting to seem real to her that there would be—and soon.

At last it was time. Once again, and for the last time, the Grand Harmonic Gate came alive, with all the people of the Solace system to bear witness. In every dome, aboard every spacecraft, in every outer-system mining camp and subterranean habitat, the people watched. They had risked everything for this moment—and if Solace-R did not arrive safely, then there could be no second chances, for the gate, or for any of them.

The gate's three rings began to move, ever so slowly starting to spin, gaining speed, until the geometric tracking patterns painted on them vanished from sight altogether. Somewhere, somewhen, if all was going well, the uptime duplicate end of this gate, a gate that had been built around the revived and reterraformed Solace, was spinning up as well, generating field strength, reaching out, establishing its own harmonic pattern, edging closer, ever closer, to a perfect phase match with the Grand Harmonic Gate of the present.

The true test of the here-and-now Grand Gate was at hand. The energy discharges it had experienced when dispatching Solace-D were a mere backwash of the system power output. As the uptime and downtime

Gates hunted closer and closer to phase-lock, the down-time Gate began absorbing detuned energy from the up-time Gate, far more energy than it could convert and put to use. That energy had to go somewhere—and it did. Lightning flashes blazed and flared all about the rings, even before momentum transfer was initiated. A plasma sheath formed, completely engulfing the rings and spanning and merging across the empty center, until the gate was a disk of fire, roaring and wheeling across the sky.

And then, faster than they could see, the angular momentum transfer formed spontaneously. The disk became a globe, a raging glowing ball of power, fire, and glory, bright enough to shine like yet another sun, rivaling Lodestar and the NovaSpot, utterly dwarfing SunSpot's focused beam of power. Plasma tubes began to form at either pole, pillars of fire reaching upward and outward. Pulsations began to form in the surface of the fireball as the gate fought to maintain its form and integrity. No one needed to look at the telemetry displays to know that the gate was straining against its limits, barely containing the unspeakable power required to form and hold so massive a link across so great a span of years.

The strain built to its maximum, the pulsations growing deeper, more profound, until the whole surface of the gate was shuddering, flickering, flaring brighter, bucking and fighting against the outrage being committed against the existing shape of space and time.

And then it happened.

The Grand Harmonic Gate of Solace exploded, a flash of light and power that burned out half the long-range cameras in the Solace system. The shock wave pulsed outward, and, just for a moment, the rings of the Gate could be seen, still holding their forms—until they burst apart, disintegrating instantaneously, smashed to bits by the power they could no longer absorb. They blasted outward, into space, utterly destroyed.

No know or theoretically possible structural material could have withstood such a massive energy transfer.

The engineers had known that, accounted for it. Any receiving gate large enough to handle a planet-sized mass would inevitably be destroyed by the act of being used. There was nothing left of the gate, no chance to try again.

And neither would there be any need—for something was left behind where once the gate had been.

A world. A green and living world, for a moment beset by monstrous lightning flashes, magnetic disturbances, transit shock waves—and then all was serene.

Solace had come home.

The first ship set down on the first morning of the first day on the new old world, in a meadow that stood between a stand of pine trees and the seashore.

Not long after, the hatches swung open, and a ramp extended, forming a gentle incline down which one could easily walk to the sweet green grass below. Two men, both of average build, or perhaps a bit below, both well past middle age, but one plainly much older than the other, started to make their way down, moving slowly, the older one steadying himself a bit on the arm of the younger. The old man moved carefully, but eagerly as well, as if toward the promised land. For so it was.

Anton Koffield let go of Oskar DeSilvo's arm and paused at the base of the ramp just long enough to make sure it was DeSilvo who first set foot on the reborn, twice-made world of Solace.

Oskar DeSilvo turned, looked back, looked down at his feet, there on solid ground, and smiled his thanks for the gesture. He looked past Anton Koffield, at the others who were coming down the ramp as well.

"And so," DeSilvo said in solemn tones, "here we are, in the world we have all made new." He paused for a moment and laughed out loud. "I suppose that discharges my duties to the history books," he said. "They always want grand words, you know. Thank heavens all that is out of the way." Anton stepped off the ramp as well, and the two of them stood to one side, in part to let the others come down, but mostly just to breathe in the fine clean air, feel the breeze muss their hair, let the sunshine warm their faces.

The others who had come along in the first contingent made their way down the ramp and onto the clean new world.

Anton had eyes especially for Elber Malloon and his wife Jassa—and their poised, coltish, twenty-two-year-old daughter, Zari, setting foot on her native planet for the first time—for she had been too young to walk when she departed. Anton watched her face as she looked up, in wonder, at an open, undomed sky, as she took her first breath of natural air, and as she looked for the first time at grass and trees and plants that grew where they wanted, and not where they were planted. It had been Malloon's ability to see another way that had brought them there. It seemed quite fit and natural for his family to be among the first to return.

Some would not be coming back. Wandella Ashdin, still engrossed in her histories until the end, had died three years too soon to see the future. Olar Sotales had died as well, under circumstances that were as murky and well hidden as his motives. Perhaps he would have wanted it that way.

But individuals died. That was as it was. Those two, and many others, had spent their lives seeing to it that a *people* would not die. A fair exchange.

Anton looked upward at the sky and watched as a dozen meteors, each easily bright enough to see in daytime, streaked across the sky in as many seconds. The barrage of fragments from the Grand Gate would keep up for months, an all-day all-night fireworks display to celebrate the rebirth of a world.

"Did you ever truly think that you would live to see this?" DeSilvo asked.

"Me?" Anton asked. "No. I never dared think about it, one way or the other."

"I couldn't help but think of it," DeSilvo said. "In any event, I'm quite glad to have broken the rules governing such matters."

"What rules haven't you broken?" Anton asked with a smile.

"Fair enough, fair enough. But I was referring to the

precedent set by Moses, of course. I was supposed to die within sight of the promised land and not quite get here. I must confess I was nervous that the universe would make sure I obeyed *that* rule, at least—but nothing much seems to have occurred."

"Oh, I don't know," Anton said, straight-faced. "It seems to me that quite a few things have happened."

"And they're going to keep happening for a while yet," Norla Chandray announced, coming down the ramp and into earshot. She moved carefully down the ramp, a wide-eyed little four-year-old girl riding on her hip. "There's the small matter of building cities, towns, roads, farms. That sort of thing." She lifted the little girl off her hip, and handed her to Anton Koffield—her husband of five years' standing. "Let your daddy hold you for a while, Theresa."

Anton lifted her up, shifted her about, and planted her on his shoulders, up where she could get a good view. But rebellion was instantaneous. "No!" Theresa announced. "You said I could go and *look*. You said I could go look by *myself*."

"So we did," Anton said, and carefully lifted her down. He set her on the ground and watched as his daughter solemnly trod her first-ever steps on living grass under an open sky.

"No more domes," Norla announced, looking first at her daughter, then up at the sky, and then at Anton. "Is that clear? No more domes, no more habitats, no more canned air, no more food put in storage before we were born."

"No argument from me," her husband said placidly.

"What?" asked Oskar DeSilvo. "Don't you ever plan to go off-world?"

Norla shook her head and looked to Anton. "We haven't been home five minutes, and already he's talking about leaving." She looked back to DeSilvo. "Are *you* planning a trip?"

"Oh no," said DeSilvo. "I'm not planning to go anywhere. I plan to stay right here. I don't want to miss anything."

Anton looked at both of them, then turned to watch

as his daughter walked away toward the booming of the waves. He moved forward, as if to intercept her, but Norla took him by the arm and held him back. "Let her go on her own," she said. "She's been talking about nothing else."

"Oh, I will," he said. "I just want to be close enough to see it."

He followed along, about a hundred meters back, and watched as his daughter climbed over the dunes, and looked for the first time upon the open sea. With a cry of delight, she ran down the other side, out of sight. Anton, with a jolt of fatherly fear, ran forward to the top of the dune. He stopped there and looked down at the fair white sand below. Theresa had sat down, and was most carefully removing her shoes and socks. She set them in a neat little pile, and rolled up the legs of her ship's coveralls. Then she stood up, let out a yell of triumph, and ran down to the sea. She charged, full speed ahead, out up to about ankle deep—and then stopped, and stood, as if transfixed, staring out across the broad vistas of sea and land, across the wide horizons of hope and promise.

The waves splashed over her feet, rushed up to meet the land, and then broke, gentle as a kiss, upon the shores of tomorrow.

THE END

GLOSSARY, GAZETTEER,
AND SHIP NAMES

ArtInt: Artificial Intelligence. Any machine or device with sophisticated decision-making ability, and the capacity to interpret and execute complex orders. Generally speaking, ArtInts are deliberately built and programmed so as to be regarded as appliances and tools. Thus, while it is possible for them to speak and understand speech, they are usually designed to discourage any tendency to treat them as human.

Autofac: Automated Manufacturer. A near–von Neumann machine, not quite capable of replicating itself, but capable of making a wide variety of machines and objects, usually working from a set of specifications written for the express purpose of programming an autofac. Much of high-end technology has been shaped by what can and cannot be built in an autofac.

Base Glister: Oskar DeSilvo's "official" name for his operations center on Glister. It is known to its visitors as "DeSilvo City."

C.P.S. *Belle Boyd IX:* CP Intelligence Command Ship. Named for a female spy active in a near-ancient war in North America.

Big Run: "The Big Run" is the name given by the peasants and rural people of Solace to the panicky attempt to evacuate Solace some years back. A rumor that there would be no more ships leaving the planet led to a rush to get out. Many did get out—but then were stranded on orbit until it was possible to send them back—and they were willing to go back. Although only a relative handful of people made The Big Run, it demonstrated just how fast and violent panic could be. It affected everything from planetary policy to the peasant's view of the government.

Burn-off suit: An isolation suit, for use in extremely hostile environments, worn completely over an inner pressure suit. At the end of a period of exposure, the wearer enters a burn-ball filled with pure oxygen. The burn-off suit is made to burn, incinerating any unwanted life-forms and—usually—leaving the inner suit and its wearer intact.

Canyon City: The diehard settlement inside Last Chance Canyon.

Chronologic Patrol: The military organization assigned to protect the timeshaft wormholes, and to defend against any deliberate or accidental attempt to abuse time travel so as to damage causality.

Circum Central Wormhole Farm: The timeshaft wormhole that once linked Glister to other worlds, usable for transit to Solace as well. The name was an optimistic misnomer. Circum Central was not central to anything, and there was only one timeshaft there, though the term *wormhole farm* usually refers to three or more wormholes clustered near each other at a main transfer point. Circum Central was supposed to be much more important than it turned out to be.

Collapse Wars: The name given to the conflicts during a final period of contraction of interstellar civilization. As available resources contract more rapidly than population, the survivors will battle all but continuously over the scraps that remain.

Comfort: A large gas giant planet in the outer reaches of the same planetary system that holds Solace. The satellite Greenhouse orbits Comfort, and SunSpot orbits Greenhouse.

Cruzeiro do Sul: Large auxiliary ship, or lighter, carried aboard the *Dom Pedro IV*.

Dark Museum: Informal name for the Chronologic Patrol's Technology Storage Facility, a vast underground complex on Mars where suppressed technology is stored for future reference. Badly damaged in an explosion centuries ago, it was assumed to be completely destroyed. The lowest level, however, is partly intact.

DeSilvo City: Informal and semi-ironic name given by the *Cruzeiro do Sul* party to Oskar DeSilvo's massive operations center on Glister. See *Base Glister*.

Diehard Habitat, diehard: A habitat, or person, that remains behind after the collapse of the planet or major habitat on which it depends. Diehards might remain for economic reasons (for example, to mine a valuable deposit) out of some emotional, spiritual, or religious motivation, or might simply have been left behind after the last evacuation, with no means of departure. Diehard habitats rarely survive more than a few generations past the collapse of the planet or main habitat.

Downtime: Referring to events in or travel toward the past as regards a timeshaft wormhole. For a hundred-year timeshaft connecting 5100 A.D. and 5000 A.D., 5000 A.D. would be the downtime end.

Founder's Dome: A large habitat dome on Greenhouse. Quite near Research Dome, it was deliberately blown, i.e., exposed to fire, heat, toxic gases, and then explosive decompression and vacuum, in order to sterilize its badly contaminated interior. Repair plans are dependent on the outcome of the NovaSpot Ignition Project. It is home to the tomb of Oskar DeSilvo.

FTL: Faster Than Light.

Gleaner Party: A group sent out by a diehard community to search a particular area—the site of a crash, a newly discovered abandoned facility, the wreckage of a nearby collapsed diehard habitat—and collect whatever is there that might be of value.

Glister: A terraformed planet near Solace that has suffered a climatic collapse.

Grand Library: The ultimate storehouse of human knowledge, housed in a massive habitat orbiting Neptune. Two Permanent Physical Collections, or PPCs, serve as backups in the event of the Grand Library's destruction. One PPC is in a different orbit of Neptune, while the other is buried in an undisclosed location on the farside of Earth's Moon.

Greenhouse: A rocky satellite of the gas giant Comfort, used as the research station and breeding support center for Solace. It is illuminated by the failing SunSpot.

Intruders: Name given, more or less by default, to the thirty-two ships that attacked and went through the Circum Central Timeshaft Wormhole, transiting from downtime to uptime, past to future.

Last Chance Canyon: Site of Canyon City, diehard habitat about seven hundred kilometers south-southeast of DeSilvo City on Glister.

Lodestar: Local name of HS-G9-223, the star around which Solace orbits.

Lodestar VII: The official interplanetary spacecraft for the Planetary Executive of Solace.

Lowdown: A slang term that keys off the term *upper,* but it has come to mean more than a lower-class person. It refers to a peasant who has not—or cannot—

escape the surface of the planet, or someone who has been so severely oppressed or manipulated that he or she is lower than a peasant.

Near-ancient, near-ancients: Referring to a period of remote human history, or the people of that period. The near-ancient period is considered to start roughly with the Enlightenment, and end roughly with the establishment of wormhole transit. Thus, from about 1740 to 3000 A.D.

NovaSpot: A replacement for the gradually failing SunSpot.

Objective time: The time or duration as measured by an outside observer. Typically used in regard to timeshaft-wormhole travel. A timeshaft ship might travel for one hundred years of self-chronologic time, and experience significant relativistic time dilation, but arrive only a week or so after departure in objective time, thanks to passage through a timeshaft wormhole. See *Self-chronologic time* and *Subjective time*.

Reiver: Any member of a reiver troop is a reiver, but the reiver is the head of the troop. By extension, the extralegal lord and master of the territory controlled by his troop.

Research Dome: A medium-sized habitat dome on Greenhouse, home to the Terraformation Research Center and other scientific and technical institutions.

Robot: An ArtInt provided with sensory inputs and manipulators that allow it to do mechanical work. Typically, robots will work under a master ArtInt, normally a sessile unit that is more sophisticated and intelligent. Much of a robot's ArtInt capacity must be given over to physical coordination and mechanical control, so it is rarely cost-effective to build a robot with much onboard intellect.

Sabot Drone, Sabot Ship: An uncrewed vessel disguised as, for example, a harmless freighter, but concealing a powerful and destructive weapon, such as a bomb or a wormhole-destruct system. The term is a merged back-formation from *sabotage,* to destroy enemy property covertly, and *sabot round,* a smaller-caliber round placed (and therefore concealed) inside an inert spacer in order to allow the smaller round of ammo to fit in a large weapon.

SCO Station: Solace Central Orbital Station—the largest and most important of the spaceside facilities in orbit of Solace. It houses thousands of people and a great deal of technical expertise in ship handling, ship repair, cargo services, and so on. A natural trading center, it is in effect the capital of the Solace System space habitats.

Self-chronologic time: The accumulated duration or age of an object, a person's life, or an event, as it would be measured by a chronometer physically attached to an object or person, and ignoring the actual calendric time and date and relativistic time-dilation effects. Put another way, self-chron is a measure of how much an object or person has actually aged, regardless of time travel, cold sleep, or temporal confinement. A person who traveled, over the course of several trips, for five centuries in cryosleep, but traveled down five one-century wormholes, would have gone through five centuries of self-chron time but experienced virtually no subjective time, and might well end up in the same objective year from which he or she started. See *Objective time* and *Subjective time.*

Settled Space: The region of worlds, centered roughly on the Sun, that have been settled by humanity.

Slowboat: A ship that travels from one star system to another without transiting a timeshaft wormhole. A timeshaft wormhole ship might take ninety years of shipboard time to travel between stars, but by using the timeshafts, it might arrive after only a few weeks of objective time. A slowboat would take ninety years to make the trip, and arrive ninety years after departure. Except in very rare instances, they are entirely robotic. They might be loaded with some sort of freshly made luxury item that improve with age, or supplies that will be needed decades later by long-term construction or terraforming projects. Large criminal organizations use slowboats for certain forms of smuggling.

Slowtime: Slang for temporal confinement. Time moves very slowly for anyone inside a temporal confinement field.

Solace: A newly terraformed planet.

Solace City: Capital of Solace.

C.P.S. *Standfast:* The downtime Chronologic Patrol Ship attacked and destroyed during the Circum Central incident.

Subjective time: The apparent time or duration as experienced. A passenger aboard a starship might be in cryosleep for a century, but only be awake to experience a few weeks of subjective time. See *Objective time* and *Self-chronologic time*.

SunSpot: A massive fusion generator, in effect a miniature sun, surrounded by an adjustable reflector, which orbits Greenhouse in the same period as Solace's day, and thus provides simulated day and night to Greenhouse.

Symbiote-mold: The generally accepted term for the complex of commingled life-forms that have, somehow, formed into a symbiotic whole that has engulfed virtually all the habitable land surface of Mars. Molds, fungi, bacteria, and other forms of various species have merged into a meta-life-form that adapts to differing landscapes and climates by expressing whatever combination of member life-forms is best suited to the local environment. It is unclear exactly how the symbiote-mold came to be.

Technology Storage Facility: See *Dark Museum*.

Terraformation Research Center: A think tank located in Research Dome on Greenhouse. At the time of the story, the TRC is mainly concerned with climate maintenance and ecosystem repair—subjects related to terraforming but on a much smaller scale. No one has really given serious thought to the question of terraforming a new, barren world since Solace itself was declared complete.

Timeshaft Wormhole: A wormhole linking past and future. A hundred-year timeshaft would allow one to travel back and forth exactly one hundred years—no more, no less. In the year 5000 A.D., the downtime end of a hundred-year timeshaft would link with the year 5100 A.D. on the uptime side. A timeshaft experiences normal duration, such that both ends are moving normally through time, from past to future at the normal rate. In 5001 A.D., the same timeshaft would link with 5101 A.D., and so on. A hypothetical twenty-four-hour timeshaft would link 4:15 P.M. Tuesday with 4:15 P.M. Wednesday. Two days later, 12:05 A.M. Thursday would be linked with 12:05 A.M. Friday. Move from the downtime to the uptime end of a timeshaft, spend five minutes on the uptime side, and then return to the downtime side, and it will be five minutes later there as well.

C.P.S. *Upholder:* The Uptime Chronologic Patrol Ship, commanded by Captain Anton Koffield, that survived the attack of the Intruders during the Circum Central incident.

Upper: Solace peasant slang. A member of the upper classes, or, anyone who outranks the person using the term.

Uptime: Referring to events in or travel toward the future as regards a timeshaft wormhole. For a hundred-year timeshaft connecting 5100 A.D. and 5000 A.D., 5100 A.D. would be the uptime end.

AUTHOR'S NOTE

Where do you get your ideas? That's the question that terrifies most writers—science fiction writers especially. The truth is, there often is no one moment of inspiration, no precise moment when the core idea of a story suddenly comes to light. For me, at least, it is often an evolutionary process, an accumulation of ideas that slowly come together. I'll read this article, and have that conversation, and see that place, and meet that person, getting a little bit of a notion from each—then reworking those bits, over and over again, into the story idea. By the time the story is worked out, the initial jumping-off points are often too murky to identify and have little or no relation to the story they inspired.

Not so with *The Chronicles of Solace*. I know *exactly* where I was when I got the core idea, and all else flowed from that moment. I was in an open boat off the coast of Maine, heading back to the mainland and a visit in New York with a certain young lady.

It was a perfect summer day. The sky was blue, the cold slate-grey water calm, the winds gentle, the air sweet, the world full of life. As our boat passed by a patch of seaweed, I saw a seal poke his head out of the water. He floated there, obviously content, happy, and comfortable with life as it was, plainly admiring the day, just as I was.

In that moment, I found myself marveling at how well adapted that seal was to his perfect world. There were such deep interactions needed to make it all work; between the seal and the sea and the climate and the food supply and a thousand other things, from the pull of the tides to the salinity of the water. I thought of the millions, billions, of years of evolution required before the Earth and life could fully adapt to each other, before that seal could poke his head out of the water and blink contentedly at the seascape.

What if life and Earth had *not* had all that time to adapt to each other? What if, because things had been *done* in a hurry on a terraformed world, that world would *die* in a hurry? I saw vast potential for a story in that idea. Three books later, you may judge for yourself if I have managed to make good use of that potential.

In between having the idea, working out its implications, writing it, and seeing it published, a good deal else has gone on. I wrote something like five or six other books. I married that certain young lady, some years later. We have just celebrated our ninth anniversary. Our son is now four and a half years old. It just goes to show—these things take time.

I might add that we've moved around a bit: I wrote *The Depths of Time* largely in Brazil, *The Ocean of Years* largely in Maryland, and *The Shores of Tomorrow* largely in Germany—and none of the books all in one place. I have lost track of the times that someone, on learning that I am a writer married to a diplomat, has brightly informed me that the great thing about my job is that I can do it anywhere. Though I suppose I've proved that's true, I've also proved it's not easy. It's my sincere hope that I manage to write my next book without a transoceanic house move during the process. It's not likely, but a fellow can dream.

Before I close, there is one more, much more melancholy observation that I must make. This volume is dedicated to the memory of Dr. Charles Sheffield. He wrote wonderful science fiction books and stories, and was one of the kindest, smartest, busiest men I ever knew. He was also the man with the greatest sense of fun, and greatest *capacity* for fun, whom I have ever known.

I was always a bit hesitant to intrude on his time because I knew he would make time for me, more than I deserved, and more than he could afford. It's worth noting that Anton Koffield is named half for him, and half for another scientist-writer friend of mine, Yoji Kondo. (Kondo-Sheffield, Koffield.)

Charles died in November 2002. Now, needless to say, I wish I had been just a bit greedier about taking what chances I had to spend time with him. I miss him terribly.

I would like to thank my wife, Eleanore Fox, and my son, Matthew, for putting up with me in the heavy-duty writing phase of this project. I'd like to offer my further thanks to Eleanore for undertaking the grim task of cutting away a great deal of needless verbiage from the first draft of this story. She made this book a lot better. Thanks, as always, to my parents, Tom and Scottie Allen, for everything and then some. Thanks to Sara and Bob Schwager, for their enthused, careful, and improving copyediting, on this and the previous volumes. Finally, thanks to my editor, Juliet Ulman, for managing me with a great deal of diplomacy during the long process of getting the book done.

And that brings this story, at last, to a close.

I guess it's time for me to go get that next idea.

Roger MacBride Allen
Leipzig, Germany
June 2003

ABOUT THE AUTHOR

ROGER MACBRIDE ALLEN was born September 26, 1957, in Bridgeport, Connecticut. He is the author of nineteen science fiction novels, a modest number of short stories, and one nonfiction book.

His wife, Eleanore Fox, is a member of the United States Foreign Service. After a long-distance courtship, they married in 1994, when Eleanore returned from London, England. They were posted to Brasilia, Brazil, from 1995 to 1997, and to Washington, D.C., from 1997 to 2002. Their son, Matthew Thomas Allen, was born November 12, 1998. In September 2002 they began a three-year posting to Leipzig, Germany.

Visit the author's website at www.rmallen.net to learn more.

Come visit

BANTAM SPECTRA

on the INTERNET

Spectra invites you to join us
at our on-line home.

You'll find:

< Interviews with your favorite authors and
excerpts from their latest books
< Bulletin boards that put you in touch with
other science fiction fans, with Spectra
authors, and with the Bantam editors who
bring them to you
< A guide to the best science fiction resources
on the Internet

Join us as we catch you up with all of Spectra's finest
authors, featuring monthly listings of upcoming titles
and special previews, as well as contests, interviews,
and more! We'll keep you in touch with the field, both
its past and its future—and everything in between.

Look for the Spectra Spotlight
on the World Wide Web at:

http://www.bantamdell.com.